THE ENIGMA OF ROOM 622

Also by Joël Dicker in English translation

The Truth about the Harry Quebert Affair
The Baltimore Boys
The Disappearance of Stephanie Mailer

THE ENIGMA OF ROOM 622

JOËL DICKER

Translated from the French by
Robert Bononno

MACLEHOSE PRESS
QUERCUS·LONDON

First published in the French language as *L'Énigme de la chambre 622*
Éditions de Fallois, Paris, in 2020
First published in Great Britain in 2022 by MacLehose Press
This paperback edition published in 2023 by

MacLehose Press
An imprint of Quercus Editions Ltd
Carmelite House
50 Victoria Embankment
London EC4Y 0DZ

An Hachette UK company

Typeset by Jouve (UK), Milton Keynes
Printed and bound in Great Britain by Clays Ltd, Elcograf S.p.A.

MIX
Paper | Supporting
responsible forestry
FSC® C104740
www.fsc.org

Papers used by Quercus are from well-managed forests and other responsible sources.

To my editor, friend, and teacher,
Bernard de Fallois (1926–2018).
Every writer should have the good fortune
to meet such an extraordinary publisher.

CONTENTS

PROLOGUE

The Day of the Murder

Sunday, December 16

Six thirty in the morning. The Hôtel de Verbier was dark. Outside, it was pitch-black and snowing heavily.

On the sixth floor, the doors of the service elevator opened. A hotel employee appeared with a breakfast tray and made his way towards Room 622.

When he reached the room, he noticed that the door was ajar. Light spilled through the opening. He knocked but there was no response. Finally, he decided to go in, assuming that the door had been left open for that purpose. He walked in and let out a scream. Running from the room, he went to alert his colleagues and call for help.

As the news spread through the hotel, the lights went on, floor by floor.

On the carpet of room 622 lay a corpse.

PART ONE

Before the Murder

1

Love at First Sight

At the start of summer 2018, when I travelled to the Hôtel de Verbier, a well-known luxury hotel in the Swiss Alps, I was far from imagining that I would spend my holiday unravelling a crime that had been committed there many years earlier.

My stay was supposed to provide a welcome break after two small personal traumas in my life. But before I reveal what happened that summer, I need to go back to the beginning of this story: the death of my publisher, Bernard de Fallois.

Bernard is the man to whom I owe everything. My success, my fame, I owe it all to him. It is because of him that people call me a *writer*. And people read my books because of him.

When we met, I was an unpublished author; he made me a writer whose books were read the world over. Bernard, who resembled an elegant patriarch, had been one of the leading personalities in French publishing. For me, he had been a teacher and most of all, in spite of the sixty-year difference in our ages, a great friend.

In January 2018, Bernard, then ninety-one years old, died, and I reacted to his death the way any writer would: I began writing a book about him. I put my heart and soul into the project, locked in the office of my apartment at 13 avenue Alfred-Bertrand, in the Champel quarter of Geneva.

As always when writing, the only human presence I could tolerate was that of Denise, my assistant. Denise was the good fairy who watched over me. Always in good spirits, she managed my schedule, sorted and filed the letters from my readers, read and corrected what I had written.

5

She also filled my fridge and supplied me with coffee. And, from time to time, she served as ship's doctor, landing in my office as if she were stepping aboard after an interminable crossing, showering me with advice about my health.

"Go outside!" she ordered, gently. "Take a walk around the park and clear your head. You've been locked in here for hours!"

"I already went for my run this morning," I reminded her.

"You need to get some oxygen to your brain from time to time," she insisted.

This had become our daily ritual: I complied and stepped out onto the office balcony. I filled my lungs with the cold air of February, then, defying her with an amused look on my face, lit a cigarette. She protested and, sounding annoyed, said, "You know, Joël, I'm not emptying your ashtray. It's the only way you'll learn just how much you smoke."

Each day I stuck to the monastic routine I adopted when I was writing, which could be broken down into three indispensable steps: rise at dawn, go jogging, write until evening. It was indirectly, through this book, that I met Sloane. Sloane was my new next-door neighbour. Ever since she had moved in, quite recently, everyone in the building had been talking about her. Our own meeting proved elusive – that is, until the morning when, returning from my daily workout routine, I passed her for the first time. She, too, had been out jogging, and we entered the building together. I understood at once why the neighbours were unanimous in their opinion of her: she was a young woman of irresistible charm. We limited ourselves to a polite hello before we disappeared into our respective apartments. Behind my door, I remained stunned. That brief encounter had been enough to make me fall in love a little.

Soon, I had but one idea in mind: getting to know Sloane.

My first attempt involved running. Sloane ran nearly every day, but her hours were irregular. I would wander around Parc Bertrand, desperate for some chance encounter. Then, one day, I saw her running down a path. Since I was incapable of catching up with her, I decided to wait by the entrance to our building. I lingered in front of the mailboxes, pretending to examine the mail whenever one of the neighbours appeared, until she finally arrived. She walked past and smiled, which made me lose my composure entirely; by the time I had found something intelligent to say, she had already gone inside.

It was the building's concierge, Madame Armanda, who told me about Sloane. She was a paediatrician. Her mother was English; her father was a lawyer. She'd been married for two years, but the marriage wasn't going well. She worked at the Geneva University Hospitals and alternated between day and night shifts, which explained my difficulty in trying to make sense of her routine.

After my failed attempt to meet her jogging, I decided to change my approach. I asked Denise to monitor the hallway through the peephole and notify me whenever Sloane appeared. Whenever I heard Denise shout "She's leaving!", I charged out of my office, dressed and abundantly perfumed, and made my way to the landing, as if my presence were the merest coincidence. Our exchanges were limited to a greeting. Most of the time, she walked down the stairs, which cut short any conversation. I followed, but for what? When she reached the street, she disappeared. The few times she took the elevator, I stood there mute, and an uncomfortable silence filled the space. In either case, I returned to my apartment, muttering to myself.

"So?" Denise asked.

"So, nothing," I grumbled.

"Really, Joël, you're useless! Make an effort at least."

"I'm a bit shy, that's all."

"Oh, please, stop. You're not very shy when you're on television."

"Because you're seeing the *writer* on television. Joël is very different."

"Look, Joël, it's really not that complicated. You ring her doorbell, offer her some flowers, and invite her to dinner. Are you too lazy to go to the florist? Is that it? You want me to do it?"

Then there was that April evening. I was at the Grand Théâtre de Genève, alone, for a performance of *Swan Lake*. During the intermission, as I stepped out for a cigarette, I ran into her. We exchanged a few words; then, as the bell announced the resumption of the performance, she suggested that we meet for a drink after the ballet. We met at the Remor, a nearby café. And that's how Sloane entered my life.

Sloane was beautiful, funny, and intelligent – one of the most fascinating women I'd ever met. After our evening at the Remor, I invited her out several times. We went to concerts, movies. I dragged her to an art opening, a strange exhibition that made us laugh out loud; we fled to have dinner at one of her favourite Vietnamese restaurants. We spent several evenings at her apartment, or at mine, listening to opera, talking, and planning the world's future. I couldn't keep myself from staring at her; I was helpless in her presence. The way she blinked, or pushed her hair aside, the way she smiled gently when she was annoyed, or played with her painted nails before asking a question – I liked everything about her.

Soon, I thought only of her. I even began to forget about my book.

"You look lost, Joël," Denise would say to me when she saw that I hadn't written a single line.

"It's Sloane," I explained behind my silent computer.

I couldn't wait to see her again and continue our interminable conversations. I never tired of listening to her talk about her life, her passions, her wants and ambitions. She loved Elia Kazan movies and opera.

One night, after dinner at a brasserie near Pâquis, where we had both drunk a good deal, we ended up back in my living room. Looking amused, Sloane surveyed the knick-knacks and books along the walls. She stopped for a long time in front of a painting of Saint Petersburg that had belonged to my great-uncle. Then she stopped in front of my bar. She liked the sturgeon in relief on the bottle of Beluga vodka. I poured us two glasses, over ice, and turned the radio to a classical music station, one I often listened to in the evening. She challenged me to identify the composer who was being broadcast. That was easy; it was Wagner. And it was during the *Ride of the Valkyries* that she kissed me and pulled me against her, whispering in my ear how she wanted me.

Our affair lasted two months – two wonderful months. But by then, my book on Bernard had got the upper hand. At first, I simply took advantage of the nights when Sloane was at the hospital to continue writing. But the more I wrote, the more I was carried forward by my novel. One evening, she asked me to go out and, for the first time, I declined. "I have to write," I explained. At first, Sloane was very understanding. She, too, had a job that sometimes kept her away more than she had anticipated.

Then, I turned her down a second time. Once again, she was sympathetic. Please don't misunderstand me; I adored every minute of the time I spent with Sloane. But I felt that with Sloane it was for the long haul – that our moments of complicity would be repeated indefinitely. The inspiration for a novel, though, could vanish just as easily as it arrived; it was an opportunity I had to take advantage of.

Our first fight took place one evening in mid-June when, after having made love, I got up from her bed to get dressed.

"Where are you going?" she asked.

"Home," I replied, as if it were perfectly natural.

"You're not going to sleep here with me?"

"No, I'd like to write."

"So, what, you come over to get laid and then you leave?"

"I have to put some work into the book," I replied sheepishly.

"But you can't spend all your time writing!" she shouted. "You spend all your days, all your evenings, even your weekends! It's insane. You never want to do anything anymore."

I felt that our relationship was at risk of withering away as quickly as it had burst into flame. I had to act. A few days later, the day before leaving on a ten-day trip to Spain, I took Sloane to dinner at her favourite restaurant, the Japanese place in the Hôtel des Bergues, located on the roof of the building and offering a breathtaking view over the entire city of Geneva. The evening was wonderful. I promised Sloane I would write less and leave more time for "us", telling her again how much she meant to me. We even made tentative holiday plans for August, in Italy, a country we were both in love with. Would it be Tuscany or Puglia? We would do some research when I returned from Spain.

We remained at our table until the restaurant closed, at one in the morning. The night, at the start of summer, was warm. Throughout the meal I had the strange sensation that Sloane was expecting something from me. And as we were about to leave, when I got up from my chair and the staff began to mop down the terrace around us, Sloane said, "So, you've forgotten?"

"Forgotten what?"

"It was my birthday today."

Seeing the look on my face, she understood that she was right. She left, furious. I tried to stop her, muttering my excuses, but she jumped into the only available taxi in front of the hotel, leaving me alone on the street, like the imbecile I was, before the astonished eyes of the hotel valets. By the time I had got into my car and returned to my building, Sloane was already in her apartment; she had turned off her phone and refused to open the door. I left for Madrid the following morning. While there, I wrote to her many times, but my messages and emails went unanswered. I had no news from Sloane.

I got back to Geneva the morning of Friday, June 22, to discover that Sloane had broken up with me.

It was Madame Armanda, the concierge, who was the messenger. She intercepted me as I arrived at the building.

"Here's a letter for you," she said.

"For me?"

"It's from your neighbour. She didn't want to put it in the mailbox because your assistant opens your mail."

I opened the envelope at once and found the following message:

Joël,
It will never work.
See you,
Sloane

The words were a stab in the heart. Head down, I walked up to my apartment. At least Denise was around to lift my spirits, I thought. Denise, a kind woman whose husband had left her for someone else, an icon of modern solitude. Nothing can help you feel less alone than to find someone more forlorn than yourself. But, entering the apartment, I ran into Denise on her way out. It wasn't even noon.

"Denise? Where are you going?" I asked.

"Hello, Joël, I told you I was leaving early today. My flight is at three."

"Your flight?"

"Don't tell me you forgot! We talked about it before you left for Spain. I'm going to Corfu with Rick for two weeks."

Rick was a guy Denise had met online. In fact, we had talked about the holiday, but I had completely forgotten about it.

"Sloane left me," I blurted out.

"I know, I'm very sorry."

"What do you mean, you know?"

"The concierge opened the letter Sloane left for you and told me everything. I didn't want to tell you while you were in Madrid."

"And you're leaving all the same?" I asked.

"Joël, I'm not going to cancel my holiday because your girlfriend dumped you. You'll find somebody else just like that!" she said, snapping her fingers. "Women are always making eyes at you. It's okay. I'll see you in two weeks. It's going to pass quickly, you'll see. Besides, I've taken care of everything, I even went shopping. Look."

She led me into the kitchen. Alerted to my break-up with Sloane, Denise had anticipated my reaction: I was going to stay locked in my apartment. Evidently worried that I wouldn't feed myself in her absence, she had stocked up on provisions. From the cupboards to the freezer, there was food everywhere.

And then, she left. And I was alone in my kitchen. I made myself a coffee and sat at the black marble counter behind which some tall chairs were aligned, all desperately empty. The kitchen could accommodate ten, but there was only me. I dragged myself to my office, where I looked for a long while at the pictures of Sloane and me. I grabbed a cardboard box and wrote "Sloane", followed by the date she had left me: "6/22, a day to forget." But it was impossible to get Sloane out of my head. Everything reminded me of her. Even the couch in my living room, where I had sprawled out, reminded me how, a few months earlier, on this same spot, on this same fabric, I had begun the most extraordinary relationship of my life, which I had managed to completely sabotage.

It took all my strength not to knock on her door or call her. Early in the evening, no longer able to contain myself, I went out onto the balcony, smoking cigarette after cigarette in the hope that Sloane would step outside and we would fall into each other's arms. But Madame Armanda, who had seen me from the pavement when she went to walk her dog and found me still there on her return an hour later, cried out from the entrance to the building, "There's no point in waiting, Joël. She's not there. She went on holiday."

I returned to my office. I had to get out of there. I wanted to get away from Geneva for a while, to erase my memories of Sloane. I needed calm; I needed peace and quiet. Then I saw, on my table, among my notes on Bernard, the note about Verbier. He loved the place. The idea of going to Verbier for a while, to take advantage of the quiet of the Alps and find myself, appealed to me at once. I turned on my computer and quickly found the home page for the Hôtel de Verbier, a legendary hotel, and the photos that scrolled before my eyes convinced me – the sun-drenched terrace, the Jacuzzi overlooking the magnificent landscape, the half-lit bar and comfortable salons, the suites with fireplaces. It was exactly what I needed. I clicked the reservations tab and keyed in the information.

That's how it all began.

13

2

Holiday

On Saturday, June 23, 2018, at dawn, I put my suitcase in the boot of my car and set out on the road to Verbier. The sun was just above the horizon, bathing the empty streets of central Geneva in a powerful orange halo. I crossed the Mont Blanc Bridge before driving along the flowered shore to the United Nations and then taking the autoroute in the direction of the Valais.

That morning, everything seemed marvellous: the colour of the sky appeared new, the landscape on either side of the autoroute more bucolic than ever before; the small villages scattered among the grapevines and overlooking Lake Geneva could have been taken from a postcard. I left the autoroute at Martigny and continued along the winding local road, which, after Le Châble, climbs all the way to Verbier.

After an hour and a half, I reached my destination. The morning had barely begun. I walked up the main street and crossed the village, then had only to follow the signs to find the road to the hotel. It was located very near the village (a few minutes on foot) but was so well situated that you felt as if you were in a special place. The building, a typical mountain luxury hotel with its turrets and broad roof, was nestled in a small swath of greenery, surrounded by the pine forest as if by a wall and looking out across the Bagnes Valley, of which the hotel had a spectacular view.

I was welcomed at the hotel by the charming and attentive staff. At once, I felt at ease in this serene setting. As I was checking in at the front desk, an employee said to me, "You're the writer, aren't you?"

"Yes."

"We're honoured to have you here. I've read all your books. Have you come to write your new novel?"

"Not at all!" I answered with a laugh. "I've come to relax. Vacation, vacation, vacation."

"I think you'll enjoy yourself here, you're in one of our most beautiful suites, number 623."

A porter escorted me and my luggage to the sixth floor. Moving along the corridor, I watched the room numbers pass: 620, 621, 621A, 623.

"That's strange," I remarked to the porter, "there's no room 622."

"No," he answered, without further comment.

Room 623 was magnificent. It was decorated in a modern style, which contrasted perfectly with the hotel's ambiance. There was a living room, with a large couch, a fireplace, an office with a view overlooking the valley, and a broad balcony. In the bedroom area, there was a large bed and a dressing room, which led to a marble bathroom with an Italian shower and an immense bathtub.

After I had familiarised myself with the suite, I started thinking about the room numbers. This bothered me.

"Why 621A and not 622?" I asked the porter who was bringing in my luggage.

"Probably an error," he replied, vaguely.

I couldn't tell whether he was really ignorant or simply lying. In any case, he had no desire to continue the conversation.

"Do you need anything else, sir? Should I send someone up to unpack your bags?"

"No, thank you, I'll do that myself." I thanked him and slipped him a tip.

He quickly disappeared. Driven by curiosity, I went to inspect the hallway. Aside from the room adjoining my own, there was no other "A" room on the floor. Strange. I forced myself not to think about it. After all, I was on holiday.

*

15

On my first day at the hotel, I went for a walk in the forest to a restaurant high on the slope, where I admired the view. Returning to the hotel, I took advantage of the heated pool, then spent the rest of the afternoon reading.

That evening, before going to dinner, I drank a Scotch at the bar. While there I chatted with the bartender, who had a number of juicy anecdotes about the other guests. That's when I saw her: a woman about my own age, beautiful, visibly alone, sitting at the other end of the bar, where she ordered a dry Martini.

"Who is that?" I asked the bartender after he had served her.

"Scarlett Leonas. A guest. She arrived yesterday from London. Very nice. Her father is an English aristocrat, Lord Leonas. Do you know him? She speaks perfect French; you can tell she's had a good education. I understand she left her husband and came here to hide out for a while."

The next few hours, we would cross paths two more times.

First, at the restaurant, where our tables were not far from each other. Then, quite unexpectedly, around midnight, when I went out to the balcony of my suite to have a smoke and noticed that she was staying in the room next to mine. At first I thought I was alone in the blue night. Leaving Geneva, I had taken a picture of Bernard with me and was holding it in my hand. Leaning against the railing, I lit my cigarette and looked at the photograph, melancholy. Suddenly, a voice tore me from my reverie.

"Good evening," I heard.

I jumped. She was there, on the balcony next to mine, discreetly curled up in an outdoor lounge chair.

"Excuse me. I scared you," she said.

"I wasn't expecting to meet anyone at this hour."

"My name is Scarlett."

"Joël."

"I know who you are. You're the *writer*. Everyone here is talking about you."

"That's never a good sign," I noted.

She smiled. I wanted the moment to go on, and offered her a cigarette. She accepted. I held the pack out to her, then lit her cigarette with my lighter.

"What brings you here, Writer?" she asked, after exhaling a puff of smoke.

"I needed to get some air," I replied, somewhat evasively. "And you?"

"Same. I left my life in London, my job, my husband. I needed a change. Who is that in your photo?"

"My publisher, Bernard de Fallois. He died six months ago. He was someone very important to me."

"I'm very sorry."

"Thanks. I'm having a hard time turning the page."

"That's got to be difficult for a writer."

I forced myself to smile, but she saw the sadness in my face.

"I'm sorry. I was trying to be witty and I failed."

"Don't worry about it. Bernard was ninety-one; he had every right to leave. I have to deal with it."

"There are no rules for sorrow."

She was right.

"Bernard was a great publisher. But he was more than that. He was a great man, a man with great qualities, who lived several lives throughout his career in publishing. He was a writer and a scholar, he was also a tough businessman, a man with a lot of charisma and rare conviction. Had he been a lawyer, the entire Paris bar would have been out of work. There was a time when Bernard was the head, feared and respected, of some of the largest publishing groups in France. At the same time, he was close to the leading philosophers and intellectuals of the time, politicians as well. In the last part of his life, after he had ruled Paris, Bernard retired, but without losing any of his aura. He started a small publishing house; it was a bit like him: modest, discreet, prestigious. That's the man I knew when he took me under his wing. Kind, curious, joyful, and luminous – he was the teacher I had always dreamed of. His conversation was brilliant, witty, light-hearted, and deep. His laugh was an enduring lesson in wisdom. He knew all the quirks of human behaviour. He was an inspiration, a star in the night."

"He sounds like an extraordinary man," Scarlett said.

"He was."

"Writer, even so, it's a fascinating line of work . . ."

"That's what my last girlfriend thought before she got together with me."

Scarlett burst out laughing. "No, I really meant it. I mean, everyone dreams about writing a novel."

"I'm not so sure."

"Well, I do."

"Then do it," I suggested. "All you need is a pencil and a stack of paper, and a whole wonderful world opens up before you."

"I wouldn't know how to go about it. I wouldn't even know where to get an idea for a novel."

My cigarette was out. I was getting ready to go back inside when she held me back, which I had no reason to complain about.

"How do you find the ideas for your novels?"

I remained silent for a moment before replying.

"People always think that writing a novel begins with an idea. But a novel begins most of all with a desire: the desire to write. A desire that grabs you and that nothing can stop, a desire so strong that you turn your back on everything else. That perpetual desire to write, I call the writer's sickness. You can have the best plot for a novel, but if you have no desire to write, you'll get nowhere."

"And how do you create a plot?" she asked.

"Very good question, Dr Watson. New writers often make that mistake. They think the plot consists of facts assembled one by one. They imagine a character, place him in a situation, and so on and so on."

"So," said Scarlett, "I had an idea for a novel. It goes something like this: a young woman gets married and, on her wedding night, kills her husband in their hotel room. But I never managed to get any further than that."

"Because you're assembling facts, as I just described. But a plot needs questions. Start by presenting your scenario as a series of questions: why does a young bride kill her husband on their wedding night? Who is this young woman? Who is her husband? What is the background of their marriage? Why did they get married? Where did they get married?"

Scarlett replied point for point.

"The husband is immensely rich but a contemptible miser. She wanted a dream wedding with white swans and fireworks, but in the end all she got was a discount celebration in a moth-eaten inn. Mad with rage, she ends up killing her husband. The judge at her trial is a woman, and she rules that there are attenuating circumstances because there's nothing worse than a stingy husband."

I burst out laughing.

"You see, simply presenting your initial story as a series of questions offers infinite possibilities. In answering the questions, the characters, places, and actions will present themselves to you. You've already sketched out some of the characteristics of the husband and wife. You've progressed the plot by introducing the trial. Is the real story the murder? Or the trial? Will she be acquitted? The magic of the novel is that even a simple fact, any fact, when presented as a series of questions, opens the door to a story."

"Any kind of fact?" she repeated, somewhat incredulously, as if she were challenging me.

"Any kind of fact. Let's take a very concrete example. Unless I'm mistaken, you're in room 621A, right?"

"Absolutely."

"And me, I'm in room 623. And the room before yours is 621. I walked the entire floor to make sure: there is no room 622. That's a fact.

Why, in the Hôtel de Verbier, is there a room 621A instead of room 622? That, that's a plot line. And the start of a novel."

She smiled. She was beginning to enjoy the game.

"Yes, but there could be a rational explanation. Some hotels skip room 13 out of concern for superstitious guests."

"If there's an immediate rational explanation, the plot fails and there is no novel. That's when the novelist goes into action. For a novel to exist, the writer has to push back on the walls of rationality, undo reality, and – especially – create a story where there was none before."

"And how would you do that for this hotel room?" asked Scarlett, who seemed not to have completely understood what I was saying.

"In the novel, the writer, in looking for an explanation, will question the concierge of the hotel."

"So go on!" she suggested.

"Now?"

"Of course, now!"

"Room 621A is typical of the hotel," the concierge explained to us, amused that we would show up at that late hour to ask such a question. "When the hotel was being built, the number 621 was attached to the doors of two rooms by mistake. All we had to do was replace one of the 621s with a 622, and everything would have been settled. But the owner at the time, Edmond Rose, an astute businessman, preferred to name it 621A. This succeeded in arousing the curiosity of our guests, who asked especially for that room, convinced there was something special about it. The trick has continued to work to this day because you're here, in the middle of the night, questioning me about it."

When we returned to the sixth floor, Scarlett said to me, "So, room 621A is simply a construction mistake."

"Not for the novelist," I reminded her, "otherwise the story ends there. In the novel, the concierge is lying. Buy why? What's the truth about this mysterious room 621A? What happened there that made the hotel staff decide to conceal it? That's one way to construct a story from a simple situation."

"And now?" she asked.

"And now," I joked, "it's up to you to move forward. I'm going to bed."

Little did I suspect that I had just ruined my holiday.

The following morning at nine, I was awakened by someone knocking on my door. I went to open it and saw Scarlett. She was surprised to see me looking the way I did.

"Were you sleeping, Writer?"

"Yes, I'm on holiday. You know, those periods of rest when people leave you alone."

"Well, in that case, your holiday is over," she announced, entering my suite, holding a fat book under her arm. "I have the answer to your so-called plot: why is there a room 621A at the Hôtel de Verbier instead of 622? Because there was a murder! Fiction is stranger than fact."

"What? How do you know that?"

"I got up early and went to a café in the village centre to ask some questions. Several people were willing to talk to me about it. May I have a coffee, please?"

"Excuse me?"

"Coffee, *please*! Next to the minibar there's a capsule espresso machine. Put the capsule inside, press the button, and the coffee flows into the cup. You'll see. It's magic."

I was completely seduced by Scarlett. I did as she asked at once and prepared two espressos.

"Nothing connects this murder and this strange business with room 621A," I noted, bringing her the cup of espresso.

"Wait till you see what I found," she said, opening the book she had brought.

I sat down next to her.

"What's that?" I asked.

"A book about the history of the hotel," she explained as she turned the pages. "Found it at the bookshop in the village."

She stopped at a photo of an architectural drawing of the hotel and put her finger on it.

"This is the sixth floor. We're lucky, all the same. You see, this is the hallway here, and there, you can see that, for every room, there's a number. They follow one another numerically. Look! And number 622 is right here, between 621 and 623."

Somewhat shocked, I saw that Scarlett was right.

"What are you thinking?" I asked, certain that she had something in mind.

"That the murder took place in room 622 and the hotel management wanted to erase the memory."

"That's merely a hypothesis."

"Which we're going to check out. Do you have a car?"

"Yes, why?"

"Let's go, Writer!"

"What do you mean, 'Let's go'? Where do you want to go?"

"To the archives of the *Nouvelliste*. It's the largest daily in the region."

"It's Sunday."

"I called the office. They're open on Sunday."

I liked Scarlett. That's why I went with her to Sion, roughly an hour away, where the *Nouvelliste*'s headquarters were located.

Behind the desk, a receptionist informed us that access to the archives was reserved for subscribers.

"You have to subscribe," Scarlett said, hitting me with her elbow.

"Um, why me?"

"Come on, Writer, we don't have time to quibble. Subscribe, please."

I hesitated and then took out my credit card, which gave us the right to access the archive room. I had imagined a dusty basement stacked with thousands of old newspapers. In reality, the archive room was a small office equipped with four computers. Everything had been digit-ised, which made life much simpler. Seated before the screen, Scarlett needed only a few keywords to find a series of articles. She clicked on the first and shouted victoriously. The story was on the front page, along with a photograph of the Hôtel de Verbier with several police cars parked in front:

MURDER AT THE HOTEL

Yesterday, Sunday, December 16, a man was found murdered in room 622 of the Hôtel de Verbier. A hotel employee discovered the body of the victim as he was bringing him his breakfast.

3

The Start of the Affair

Sunday, December 9, seven days before the murder

The plane was stuck on the tarmac at the Madrid airport. Over the loud-speaker, the captain had announced that a large snowstorm in Geneva had forced the airport to close briefly, at least long enough to clear the landing strip. The plane should be able to leave in about a half hour at most.

This was a minor inconvenience for most of the passengers on board, except for one Macaire Ebezner, a passenger in business class, sitting in the first row. His eye fastened on the window, he quickly swallowed the glass of champagne the hostess had offered him while he waited. He was nervous. Something wasn't right. He was convinced that the plane's being held had nothing to do with the snow: they had found it. They were going to pick him up on board the plane. He could feel it. He was trapped, like a rat. There was nowhere to run. Examining the tarmac through the window, he suddenly caught sight of a police car travelling at high speed towards the aircraft, its lights blinking. He felt his heart rate increase. He was trapped.

* * *

The previous day, in the middle of the afternoon, in the neighbourhood of Salamanca, in the centre of Madrid.

Macaire and Perez exited the Serrano metro station. They had identified the informer and recovered the documents from his apartment, then fled into the metro to avoid being seen. But exiting the car, Perez had the impression that they were being followed. Walking up the stairs to the street, he discovered he had been right.

"Don't turn around," he ordered Macaire. "Two guys are tailing us."

By the tone of his voice, Macaire knew that it was over. Yet, they had been careful to pay attention to the signs; they would pay dearly for their lack of vigilance.

Macaire felt a rush of adrenaline.

"Go right," Perez told him. "I'll head left. I'll meet you at the apartment later."

"I'm not leaving you alone!"

"Now!" Perez ordered. "Do as I say. You're the one with the list."

They separated. Macaire turned right and walked down the street at a brisk pace. He noticed a taxi by the kerb that had just dropped off a passenger, and he jumped inside. The driver took off, and Macaire turned around. Perez had disappeared.

Macaire had himself dropped off at Puerta del Sol and mixed in with the mass of tourists. He entered a clothes shop from which he emerged completely changed, just in case someone had noted his appearance. Not knowing what he was supposed to do, he called the emergency number. It was the first time in twelve years that he had used it. He found a phone booth near the Retiro and dialled. He knew the number by heart. He identified himself to the receptionist and was connected to Wagner, who told him the bad news.

"Perez was picked up by the Spanish police. They have nothing on him; he'll get out. In any case, he has a diplomatic passport."

"I have the list," Macaire said. "It was our man."

"Perfect. Burn the list and follow the protocol. Go back to your apartment and return to Geneva tomorrow as planned. Don't worry. Everything's going to be fine."

"Perfectly fine," Macaire agreed.

Before hanging up, Wagner remarked, in a somewhat amused tone of voice, which was like an explosion given the gravity of the situation, "Oh, since I have you on the line, you're in the paper. It's official."

"I know," Macaire replied, slightly annoyed by the light-hearted comment.

"Bravo!"

The line suddenly went dead.

Following the directions he had been given, Macaire returned to the apartment, taking every possible precaution, and burned the list. He greatly regretted having agreed to this trip, which was supposed to be his last. He was afraid that it was one too many. He had a lot to lose: his wife, his dream life, and the expected promotion. One week from now, he would be president of the family bank, one of the largest private banks in Switzerland. The news had made its way into the weekend edition of the *Tribune de Genève*, which had come out that very day. He had received congratulatory messages from everyone – except his wife, Anastasia, who had remained in Switzerland. As always with this type of trip, he had arranged it so that she didn't come along.

* * *

On the tarmac of the Madrid airport, the police car passed in front of the plane and continued along the service road without stopping. False alarm. Macaire collapsed in his seat, relieved. Suddenly, the plane shook and began to roll slowly in the direction of the departure runway.

A few minutes later, when the plane finally rose into the air, Macaire, feeling he was out of danger, breathed a long sigh of relief. He asked for a vodka and some nuts, then unfolded his copy of the *Tribune de Genève*, one of the newspapers available in the cabin. Turning to the business pages, he saw his picture.

MACAIRE EBEZNER TO BE NAMED PRESIDENT
OF THE EBEZNER BANK THIS SATURDAY
A decision has been made. Macaire Ebezner, 41 years old, will take over the reins of the largest private bank in Switzerland, to which he is the sole heir. The news was confirmed – although not in so many

words – by an influential member of the bank, who preferred to remain anonymous. "Only an Ebezner can lead the bank," he stated.

He asked for another vodka and swallowed it fast. He sighed.

He thought he had closed his eyes for no more than a few minutes but, when he awoke, the plane was already on its final approach to Geneva. He saw the chiselled contour of Lake Geneva and the lights of the city. It was snowing heavily, and snowflakes were spinning through the air. They were well into winter; Switzerland was covered in white. The flight from Madrid was one of the first to arrive at the Geneva airport after the lengthy delay caused by the weather.

It was nine thirty p.m. when the plane touched down at the newly cleared runway. Once he had disembarked, Macaire quickly crossed the interior of the airport, which he knew by heart, his briefcase in hand. He left the arrival area, looking relaxed. The customs agents didn't question him.

Because the snow had slowed air traffic for the last hour, a long line of taxis waited at the exit for the few travellers who had showed up. Macaire got into the first car. The driver set aside the newspaper he had finished scanning.

"Chemin de Ruth, Cologny," Macaire said.

Glancing at his customer in the rear-view mirror, the driver, waving his copy of the *Tribune de Genève*, asked Macaire, "That's you in the paper, isn't it?"

Macaire smiled, flattered to be recognised.

"Yes, it's me."

"It's a great honour, Monsieur Ebezner," the driver said, his face filled with admiration. "It's not every day that I get to carry a star of high finance."

Examining his face reflected in the glass, Macaire was unable to suppress a broad smile. He was at the peak of his banking career. The tension he had felt in Madrid was forgotten. He had managed to extricate himself from that business, and his future looked splendid. He was looking forward to being at the bank the next day – anxious to see the expressions on all their faces. Even though his rise to the presidency had been known for months, the article was going to generate gossip. Starting tomorrow, they would be fawning all over him. Just a few more days of patience. Saturday evening, during the bank's big annual weekend bash at the Verbier, he would be named as the head of the prestigious establishment.

The taxi went down rue de la Servette, then avenue de Chantepoulet, and crossed the Mont Blanc Bridge. The shores of Lake Geneva were glittering. The large fountain, the Jet d'Eau, rose majestically among the snowflakes. Between the snow and the Christmas lights, Geneva was a fairyland. Everything looked calm and serene.

The car then drove up quai du Général-Guisan and continued on towards Cologny, one of Geneva's most affluent communities, where Macaire lived with his wife, Anastasia, in a magnificent house overlooking Lake Geneva.

In the Ebezner kitchen, at that moment, Arma, the maid, tasted the veal roast she had been lovingly preparing for the past few hours; it was perfect. She again looked admiringly at the newspaper article she had placed on the work surface to keep her company. It was official. Monsieur would be named president of the bank next Saturday. She was so proud of him. She never worked weekends, but last night, as soon as she had seen the article in the café she patronised, she had decided to come to work so she could greet him upon his return from Madrid. She knew he was alone because his wife was spending the weekend with a friend (Madame Anastasia didn't like to be alone in the large house when her husband was travelling). Arma thought it was sad that no-one would be there on his return to celebrate such important news.

When she caught sight of the headlights of the taxi as it entered the property, she rushed outside to greet her boss, not bothering to put on her coat, in spite of the falling snow.

"You're in the paper!" she cried proudly, waving the article before Macaire, who was trying to get out of the taxi.

"Arma, what are you doing here? It's Sunday!"

"I didn't want you to come home to an empty house with nothing on the table."

He smiled affectionately.

"*President*. So, it's official." Arma beamed.

She grabbed the small suitcase that the driver removed from the boot, then followed her employer into the house as the taxi drove off. The car had barely passed the entrance gate to the property when a man appeared in its headlights. The driver stopped and lowered the window.

"I did as you said," he told the man, who appeared unconcerned by the falling snow.

"Did you show him the article?"

"Yes, I followed your orders to the letter," the driver swore, as he waited for his compensation. "I pretended to recognise him, just like you told me."

The man appeared satisfied and handed a bundle of hundred-franc notes to the driver, who left immediately.

In the house, seated at the kitchen table, Macaire had Arma serve him a thick slice of the roast. He was preoccupied – mostly because of Anastasia. He had sent her a message to let her know he had arrived in Geneva. She had replied, laconically:

Pleased that your trip went well.
Congrats on the article in the Tribune.
Returning tomorrow, better not to drive with all this snow.

Rereading the message, Macaire wondered who was lying to whom. He had been doing so for twelve years now. For twelve years a secret had been burning his lips. Arma recalled him from his thoughts.

29

"I'm very happy for you. When I saw the article, I nearly cried. *President of the bank!* You were in Madrid for work?"

"Yes," Macaire said, lying.

His mind was elsewhere and he wasn't paying the least attention to Arma. She went off to clean the pots and pans, furious with herself. What an idiot she had been to come here to meet him this evening. She thought he would be pleased. It would have been an opportunity to spend a special moment together. But he couldn't care less. He hadn't even noticed that she had been to the hairdresser and painted her nails. She decided to go home.

"If you have no further need of me, sir, I'll be going."

"Of course. Please go, Arma, and thank you for this delicious meal. Without you I would have gone to bed on an empty stomach. You're a pearl. Speaking of which, don't forget that I'll need you here all of next weekend."

"Next weekend?" Arma gasped.

"Yes. You know it's the big weekend banquet, off limits to the wives. I'm worried about leaving Anastasia alone again. Two weekends in a row, that's a lot. You know how much she hates being alone here. You could even sleep in one of the guest bedrooms. It would mean a lot to her."

"But you told me I could take next Friday off," she reminded him. "I was planning to take off until Monday."

"Oh, damn, I completely forgot. Can you cancel your plans? Please, it's very important that someone be here with Anastasia. She may want to have some friends over, and it would be good if you were here to take care of the house and do some cooking. I'll pay you double for your time from Friday to Sunday evening."

She wouldn't have agreed for all the money in the world. That weekend was very important. But since she was incapable of refusing her boss anything, she reluctantly accepted.

*

When Arma had left, Macaire locked himself in his office, a small room on the ground floor. He unhooked a picture from the wall (a watercolour of Geneva), which hid a small safe whose combination only he knew. He opened it. Inside was a single object: a notebook. For several weeks he had been writing down his secrets, just in case – so that someone would know. Recently, he had felt that he was being watched – surveilled. Events in Madrid seemed to confirm this. For twelve years, he had taken risk after risk. Writing down the truth somewhere could prove vital.

He flipped through the notebook. The first pages showed columns of numbers and sums of money, as if it were an accounting document. Maybe undeclared funds, someone might assume if the notebook were to fall into the wrong hands. That was a ruse. The following pages appeared blank, but were covered with his confessions. For greater security, Macaire had been writing with invisible ink. It was an old trick, but it still worked. Using a fountain pen, intentionally left empty, whose tip he dipped into a mixture of water and lemon juice, everything he wrote immediately disappeared into the pages. Although filled, they remained blank. If, one day, Macaire wanted to recover his invisible text, he simply had to put the pages near a source of light and heat, and his entire story would appear.

At first, it had been a tedious business, but with some training, his hand had become agile. Even without seeing his text, Macaire wrote quite legibly. He opened his notebook and located the last page of the text, whose corner was folded over, and dipped his pen into the bowl of lemon juice. He didn't notice the shadow hidden in the darkness a few feet away. Someone was watching him through the bedroom window.

The man remained motionless as he observed Macaire for more than an hour. He watched Macaire write, then return the notebook to the safe behind the painting before leaving the room – no doubt to go to sleep, given how late it was.

The man disappeared into the night, silent and invisible, making his way outside the property by slipping over the wall. Snow continued to fall and would soon cover his tracks. When he arrived at chemin de Ruth, the man got into a car parked near the shoulder. There was no-one in sight. He started the car and drove for a few minutes until he was some way off, then stopped to make a call.

"He returned home, and he suspects nothing," he assured his contact. "I even arranged for a taxi driver to discuss the article with him."

"A very good idea! Excellent."

"How did you manage to get the article published? With a picture, no less!"

"I have my contacts. Poor guy, tomorrow he's going to fall from his perch."

A kilometre away, the Ebezner home went completely dark. Macaire, in his large bed, quickly fell into a deep sleep, the article extolling his rise by his side. He had never felt so happy. He had no idea that his problems were only just beginning.

4

Agitation

Monday, December 10, six days before the murder

Six thirty in the morning. Awakened by the sound of his alarm, Macaire needed a few moments to remember that he was home. Opening his eyes, he jumped at the memory of the events in Madrid. Then, realising he was safe in his bed, he allowed himself to be overcome by a feeling of calm. Everything would turn out well.

He hadn't closed the shutters. Through the window, he saw that it was still dark outside and continued to snow heavily. He had no desire to engage with the cold. Wrapped in his duvet, he decided to spend a few more minutes in bed and closed his eyes.

At that moment, on rue de la Corraterie, in central Geneva, his secretary, Cristina, entered the imposing Ebezner Bank building with her usual punctuality. Since she had been hired six months earlier, she would arrive for work every morning at six thirty, when the tellers opened the building. She did so mostly to show her employers she was serious but also, especially, to have time to look through the files without being disturbed and without anyone asking questions.

Because of the snow, she had come on foot, unwilling to risk being caught in traffic on the poorly cleared streets. Wearing boots, her heels in her bag, she had walked from her apartment in Champel across the still sleeping city.

She strode across the broad entrance hall of the bank, elegant in her tightly belted coat. The tellers, in a row behind the counter, all of them a bit in love with her, marvelled at how nothing could diminish the zeal of this young employee, whose beauty was matched by her dedication.

"Good morning, Cristina," they all shouted with one voice.

"Good day, gentlemen," she smiled, placing before them a bag of croissants she had bought in a nearby bakery.

Touched by her gesture, they thanked her profusely.

"Did you see the weekend paper?" one of them asked, as he swallowed half a croissant. "You're going to be secretary to the president!"

"I'm very pleased for Monsieur Ebezner," she said. "He deserves it."

She headed for the elevators, then got off on the fifth floor, the centre of operations for wealth management. Following a long hallway whose walls were tastefully decorated, she arrived in the antechamber that served as her workplace and that led to the offices of her two superiors: Macaire Ebezner and Lev Levovitch.

This antechamber wasn't very large or very practical. A large desk blocked the passage; there was an armoire in one of the corners and a large photocopying machine. Cristina was the one who had asked that she be placed there. In all the departments, including wealth management, the secretaries occupied large, comfortable offices. But she preferred to be in direct contact with her superiors.

Cristina had quickly made herself indispensable at the bank. She worked hard and never complained. Intelligent, perceptive, charming. Always in a good mood, always willing to help out. She screened calls, carefully sorted the mail, handled meetings and scheduling.

Ever since her first day at the bank, she had been very impressed by Lev Levovitch. He was one of Geneva's most esteemed bankers, revered for his business acumen. He was the most feared as well. About forty years old, arrogantly good-looking, he had the allure of an actor and the bearing of royalty. Charismatic, gifted, fluent in six languages, he was annoyingly perfect. No-one was indifferent to him; everyone was envious.

He was familiar with his accounts down to the slightest detail. He understood the markets better than anyone and could anticipate their movements. Even when the stock markets unwound, his customers made money.

Oddly enough, Levovitch wasn't born into this world; he didn't come from a patrician Genevan family. Starting from nothing, he had worked hard to get where he was, which earned him the respect of the big players with whom he now rubbed shoulders and the sympathy of the staff, who saw themselves reflected in his modest origins.

Both secretive and discreet, cultivating an air of mystery, he never boasted about his work, letting the facts reported by the journalists speak for him – gossip as well. He was an adviser to the richest clients, intimate with the powerful, the friend of presidents, but, never forgetting where he came from, he was always available for those in need, came to the assistance of those without resources, and was generous to those who sought his help.

In Geneva everyone talked about him; everyone dreamed about calling him their friend. In spite of it all, he was a solitary man, without attachments. He lived in a very large suite on the fifth floor of the luxurious Hôtel des Bergues, located on the shore of Lake Geneva. His private life was well hidden; he didn't seem to have any friends, and his only confidant was his chauffeur and butler, Alfred Agostinelli, the epitome of discretion. A desirable bachelor, Levovitch's name was on the lips of every young woman of Geneva's best families, and the great families of Europe hoped he had eyes for one of their daughters. But Levovitch seemed to be completely detached from such ordinary needs. His heart was an impregnable fortress. It was said he had never fallen in love.

Levovitch arrived at the office every morning at seven sharp. But on that day, by 7:40 a.m., he still hadn't shown up. Yet Lev lived no more than a ten-minute walk from the bank; snow couldn't have been the reason for his absence. Struggling to find a good reason for the delay, Cristina assumed he had had a meeting outside the bank. Checking her boss's schedule, she saw that the page was empty until four p.m., where he himself had written – she recognised his handwriting – an enigmatic note in capital letters: VERY IMPORTANT MEETING. She was nonplussed. In general, she was the one who entered all the appointments on his calendar. This must have been added at the last minute. Cristina was intrigued and wondered what it could possibly mean.

Suddenly, she heard a voice in the hallway. She knew that the floor was always deserted at that hour. She listened, then stepped quietly forward along the hallway. In the stairwell stood Sinior Tarnogol, one of the members of the bank's board, who was walking up the stairs to his office on the sixth floor and had stopped to catch his breath. He was talking on the phone and spoke freely, convinced that, at that early hour, he was safe from eavesdroppers.

Cristina, keeping out of sight, listened to the conversation. She was stunned. The news would go off like a bomb.

5

The End of the Holiday

At the offices of the *Nouvelliste*, Scarlett had printed out all the articles concerning the murder in room 622. She had discovered that the crime had never been resolved. And in the car on the way back to Verbier, she had only one thought in mind: to convince me to write a book about it.

"Hey, Writer, there was a murder in this hotel! That's crazy. Think about it – the cosy atmosphere, the guests under suspicion, the detective questioning witnesses sitting by the fireplace."

"So, Scarlett, what do you want to do? Reopen the case? Solve a murder that the police couldn't solve?"

"Exactly! You're better than a cop, you're a writer. We'll conduct the investigation together and you'll write a book about it."

"I'm not going to write a book about it," I told her.

"Come on, Writer. I'm certain that Bernard would have wanted you to write about it."

"Nope. My next novel will be a crummy police procedural."

"Don't be so grumpy. There's even a novel within the novel: how we discovered that the number of room 622 was changed after the murder. Aren't you curious to find out why the concierge lied to us last night?"

"That's all we need."

"Yes, in fact. And I'll help you."

"You'll help me? You've never written a book."

"I'll be your assistant."

"I already have an assistant and, believe me, you don't want to be like her."

"Then from now on you'll have two assistants."

"I'm supposed to be on holiday. I'm supposed to be relaxing."

"You can relax when you're dead."

"In any case, I'm not available. I have commitments."

"Oh? What?"

"Why, this afternoon, for example, I'm getting a massage. After that I'm going to the spa to sit in the Jacuzzi and enter a state of absolute relaxation."

"That's a good plan, Writer. Take care of yourself, build up your strength. The more relaxed you are, the better your book. Just tell me what I can do to help out."

After remaining silent for a long while, I said, "You need to find the pieces of the puzzle that will help us follow the thread of this story."

Scarlett's face brightened.

"That means you accept!"

I smiled. Of course, I accepted, if only to spend some time with her.

That afternoon, while Scarlett was supposed to be gathering material for our investigation, I took advantage of the hotel's spa services. Upon returning to my suite, I discovered that Scarlett had taken possession of the room. She had covered the wall with the articles we had found about the murder.

"How'd you get in?"

"I asked reception to open the door."

"And they did?"

"I told them I was your assistant. The great writer's assistant. Can you imagine? They were quaking in their boots. Take a look at what I found."

I sat on one of the armchairs, and she pointed to a sheet of paper on which she had written: "Ebezner Bank."

"Are you familiar with the Ebezner Bank in Geneva?" she asked.

"Yes, of course, it's one of the largest private banks in Switzerland. They're located on rue de la Corraterie."

"Does the name Macaire Ebezner mean anything to you?"

"No, but with a name like that, there has to be some connection with the bank."

"Bravo, Sherlock Holmes!"

She held out an article from the *Tribune de Genève* published eight days before the murder, which she had dug up on the internet. I read the title:

MACAIRE EBEZNER TO BE APPOINTED PRESIDENT OF THE EBEZNER BANK ON SATURDAY

"Ebezner was supposed to be named president of the bank on the weekend of the murder," Scarlett explained. "He was supposed to succeed his father, Abel Ebezner, who had died a year earlier. Except that, contrary to what the article states – you should always be suspicious of the press – the announcement had to be postponed."

"How do you know?"

"It wasn't easy, but I finally managed to get hold of last night's concierge. He explained that, if there were any questions from guests, management told him to invent this story about the wrong room numbers. Because a murder in a hotel is bad for business. I asked to speak to the manager but, as if by coincidence, he's not around this week. I suspect he's not too eager to be questioned. And the concierge was already working at the hotel at the time of the murder. At first, he told me he didn't remember anything, but a few francs succeeded in clearing up his amnesia. He told me that, at the time, Ebezner had a serious competitor by the name of Lev Levovitch, another banker, a rather flamboyant individual, known to the hotel, who had been Abel Ebezner's right-hand man."

"That's Macaire Ebezner's father, right?"

"Exactly," Scarlett confirmed. "The concierge had earned the confidence of the manager of the hotel at the time, Edmond Rose, who was apparently very close with Levovitch. On the weekend of the murder, there was already some unusual commotion at the hotel."

"Wait a minute. I don't get it. What connection is there between the hotel and the bank?"

"The Gala Weekend."

"The Gala Weekend? What's that?"

"It's been a tradition of the Ebezner Bank for decades. It's their annual celebration. Every year, in December, all the bank's employees are invited to spend two days at the Verbier. Everyone is given a room here. The days were kept open so employees could go skiing or hiking or play curling. On Saturday evening, there was a gala dinner in the hotel ballroom. That's when the official announcements were made – internal promotions, transfers of power, or retirements."

"So, the murder took place during one of the bank's Gala Weekends?"

"Yes, and not just any weekend. Look."

Scarlett showed me another article from the *Tribune de Genève*. It was dated almost one year before the murder and discussed Abel Ebezner's funeral, held in early January at the Cathédral Saint-Pierre in Geneva. There was a photograph of three men, described as members of the bank's board: Jean-Bénédict Hansen, Horace Hansen, and Sinior Tarnogol.

"The bank's board?" I asked, realising that Scarlett had written those same words on a piece of paper taped to the wall, as if it were something important. "How do they fit in?"

She smiled victoriously.

"I asked myself the same question. So I did some research. At the time, the bank hierarchy was as follows: at the bottom, the ordinary employees; above them, the department heads; above them, the signing officers; above them, the assistant directors; above them, the directors; and, above them, at the top, dominating all the others, the bank's board of directors. There were four members: two ordinary members, a vice president, and a president. According to the article in the *Tribune de Genève*, the presidency of the Ebezner Bank has always been handed down from father to son. This means that the presidents and vice presidents of the bank have always been Ebezners, father and son, passed down from generation to generation."

"So, logically, Macaire Ebezner should have been appointed president, following his father."

"Logically, yes. Now look at the photo from the article on Abel Ebezner. Look at the three other members of the board of directors: Macaire Ebezner is not among them."

"Why not?"

"I don't know. But based on what I was able to find online, before his death, Abel Ebezner changed the rules. He had assigned the board the task of choosing his successor, giving it about a year to make its choice. The announcement of the new president should have taken place at the Gala Weekend following his death – the weekend of the murder."

6

The Race to the Top

In the month before the murder, the succession of the presidency of the Ebezner Bank had become a minor epic that captivated the city.

It had started in January, during the very first days of the year, when Abel Ebezner, president of the bank for the past fifteen years, had died at a respectable age, carried away by cancer. When his death was announced, everyone assumed that the presidency would rightfully fall to Macaire, his only son. Ever since the founding of their family bank, three hundred years earlier, control of the business had always been passed from father to son. "Only an Ebezner can run the Ebezner Bank," was the refrain repeated to employees and clients alike, as if it were a guarantee of some extraordinary ability. But before his death, Abel Ebezner had decreed in his will that this tradition of filial descent would be buried with him and that the next president of the prestigious bank would be appointed not for his name but for his abilities.

Taking the advice of his lawyer, old man Ebezner had thought of everything, down to the smallest detail. The method of choosing the bank chair would be governed by three requirements. First, the three remaining members of the bank's board would be responsible for appointing a new fourth member who would act as president and chairman. Second, the board could not choose among themselves but had to appoint a new member. And third, the decision would be announced only during the traditional Weekend Gala at the end of the year, and the new president would assume his functions on January 1 of the following year.

Abel Ebezner's last will and testament went off like a clap of thunder inside the bank. Far from destabilising the business, it galvanised it.

From the tellers to the directors, everyone suddenly believed that they, too, could rise to the top of the pyramid. At every level, the employees worked harder to attract the attention of the members of the board. The bank had never been so productive. No-one requested sick days, and many of the employees even avoided taking a holiday.

The frenzy surrounding the succession was so intense that its repercussions were felt throughout the city. The Ebezner Bank was one of the city's great institutions, and its president was one of the city's most prominent personalities. The fact that, for the first time, the succession wouldn't be hereditary was a subject of heated discussion.

As the weeks passed, excitement rose to a crescendo. At last, December arrived. Everyone was dying to know who would join Jean-Bénédict Hansen, Horace Hansen, and Sinior Tarnogol on the board and preside over the bank's future.

So, on Monday, December 10, at ten thirty a.m., when Macaire Ebezner finally made his appearance on the pavement of rue de la Corraterie, he rejoiced upon seeing the imposing building rise before him. He gazed proudly at the façade.

EBEZNER & SONS, SINCE 1702

He was going to be a star. He knew it. Over the following days, his name was going to be on everyone's lips; everybody would know who he was. But he had to keep a cool head and appear unassuming. He had to remember that, before Saturday, all options were still open to the board. Obviously, he couldn't say that he had known for a long time that he would be the next president. But he couldn't wait for Saturday to arrive. Just six short days and it would be official. He had to remain patient.

He admired the pediment of the bank and breathed deeply of the winter morning's revivifying air. The sun was shining on the snow; the sky was a brilliant blue.

43

He regretted not getting out of bed when he had first awakened. Thinking he would close his eyes only for a few moments, he had fallen into a deep sleep again. Because everyone was expecting him, they would note his late arrival. It wouldn't look good for a future president of the most important private bank in Switzerland to arrive so late for work. It was bad enough that he never arrived early, but this was the icing on the cake. He would blame the snow this time but made a New Year's resolution that once his appointment was official, he would be one of the first to arrive at the bank every morning.

Passing through the bank's heavy entrance door, with its ornate gilt decorations, Macaire Ebezner self-importantly entered the large reception hall. He felt all eyes were upon him. Behind their windows, the tellers greeted him deferentially. "Good morning, Monsieur Ebezner," they repeated in chorus, slightly inclining their heads.

Macaire noticed at once that they were looking at him differently. He suddenly felt more important than the Pope. Everyone he passed congratulated him, offered obsequious greetings, and winked complicity. Soon he would be confirmed in his role – he had the right to be flattered. The most sycophantic even went so far as to say, "Good day, Mr President."

He took the elevator with a knot of bootlickers, who squirmed before him. They're just a bunch of flunkies, he thought, watching them as they twisted and turned. But he was nobody's fool. Some of his courtiers had changed their stripes at the last minute, assuming that he would be overlooked by the board. He knew he wasn't always taken seriously, especially this past year, because of the stipulations his father had made just before his death. His father's decision to have him voted in by the board rather than appointing him directly had bothered him at first. He would have preferred that Abel Ebezner had done as all his predecessors had done for the past three hundred years and simply passed the torch to his son, to be in charge immediately without having to be subjected to such formalities as an election. But, in the end, he understood the reason for his father's final decision: it was to better establish his legitimacy. Macaire would be appointed for his talent, not for his name. He would come out of this more powerful than before. His father had thought of everything.

On the fifth floor, Macaire got out of the elevator, strutting through the antechamber where his secretary, Cristina, worked. What a party she would throw for him. But Cristina looked mortified.

"Monsieur Ebezner, you're finally here."

"What's wrong, Cristina?" he asked, with a mocking expression. "You look like you've seen a ghost."

"I don't know how to say this . . ."

"Say what?" He smiled. "If it's about my appointment as president, the weekend paper already informed me."

With an amused smile, Macaire stepped into his office, removing his heavy winter coat. Cristina followed him into the room and, since she stood there in silence, he frowned.

"You're worrying me, Cristina. You look pale. I hope it's not your health."

After a moment's hesitation, she said, "Monsieur Ebezner, they're not going to appoint you head of the bank."

"What are you talking about? Haven't you seen the weekend paper?"

"The article's a fake!" she shouted. "Levovitch is going to be appointed president."

This last statement rang out like a gunshot. Macaire stood there, stunned.

"What are you saying?"

"Levovitch is going to be elected president. I'm so sorry."

"Oh, that little shit!" Macaire muttered.

He wanted to run into Levovitch's office and demand an explanation, but Cristina stopped him.

"Monsieur Levovitch didn't show up at the bank this morning. I tried to reach him. I'm very worried. I absolutely must talk to him. Do you know where he is?"

Macaire, composing himself, assumed a disinterested air.

"There's no point getting excited over poor Levovitch. There's no question of him becoming president. What's got into you to spread such idiotic rumours? I know who the source was for the article. It's a member of the board with whom I'm very close and who has assured me for months that . . ."

"Is it your cousin, Jean-Bénédict Hansen?" she interrupted.

"Excuse me?" Macaire hated to be cut off in mid-sentence by underlings.

"The member of the board with whom you're so close, it's Monsieur Hansen, isn't that right?" she asked.

"It's Jean-Béné, yes," he confirmed. "Is that a problem?"

"This morning I heard Monsieur Tarnogol talking on the phone with Monsieur Hansen. He told him that he mustn't vote for you, that it would be against your father's wishes. Because of what happened fifteen years ago at the Verbier. He said your father had never forgiven you, that if he had wanted you to be president, he would have appointed you directly. As far as I can tell from the conversation, the board met on Friday and agreed to appoint Levovitch."

"No, no, no. Jean-Béné wouldn't do that to me."

"That's what I said to myself, too. So, I went to wait for Monsieur Hansen outside his office to ask him, and, unfortunately, my assumption was correct. I'm really very sorry, Monsieur Ebezner. I think it's very unfair."

Refusing to believe that any of this was true, Macaire rushed to the floor above to question his cousin himself.

The offices of the board's members were situated on the sixth floor of the bank. At the end of an impressive corridor, four doors followed one another in succession. The first was the office of the president, left vacant since the death of Abel Ebezner. Next was that of the vice president, which should have been Macaire Ebezner's for the past fifteen years but which, following the events that occurred back then, was instead occupied by Sinior Tarnogol, a shadowy, mysterious presence, who spent the majority of his time travelling between Switzerland and Eastern Europe. Then there were the offices of the two other members of the board: Horace Hansen, a member of another, younger branch of the Ebezner family, and his son, Jean-Bénédict Hansen, a man of about forty, like Macaire.

At that moment, Jean-Bénédict Hansen was pacing anxiously in his office, staring at the door, fearing the furious arrival of his cousin, Macaire, once he had been informed by Cristina.

"The filthy little busybody!" Jean-Bénédict complained aloud. Two hours earlier, upon his arrival at the bank, he had found her outside his office.

"Is it true?" she had asked. "You're not going to elect Monsieur Ebezner president?"

He blanched.

"How do you know that?" he mumbled. "Really, Cristina, are you spying on the board? That's unacceptable!"

"Don't be ridiculous. You'd do well to tell Monsieur Tarnogol to be a little more careful if you don't want your secrets getting out. How could you do something like this to your cousin?"

"It's none of your business, Cristina," he shot back at her. "I think you're completely overstepping your role here. Please don't talk about Macaire."

"You don't want me to say anything? And let him hear the news on Saturday evening in front of all the bank's employees? That would be so humiliating for him."

"It's more complicated than that."

"I can't just pretend that nothing has happened."

"You have no reason to tell him anything. You're letting yourself get carried away by your affection for him. Please, Cristina, hold your tongue. Otherwise, there will be serious consequences. Trust me."

"Everyone should do what they feel is right," she concluded.

She walked out of the office, looking defiant, and he scowled at her all the way to the elevator. She was unquestionably the biggest pain in the arse around. He regretted having helped her get a start at the bank, finding a position that was perfect for her. Then she had asked to be moved into the antechamber, arguing that she couldn't do her job properly if she was with all the other secretaries in a shared office. And he had agreed to everything. Now this was his thanks.

The door to Jean-Bénédict's office suddenly flew open, and Macaire appeared.

"Jean-Béné, tell me it's not true. Tell me the board isn't going to make Levovitch president."

"I'm really sorry," Jean-Bénédict said, staring at the floor.

A glacial silence spread through the room. Macaire, in shock, let himself collapse into an armchair and closed his eyes, as if to shield himself from the unbearable reality. He was being denied his birthright! Such shame! Such humiliation! What would people say? What would his wife say? Until today, if he was someone important in Geneva, it was because he was the heir to the Ebezner Bank. But now, shoved aside by his father, shoved aside by his peers, he would be the laughing stock of the entire city. His whole world was collapsing. There would be no honours, no applause. He pictured the large boardroom, the holy of holies, where he had imagined his portrait looking out beside that of his ancestor, Antiochus Ebezner. And he wondered what old Antiochus would have thought about all this.

Antiochus Ebezner had founded the bank in Geneva in 1702. He had requested financing from a younger branch of the family, the Hansens, miserable cousins as tight-fisted as rats, who had fled France for

Switzerland after the Saint Bartholomew's Day massacre and, in Ebezner's opinion, would have been better off massacred, because, instead of making an ordinary loan, they had demanded participation in the bank in exchange for the money.

Antiochus had no choice but to transfer shares to his cousin Wilfried Hansen while keeping control of the majority. But, because he didn't trust Hansen, and to forestall a putsch within his own bank, he decided to establish a board of directors and transfer nearly half of his shares to his son, Melchior, thereby appointing him vice president. In this way he could train Melchior and prepare him to run the business when the time came. To prevent a two-against-one situation, Wilfried Hansen demanded to be allowed to do the same and transferred half of his shares to his eldest son, who also became a board member.

Afterwards, to finally put an end to an internal struggle that had begun to harm the bank's reputation, Antiochus and Wilfried agreed that the bank's board would consist of only four members, who held all the shares: two Ebezners (father and son), who would hold the majority, and two Hansens, who would remain minority shareholders, with generous dividends to compensate for their subaltern status. This enabled the Ebezners to maintain control of their bank, transferring their shares from father to son and generation to generation, while the Hansens, considered an inferior branch of the family, were condemned to remain in the background.

For ten generations, the family's fertility allowed the Ebezners to ensure that the line of succession, begun in 1702, continued uninterrupted, for every president had had at least one male heir (as the patriarchy demanded). In more recent times, Auguste, Macaire's grandfather, upon becoming president, had transferred the position of vice president to his son Abel, Macaire's father. And when Auguste passed away, it was quite natural that Abel would offer his seat as vice president of the board to his only son, Macaire, then twenty-six years old.

It had all begun to unravel fifteen years earlier; Macaire remembered it all as if it were yesterday. At the time, the traditional annual Gala Weekend at the Verbier had been a fixture for years and, on this occasion, during the Saturday evening ball, the weekend's highlight, he had received from his own father, in front of everyone assembled, the remaining shares that would raise him, according to a tradition established three hundred years earlier by Antiochus Ebezner and Wilfried Hansen, to the rank of vice president of the board.

But Macaire Ebezner never had the opportunity to sit on the board, because he had the misplaced idea, for reasons no-one could ever comprehend, of transferring his shares to a certain Sinior Tarnogol, an unscrupulous businessman originally from Saint Petersburg, who had been looking to invest his money in Switzerland. Of course, when Abel Ebezner learned the news, he did everything he could to recover his son's shares. First, he sued – unsuccessfully, because the sale had been conducted legally. He then tried to negotiate, prepared to offer an astronomical sum to recover the precious shares, but Tarnogol had refused to sell. In this way he became a member of the board in Macaire's place and, because he was also vice president, overturned the order that had been established by Antiochus Ebezner three hundred years ago. Antiochus had thought of everything in his efforts to ensure that ownership of the bank would stay in the family – everything except the possibility that an Ebezner might one day sell his shares.

The voice of his cousin Jean-Bénédict brought Macaire back to his sad reality.

"Levovitch is best equipped to run the bank. You have to face facts. The numbers speak for themselves, and the customers love him."

"I've had a bad year, it's true," Macaire admitted, "but you know very well why – my father's death in January, his decision not to name me directly as his heir."

"Yes, his decision not to name anyone at all," Jean-Bénédict dared reply.

"What are you implying?"

"I don't suppose your father ever forgave you for what you did fifteen years ago. What were you thinking, anyway?"

"It doesn't matter, you wouldn't understand."

"But one day you'll tell me, won't you? Really, Macaire, do you have any idea what you did? You broke the Ebezner pact, you sold your shares!"

"And you, you lied to me all year long," Macaire replied. "You told me I'd be named president by the board. And in the end, you stabbed me in the back! I thought we were friends!"

"I never betrayed you, Macaire. I never lied to you. You're my cousin . . . and my friend. Back in January, the board had decided that you would succeed your father. We were all in agreement. You would be president; there wasn't the shadow of a doubt. Not only because we wanted to maintain the tradition, but also to reassure our customers. But your earnings continued to drop. All year long. I did everything I could to help you; I defended you tooth and nail. In June, when the board grew concerned about your poor mid-year earnings, I brought in an additional assistant to help you, and you alone."

"An assistant for Levovitch and me," Macaire replied.

"Look, you knew very well that she was hired for you, to help you crawl back up that hill. We were trying to prevent your humiliation; that's why we pretended she was an additional resource for you *and* Lev, given the number of clients you both had."

"But Levovitch was the one who used her the most!"

"Well, you're an idiot!" Jean-Bénédict shouted. "You don't know how to manage your resources – one more reason not to entrust you with running a bank!"

Jean-Bénédict's sudden change of tone unsettled Macaire. In a strangled voice he replied, "But just last week, after the board meeting, you assured me that I was the one."

"Last Wednesday you were the board's choice," Jean-Bénédict confirmed. "I'm not making this up."

"So what happened?"

"On Friday morning, Tarnogol asked to see us, my father and me. It was 'urgent', he said. And then, he showed us a file he had put together. It was about you."

"A file? What was in it?"

"Your annual earnings – catastrophic. And letters from unhappy clients. Some of them had changed advisers; others simply found a new bank. We had no idea."

"Look, Jean-Béné, I screwed up, I had a bad year, it's true. But, until now, my record has been faultless. I'm the top wealth manager at the bank."

"Levovitch and you were the top wealth managers at the bank," Jean-Bénédict corrected. "But even in your best years, you were never at Levovitch's level. Anyway, Tarnogol showed us the numbers and said we were making a serious error in appointing you president when all the indicators were flashing red. He said that we had chosen you out of respect for tradition, without thinking about what was best for the bank. And he pointed out that if your father had decided not to turn management of the bank over to you, there must have been a good reason. That's why we have to elect Levovitch president."

"And you didn't defend me?"

"Of course, I defended you."

"Then why didn't you warn me about what was going on? Why did I have to hear it this morning from my secretary?"

"I did try to warn you, last Friday. But you weren't at the bank that day, and I couldn't reach you by phone."

"I was travelling."

"For the bank?"

"Yes."

"Travelling where?"

Macaire, sensing he was being led into a trap, chose not to lie.

"Madrid."

"You have no Spanish clients, Macaire. And that's the one thing that stands out in Tarnogol's file on you. He discovered you've been travelling at the bank's expense for years to places where you have no clients."

* * *

Three days earlier

In the boardroom, Horace and Jean-Bénédict, both in a state of shock, studied the documents Tarnogol had placed on the table: dozens of pages he had obtained from the accounting department.

"I didn't want to speak to you before I had done all the research," Tarnogol explained. "I didn't want you to think I was orchestrating a campaign to denigrate Macaire. But we're at a critical juncture. The man you want to appoint as president has been stealing from the bank for years; we've been paying for his expensive trips all over Europe, without any justification."

"Have you spoken to Macaire about this?" Jean-Bénédict asked.

"I would have preferred if he were here, with us, so he could explain himself. But he's not at the bank this morning. He's in Madrid. I know this because, as you can see on this receipt, the bank paid for business-class tickets and an apartment for the weekend. But Macaire has never had any clients in Madrid. He doesn't speak a word of Spanish. You can go back years: London, Milan, Vienna, Lisbon, Moscow, Copenhagen, and on and on. We're talking about astronomical sums of money spent without the least explanation."

Horace and Jean-Bénédict looked over the documents, gradually coming to appreciate the magnitude of the expenses.

"Look at this. He had the bank pay for suites at the Hotel Grande Bretagne in Athens, the Bayerischer Hof in Munich, the Plaza Athénée in Paris," Horace commented with an air of disgust.

"Always weekends, always the best hotels, the best restaurants," added Tarnogol. "Macaire has been dipping into the till to pay for his good times."

"How is it that no-one noticed anything all this time?" Horace asked.

"Do you think the people in accounting were going to go combing through the receipts of the future president to find out whether his expenses were justified?" Tarnogol replied. "They're not crazy. They all understood what he was doing, but they preferred to sweep it under the carpet."

"Is Macaire leading a double life?" Jean-Bénédict wondered. "Is he cheating on Anastasia?"

"What does it matter?" Horace objected. "Macaire can do what he wants in his private life, but not with the bank's money. It's our money he's been stealing."

"Am I to understand that you're changing your mind?" Tarnogol asked.

"Yes – yes, I am," Horace admitted. "I'm giving my vote to Levovitch. It's time that the Ebezners stopped behaving as if everything belonged to them."

* * *

Listening to his cousin, Macaire broke out in a cold sweat. Having the bank pay for his travel was a grave error.

"But Macaire, what were you thinking?"

"I'm going to reimburse the bank. Down to the last penny. Organise a meeting with Tarnogol and your father, I'll explain everything."

"If I were you, I'd wait a while. I had both of them on the phone this morning. The article in the *Tribune* announcing your appointment didn't amuse them at all, as you can imagine. Why announce it when nothing has yet been determined?"

"Me?" Macaire said, letting his arms fall to his side. "I didn't alert the *Tribune*! Why would I have done something like that?"

"I have no idea. In any event, your chances have been highly compromised."

"For God's sake, I'm an Ebezner!" Macaire shouted. "That's my name engraved on the front of the bank."

"You'd be president today if you hadn't sold your shares to Tarnogol fifteen years ago. You've only yourself to blame."

Macaire stared darkly at his cousin and thought, Oh, that filthy little prick. Now he's trying to give me advice! When Jean-Bénédict had joined the bank, Macaire had taken his cousin under his wing. Macaire had always been there for him, always ready to help, always ready to bail him out with his clients when the numbers weren't good and they needed to be massaged a little. And one fine day, Grandpa Hansen dies and here comes cousin Jean-Bénédict, trotting up to the top floor to assume the second Hansen seat on the board. And now, he's the big man all of a sudden, strutting around the hallways of the bank!

All the same, Macaire felt it would be better to avoid showing his true feelings. He preferred to bluff his way out.

"What do you think, Jean-Béné? Should I just let them do this to me? If you think that's going to happen, you don't know me very well. I'm going to annul the election. Do you think I've wated a whole year, quietly biding my time, waiting to discover whether the board would name me president, just to place my fate in the hands of Tarnogol, your father, and you? I've been preparing my strategy for a year."

"What do you mean, your *strategy*?" Jean-Bénédict asked, his voice betraying his uncertainty.

Macaire didn't reply to his cousin, and a mysterious silence filled the room. Macaire was trying to decide what he would say next, but also wanted to enjoy the authority he had always held over his cousin.

"It wouldn't be wise to talk about it. Good day."

He made a move to leave, but his cousin stopped him.

"Wait, Macaire. You can tell me everything. You've never had a reason to doubt my discretion. I had planned to talk to you about this today. Since the start of the year, I've been the one defending you tooth and nail during the board's meetings."

Macaire nodded, as if he had only then been convinced by Jean-Bénédict. "There's going to be a purge within the bank."

"A purge? I don't like that word." Jean-Bénédict looked concerned.

"You might," Macaire replied, digging deeper into his lie. "A year ago, my lawyers put together a working group. They examined the files secretly, ruthlessly, looking for a way to neutralise my father's last wishes. And they found a weak spot: his will has no legal value. It doesn't matter what this two-bit board decides; all I have to do is bring the matter to court, and your ruling will be revoked. One way or another, I will be the majority shareholder and, therefore, president."

"Why didn't you say something before?"

Macaire smiled, half angel, half devil.

"First of all because I had hoped that the board would be loyal to me, which would have allowed for a smooth transition, with the bank's best interests in mind. I didn't want to make trouble unnecessarily. And, of course, it gave me an opportunity to see who would be loyal and who would stick a knife in my back. Your father and Tarnogol can crow all they like. Once I've taken control, I'll throw them out, along with all the hypocrites who refused to believe in me after my father died and took me for granted. Yes, a purge!"

"I've always supported you," Jean-Bénédict reminded him, hoping to save his own skin.

"I know, cousin. I haven't forgotten. But you're going to have to work a little harder to make sure I get to the top."

After a brief moment of reflection, Jean-Bénédict replied. "The dice haven't been thrown yet. The presidency is between Levovitch and you; of course, right now, he has the clear advantage. But all that can change. The board's final decision won't be made until this Saturday afternoon at the Hôtel de Verbier. Between now and then, anything can happen."

At those words, Macaire saw a glimmer of hope. He felt his confidence begin to return. "If I understand correctly, I still have five days to convince Tarnogol to vote for me."

"If you can convince Tarnogol, then you'll come out on top. My father will add his vote. You know that you already have mine."

The skies suddenly cleared for Macaire. He needed to convince just one man to be unanimously elected.

In a magnanimous tone of voice, Macaire said, "Thank you for your support, my dear Jean-Béné." He then returned to his office to calmly work out a plan to convince Tarnogol. Reaching the antechamber, he saw Cristina getting ready to leave.

"Leaving already, Cristina?"

"I'm going to the Hôtel des Bergues. I've still had no news from Monsieur Levovitch. It's not like him to keep silent. He's been unreachable. I've even contacted the concierge at the hotel, but he told me that no-one is answering and he didn't see Monsieur Levovitch go out this morning – almost as if he had disappeared. The concierge refuses to go to Monsieur Levovitch's suite to check on him. 'Hotel policy,' he said. What if something terrible has happened?"

Hearing the words "something terrible", Macaire's face brightened. If Levovitch had had a devastating heart attack in his bath, Macaire would be named president without having to convince Tarnogol. Life was good after all. Macaire wanted to rush over to the Hôtel des Bergues and be the first to discover the body on the marble floor. But not so fast! At the very least, Levovitch needed to remain paralysed for the rest of his life. It would be a waste if the ambulance arrived in time. Macaire, looking at his watch, saw that it was only 11:15 and decided that his rival deserved to remain on the floor for another forty-five minutes at least.

"You're not going anywhere, Cristina," Macaire ordered. "I need you here. This is no time to be going for a walk."

Frowning, she removed her coat. She should have lied and said she had a doctor's appointment. A rookie error. She thought about asking a co-worker to go to the hotel for her but decided against it. If Macaire discovered what she had done, it might backfire. She had to stick to being a secretary.

Noticing that Cristina was upset, Macaire said, "I promise, if by noon we haven't heard from him, I'll go to the hotel myself and order the concierge to open the suite. But now, let's get back to work."

Cristina resigned herself. She had no choice, anyway. She went through the day's mail, stacking the newspapers that Levovitch received every day: the *Financial Times*, *Le Figaro*, the *Neue Freie Presse*, *Corriere della Sera*, the *Tribune de Genève*. Looking at the *Tribune*'s headline, she saw there would be a large conference that afternoon at the United Nations about the refugee crisis. Presidents and prime ministers from around the world would be attending.

She then opened the day's correspondence, scanning the pages before stamping them with the date for any administrative follow-up.

She brought Macaire his mail. He looked uneasily at the two stacks of letters that were piling up before him, which Cristina added to each day. Maybe Jean-Bénédict was right. He had neglected his work throughout the year. He had allowed himself to fall far behind. It was time to climb back up the slope, and he had to do it fast. If Tarnogol found out that he wasn't answering his mail or, worse, if Tarnogol entered his office and saw those stacks of waiting letters, it would certainly work against him.

Through the open door, Cristina observed her boss tenderly. She felt a deep sympathy for Macaire. He was loyal and good-natured but had the slightly blasé attitude of those who have never had to struggle to get to the top. He had never had to do anything for himself. His name alone had allowed him to enter the bank by the front door and quickly get a foothold as a wealth manager, without having to prove himself. And this was at a time when the markets were doing most of the work for him.

She felt bad for Macaire. He didn't deserve this. And he didn't deserve to be barred from becoming president of the bank. He was a gentle man, affable. Always kind, always ready with a compliment, fascinated by everything. She liked him very much.

When she had started at the bank, she had never imagined that Lev and Macaire would charm her, each in his own way. And sometimes she had to control herself. There was a reason why Jean-Bénédict had hired her, and she mustn't forget it. She had to remain professional. She couldn't risk compromising her job.

At twelve sharp, Macaire left his office, wrapped in his long winter coat.

"I'm going," he said, as if he were leaving on a dangerous mission.

"I'll go with you," Cristina said, rising from her chair.

"No," Macaire said firmly, to dissuade her. "You have to stay here in case Levovitch calls. I'll call as soon as I have any news."

Macaire stepped out of the bank and walked down rue de la Corraterie before reaching place Bel-Air. He then walked along quai Bezanson-Hugues to the Bergues pedestrian bridge. He stopped to take in the snow-covered expanse: the lake reflecting the blue sky, the mountains overlooking the city, Rousseau Island, and in the background the spray from the Jet d'Eau rising up like a flag. At the other side of the bridge appeared the Hôtel des Bergues. Macaire admired the majesty of the building, without suspecting for a second what was then happening inside.

7

At the Service of the Confederation

On the fifth floor of the Hôtel des Bergues, in suite 515, which he rented by the year, Lev Levovitch was knotting his tie as he looked out the window at Lake Geneva before him. He was lost in thought, thinking about her. He could think only of her. He wondered if she had come to spend the weekend with him because she really loved him or out of boredom.

He adjusted the jacket of his three-piece suit, then checked his tie in the mirror, taking advantage of it to consider his insolent beauty. On a silver platter was a pot of filtered coffee. Levovitch poured himself a cup but drank little. He was very late; he had to leave. He grabbed the basket of croissants he had ordered earlier and headed for the bathroom.

In a very large bathtub with a view overlooking the city, a woman was relaxing, lost in thought. She had made a decision. She was madly in love with Lev, but she had to break it off before it went too far. She couldn't go on like this. If word got out, her husband would be terribly humiliated, and Lev would run into problems at the bank. He had worked so hard to get where he was. Better to cut it off immediately, before three lives were destroyed. It broke her heart, but it was best for everyone involved.

At that moment, Lev appeared in the bathroom, dressed like a prince. She couldn't help but admire him. He had brought coffee and croissants, which he placed on the edge of the bathtub.

"Breakfast is served, Madame." He smiled. "Unfortunately, I have to leave, I'm already very late. Stay as long as you like. Make yourself at home."

She turned her blue eyes on him and said, dryly, "It's over, Lev."

He was taken aback.

"Anastasia, what are you saying?"

"I'm saying that I'm breaking up with you. It's over."

Upon hearing these words, Levovitch burst out laughing.

"You can't do that," he said, amused.

"And why not?"

"Because we love each other," he replied, as if it were a reason. "We've always loved each other. We love each other like we've never loved before. This love that binds us is the only meaning in our lives."

Without denying it, she swept the argument away, annoyed.

"I have a husband, Lev! And I have no intention of hurting him. I can't spend the weekend in your hotel, whenever you please. People will see us, and the entire city will find out. You know how fast rumour travels. And it would cause problems for you, too. Serious problems."

He made a face. "I don't give a damn about problems. I won't put my career before our feelings."

She felt he was getting the upper hand, that he would end up convincing her. She forced herself to be cruel.

"What feelings? I don't love you, Lev," she lied. "If I did, I would have married you fifteen years ago."

He remained silent for a while as he absorbed the shock. Then, very calmly, he said, "Let's have dinner together this evening and talk about it properly."

"No, no. We won't be seeing each other again. I don't want to go on like this. Do you understand what I'm saying? I can't do it any longer."

"It wasn't a question, it was a statement. I'm delighted to be meeting you later. Let's say eight o'clock tonight, at the hotel?"

"I said no, Lev!" Anastasia shouted.

She got out of the tub and wrapped herself in a robe. She retrieved her phone from the vanity and dialled her husband's number. He picked up almost at once. She forced herself to sound tender and loving.

"How are you?" she asked. "Yes, I missed you too . . . My weekend? . . . No, it wasn't great. I never want to see her again. It's not important, though; I'll tell you all about it. How about a quiet, romantic dinner this evening? You choose the restaurant; you can surprise me . . . Me too. See you later. I can't wait."

Anastasia hung up and turned to Lev with a satisfied look on her face.

"You'll dine alone this evening, Lev. As you heard, my husband and I are going out together."

Lev turned to stone.

"Tonight, Anastasia, eight o'clock. Knowing that I'll be meeting you in a few hours makes me very happy."

He left and went down to the hotel lobby, where his chauffeur was waiting.

"Hello, Alfred. How are you doing on this beautiful day?"

"I'm well, sir, thank you." Agostinelli escorted Lev to the car. "And you?"

"I'm on cloud nine, Alfred. I'm completely in love."

"You, sir?" Agostinelli smiled. "You swore to me that love didn't exist and that you'd never fall for anyone."

"She is so wonderful, Alfred."

The chauffeur started the engine and drove down the quay as Macaire arrived at the Hôtel des Bergues, just missing them. In the car, Agostinelli asked, "Are you going to the bank, sir?"

"No. Head for the Palais des Nations, Alfred. There's a conference on refugees at the United Nations. But first, call Cristina. I forgot to tell her that I wouldn't be coming to the office this morning. The poor thing must be worried sick."

* * *

"A conference on refugees at the United Nations," Cristina repeated aloud, as if it were obvious, hanging up the telephone.

Levovitch had just called. Busy with his day, he had forgotten to call her. She felt like an idiot for being so worried. She had read the headline in the *Tribune de Genève* about the UN conference. She should have realised he might have gone there.

She immediately dialled Macaire's mobile and reached him just as he arrived at the fifth floor of the hotel, escorted by the concierge, whom Macaire had convinced to open Levovitch's suite.

"False alarm," she said, "everything's fine. I just spoke to Monsieur Levovitch; he's at the United Nations."

"You see, there was no reason to be worried," Macaire replied in a perky voice. "I was just heading for his suite."

Macaire made a sign to the concierge that the mystery was solved, and they turned around.

"You seem to be in a better mood, Monsieur Ebezner," Cristina remarked.

"Tonight, I'm having a romantic dinner with Anastasia. Can I ask you to reserve a table at the Lion d'Or in Cologny? A table for two with a view of the lake."

Macaire and the concierge reached the elevator. Just as the doors closed, a few feet away, the door to Levovitch's suite opened, and Anastasia stepped out.

In the elevator, Macaire looked at the concierge with an affected benevolence that did little to hide his sense of superiority. He felt important. He, the future president of the Ebezner Bank, would be taking his wife to the Lion d'Or, one of the best restaurants in Geneva. A table with a magnificent view of the lake. Of course, when they arrived at the restaurant, everyone would be looking at them.

He felt galvanised and imagined he had already convinced Tarnogol to back him for president. Since it was lunch, he headed for the hotel bar. He entered just as Anastasia appeared in the lobby and walked quickly out of the hotel.

*

Macaire asked to be seated at a table off to the side. He needed to think calmly, determined to find a way to convince Tarnogol to give him his vote. Macaire considered all he had accomplished these past twelve years in secret and reflected, once more, on the fact that the bank was causing him to lose money. It was all his father's fault. Thanks to him, Macaire was in therapy twice a week. His father had always considered him incapable. At his deathbed, a year earlier, Macaire had nearly revealed his secret, to show his father who his son really was. But he had backed down at the last moment. Ever since, he had regretted it and relived in his mind the scene that had never taken place. He should have said, "You know, Father, for twelve years now, I haven't just been a banker. I've been living a double life, and no-one knows what I am about to reveal to you." He imagined the look on his father's face when he learned his son's secret.

With that thought, he observed the other customers in the restaurant, taking satisfaction in the fact that none of them suspected that the quiet, elegant banker in their midst worked for the Swiss intelligence services. The whole business had the air of a spy novel. He told himself that the notes he had jotted down in his notebook would make an excellent basis for his memoir. It would appear when he was quite old and had retired from the bank, but before his death, so he could contemplate the shock wave it would cause. He could imagine the headlines in the papers: *Macaire Ebezner, President of the Ebezner Bank and Member of the Intelligence Services.*

Macaire quickly swept his daydream aside. They would never let him reveal anything.

For twelve years, under the guise of doing business abroad, he had been gathering intelligence on behalf of the Swiss government. More specifically, he worked for P-30, a section within the Department of Defence financed by a secret account, which was virtually unknown – including to the powerful parliamentary intelligence committee – and which reported directly to the Federal Council.

P-30 originated as a secret programme set up by NATO during the Cold War. Fearing an invasion of Western Europe by the armies of the Warsaw Pact, the Allied countries organised clandestine networks composed of civilians trained to resist an occupation by the Eastern Bloc. From Portugal to Sweden, sleeper cells were set up more or less everywhere: there was the Greek LOK, the Italian Gladio, the Parsifal Plan in France, the Belgian Committee P, and Switzerland's P-26.

The Swiss government, inspired by this model, decided to apply it to defending Swiss interests abroad. Thus was created P-30, whose mission was to send civilians to conduct intelligence-gathering operations for the government.

Whereas an agent from the intelligence services had to construct a new identity wholesale, with all the difficulties and pitfalls inherent that entailed, the ordinary citizens who made up the staff of section P-30 could conduct operations without having to invent an alias or lie, because their real existence was their cover.

Macaire, as a banker apparently on a business trip, could travel without arousing suspicion.

Since he had been recruited, he had worked within P-30's finance division, gathering key information about the intentions of European countries that were fed up with their citizens avoiding taxes by hiding their money in Swiss bank accounts. This delicate matter had been turned over to P-30 because it largely concerned neighbouring countries and close allies, which Switzerland had no intention of embarrassing by sending out members of its official intelligence services.

So Macaire had travelled across Europe to various colloquia and official conferences devoted to new banking regulations, tax havens, or international cooperation on taxation. Between meetings, he had cultivated high-ranking officials, ambassadors, corporate lawyers, and employees of local tax agencies. None of this exposed Macaire to any risk: if he aroused suspicion, if the police questioned him, he could claim to be a banker seeking to add to his client roster. In this way, there was no danger of a scandal or diplomatic incident that might tarnish Switzerland's image as a country of polite, well-brought-up people – a protector of international agreements and the homeland of early risers and hard workers.

Even if there was an in-depth inquiry, it was impossible to trace a link between Macaire and any government agencies. Out of a concern for security, his only connection to P-30 was his case officer, a fellow from Bern with a disjointed accent named Wagner, whom Macaire would meet in a public place. Otherwise, he knew nothing of the operations of P-30, nor the location of its headquarters in Bern. It was an arrangement that was completely impermeable and undetectable.

For Macaire, his time at P-30 had begun in the secrecy of a private room in the Ebezner Bank, where Wagner, claiming to be a prospective client, had come to meet and recruit him. It was the only time Wagner had come to the bank. That day, as soon as they were alone, Wagner had explained that he was not there to open an account but had been sent by the Swiss government.

"Switzerland needs you, Macaire. We'd like you to perform a small service for us."

Wagner had limited himself to speaking in these vague terms, without mentioning P-30 or anything else. He had then explained that a minor diplomatic conflict was brewing between the United Kingdom and Switzerland.

An Indian diamond dealer, Ranjit Singh, based in London, was suspected by Scotland Yard of using his business to launder money from arms sales. The British assumed that the money passed through an account at the Ebezner Bank and, behind the scenes, they were putting pressure on Switzerland not only to confirm this but also to grant them access to the various transfers.

Bern refused to officially force a bank to release client information; it would have jeopardised the credibility of the entire Swiss banking system. But refusing to assist in an international investigation on money laundering might damage the reputation of the Swiss financial community. On the other hand, if the British were to receive such information from an anonymous third party, that would settle the matter once and for all.

Having understood his interlocutor's insinuations, Macaire, eager to help his government, agreed to examine the bank's files and send Wagner copies of the diamond dealer's account statements.

The operation was codenamed Diamond Wedding and was an undisputed success. A few days later, Macaire discovered the following story in the *Tribune de Genève*:

INTERNATIONAL ARMS SMUGGLER
HAD CONNECTIONS IN GENEVA

Yesterday, in London, Scotland Yard arrested an important international arms smuggler. Using his business as a diamond dealer as cover, the man transferred money to a private bank in Geneva. His accounts have since been frozen.

The day the article appeared, Jean-Bénédict had showed up in Macaire's office with a copy of the paper.

"Did you read this?" Jean-Bénédict asked his cousin.

"Yes."

"Well, that private bank happens to be ours."

"Really?"

"Like I was saying. The federal police informed the board of the situation a few weeks ago. Obviously, I couldn't tell you anything; it was top secret."

"Top secret, of course," Macaire repeated, continuing to play dumb.

That same day, Macaire settled into a chair in his usual café. He turned and was surprised to see Wagner seated at a neighbouring table.

"Diamond Wedding was a success because of you," Wagner said, without lifting his eyes from the menu. "You're the type of man we're looking for. Do you think you might volunteer your services again?"

Macaire had accepted the offer – without fully understanding what he was agreeing to but conscious of the impact the decision would have on his life.

He had received some basic training, given over the course of a week in Flims in the Grisons Alps. His wife and colleagues thought he had gone hiking, alone, to restore his energy. He had made a reservation at the Hotel Schweizherof, where he spent his nights and ate supper in the evening. Every morning he would leave, wearing his cleats and carrying his trekking poles to maintain the deception. But instead of spending the day hiking, he went to an isolated chalet where Wagner was waiting for him. There Wagner taught Macaire methods of surveillance and evasion, how to react if questioned by the police, how to install a bug, and how to make a key from a tin can.

When his training was over, Macaire, on the morning of his departure, had asked the hotel to arrange his transportation to the railway station in Chur. Climbing into the shuttle that arrived to take him, he found Wagner behind the wheel.

During the journey, Wagner explained to Macaire everything he needed to know about P-30. Then, dropping him at the station, Wagner said, "I'll be in touch soon about your first mission."

"How will you contact me?"

"Music. I'm not called Wagner for nothing."

When a mission was imminent, Macaire would receive in the mail a ticket for the opera at the Grand Théâtre de Genève. That was the signal. Macaire went, alone of course, and during the intermission, he would meet his case officer in a quiet corner. During the second half of the performance, Wagner would give Macaire his orders.

As he gained experience, Macaire had advanced within P-30. After a few years, he was asked to produce analytical reports that were, he had been made to understand, quite highly regarded. Based on his observations, he prepared summaries that he sent in the form of a long letter, by ordinary mail, directly to the Federal Council, written in an unassuming style that made his document appear completely harmless.

Dear Sir or Madam
Based on my activities as a banker and interviews with my clients,
I would like to draw attention to the current situation and the
intentions of neighbouring countries and friends, et cetera.

Following Wagner's recommendations, Macaire was careful not to put in writing anything that couldn't be read by anyone. If someone found the letters, they would simply assume that Macaire was a banker concerned about the future of his profession who wished to convey his views and concerns to the country's leaders.

In this way, Macaire had alerted the Swiss authorities to various potential flashpoints: *The French want to recover their tax exiles; The Italians are looking at the money hidden in Tessin; The Germans are going to look closely at the situation; The Greeks are trying to prevent capital outflows.* The Federal Council never failed to acknowledge receipt of his reports with elegant letters filled with gratitude but as anodyne in their use of language as his own correspondence.

Macaire had loved his years with P-30. Besides the satisfaction of serving his country, they made him feel alive. His missions gave him a feeling of intoxication. As he approached the Gala Weekend and his rise to the presidency of the bank, which at the time had seemed a certainty, Wagner had indicated that he would no longer be sent on missions once appointed. He would be too exposed. His career with P-30 was reaching its natural conclusion.

For his final mission, he had been sent to Madrid. A retired IT specialist from the Ebezner Bank, now living in Spain, was suspected of trying to sell to the Spanish tax authorities a list of clients who hid their money in Switzerland. This type of informer was the bane of the Swiss banks, a scourge that threatened to undermine their very existence. Macaire was ordered to determine whether, as the Swiss intelligence services believed, this IT specialist was, in fact, a traitor; and, more crucially, he was required to recover the list of clients before the transaction with the Spanish tax authorities could take place.

The operation was conducted in collaboration with the Swiss Confederation's intelligence services, which was unusual for a P-30 mission. Once in Madrid, Macaire would make contact with a certain Señor Perez, an agent who had infiltrated Spain under cover as an employee of the Swiss embassy.

The instructions were simple. Macaire was to alert his former colleague, the IT specialist, that he was coming to Madrid and suggest that he pay him a friendly visit. The former colleague had gladly agreed to this and seemed delighted to hear from Macaire, whom he remembered very well.

The day before the visit, Macaire met Perez in the Museo del Prado, in front of Goya's *The Third of May 1808*. After making contact, Perez followed Macaire at a distance until he reached the apartment he had rented for the weekend (more discreet than a hotel, which would be heavily monitored with cameras and where guests' passports were photocopied at check-in). It was in the secrecy of this comfortable furnished apartment in the Salamanca district that Perez had laid out the operational details.

"When you meet him, tell him you have to use the toilet so you can look around the place."

"What am I looking for exactly?"

"A list of names, mail, notes, anything that allows us to establish with certainty that he's the mole. Don't forget to look inside the flow tank behind the toilet."

The next day, arriving in front of the man's building, Macaire had seen Perez, reading a newspaper on a bench, keeping watch – as if he were worried about something.

The two men had, of course, pretended not to know each other, and Macaire rang the buzzer to the computer specialist's fourth-floor apartment. He was warmly received by his former colleague and the man's wife, who had fond memories of Geneva. The meeting was so enjoyable that Macaire felt certain that this man couldn't be the mole. Nonetheless, Macaire followed his instructions. Claiming to need the toilet, he gave his hosts the slip, allowing him to make a quick tour of the apartment. He went first to the bedroom, where he quickly rummaged through the wardrobes and a small dresser. He found nothing. He wanted to inspect the next room, set up as an office, but as he was about to pass through the doorway, his host's voice surprised him.

"The toilet's at the end of the hallway, on the right."

Macaire jumped.

"Oh, thanks – thanks, I had misunderstood."

There, behind the toilet, Macaire found a long list of Spanish clients of the Ebezner Bank in a sealed plastic bag. He couldn't believe it: this man was the traitor.

He threw the bag in the toilet, stuffed the list into his underwear, then returned to the living room, trying to conceal his nervousness. He drank his coffee and said goodbye.

He had left the building quickly. As he walked down the steps of the nearest metro station, Perez caught up with him.

"So?"

"He's our man," Macaire confirmed. "I recovered the list of clients."

They took the metro together, which was a mistake. As they stepped off the train, Perez realised that they were being followed.

At his table in the restaurant of the Hôtel des Bergues, Macaire, reflecting upon the Madrid operation, which he had executed quite well, had

71

convinced himself that he had the necessary resources to persuade Tarnogol to make him president of the bank. He just had to act as if it were a mission for P-30. What advice would Wagner have given him if that were the case? Lost in thought, Macaire wondered if there was a manual that might help him. Suddenly, he had an idea.

* * *

At three p.m., Macaire rushed into Jean-Bénédict's office and tossed onto his desk one of the four copies of the book he had just bought in a local bookshop.

"I have the solution," Macaire exulted.

"What solution?"

"I found the perfect method for convincing Tarnogol."

Jean-Bénédict picked up the book: *Twelve Angry Men*.

Macaire explained. "It's the story of the trial of a young man accused of murdering his father, whom the twelve members of the jury are getting ready to declare guilty and send to the electric chair. While eleven of the jurors are convinced of their verdict, one of them, who still has doubts, manages to change their minds. Well, I'm going to take my cue from the book. I'm going to flip Tarnogol like a pancake; you and your father will follow, and the scales will tip in my favour."

"Have you read it?" Jean-Bénédict asked.

"Some of it, why?"

"You didn't see the movie that was based on the book, by any chance? I think it was on television last week."

"Okay, it's true, I saw the film the other day," Macaire admitted, somewhat annoyed at having been found out. "But I knew it was based on a book!"

"A play," Jean-Bénédict specified, opening the book and pointing out the layout.

"Yes, fine, who cares!" Macaire replied. "And to be quite honest, I slept for half the film, and I have no idea what happened. So, we have to read this thing right away. We have to examine the arguments, make lists . . . that sort of thing."

"I have to take the four o'clock train to Zurich," Jean-Bénédict said, looking at his watch. "I'll read it on the train."

"Are you and Charlotte still coming for dinner tomorrow evening?" Macaire asked.

Once a month, the Hansens and the Ebezners met for dinner.

"Of course, we'll be there. I'm only going to Zurich for the evening – a dinner with clients – and tomorrow morning I'll be returning on the first train."

"So, tomorrow evening, I'll expect a reader's report, dear cousin."

"At your service, sir, the future president!" Jean-Bénédict replied, clicking his heels before grabbing a small rolling suitcase and leaving the bank for the station. Macaire returned to his office, swollen with presidential energy, convinced that he would find arguments in his favour that would change Tarnogol's mind.

On his table, the delayed mail was still waiting. Instead of opening it, Macaire began reading *Twelve Angry Men*, trying to find a few arguments that would help him in the event he met Tarnogol in the hallway. But at three forty-five, Cristina came hurtling into his office.

"What's going on now?" Macaire asked, slightly shocked. "I'm working."

"Pardon me, Monsieur Ebezner, but, in Monsieur Levovitch's calendar, there's a note about a 'VERY IMPORTANT MEETING' at four o'clock. But it's almost four now, and Monsieur Levovitch isn't here and he's completely unreachable. He must have been detained at the Palais des Nations. What should I do?"

"He could have done a better job with managing his diary," Macaire said, annoyed, already aware of what Cristina was hinting at and not wishing to be of service.

"Can you handle the appointment for him?"

"No. I'm up to my ears."

"It must be an important client," Cristina pleaded. "He'll be furious if he finds out we've forgotten about him. I can say that Levovitch has been detained and that you'll meet him instead."

"I'm not going to save face for Levovitch and then watch him be named president instead of me. If it's an important client, let him complain to the board. Tarnogol will learn that Levovitch is far from perfect."

With that, Macaire dismissed his secretary.

When, fifteen minutes later, the "important meeting" walked into the antechamber, Cristina sat there stupefied. This was the last thing she had imagined.

8

Small Arrangements Among Friends

Before Cristina stood an imposing old man, someone she knew well: that unique face, the rough skin, the disapproving expression, the twisted nose and bushy eyebrows. In his hand he held a cane whose handle was encrusted with brilliant diamonds, said to be worth several million francs. The man was Sinior Tarnogol.

"Is Levovitch here?" Tarnogol asked. Although he spoke perfect French, he had never lost his heavy Eastern European accent.

Since Cristina remained silent, he stared at her with his bad eye. She decided to play dumb.

"Did you have a meeting with him? I don't see anything on his calendar."

"Yes, a meeting in my office. When he didn't show up, I came over to see what was going on. All the same, it's irritating to be made to wait like this."

"Monsieur Tarnogol," Cristina said in her friendliest voice, "can I ask you to wait a moment in the pink room?"

With that, Cristina rushed back into Macaire's office.

"What is it now, Cristina?" he said, laying down his copy of *Twelve Angry Men*. "I told you I was busy."

"The four o'clock appointment is with Tarnogol!"

Macaire opened his eyes wide, uneasy.

"Tarnogol? What did you say?"

"That Levovitch was unavailable but that you would meet with him."

He looked very satisfied.

75

"I'm sorry, Monsieur Ebezner, I disobeyed your instructions, but I can't just throw him out."

"Well done, my dear Cristina, well done," Macaire replied, sensing that this was the opportunity he had dreamed of to talk to Tarnogol about the presidency and about firing Levovitch. "Where did you put him?"

"The pink room."

"Excellent! The pink room." He seemed delighted. The pink room was the most elegant waiting room on the floor. "Tell Tarnogol I'm coming."

Cristina left at once. Macaire took a moment to grab his mountain of unread mail and move it to Levovitch's office. Then he trotted to the pink room like a hound dog on the trail of its quarry. He entered the room looking pleased and bent towards Tarnogol as if he were the golden calf.

"Dear Sinior, what a pleasure to see you. I absolutely must speak to you about this misunderstanding concerning my travel expenses and the article in the *Tribune*, which . . ."

"I don't have time for that now." Tarnogol cut him off. "I have to see Levovitch. It's very important."

"Levovitch isn't here."

"And where is he?"

"I have no idea. You know, he's not in his office very often."

"Really? I thought he came in very early and worked tirelessly all day long."

"Oh no, dear Monsieur Tarnogol, that's a myth. Him? Work all day?" He forced himself to smile to emphasise the irony of the situation. "Lazy is his middle name. We're happy if he shows up before eleven o'clock. And often we don't see him at all after lunch. Look, it's only four and that animal has already gone home. How serious can he be?"

"Not very serious at all," Tarnogol huffed.

Macaire, satisfied with his approach, pressed on.

"I shouldn't tell you this because I don't want to speak ill of Lev, but I'm the one who does everything around here. He never makes a move without consulting me. His kind has no initiative. Have you seen his office recently? It's overflowing with unread mail. His clients must be furious. Shameful! I've never seen such laziness."

"But why haven't you told the board about this?"

"Because I didn't want to undermine Lev," Macaire explained in an ingratiating tone. "I felt sorry for him. And my father liked him very much, so I took pity on the guy. I mean, really, he's not hurting anyone; and it's not as if he's going to be the next president of the bank."

"But this is shocking!" Tarnogol looked upset.

"Shocking, yes," Macaire repeated, nodding his head.

"Can you imagine, I was on the point of nominating him for the presidency!"

"Oh, really?" Macaire pretended to look surprised. "Levovitch, president? But he's going to sink the bank. Well, you're the shareholder, not me."

"But he made such a good impression on me," Tarnogol replied.

"You know, Sinior, the biggest imposters are often like that."

Tarnogol rose and took a few steps. He looked perplexed.

"Is everything alright, Monsieur Tarnogol?" Macaire asked.

"No. Not in the least. I was supposed to see Levovitch today about a very important matter. I made that clear. And he isn't here! I'm very disappointed."

"Perhaps I can help you," Macaire suggested.

Tarnogol looked at Macaire for a moment. "I'm not so sure. It's a rather delicate matter."

"We've put our trust in one another for fifteen years," Macaire pleaded. "That's why you're vice president of the bank today."

"I've respected the agreement as well. You got what you wanted in exchange for your shares."

"Precisely, my dear friend," Macaire replied, pushing his argument even further. "We should have complete trust in one another. So why don't we make a new agreement?"

After an interminable silence, Tarnogol said, "Very well. I propose the following, Macaire. The service I was going to ask of Levovitch will be your responsibility. In exchange, I'll make you my choice for president."

"Agreed!" Macaire rushed to take Tarnogol's hand and shook it vigorously. "What can I do for you?"

"You simply have to accept an envelope for me. Nothing illegal, nothing dangerous."

"Is that all?"

"That's all. Very easy."

"Very easy," Macaire parroted. "And then?"

"And then you'll bring me the envelope."

"That's all."

"That's all."

"Very easy!"

"Very easy."

The two men left the pink room, satisfied. Macaire, accompanying Tarnogol to the elevator, noticed as they were passing the antechamber that Cristina was not there. He suggested that Tarnogol take a look in Levovitch's office. From the doorway, Macaire pointed to the desk, piled high with mail.

"Look at all that unopened mail," Macaire clucked. "It's revolting."

"Scandalous!" Tarnogol huffed, too far away to notice that the letters were addressed to Macaire. "How could I have entertained the idea of Levovitch as president?"

"Everyone makes mistakes, Sinior. To err is human."

Once Tarnogol was gone, Macaire hurried to gather the mail from Levovitch's office and put it back on his own desk. He then collapsed into his armchair and let the euphoria fill him slowly. He had never felt so happy. He would be president. He had managed to change the course of his destiny without even needing to resort to subterfuge. He grabbed his copy of *Twelve Angry Men* and looked at it with contempt. There was no need to read it now. He would perform a trivial service for Tarnogol and in return he would be made president. Life was beautiful. Leaning back in his chair, he looked at his watch: four thirty. He could go home. "One hell of a day, all the same."

At that same moment, in Cologny, in the Ebezners' magnificent mansion, Arma had her ear glued to her employers' bedroom door. Anastasia had just received a mysterious phone call.

As always, it was Arma who had picked up the phone. "Ebezner residence, good day," she had politely announced, as she had been taught. The man at the other end of the line had asked for *Madame*, without introducing himself. Anastasia was standing next to her and Arma passed the phone to her, but when *Madame* heard the voice on the line, she had immediately transferred the call to her bedroom and closed the door behind her. Very strange. Madame never did that sort of thing. Intrigued, Arma had decided to eavesdrop.

"You're crazy to call me on this number, Lev!" Anastasia complained in what she assumed was the secrecy of her bedroom.

"I assumed you wouldn't answer your mobile," he explained.

"You're right – because I don't want to talk to you or see you."

"But I'm looking forward to seeing you this evening, darling."

"Don't call me 'darling'! Don't call me ever again. I told you it was over."

"I just wanted to let you know that I would send my driver at seven forty-five to take you to the Hôtel des Bergues. See you later."

"Did you hear what I said? There won't be any dinner this evening. And certainly not at the hotel. It was a mistake to meet this weekend. I have a husband. All Geneva could have seen us."

"You have nothing to worry about."

"Yes, I do have something to worry about."

"This evening, then."

"Never!"

Anastasia hung up. Hearing the phone slam down, Arma quickly went down to the ground floor and returned to the small living room where she was supposed to be dusting. She was in shock. Madame was cheating on Monsieur.

*   *   *

That evening at seven p.m., Macaire Ebezner proudly pulled up in the car park of the Lion d'Or in Cologny, hoping to be seen at the wheel of his luxury sedan, which had cost him a small fortune. He entered the restaurant assuming an air of importance, parading around with his wife on his arm, realising that Anastasia was attracting all the attention. They were seated at a table facing the lake, as he had requested. Geneva glittered in the night, spread before them like a treasure.

"It's champagne tonight," Macaire told the sommelier. "A vintage Pol Roger, Winston Churchill's champagne. The champagne of victory!"

Anastasia was amused. Her husband appeared to be in very good spirits.

"What are we celebrating?"

"Chouchou, tonight you're dining with the future president of the bank," he announced with a sly smile.

She pretended to be delighted. "Oh, that's wonderful. Did you get confirmation from Jean-Bénédict?"

"No, nothing official before Saturday. Actually, I wanted to wait until it was definite before announcing it, but I can't hold my tongue, I'm too excited. It's in the bag."

"Never count your chickens before they hatch," Anastasia replied.

"Indeed. After all, only this morning I learned that the board was, in fact, about to appoint Levovitch."

"Levovitch?" Anastasia choked.

"I can understand your shock, Anastasia. I was completely

dumbfounded, myself. Can you imagine a Levovitch as the head of the bank? It's the *Ebezner* Bank! It was one of Tarnogol's fantasies. These foreigners are always getting strange ideas."

"So, Tarnogol changed his mind?"

"Just about. Let's say that we came to an understanding, him and me. There's one small detail to settle, but we can consider it a done deal."

"Meaning?"

"Let me explain. You know, deep down, Papa wanted me to become president. This election business was designed to give me ironclad legitimacy."

Anastasia didn't know what to say. For her, the reality appeared to be just the opposite. Abel Ebezner had spent his life discrediting his son. If he had wanted Macaire to be president after him, he would have simply bequeathed his shares to him. But she preferred to say nothing and just raised her glass of champagne to toast her husband's health.

She was concerned about Levovitch and about the election. She was no longer hungry – she wanted to go home. But she didn't want to ruin her husband's evening, he seemed to be in such a good mood, not to mention ravenous. He ordered the tagliatelle with white truffles, followed by the rack of lamb. She ordered the tuna tartare and the scampi. He ordered a second bottle of Pol Roger for their ice bucket.

"A champagne dinner – make sure it's well chilled," he ordered the sommelier.

At seven thirty, when the appetisers were being served, the maître'd interrupted Macaire.

"Excuse me, Monsieur Ebezner, but there's a call for you."

"For me? But no-one knows I'm here."

Intrigued, he followed the employee to the cloakroom and was handed the phone. To collect himself, Macaire announced in an authoritative voice, "Yes, hello? Macaire Ebezner speaking."

He listened carefully as the voice on the line gave him lengthy instructions, then yelled into the phone, like a soldier confirming an order, "I'll set out at once!"

He ran to his wife and, without even taking the time to sit down, made his excuses. "Chouchou, I'm terribly sorry, but I have to go. It's extremely urgent. It concerns what I told you about earlier. Finish your dinner in peace and take a taxi home if you like. I can't risk being late. I'll explain later."

Without waiting for her reply, he left.

She remained alone at the table, upset, staring at the lake illuminated by the moon. She played with her tartare with the end of her fork. The other customers couldn't help staring. The woman exuded beauty from every pore – a beauty enhanced by her air of melancholy.

She finished her glass of champagne without touching her food. What was the point of eating alone? She hated eating alone. She hated being alone. She took her phone from her bag and hesitated a long time about calling Lev. She didn't dare. She decided to return home. She asked a waiter to call her a taxi and went outside to wait. A bit of fresh air would do her good. It was now 7:45. As she left the Lion d'Or, she saw a black limousine waiting in the car park. Levovitch's chauffeur, Alfred Agostinelli, stood by the open passenger door and presented her with an enormous bouquet of white roses.

"Good evening, Madame Anastasia," he said, smiling. "How are you?"

"Fine, Alfred," she replied uneasily.

She settled into the rear seat without even realising what she was doing. Then, as the good-natured chauffeur got into the driver's seat, she asked, "How is he?"

9

The Start of the Investigation

If the enigma of room 622 had its roots in Geneva, as appeared to be the case, that was where we would have to travel. So, on the morning of Wednesday, June 27, 2018, Scarlett and I set off for the city. During the trip, she said to me, "In your suite, I found some notes concerning Bernard."

"You searched my room?"

"No, they were on your table. I thought it was for the book; I wanted to tidy up."

"Did you read them?"

"Yes. I found your relationship quite moving. I wanted to know more."

"What do you want to know?"

"Everything! Tell me about Bernard. Who was he?"

"I wouldn't know where to begin."

"Begin at the beginning. That's usually the easiest place to start. Tell me how you met. How does an unknown young author become friends with an elderly publisher?"

"It's a long story."

"I'm not in a hurry."

I smiled.

"Bernard and I met seven years ago. I can still recall that sweltering day at the end of July, the day it all began. Paris was suffocating. I had arrived that morning from Geneva. I had dressed for the occasion: shirt and blazer, as if I were going for a job interview. I wanted to convince him that I was serious. He said we should meet at the L'Âge d'Homme, the bookshop on rue Férou, which is now an ice cream parlour. I arrived in a sweat, overwhelmed by the heat. He was already there, in a small meeting room downstairs.

"I was twenty-six at the time and had just finished law school – with great difficulty – I had often skipped classes to write novels. Instead of going to the university, I went to my grandmother's; she had freed a room in her apartment so I could use it as my office. My grandmother was the first person to believe in me and take me seriously. Thanks to her, during my five years at school, I had written five novels and sent them to every publisher I could think of, and all of them had been rejected. I was desperate. Then, in January 2011, my fifth book, a historical novel devoted to the Special Operations Executive, a branch of the British secret service, which had operated successfully during the Second World War, was picked up by Vladimir Dimitrijević, the founder of Éditions L'Âge d'Homme in Lausanne. But before the book was published, Dimitrijevic was killed in a car accident. At the funeral, I met Lydwine Helly, a Parisian friend of Dimitrijevic's, who told me that she had spoken to Bernard de Fallois about my book and had suggested they publish it jointly. 'You have to meet Bernard de Fallois,' Lydwine said after the ceremony. 'Maybe he will agree to publish your book.'

"Lydwine became my sponsor. She took me under her wing and organised a meeting with Bernard. That's how I came to meet him, that sweltering month of July, in Paris. And as is often the case with great friendships, it started off badly."

* * *

Paris, *seven years earlier*

"I don't think I'm going to publish your novel."

He looked like a general – elegant, lordly, sharp-eyed. The legend of French publishing: Bernard de Fallois. Inevitably, I felt a generation gap between him, eighty-five years old, and me, a young, unpublished author of twenty-six.

"Why not?" I dared to ask.

"You've presented your book as a historical novel, but I don't think what you've written is accurate. The British couldn't have done all that."

"I assure you it's true."

"And why does the war interest you?" Bernard asked suspiciously. "You didn't live through it."

"So what?"

He made a face.

"Still, you're not going to make me believe that it's thanks to the British that the French Resistance was able to fight the Germans?"

"I can prove it. It's a misunderstood subject, which is what makes the book interesting."

"I'm sorry, but I don't think I'll publish your novel."

Leaving the meeting, I wandered around Saint-Germain, depressed and overwhelmed. It had gone all wrong. I might as well stop writing; my books would never be published. I'd never be a writer. I would be better off throwing myself into the Seine rather than walking over, as I did, to the Gibert Joseph bookshop on boulevard Saint-Michel, where I looked through the history titles. I found several books on the activities of the British secret services between 1939 and 1945. I looked at the references and prepared a short bibliography, to which I added the sources used for my novel, then sent it to Bernard.

I didn't hear back from him – until Friday, August 26, 2011. At the end of the day, I received a call from Lydwine Helly. "Bernard is going to publish your book!" she announced. Lydwine had managed to convince Bernard. And that's how my first novel finally appeared in January 2012.

"And it was an immense success," Scarlett interrupted, in a burst of enthusiasm.

"Not at all. It was a catastrophe."

She burst out laughing.

"Really?"

"Really. Bernard was very tough on me; I couldn't take it. And I behaved badly. The novel sold poorly. A few hundred copies. I swore I'd never work with him again."

"And then?"

"That will have to wait. We're almost in Geneva."

We left the autoroute and headed for the city centre, driving past the offices of many international organisations. We soon caught sight of the lake and the Jet d'Eau in the background.

"You know, Scarlett, I was on this road heading in the other direction exactly four days ago."

"Don't be a spoilsport, Writer, it doesn't suit you. And you can always run home to get more socks if you've run out of clean ones."

"I could just go home and put you on a train to Verbier."

She burst out laughing.

"You wouldn't do that. You'd rather be in Verbier, with me."

She noticed I was smiling.

"Don't always try to be so serious, Writer. You're not convincing anyone."

We crossed the Mont Blanc Bridge and headed to Cologny, the smart neighbourhood overlooking Geneva. This was where Macaire Ebezner was living at the time of the murder. I had to admit that I was very impressed by Scarlett. She had scoured the furthest reaches of the web and dug up an impressive amount of information – for example, an article in *L'Illustré*, one of the large Swiss weekly papers, devoted to Macaire Ebezner and published a few months before the murder. The text was illustrated with a picture of Macaire and his wife, Anastasia, posing in front of their home.

We didn't have the exact address, but the name of the street was mentioned: chemin de Ruth. That's where we were heading. I drove slowly, and we inspected the houses on either side of the road. Suddenly, Scarlett cried out: "It's there!"

Before us, through a large iron gate could be seen the house from the magazine: a magnificent structure of white stone overlooking the lake and surrounded by a vast expanse of greenery.

10

An Angry Man

Tuesday, December 11, five days before the murder

Anastasia, wearing a bathrobe, sat alone at the breakfast table in Cologny, playing with a piece of bread. She was too busy reflecting on the events of the previous evening to eat. A wonderful evening that had brought her to the suite at the Hôtel des Bergues occupied by Lev Levovitch. He was waiting for her, looking grand in his smoking jacket. A table had been set for two; the food was refined and the wine a grand cru.

They had dined by candlelight, more in love than ever before. She felt so alive when she was near him. Then they threw themselves at each other and made love.

Around midnight the phone rang. Anastasia froze with fear; it must be Macaire! He had had her followed, he knew everything and was going to create a scene. She was relieved to learn that it wasn't her husband but the president of France, who had come to Geneva for the UN General Assembly. The president, an insomniac, wanted to talk. He wanted Lev to meet him at the French Mission near the United Nations, situated on an immense estate in Chambésy, where the president stayed when he was in town.

Lev had politely put him off, indicating that a woman was involved, but Anastasia felt uncomfortable. "He's the president of France, after all!"

Lev then called the French premiere to tell him he would come over. They dressed and he brought her with him, in his black Ferrari, a one-of-a-kind model. They found themselves in a large, gilded salon with the president of the Republic, who received them in his bathrobe.

Drinking tea and smoking a cigar, and chatting with them like old friends, the president took advantage of the occasion to ask Lev's advice about a speech he was due to give at the United Nations the following day.

At two in the morning, Lev had taken Anastasia home. He dropped her in front of the property on chemin de Ruth and, in the dark of night, kissed her once more – a long, passionate kiss – before letting her go.

Passing the gate, she had experienced a brief moment of anxiety: what would Macaire say, seeing her return at such a late hour? He must be sick with worry. Had he called the police? Or maybe he suspected something and was now lying in wait in the living room? She would tell him that she ended up going out with some friends – that they had gone for a drink at the Hôtel des Bergues and she lost track of time. That's all. She had the right to enjoy herself, didn't she? And he was the one who had left her alone at the restaurant. But as she stood before the house, she noticed that Macaire's car was gone. He still hadn't returned from his mysterious rendezvous. Where could he be? She went to bed at once, without asking too many questions, relieved at not having to explain herself and happy for the hours spent with Lev.

In the morning, she could still feel his body against hers, his fingers on her skin, the pleasure he gave her. Closing her eyes for a moment, she saw him before her, kissing her and whispering in his highly accented French, "More orange juice, Médéme?" When she opened her eyes, Arma was standing before her.

"More *juice*, Médéme?" Arma asked again, presenting Anastasia with a pitcher filled with freshly squeezed juice.

Anastasia forced herself to smile.

"You look well this morning, Médéme," Arma said, filling her glass.

Anastasia remained silent, imagining that she couldn't have looked very radiant and fearing that this might make her husband suspicious. And at that moment, Macaire entered the kitchen, shouting furiously: "That damn Levovitch!"

Anastasia thought she would faint, assuming her husband knew everything.

"That damn Levovitch," he repeated.

"What . . . who?" she mumbled.

Macaire held in his hand that day's edition of the *Tribune de Genève* and placed it before his wife.

"Look at that, chouchou," he shouted, in a tone that fell somewhere between annoyance and admiration.

The headline advertised a long interview with the president of France, and there was a photo of him with Levovitch, taken the night before, as they were walking along the shore of Lake Geneva, near the United Nations. Macaire read from the article:

Leaders from around the world have been gathering at the United Nations for a major conference on the refugee crisis. Today, the president of France is scheduled to give a long-awaited speech. Visitors to the Parc de la Perle near the lake were surprised last night to see the president, followed by his bodyguards, as he walked with a well-known investment banker from Geneva, Lev Levovitch . . .

Arma interrupted his reading.

"Orange juice, Moussieu?"

"Yes, thank you."

He put the paper down and grabbed a piece of toast, which he buttered generously.

"What a character, that Levovitch: 'Here I am walking arm in arm with the French president, and here I am making the front page of the newspaper.' And you know what's worse? He's not in the least bit pretentious. Yesterday, he wasn't in the office, but he did he tell anyone that he was busy at the United Nations? No! Cristina had to track him down to find out what he was up to."

Anastasia looked at him with disappointment: Macaire and his limitless admiration for the man who had cuckolded him. In a sense, the two of them were in love with the same person. Ill at ease, she tried to change the subject.

"And your evening? You got back late, didn't you?" she asked, innocently.

"I got in at three thirty in the morning. I'm a wreck."

"What were you doing until three thirty?"

"I can't tell you. Well, yes, you I can tell. So, yesterday, Sinior Tarnogol asked me to do something for him. Something very important. That was part of the agreement I mentioned at the restaurant."

"What kind of something?" she asked, concerned about what her husband might have done to change Tarnogol's mind.

"Not much, really. I had to pick up a letter for him and bring it to him at once."

"A letter? You're not a postman, as far as I know."

Macaire glowered at her.

"You don't understand anything. You see, I should have kept quiet. A very important letter that Tarnogol couldn't accept directly. He needed a man he could trust."

"He needed a postman," she repeated.

"A man he could trust!" Macaire insisted. "I had to go all the way to Basel to get the envelope, if you must know."

"You made a round trip to Basel last night? Now I understand why you got home so late."

"Oh, it's not that far if you drive fast. I picked up the envelope around eleven, at a large hotel. I had time to drink an espresso and then left. At two thirty, I delivered the letter to Tarnogol. Imagine, he asked me to bring it to his home. No-one from the bank has ever been invited to his home. A magnificent town house on rue Saint-Léger, opposite the Parc des Bastions. Very chic. He treated me with the respect I deserve. Welcomed me like a king, calling me 'my brother'. *My brother*! Imagine. He had prepared something to eat just in case. Well, that 'in case' ended up being enough food to feed a starving village. Outstanding caviar from Iran, smoked wild Alaskan salmon like you've never eaten, toasted brioche that melts in your mouth, a platter of cheese, delicate fruit tarts, sweets. I wish you could have seen it. It really was something. And then he opened a bottle of Beluga vodka to celebrate the 'great occasion'. He said, with his awful accent, 'Beluga, the vodka of victory!' We spent some time together, talking and laughing. We totally understood each other. And when I left, he said to me, in English, 'Thank you, Mr President.'"

"*Mr President*?"

"Yes! I'm to be confirmed on Saturday. My evening wasn't a total dead loss."

Macaire looked lovingly at his wife. Recently, something about her had changed. Her face had become more luminous. She was happier. He often found her in a particularly good mood. Different, indeed! Happy. Yes, he made her happy. They'd had their highs and lows, but now he knew what to do. All you had to do was look at her – she was resplendent.

That morning, Macaire, who ordinarily spent a long time at breakfast, wolfed down his food, in a visible hurry.

"To work," he declared, rising from the table.

"Are you leaving for the bank already?" Anastasia asked, surprised.

"No," he said, somewhat mysteriously. "I'm going to my office. I'm working on a project."

She looked intrigued. He was satisfied with the effect he had produced. She had taken him for an idiot with her postman jibe; she would find out who he really was when she discovered the truth. Still waters run deep, after all. He noted, in some corner of his mind, that the expression would make a good title for his memoir.

Locked in his bedroom, Macaire began to admire the object he had brought back from his visit to Tarnogol: a silk handkerchief embroidered with the words "Sinior Tarnogol, Vice President". He had noticed it on a side table and couldn't prevent himself from taking it. He found it extremely stylish and had decided to use it as a model for his own handkerchiefs, which would read "Macaire Ebezner, President".

He put the piece of fabric at the bottom of a drawer from which he withdrew a bottle of lemon juice. He poured some into a copper bowl and added water to produce invisible ink. He then took out his notebook from the safe and sat at the desk to resume his story.

The accounts I sent to the Federal Council were right on target: the Swiss financial market, our economic lungs, was threatened and it was essential to protect it. If the countries of Europe were planning actions not only to prevent the flight of capital to Switzerland but also to identify the Swiss accounts of some of their nationals, then, as the saying goes, we would have to prepare for war to ensure peace.

The Swiss government asked the intelligence services to set up a large-scale surveillance operation targeting the economic ministers of European countries and to be ready to anticipate any possible retaliatory measures against Switzerland.

Because sending intelligence agents to friendly countries and allies remains dangerous in terms of image and diplomacy, P-30 was sent out first to prepare the terrain. The finance division, of which I am a part, redoubled its activity. London, Paris, Lisbon, Vienna, Athens, Munich, Milan, Madrid, Stockholm – all the major cities of Europe were in our sights. In each of them, we had to identify the relevant administrative buildings, such as their ministerial offices and the headquarters of the tax authorities, and gather as much information as possible about them: access, floor plans, the presence of security cameras, security checks at the entrance. We also needed to identify all the licence plates of cars entering or leaving their parking facilities in order to create a database and to identify the local restaurants that are patronised by their staff. This detailed, fastidious, and tedious work was nonetheless essential in order to open the path for the intelligence agents who would then be sent on location to install listening devices, remove or destroy documents, or even make contact with employees who, motivated by greed, would agree to provide us with information.

Upon returning from a mission, I would receive an invitation to the opera, where I would meet Wagner and give him my summary reports and my observations.

Unfortunately, all these efforts proved to be useless. In reality, our worst enemy was found not outside our borders but in our very country. We were being attacked from the inside, as shown by an event that would traumatise our entire banking system: an employee of a large Zurich bank, in retaliation for being fired, had left with a list of foreign clients who held hidden accounts in Switzerland, a list he had sold to the German and French tax authorities.

For the banks, known for their discretion and their respect for their clients' privacy, this was devastating. For the intelligence services, it meant being on heightened alert: this unprecedented betrayal could have serious repercussions. It was essential to take robust action, to make sure that this was just an isolated case and to dissuade others from trying to follow the former employee's example.

P-30 was tasked with finding out whether the tax authorities of each of the large European countries were actively seeking to buy information from Swiss bankers. After the death of my father, taking advantage of my supposed resentment as the legitimate heir stripped of the presidency, Wagner sent me to different European cities to infiltrate the tax authorities. Throughout the year, I made numerous round trips to Paris, London, Munich, Milan, and Athens. The protocol was simple. In each of those cities, Wagner introduced me to a lawyer who worked for us. The lawyer put me in touch with a local representative of the tax authority, whom I met in a discreet location and to whom I was introduced as a disillusioned banker. For each of them I concocted the same story. "My father didn't name me president. I want to get back at him and I'm ready to collaborate." They *could verify the information: it was all true and had appeared in the papers. Once they had done so, they would set up another meeting, always through a lawyer out of a concern for absolute anonymity. During the meeting, negotiations would take place, during which I would gather important information: how much were they willing to pay for the list of my clients? What were they going to do with it? What guarantees of protection could they offer? Were they willing to grant me residency, since I would no longer be able to remain in Switzerland? In general, when I had enough information, I would demand from them a commitment in writing, which they always refused, and I could then break off negotiations without arousing suspicion.*

Since I am ending my career with P-30, I want to state the following: I have been proud and honoured to serve my country. I feel I have really lived.

The only trace of those exhilarating years is a letter sent a few years ago by Wagner, signed by the president of the Swiss Confederation. Three handwritten lines that I join to this report:

Dear Macaire,
May these few words serve to remind you of our eternal gratitude for your faultless commitment on behalf of your country.

Gratefully,
Beat Wunder
President of the Swiss Confederation

"*Eternal gratitude,*" Macaire said aloud, rereading the letter he had slipped between the pages of his notebook.

Oh, if his father had known what stuff his son was made of! He looked nostalgically at the photograph on his desk. "Your son, Papa," he said to his father looking out from the glossy paper, "is not just anybody."

Macaire heard the telephone ringing in the bedroom and Arma's footsteps as she ran to pick it up. This was followed by even faster footsteps in the direction of the office and, suddenly, several knocks on the door.

"Moussieu," Arma yelled, "I'm sorry, but you have an urgent call!"

Macaire didn't open the door to Arma until he had put his notebook back in the safe.

"What is it?"

"It's the bank."

He went to take the call from the phone in the entrance hall. At the other end of the line, he heard Cristina.

"Monsieur Ebezner," she excused herself at once, "I was unable to reach you on your mobile, so I took the liberty of calling you at home."

Perceiving the panic in her voice, Macaire hurried to reassure her.

"It's fine, Cristina, it's fine. What's going on?"

"You have to come to the bank at once."

"But what exactly is going on?"

"Come," she pleaded. "Monsieur Tarnogol is in your office. He's beside himself with anger and calling you names! I have no idea what he's talking about, but it sounds serious."

11

A Favour

Back at the bank, Cristina was trying to listen behind the closed door of Macaire's office; he had hurried in once she had alerted him. Though she couldn't make out the exact words, it was clear that Tarnogol's fury hadn't abated.

"You dared play me for a fool! You dared lie to me."

"Me? Lie to you?"

"Yesterday, you said that Levovitch was lazy and never in the office. But Levovitch was at the United Nations. With the French president!"

"How . . . how do you know this?" Macaire asked, clicking his teeth.

"Because it's in the paper," Tarnogol yelled, waving a copy of the *Tribune de Genève* at him.

"It was a misunderstanding," Macaire implored, trembling like a leaf.

"Oh, really? And you told me that he never opened his mail, was that a misunderstanding as well? That mail was for you. It's on your desk with your name on it," Tarnogol raged, grabbing a handful of letters lying on the table and throwing them in the air. "It's over, Macaire. You can forget the presidency."

"But Sinior, what about yesterday evening? We got along so well. You even called me 'my brother'."

"That was before I discovered that you had deceived me, that you'd lied to me. Levovitch will be the next president."

With those words, Tarnogol left the office, slamming the door behind him as Cristina looked on, terrified. Macaire collapsed in his chair. He was crushed.

After several long minutes, there was a gentle knocking on the door. Lev Levovitch's face appeared in the doorway.

"Everything okay, Macaire? It seems like things didn't go well with Tarnogol."

"No, not at all," Macaire whined, on the verge of tears.

"What happened?" Levovitch enquired, deciding to enter the room, followed by a cautious Cristina.

"Something serious."

"But what is it?" Cristina asked, overcome with anxiety. "Tell us, Monsieur Ebezner – you look pale."

Levovitch and Cristina looked at Macaire with compassion. He desperately needed to get it all off his chest, but how could he admit to his lies about Levovitch and the story about the mail?

"I'm very stressed out right now."

"Why are you stressed?" Cristina insisted. "Is it because of the presidency?"

"No, it has nothing to do with that," Macaire lied, hoping Cristina hadn't told Levovitch what she had heard the day before. He tried to change the subject: "I think I'm depressed, that's all. The usual winter blues."

"Are you still seeing the psychoanalyst I recommended?" Levovitch asked. "He's really very good."

"Yes, Dr Kazan. Every Tuesday, at twelve thirty. Today is the perfect day for it, in fact." He laughed, trying to appear light-hearted. "Thursday as well."

"I didn't know you were seeing a psychoanalyst," Cristina remarked.

"Well, it's not important," Macaire said, eager to change the subject. "How about we go for coffee? It's on me."

* * *

At twelve thirty that afternoon, Macaire entered the office of Dr Kazan at 2 place Claparède.

"I'm not doing well, Doctor," Macaire announced as he threw himself onto the couch.

He had been seeing Kazan for fifteen years – ever since the business with the bank shares. When his father had learned that Macaire had transferred his shares to Tarnogol, he had been so angry that he had stopped talking to his son for several weeks. Macaire had contacted Dr Kazan on Levovitch's recommendation; he had assured Macaire that the doctor was the right man for the job. Levovitch had assessed the matter correctly. Thanks to Kazan, Macaire had reached an understanding with his father. But since his death, Macaire had experienced bouts of serious depression and felt he needed two sessions a week to climb out of the hole he was in. He was fond of the doctor, who had helped him regain confidence in himself. He liked Kazan's serenity, his gentle gaze, and his way of chewing on the sides of his eyeglasses when he was listening.

"As I was saying, Doctor, I thought there was little doubt that I would be named president."

"I seem to have read something about that in the paper. I was getting ready to congratulate you."

"Yes, well, there's been a bit of a falling out."

"Oh?"

Macaire related the events of the past twenty-four hours.

"If I understand you correctly, Monsieur Tarnogol no longer wants to speak to you?"

"Yes, and all because of a mistake on my part," Macaire lamented. "Oh, Doctor, help me find a way to convince him, please! I have to get him to change his mind. If I'm not appointed president, I'll kill myself."

"Don't say that," Kazan replied. "It would be very bad for my reputation."

"Speaking of your reputation, you were contacted by a Jean-Bénédict Hansen; that's my cousin, Jean-Béné. He's looking for a therapist for his wife, who suffers from mood swings. I recommended that he call you. I told him you were the best. But, apparently, you told Jean-Béné that you weren't able to accept new patients."

"That's correct. I haven't been taking on new patients for years. I made an exception for you because, at the time, you were referred by Levovitch."

"Levovitch again," Macaire groaned. "I hate the man. So perfect. So extraordinary. I want to be him!"

"Do you hate him or admire him?"

"Do I have the right to hate someone because I admire them so much?"

"Yes. It's called jealousy."

"So, I'm jealous?"

"To be specific, I'd even say that you suffer from *invidia maxima*, a condition identified by Freud in the well-known case of Lucien K. Lucien K was a rich Viennese industrialist's son who had always sought recognition from his father. But his father had always reproached his son and had, in the end, preferred another young man, whom he treated like a son and to whom he turned over control of his empire."

"That's exactly what's happening with Levovitch!" Macaire exclaimed, feeling relieved to learn of the existence of a well-known precedent. "So what happened in the case of Lucien K?"

"He killed his father, his mother, his wife, the dog, everyone. He ended up in an asylum. That's how Freud was able to study him."

"Damn! Do you think I'll end up like him?"

"No," Kazan reassured him. "In your case, what's different is that fifteen years ago you had everything under control. Your father had passed the torch and acknowledged you as his successor by publicly handing over, in front of everyone, the shares that guaranteed that you would become president. And you gave them, for a reason that escapes me even now, to Sinior Tarnogol. But you didn't get any cash in return, isn't that correct?"

"I exchanged them," Macaire acknowledged.

"But for what? I'm trying to understand what could be equal in value to being president of the bank."

"Something that everybody wants but no-one can buy."

"Which is?"

"You wouldn't believe me."

"I might."

"You wouldn't believe me," Macaire repeated.

Kazan didn't insist.

"What are you going to do about Tarnogol?"

"I don't know," Macaire sighed. "What would you do in my place, Doctor?"

"Macaire, we've been working together to prepare you for the Gala Weekend for almost a year. Do you remember what it means for you?"

"The separation with my father."

"Exactly. You're finally going to cut the cord. Do you remember what we discussed during our sessions? It's not your father who decides your life; it's you, Macaire. You're in control of your own destiny."

Macaire continued to look confused.

"What I'm trying to explain to you is that Tarnogol's desire to ensure that Levovitch is appointed is your chance to discover who you really are."

"I'm not certain I follow you, Doctor."

"Well, if you had been appointed without having to fight for it, you might have ended up telling yourself that you didn't deserve it. But now you have to convince Tarnogol. And I know that you'll manage it. I know you're capable. You're going to find out what you're really made of, and you'll be named president of the Ebezner Bank. And after the election, you'll be a new man, free of your father at last, you'll owe your position to yourself alone. During our sessions, you have slowly revealed your true identity: that of a fighter, a winner. It's time to show the world, beginning with Tarnogol."

"You're absolutely right, Doctor," Macaire cried out, suddenly galvanised. "But you haven't told me how to convince Tarnogol. As a psychoanalyst you're skilled in the art of persuasion, I would assume."

"In principle, I'm not supposed to suggest ideas; you need to arrive at them yourself," the doctor reminded him. "That's the whole point of psychoanalysis."

"Doctor, please, a little help wouldn't hurt. I imagine you must have some idea."

Dr Kazan, seeing his patient's distress, then suggested the following:

"Make it so Tarnogol owes you something – something important. He'll be forced to name you president. I believe our session is over. I'll see you on Thursday."

12

Adultery

That Wednesday, June 27, 2018, Scarlett and I spent a good deal of time on chemin de Ruth by the gate to the Ebezner property. We had rung the bell but no-one had answered. Scarlett wanted to wait until someone showed up. Finally, a neighbour who had witnessed our vain attempt to gain access came out to meet us.

"Can I help you?" she asked in a tone that made us understand that she assumed we were up to no good.

Then she recognised me, and her face softened at once.

"But it's you . . ."

"The *writer*," Scarlett replied. "I'm his assistant, Scarlett Leonas."

"Delighted," the neighbour replied. "The house is no longer for sale, though; it was finally bought almost a year ago. The new owner is on holiday."

"Wasn't this Macaire Ebezner's house?" Scarlett asked.

"Yes. It was up for sale for years. Ever since . . . You're familiar with what happened, I assume."

"Yes," I answered. "Well, to a certain extent. That's why we're here."

The neighbour was kind and in a talkative mood. She invited us over for a drink. She'd been a widow for several years and welcomed a bit of company from time to time.

"I remember that time very well. We had a great deal of snow that year. Do you want to see some photos?"

"No, thanks."

"Yes, we would," Scarlett corrected me.

The neighbour pulled a volume from a shelf filled with albums arranged by year. She showed us her garden covered with snow, chemin de Ruth covered with snow, the main street of the village covered with snow, the shore of Lake Geneva covered with snow.

"Fascinating," I gushed sarcastically.

"Don't pay attention to him," Scarlett said to her. "He pretends to be a grouch but he's actually quite friendly. How well did you know Anastasia and Macaire Ebezner?"

"Not very well. We weren't exactly close, but we were good neighbours. Very nice people. At the time, I had a dog who used to run away – a Hungarian short-haired pointer, a male. It's better with a female, much simpler. The males are always running off. If they smell something they like, they'll find a way to get outside. The Ebezners used to bring Kiko back all the time when they found him in the street."

"Kiko, that was your dog?"

"Yes. Magnificent animal. I have some photos I can show you."

"No, thanks," I said.

"Oh, yes, of course," Scarlett replied.

The neighbour got up to find an album dedicated to Kiko. As she turned the pages, Scarlett asked her, "What can you tell us about Anastasia and Macaire?"

"By the end, their marriage was in a bad shape. Well, to put it bluntly, she was cheating on him."

"How do you know?"

"One day, Anastasia received some flowers. She told her husband that I had sent them over to thank them for bringing Kiko back home. I know because Macaire came over to thank me for the roses I was supposed to have sent. I understood at once that Anastasia had a lover. When a woman lies to her husband about a bouquet of flowers, the explanation is generally very simple."

"Do you know who he was? Her lover?" I asked.

"No, but I think that Arma, their maid, knew. She alluded to it once."

I wrote down the name.

"Arma what?" I asked.

"I don't know, but I can give you her number. A lovely woman. The poor thing. When it all fell apart, she was left without a job. I hired her from time to time, but she needed something more stable. Now she's working for a cleaning company. But I get in touch with her whenever I need help for entertaining. Call her, she can certainly help you out."

13

The Book of Esther

Tuesday, December 11, five days before the murder

"A favour," Macaire repeated as he considered the advice that Dr Kazan had given him a few hours earlier. It was 6:40 p.m., and Macaire was pacing in the kitchen, orbiting like a satellite around Arma, who was preparing dinner. "What do you do to ensure that someone owes you a favour?" he continued to repeat.

In his hand he held the copy of *Twelve Angry Men*, which he waved in the air as if doing so would somehow miraculously enable him to absorb its contents. It seemed to him that, in the play, the jury, which surprised everyone, had no need of a favour from anyone to achieve its ends. How did the jurors do it? Damn it, Macaire despaired; he had fallen asleep during the film and he didn't have the patience to read the play. Anastasia had certainly read it – she knew everything. He needed to speak to her, but for the past two hours she had been locked in the bathroom. What was she doing in there? He had tried to share his anxiety with her through the door, shouting to be heard over the noise of the water flowing into the tub. "How do you get someone to owe you a favour?" But she had shrugged him off: "This is no time for guessing games." Next, he appealed to Arma.

"*How do you obtain a favour?*" Arma replied, lifting her eyes skyward while basting the lamb. "If I only knew . . ."

"What are you implying?" asked Macaire, suddenly testy.

"I asked you if I could take off this Friday, and you said no."

"Yes, but I explained how it wouldn't work because I'm leaving early on Friday for the Gala Weekend and Anastasia will be home alone. And it's the first time I've refused to give you the day off; I find it rather disrespectful that you even complain about it."

"*Pardon*, Moussieu, but it was you who asked me the question," Arma replied.

"'*Pardon, pardon.*' Nice of you to apologise. You want your Friday off? Take it, then. I hope you're satisfied. You see, once more I've let myself be talked into something. I'm too considerate, with a capital C! That's what I am. Go on, enough chit-chat – finish preparing dinner, the guests will be here in fifteen minutes."

Deeply annoyed by his situation, Macaire sought another pretext for taking his frustration out on Arma. And he found one in the fact that the outside Christmas lights were on, illuminating the snow-covered trees.

"Please, my little Arma, shut off those lights until the guests have arrived, will you? I've told you a thousand times that it's pointless to light everything up when there's no-one around to impress. What is this obsession with wasting electricity at every opportunity?"

"It's to make it look pretty," Arma explained.

"It is pretty, but it costs money too! Obviously, you're not the one who's paying. Shut them off. Now!"

Arma hurried to obey. Macaire was suddenly angry with himself for having raised his voice. There was nothing wrong with Arma. She was hardworking and loyal and had been in their service for ten years now. Honest, never sick, always willing. And she didn't ask for that much time off to begin with. She almost never took a holiday. So, while Arma was busy with the lights, he ducked into the small pantry next to the kitchen, where she changed and kept her belongings, and slipped a hundred-franc note into her handbag. When he reappeared in the kitchen, Arma, back at her stove, was in the process of roasting fingerling potatoes.

"Are you worried about something?" she asked in a soft voice.

"Yes, you could say that."

"What is it? You left so quickly this morning; you looked very stressed."

"Complicated business," he replied evasively. "You have no idea how lucky you are to lead a simple life – no problems, no concerns."

He let himself flop into a chair with a long sigh, then got up immediately in a state of great agitation. He left the kitchen to inspect the dining room and returned at once.

"Arma, what's that enormous bouquet of white roses in the salon?"

"They were sent to Médéme."

"Oh? Who sent them?"

Arma wanted to tell him everything. She had no further doubts about Madame Ebezner's behaviour. Yesterday, the phone call. Today, this enormous bouquet of roses. But how could she tell Monsieur? And, besides, she needed proof, for Madame would certainly deny it. She would claim, sounding offended, that the phone call was Arma's fabrication; she would invent some reason for the flowers. "Why lie, Arma, when we have always been so good to you?" she would say. Macaire would be furious as well, and she would be fired.

Just as Arma was telling herself it would be better to hold her tongue, Anastasia appeared, more beautiful than ever, wearing a dress of midnight-blue chiffon that Macaire had never seen on her.

"Wow!" he gushed, thinking his wife had dressed up just for him.

"I'm going out to dinner with some friends," she told him.

"What do you mean? Jean-Béné and Charlotte are coming for dinner."

"I'm so sorry, I thought that was next Tuesday!"

"But our dinner is always the second Tuesday of the month. You know that."

"We should do it on the first Tuesday of the month rather than the second to avoid this kind of confusion. Why didn't you remind me this morning? You were in such a hurry to lock yourself in your office."

"So it's my fault now?"

"Partly. I can't cancel my dinner at the last minute."

"You're not going to just leave me here."

"We see Jean-Béné and Charlotte every month. For once, I can miss it."

"You're going to miss an interesting dinner, you know. We're going to be talking literature. *Twelve Angry Men*. Do you know it?"

"Of course."

"You see, brilliant, you know everything. So, you've read the book?"

"It's a play," Anastasia corrected. "I've seen it, yes, but a long time ago. Why?"

"Do you remember what the guy did to convince all the others he was right?"

"It's not a question of right and wrong. He forced the other jurors to confront their own beliefs. He sowed doubt in them and gradually chipped away at their convictions."

"That's exactly what I tried with Tarnogol. I tried to chip away at his convictions. But it didn't work. You wouldn't have any advice for me, would you? You always have good advice. I need to . . ."

"Later," she interrupted. "I have to leave – I'm going to be late."

She made for the large entrance hallway. Macaire followed her like a little dog.

"You know," he whined, "I've had a bad day at work. It would have made me happy to have you with us tonight."

Without a word, she took from the closet an elegant coat, which she slipped into. Macaire tried again.

"You could always go out another time. Your friends would understand."

She told herself she would have been better off leaving without telling him anything, to avoid having him play the victim or bombarding her with questions – which he never failed to do. As she was about to open the front door, he mentioned the flowers he had noticed.

"By the way, who sent those roses?"

108

"The neighbour," she quickly replied.

"The neighbour? Why would she send you a bouquet like that?"

"I found her dog in the street the other day and brought him back to her. You know how much she loves that dog."

"You never told me – why didn't you tell me? I tell you everything."

"I thought I had."

"Nice of her, in any case. I'm going to thank her."

"It's not necessary; I already did."

"Oh. You didn't tell me where you're going tonight."

"I'm meeting for cocktails at the bar of the Hôtel du Rhône," she lied. "After that we'll find a place somewhere in town."

"I can drop you off, if you like . . ."

"No, that would be ridiculous. You'll keep your guests waiting if you do that. Have fun tonight. I might be back late. Say hi to Jean-Béné and Charlotte for me."

"They'll be very disappointed not to see you," Macaire remarked, in a final attempt to make his wife feel guilty and keep her home.

"I'm sure they'll understand," Anastasia said as she walked out.

Macaire, annoyed, collapsed into one of the large armchairs in the hall, fanning himself with his copy of *Twelve Angry Men*, which he still had in his hand, and looked out the window at his wife as she climbed into her sports car and sped off.

Once she had passed through the front gate to the property, Anastasia drove along chemin de Ruth. After a couple of minutes, she parked on the shoulder of the empty residential street, quickly removed her leather gloves, and took from her handbag the letter that had accompanied the large bouquet of roses that Agostinelli, Lev's chauffeur, had brought that afternoon.

Tonight at 7 in the car park at the Promenade Byron.
I'll be waiting for you.
Lev

The Promenade Byron was only a few minutes' drive from the Ebezner home. It was the ideal romantic spot, set in a clearing on Cologny Hill, a place where lovers met to enjoy an extraordinary view of Lake Geneva and the city.

When Anastasia arrived, the parking area was empty. Eager to see Lev, she had arrived ten minutes early. She knew she should have showed up late or, even better, not showed up at all. Let him cool his heels. Leave him to stew. He would have desired her more. But when she received the flowers and the note, she couldn't keep still. She'd spent the afternoon getting ready, preparing, making herself look beautiful. She tried on ten dresses, fifteen pairs of shoes. She wanted to be perfect.

For the third time, she looked at her watch. Then she fixed her hair in the rear-view mirror. Only a few minutes before he would arrive.

At precisely seven p.m., Jean-Bénédict appeared at the Ebezner house without his wife.

"Dear cousin," Macaire greeted him, "isn't Charlotte with you?"

"She's not well. Another of her mood swings. The past few days, she seemed fine. But just now, returning from the bank, I found her sitting at home in the dark. She said she needed rest. I told her that it was very impolite to cancel at the last minute."

"Well, Anastasia did the same to me. She said she got the date of our dinner mixed up and went out to meet with friends."

"You know what? So much the better for us, and so much the worse for them. This way we can discuss important matters in peace."

Macaire led Jean-Bénédict into the living room to serve him an aperitif. Macaire told his guest what had happened the day before with Tarnogol and how, after having convinced the old man to vote for him in exchange for going to get a letter in Basel, he had ruined everything because of a stupid misunderstanding.

"What kind of misunderstanding?" Jean-Bénédict asked.

"Not important," Macaire replied, gesturing broadly with a sweep of his hand. "Some business about unread mail. Whatever. What I need to do now is find a way to win him round. We have the evening to figure it out."

At that moment, still in her car at the Promenade Byron, Anastasia was waiting patiently. It was fifteen minutes past the time of their rendez-vous, and Levovitch hadn't yet shown up. A little delay . . . it happens.

At eight p.m., in the large dining room of the Ebezner home, Macaire and Jean-Bénédict were feasting on the roast lamb and fingerling potatoes with garlic and sea salt that Arma had prepared, as they devised a strategy for securing Tarnogol's support.

"I read *Twelve Angry Men*, as you asked, but I don't think I can make a connection with your situation."

"It's a question of sowing doubt in his mind and gradually chipping away at his belief in Levovitch," Macaire explained, repeating what his wife had told him about the play. "But I already did that, just like in the book, and it didn't work. We need something else. And soon. Time is not on our side. The vote is in four days."

"Do you have any ideas?"

"I spoke to Dr Kazan today and he had a brilliant suggestion. I have to put Tarnogol in the position of owing me a big favour."

"And that favour would be the presidency?" Jean-Bénédict replied.

"Exactly."

"I really wish Kazan would take Charlotte as a patient," Jean-Bénédict remarked, now the doctor's name had come up.

Filling his cousin's glass with Cheval Blanc, Macaire announced confidently, "It's a waste of time, Jean-Béné. He told me he's only seeing important clients. But one hand washes the other. So let's hurry up and find a solution. How can we secure that big favour?"

"By providing a great service," Jean-Bénédict suggested.

"I've already done that by going all the way to Basel in the middle of the night! We need to think of something else."

Still parked at the Promenade Byron, Anastasia continued to wait inside the car's chilly interior. Lev was now an hour late. He must have been held up by something. Maybe the French president. There must be a good reason. She decided wait a little longer.

It was now nine p.m. in the Ebezner dining room. Jean-Bénédict and Macaire were well into Arma's celebrated apple tart – a favourite of guests – and a second bottle of Cheval Blanc, when Jean-Bénédict had a sudden brainwave.

"Two weeks ago, Pastor Berger came over to the house for tea. He talked to us about the Book of Esther."

"Him again, that nuisance," Macaire grumbled. He saw no connection with the rest of the conversation, unless this Esther woman had written a book on mind control.

"The Book of Esther is part of the Old Testament," Jean-Bénédict explained, with the tone of a zealot. "It tells how, five hundred years before Jesus Christ, a Persian king, Ahasuerus, took as his new wife a woman called Esther, one of the most beautiful women in the kingdom but one who, unfortunately, was Jewish. Mordecai, Esther's uncle, advises his niece not to reveal this, to avoid complications. When Esther becomes queen, her uncle visits her regularly and, as a result, is often found hanging around the palace. One day, Mordecai surprises two soldiers who are plotting against Ahasuerus. Mordecai denounces them and saves the king's life. Meanwhile, Haman, the king's cruel viceroy, is growing increasingly annoyed with Mordecai, who refuses to bow to him. When Haman learns that Mordecai is Jewish, he decides to have all the Jews in the kingdom massacred and manages to persuade Ahasuerus – who does not know his wife is Jewish – to sign a decree ordering it to be done.

Learning the terrible news, Mordecai informs Esther that she is the only one who can convince Ahasuerus to change his mind."

"And so, what does she do, this Esther?" Macaire exclaimed, suddenly fascinated.

Jean-Bénédict resumed the story.

"Esther invites Ahasuerus and his viceroy, Haman, to join her for two large banquets. After the second meal, Ahasuerus, who has eaten like an ogre and is in high spirits, asks his wife, 'What can I do for you, Esther, my darling?' And Esther tells him everything – that she is Jewish and that Haman wants to kill all her people and her along with them. Ahasuerus suddenly realises what has happened ('Esther, you're Jewish? And your uncle, Mordecai, is Jewish too?'). Obviously, Ahasuerus cancels the decree for the massacre. The Jews of Persia are saved and cruel Haman is a goner."

"That's a story to put you to sleep on your feet," Macaire complained, unconvinced.

"It's the Holy Bible," Jean-Bénédict reminded him.

"All the same, the wife invites her guy over to eat twice and, just like that, he changes his mind? That's just nonsense. And tell me, how is this nutty story supposed to help me convince Tarnogol?"

"Don't forget that Mordecai saved the king's life," Jean-Bénédict interjected. "Surely that gives you an idea."

"What are you trying to say?"

"If you save Tarnogol's life, he'll have to vote for you."

"Save his life? Between now and Saturday? How?"

There was a lengthy silence. Macaire began to think. He walked around the table, wondering what Wagner would have suggested if this had been a P-30 operation. Suddenly, he cried out:

"I have an idea! The idea of the century! We're going to try to kill him and save him at the same time."

14

A Secret

It was ten p.m., and a secret plan was being hatched in the Ebezner home.

Arma had been dismissed for the evening, even though she hadn't finished the dishes. Macaire told her she could do it the next morning – that she had worked hard enough for the day. This was highly unusual, and Arma assumed that something serious was underway; her employer never let her go home early. As she was leaving, waiting by the closed door to the dining room, she heard Macaire yell through the wall, "I won't let Lev Levovitch steal my place as president!" So, Monsieur wasn't sure of becoming president of the bank? Was that what had been worrying him the past few days? She decided to find out for herself.

In the dining room, Macaire and Jean-Bénédict were finalising their plans for what they were calling Operation Turnaround, developed by Macaire for the most part – a scenario worthy of P-30 itself.

After a lengthy discussion, to make sure that everything worked as planned, Macaire and Jean-Bénédict carefully rehearsed their roles.

The operation would take place the day after next, Thursday evening, December 13, during the annual gala dinner of the Association of Bankers of Geneva in the ballroom of the Hôtel des Bergues. It was an important event, which brought together board members and associates of local private banks – the crème de la crème. Jean-Bénédict was invited, together with Charlotte. Horace Hansen had declined the invitation, but Tarnogol would be there.

"Anastasia and I will attend the dinner in your place," Macaire repeated.

"Yes, Charlotte will be delighted not to go; she has tickets to an organ concert at Victoria Hall with her sister."

"And you're sure that Anastasia and I will be seated at Tarnogol's table?"

"I'm sure. It's always like that at this dinner. Bankers from the same bank are always seated at the same table."

"I'll use the dinner to make a good impression on Tarnogol. Then, shortly before the end of the evening, I'll tell him I'd like to speak with him privately, and I'll lead him outside for a short stroll along the river in front of the hotel.

"The evening ends at ten; it's written on the invitation. I'll lead Tarnogol outside at nine thirty, that's when they'll be serving coffee. Everyone will be busy in the ballroom and there'll be no-one outside the hotel.

"Once outside, I'll take a walk with Tarnogol. We'll have a very serious conversation. I'll tell him that it's imperative I'm named president. We'll walk to the centre of the Bergues Harbour, along the Rhône. At that hour, it's deserted, especially in December. We'll be alone on the quay; it will be dark and there won't be a soul around."

"Between the bad lighting and the fog rising from the river, you won't be able to see much," Jean-Bénédict noted. He often took the quay when he returned home on foot from the right bank of the city. "I'll be in my car, waiting in ambush. Make sure you walk in the centre of the quay. You'll both be too distracted by your conversation to notice the car that's advancing behind you, whose driver has forgotten to turn on the headlights."

"When you're in position behind us, you'll turn on your lights and honk the horn. That will be my signal. I'll grab Tarnogol by the arm and pull him towards me with all my strength. We'll both end up on the ground, it'll be a spectacular fall. You'll accelerate quickly and pass by us at high speed, as if you hadn't seen us, and then continue on your way, like a rocket. At last he'll see what I'm made of. After an episode like that, I don't see how he couldn't give me his vote."

After a long silence, Jean-Bénédict said, "What if I screw up and hit Tarnogol?"

"Impossible. Don't forget the plan: you'll drive very slowly until you reach us. It's important that we don't hear you. You only accelerate after sounding your horn, just as I pull Tarnogol towards me. That's when you step on it; we'll be out of the way by then. You'll pass right by us, which will make it seem like you're going very fast, but it will only be an illusion. Nothing can go wrong."

"What if someone sees my licence plate?"

"Position yourself far enough from the hotel so that the employees can't see you. And before you approach us, make sure no-one's walking in the street. The quay is long enough that I can extend our walk until you're sure there are no witnesses. As for Tarnogol, he'll be on the ground with me; he won't have time to see anything. By the time he gets up, you'll be far away. In any case, your car is like every other car around. No-one will make the connection. And you can always put some snow on your licence plate, if you know what I mean!"

"What if Tarnogol wants to walk on the pavement?" Jean-Bénédict asked.

"It's up to me to get him to walk where we need him to. That's my job. You have to make sure there are no witnesses. When those two elements come together, you give the signal with your horn, I'll suddenly pull Tarnogol against me, and you disappear. It's quite simple."

Jean-Bénédict was not reassured.

"I'm not sure I want to get involved. It could turn out badly. Don't you think you're going a bit too far?"

"Don't be silly, it's nothing more than a bit of theatre," Macaire said, trying to convince his cousin.

"It's a bit more than theatre," Jean-Bénédict replied. Macaire looked upset.

"You know what? If you don't want to help me, don't. I thought our friendship was stronger than that. Yesterday, you said you'd do whatever it took. It seems you've changed your mind. In that case, don't expect anything from me when I'm president."

The threat was enough to convince Jean-Bénédict.

"Of course," Macaire added, "our little operation must remain absolutely secret from everyone, including our wives. No-one can know."

Macaire had, in spite of himself, spoken those last words in a tone of extreme gravity. He at once forced himself to laugh out loud to clear the air. He didn't want to say so in front of Jean-Bénédict, but it hadn't escaped him that there were serious risks associated with the operation. However, it was also his last chance.

Arma had just returned to her small apartment in Eaux-Vives. She lived alone in two rooms at the corner of rue de Montchoisy and rue des Vollandes. She had discreetly left the Ebezner home after listening to Macaire and Jean-Bénédict's plan through the wall. She was upset and couldn't help wondering how the affair would turn out.

She made herself a cup of tea and went to the living room to look at the copy of the *Tribune de Genève* she had brought back from her employers' home. They always let her take the paper home with her.

She looked carefully at the large photo on the front page, the one that Monsieur had got so agitated about during breakfast. In the picture, two men were walking side by side in the Perle du Lac Park, smiling like two close friends, surrounded by bodyguards and attracting the amazed stares of passers-by. Arma recognised one of the two men: he was the French president. The second, a handsome, elegant man was, according to the caption, Lev Levovitch.

Upon reading the name, Arma looked up from the paper, terrified. All the pieces of the puzzle were suddenly coming together.

If the character in the paper, this Lev Levovitch, was the reason Monsieur was so upset this morning, it was because he wanted to take Monsieur's place as president of the bank. That was the name that Macaire had pronounced half an hour earlier, in the dining room: "I won't let Lev Levovitch steal my place as president!" Lev Levovitch – with a name like that, there couldn't be two of them in Geneva. That meant that the man in the paper was also Madame's lover. Without a doubt. Yesterday, during that mysterious phone call, Madame had said – Arma recalled it all perfectly – "You're crazy to call me here, Lev!" The same Lev who sent that immense bouquet of white roses today. When Madame opened the door, a while ago, she looked like she knew the man who brought the flowers, who was dressed like a chauffeur. "This is from Lev," he had said. Madame thought that Arma hadn't seen him, but Arma had seen everything! There was a note with the bouquet. As soon as Madame saw it, she went and locked herself in the bathroom, before leaving shortly afterwards; she was going to meet Levovitch, that much was certain.

Levovitch was Madame's lover and the one who wanted to steal the presidency from Monsieur.

Arma was fuming. She grabbed a pen and, in a rage, covered Lev's face with black lines until he disappeared before tearing up the picture. She hated him, this home wrecker who was ruining her boss's life.

In distress, she grabbed the photo of Macaire that she kept in a pretty silver frame on the living-room table. She looked at the picture for a long time. It must have been taken a few years ago; Macaire looked so calm. He was elegantly dressed in a tuxedo, probably for some gala evening. She had found the photo in a box at the back of a wardrobe overflowing with photos that had been waiting to be sorted for years. Macaire looked so handsome in the picture, and there was no-one to admire him. That was terrible. She had given herself permission to take the photograph, which she had kept reverently ever since.

Arma caressed the face in the picture, then kissed it. Her Macaire, such an exceptional man. She smiled at him, then murmured that gentle word he loved so much: "kitten". She was the only one who really loved him.

She grabbed a stiff album from the table, a scrapbook of all the articles she had read about Abel Ebezner's death and the succession, which she had assumed would be decided in Macaire's favour. As she did almost every evening, she looked through the collection.

DEATH OF THE BANKER ABEL EBEZNER

The president of the Ebezner Bank passed away on Sunday evening. He was 92 years old. He left his imprint on the banking world of Geneva.

ABEL EBEZNER: THE DEATH OF A GREAT BANKER

Charismatic and brilliant, but also irascible. That's how Abel Ebezner has been described. He was a man ahead of his time but respectful of tradition. Under his guidance, the Ebezner family bank has become the leading private bank in Switzerland, clearly distancing itself from its competitors. In keeping with a tradition that has been followed at the bank since its founding, Abel's son, Macaire, who currently holds the position of wealth manager at the bank, is expected to replace him.

WHO WILL SUCCEED ABEL EBEZNER?

Rumour has it that Abel Ebezner has intentionally not named his son, Macaire, as the next president of the Ebezner Bank, and has left it up to the board of directors to choose his successor.

SHAKE-UP WITHIN THE EBEZNER BANK

A lawyer for the Ebezner family, Mr Peterson, confirmed Abel Ebezner's wishes during a press conference. The bank's board of directors will now be responsible for appointing the bank's next president.

"Abel Ebezner remained a visionary up until his demise," Peterson explained with his customary flair. "It was his wish, for the good of the bank, that we break with obsolete and nepotic traditions and move towards a system that will no longer award the presidency on the basis of heredity but on the ability to manage a bank of this importance."

MACAIRE EBEZNER WILL BE APPOINTED PRESIDENT OF THE EBEZNER BANK ON SATURDAY

Well, the wait is over. Macaire Ebezner, 41 years old, will assume the helm of the most important private bank in Switzerland, to which he is the sole heir. The news was confirmed, although not in so many words, by an influential member of the bank, who wished to remain anonymous. "Only an Ebezner can manage the Ebezner Bank," he stated. Certainly the board's role in the appointment is a brilliant move by the late Abel Ebezner. Without breaking with tradition, it offers increased legitimacy to his son. It has also stirred up considerable publicity for the bank, which has succeeded admirably in focusing attention on itself.

Arma slammed the album shut.

How could Madame do such a thing to Monsieur? Cheat on him – with the man who wanted to take his place as president. How could she deceive him like that? For the ten years Arma had been working for the Ebezners, she had been proud to share the day-to-day life of two people she considered a model couple, who reflected her own aspirations. But Madame had ruined everything, and Arma's disappointment was equal to the admiration that had preceded it. Until then, Arma had considered Madame to be an exceptional woman: beautiful, lively, intelligent, funny, gifted in everything she did – the kind of woman people noticed at once at dinners and cocktail parties. Only a woman like her could have seduced a man as extraordinary as Monsieur Macaire. And it was for that very reason that, in spite of the feelings she had for her employer,

Arma had always been incapable of experiencing the least jealousy towards Madame Ebezner. She was superior, untouchable. What did Arma have compared to this Russian princess? Arma, the little Albanian maid, in an apron all day long.

But Madame was clearly not aware how lucky she was to have married a man like Macaire Ebezner. She didn't deserve him. Monsieur had to be told.

Arma regretted not having said anything to Macaire that day. She had been weak. She had been cowardly. But that was over!

Tomorrow, she would speak to him.

Tomorrow, she would tell him everything.

* * *

When Anastasia returned home at eleven thirty, Jean-Bénédict had been gone a while. Macaire was waiting for her in the living room. He had to talk to her about Thursday's dinner. Hearing a key in the lock, he hurried to greet her.

"Good evening, chouchou. Did you have a good time?"

Anastasia, her face unmoving, simply slammed the front door and grunted. Clearly, she was not in a good mood.

"I'm going to bed," she said, heading for the stairs.

By the time Macaire had switched off the lights in the living room and joined her upstairs she had locked herself in the bathroom. He knocked gently on the door.

"I just want to brush my teeth."

Anastasia pretended not to hear him. She opened the tap as far as it could go and sat on the toilet. Lev had stood her up. She had waited for hours like an idiot. She had tried to reach him on his mobile; she had left messages at the hotel. Nothing. Not a thing. She hated herself for having believed him; she hated herself for being so eager. She no longer knew whether she was sad or furious. And now Macaire wanted to talk.

She left the bathroom only when she was ready to go to bed. Macaire rushed in to quickly brush his teeth so he could get into bed and speak with his wife. But she threw herself under the covers, pretending to be asleep to avoid speaking to him. When Macaire reappeared in his pyjamas, he found her on her side, curled up in a fetal position.

"You asleep already, chouchou?" he said, sliding between the sheets.

She didn't reply. Uncertain, he decided to talk to her back.

"There was a bit of trouble at the bank today. Tarnogol laid into me. He said he wouldn't vote for me. I still have a few days to convince him I'm the right man for the job, though – which reminds me, can you set aside Thursday evening for the Association of Bankers of Geneva dinner at the Hôtel des Bergues? Jean-Béné and Charlotte are giving us their seats. It's very important."

Right, she thought, trying to remain motionless. Another one of his ridiculous bankers' dinners. He continued.

"Tell me, chouchou, if I weren't president of the bank, would you love me all the same?"

She didn't move. She must be sound asleep. He was sad. His wife was ignoring him. He swallowed a sleeping pill and quickly fell asleep.

She was still awake when her husband's snoring filled the bedroom. She turned and observed her gentle sleeper. She felt mean. She was annoyed with Lev, and Macaire had paid the price. She'd go to that Thursday dinner, and she would try to make a good impression on Tarnogol. Would she still love Macaire if he wasn't elected president? President or not, it had been a long time since she had felt anything for him. Had she ever? What had attracted her was his kindness. Beneath his sometimes uncouth exterior, Macaire was fundamentally a good person, reasonable and generous. When she had agreed to marry him, she was so young, so lost. She desperately needed kindness. She needed someone to take care of her – to heal her wounds. And she needed to get as far from her mother as possible. Macaire would never hurt Anastasia. He was always attentive. He'd bend over backwards for her. But men who bend over backwards are men who are tamed, and passion never survives conquest.

Now, she needed passion. She was thirty-seven; her whole life was ahead of her – a life that she no longer saw herself sharing with Macaire. She wanted children, but not with him. She understood that now. All these years she had taken the pill secretly, believing it was because of her mother that she didn't want children. And Macaire was always going to see specialists, convinced that he was the problem! But now she found herself dreaming about having a child with Lev.

Why the hell had he stood her up? Was he laughing at her? And what if she left Macaire, and it didn't work out with Lev? She would end up with nothing. That was her greatest fear. She tried to reassure herself by imagining she would get a job; she would work it out. She would live a simple life, without lies. But that was nothing more than self-deception, because of her mother. Maybe she should make an appointment with Dr Kazan; Macaire couldn't stop talking about him. A doctor of his calibre would certainly help her sort things out.

All that thinking kept her awake. Macaire, judging by his snoring, was sound asleep. She decided to go the kitchen to make a cup of herbal tea. Before leaving the bedroom, she grabbed the small gold-plated pistol she kept at the bottom of her dresser drawer. She was afraid at night in that big house. There had been several robberies in the neighbourhood. Macaire was the one who had bought the gun, two or three years ago, after someone had entered the neighbours' home while they slept. He wanted her to feel safe when he was away on his business trips. He even had "Anastasia" engraved on the grip. It was a beautiful gun.

She slipped it into the pocket of her bathrobe and went down to the kitchen.

Would she still love him if he wasn't president of the bank? But ever since the death of old man Ebezner, she had known that Macaire wouldn't be president. She often thought of that last evening with Abel Ebezner.

*　*　*

Early January, a year earlier

The doctor had called Macaire and Anastasia to Abel's bedside, telling them he had no more than a few hours to live. Entering the large patrician dwelling in Collonge-Bellerive, Anastasia was struck by the odour of death that filled the rooms.

Abel was in bed, dry and stiff, but his mind was still alert. She kissed him on the forehead, and he took her hand, complimenting her as always. They smiled affectionately at each other. She had always got along well with her father-in-law. After kissing him once more, she left the room so he could be alone with Macaire, but as she stood behind the half-open door, she heard their final discussion.

Abel Ebezner assumed the unpleasant tone he often used with his son.

"I'm at the end of my life. I had only one child. Had I known how you'd turn out, I would have tried to have at least two. You caused your mother a lot of pain, you know. May she rest in peace."

"I tried to do my best, Papa."

"Well, you could have made more of an effort!"

"I'm sorry, Papa."

"It's easy to be sorry, but that doesn't change anything. Now, before it's too late, I wanted to talk to you about the bank."

"I'm listening, Papa," Macaire replied, his voice betraying his excitement.

"As you can imagine, I'm not about to let Tarnogol get control. In my will, I've stipulated that the method of appointing the president, which we've used at the bank since the days of Antiochus Ebezner, will be changed."

"That's a very good idea, Papa," Macaire replied, like a small dog waiting for a treat.

"There's no point in flattering me, Macaire, I'm not naming you president. You humiliated me fifteen years ago when you transferred the shares I had given you to Tarnogol. You dishonoured your name and your family by allowing that lunatic on the board – that shameless boor who stinks of dirty money. I'll make you pay for it as long as you live. Obviously, it's out of the question that Tarnogol, or your idiot cousin, Jean-Béné, much less his arrogant father, should become president. So, I've decided that the board will appoint my successor, with the condition than none of its members can be considered. That way I can leave in peace. As for you, I've already given you a great deal of money: I paid for your gigantic house, you have your mother's inheritance, you'll inherit everything I have. You'll have nothing to worry about for the rest of your life, and for several generations after that, assuming you have children one day, Anastasia and you. And that's without counting the money you made selling your shares to that shit Tarnogol. You know, that's what disappointed me the most about you. That you would be so venal. No sooner did I give you my shares than you sold them to the highest bidder."

"I didn't sell my shares, Papa. I've told you that already! I would never do that. It was never about the money."

"That's hard to believe, Macaire. Because you never explained to me why or under what terms you sold your shares to Tarnogol, if it wasn't about the money."

"You'll think I'm crazy, Papa."

He got up from the chair and kissed his father on the forehead for a last goodbye.

* * *

The whistling kettle drew Anastasia from her thoughts. She poured the water into the teapot and let the tea steep.

125

She thought often about those last moments between Macaire and his father. What could Macaire possibly have exchanged his bank shares for? He had never told a soul, not even her.

Abel had died shortly after they left the house, as if he had been waiting to die alone. Anastasia imagined that Abel had always been a man surrounded by people – someone to whom others came for advice but who was, at bottom, very alone. His funeral was held in the Cathédral Saint-Pierre on a bitterly cold morning. There was an overflow crowd: friends, city and local officials, members of Geneva's high society, representatives of different banks, curious onlookers. One simply had to be there.

Then, as per Abel's wishes, the burial took place in private. Only three people accompanied the casket to the Saint-Georges Cemetery: Macaire, Anastasia, and Lev. Anastasia would never forget that moment. The three of them, side by side, standing in silence as the casket was lowered. Suddenly, Lev, without Macaire noticing, had taken her hand. She felt a shiver. It had been fifteen years since they had spoken. That day, when his skin touched hers, she had felt more alive than ever. They had finally found each other. After fifteen long years.

Standing in her kitchen, she drank her tea, gazing out the window. She wondered where Lev was. She tried to convince herself that he had a good reason for standing her up – an important meeting maybe. Something very serious – at the United Nations, perhaps. He was unable to call. There had to be a good reason.

She couldn't see the man who was squatting on a branch of an enormous cedar at the edge of the property, watching the brightly lit kitchen, his eyes glued to a pair of binoculars.

"She looks sad," Lev murmured from his perch to Agostinelli, who was keeping watch on the other side of the garden wall.

"You should get down now," the chauffeur said, as he looked uneasily around. "You're going to hurt yourself. And if someone sees us, won't you look clever!"

Lev hesitated, then left his observatory the same way he had climbed up. Remaining seated on the branch for greater stability, he slowly slid, using his arms, without worrying about the damage to his trousers, until he reached the trunk of the tree, which almost touched the wall. Grabbing the trunk, he stood up and stepped onto the wall, from which he jumped down easily onto the roof of his car, which was parked directly below him.

Agostinelli then asked, "If I may, sir, why did you stand Anastasia up and spend your evening spying on her? You obviously wanted to see her."

"I had to, Alfred. Do you know why love is so complicated?"

"No, sir."

"Because love doesn't exist. It's a mirage, a social construct. Or, if you prefer, love exists only if it isn't materialised. It's a spiritual emanation made of hope, expectation, and projection. What would have happened if I had met Anastasia? She might have been bored. She might have found my conversation banal. Maybe a piece of salad would have got stuck in my teeth, and she would have thought of me differently."

"Or maybe not, sir," Agostinelli observed.

"Alfred, you know it as well as I do – tonight was perfect because it didn't happen."

"But, sir, why does it have to be perfect?"

"Because I've been waiting for this for fifteen years, Alfred. Fifteen long years."

"What happened fifteen years ago?"

"I made the worst mistake of my life. Like poor Macaire. The same day, we both paid the price for a decision that ruined our lives."

15

A Faux Pas

Geneva, Wednesday, June 27, 2018.

Following our visit to the neighbour in Cologny, Scarlett tried to contact Arma, the Ebezners' former employee, but without success. Scarlett left Arma a voicemail, asking that she call back as soon as possible. We then took advantage of our presence in Geneva to visit the Ebezner Bank on rue de la Corraterie. In the bank's immense entrance hall, we were greeted by a teller.

"How may I help you?"

"We'd like to meet the president of the bank," Scarlett announced.

"Do you have an appointment?"

"No."

"I'm sorry, Madame, but you'll need an appointment. What is it about?"

"The murder that took place in room 622 at the Hôtel de Verbier. I assume you know what I'm referring to?"

The teller showed no sign of surprise. He stepped aside to make a phone call. I caught a bit of the end of his conversation: "I'll have them come up at once."

A few minutes later, we were met in a private reception room by the president, who didn't seem very pleased to receive us.

"You do have a nerve," he burst out, "to come here without warning and demand to see me."

"We haven't demanded anything," Scarlett clarified. "We were near the bank, and we simply stopped by to see if you were available. Of course, if it's not a good time for you and you'd like us to make an appointment, we'd be happy to come back."

"You will not come back!" the president retorted in a tone of voice that brooked no dissent. "I've interrupted a very important meeting to say one thing: that business is over, and I have no intention of letting you cause problems for the bank."

"Who's talking about making problems?" I remarked.

"If you're here, it's because you're planning to write a book, isn't that right? About what happened. You were looking for something to write about, and you thought you might as well reopen an old case, isn't that correct? I'm surprised at you. I'm embarrassed to say that I liked your books. But I won't be reading any more of them."

"The case isn't over," Scarlett offered. "The murderer was never found."

"It's over for the public, and that's what counts. Everyone has forgotten about it, and it's better that way for us and for everyone concerned. You may not know this, but after the murder, the bank had to climb back out of a hole. Our clients were unhappy; the bank was on shaky ground; we had all been through a crisis. Now that everything is back to normal, it is out of the question for you to come here and reopen that old wound. Think what it would do to the bank. I'm going to inform my lawyers immediately. I'm warning you, if you persist in this, you'll never get that book printed. And trust me, I have connections."

As we were leaving the bank, the teller who had greeted us stopped us in the large entrance hall.

"I hope your meeting was fruitful."

"Not really," Scarlett remarked.

The teller slipped a piece of paper into her hand. He turned around and walked back behind the reception desk.

* * *

"I'm not sure I understand what just happened," I said to Scarlett as we quickly walked away from the bank.

"Me neither, but we're not going to have to wait long to find out." She showed me the note the teller had given her.

Meet in 1 hour, tearoom, rue de la Cité.

Rue de la Cité was a pedestrian street in the old part of Geneva, located behind the Ebezner Bank. There were several shops and a few restaurants there, but only one tea room. We sat down and had lunch while we waited for the teller.

After an hour, a concealed doorway in the building opposite opened; we realised it was the rear of the bank. The teller appeared and quickly walked across the narrow street.

"Some customers use that door to exit without being seen," he explained.

"Some employees as well," Scarlett noted. He smiled.

"Why are you interested in that last Gala Weekend and the murder?"

"It's the writer," Scarlett said, nodding in my direction. "He's writing a book about it."

"It was mostly your idea to investigate this story," I clarified.

"The murder has never been solved," the teller reminded us.

"Exactly, and we want to figure out what happened," Scarlett replied.

"I have to admit, I'm curious to find out myself. The story has haunted me all these years. I'm six months away from retirement and I can't help feeling that something has got away from me. I want to find out what happened back then. But look, it's not exactly good form for a bank employee to talk about these things. My name can never appear in your book; that could cause trouble for me."

"I can just call you the teller, if that's okay with you," I suggested, as I took out my notebook.

"That's alright, then."

"Did you know the victim?" Scarlett asked.

" 'Know' is a strong word. I ran into him at the bank. No-one pays much attention to the tellers. But, a few days before the murder, something strange happened at the bank – I remember it well. A man showed

130

up at the reception desk. It sticks in my mind because he was dressed rather oddly. He left an envelope and disappeared without saying a word."

"Who was it for, this envelope?" Scarlett asked.

"Macaire Ebezner. It was marked 'Urgent'. I immediately brought it upstairs to Monsieur Ebezner. He got very upset."

16

An Anonymous Letter

Wednesday, December 12, four days before the murder

It was seven thirty in the morning when Macaire Ebezner, having decided to change his behaviour to prove to Tarnogol that he would make a good president, arrived at the bank. Cristina was very surprised to see him there so early.

"Monsieur Ebezner, is everything alright?"

"And why shouldn't it be?"

"Well, we've never seen you here at this hour before."

"This is the new me, dear Cristina," he said as he arranged himself behind his desk. "From now on, call me Stakhanov!"

He felt confident. He had woken up with a good feeling. Operation Turnaround was going to work. On Saturday, he would be president.

After Cristina, it was Levovitch's turn to appear in Macaire's office, asking whether he wanted to have a coffee. Macaire declined: "Too much work. Important week." Judging that it was time to finally attack his pile of mail, he grabbed a letter. But at that very moment, Cristina walked into his office. "Monsieur Ebezner, this just arrived." She handed him an envelope on which was written, in capital letters in red marker:

ATTN. MACAIRE EBEZNER
VERY URGENT
PERSONAL AND CONFIDENTIAL

There was no address, no stamp – no return address either. Intrigued, Macaire opened the envelope at once. Inside, there was an anonymous message:

Rendezvous this evening at 11:30, Parc Bertrand, by the big pond.
  If you want to be named president of the bank, don't be late.
  Your future depends on it! Speak to no-one about this!

Macaire rushed to Cristina.

"What is this letter? Who gave it to you?"

"One of the employees in the post room just brought it to me. Why? You look pale, Monsieur Ebezner. Is everything alright?"

Without answering, Macaire went down to the first floor, where the post room was located.

"Yes, I just brought the letter up," one of the employees said to Macaire.

"And who gave it to you?" Macaire asked nervously.

"A teller. When someone leaves mail at the reception desk, a teller brings it to us and we bring it to the recipient. Why? Is there a problem?"

Without answering, Macaire walked to the reception desk.

"Good morning, Monsieur Ebezner," the tellers sang in chorus.

"Who accepted this letter?" Macaire asked, waving the letter around.

"I did," one of the tellers remarked.

"And who gave it to you?"

"A strange-looking man. He was wearing a cap and sunglasses. I thought it a bit unusual for December, but you know, you see all kinds here. He didn't say a word, just handed over the letter. I asked for his name, but he just nodded and left. I immediately brought the letter to the post room, as we always do. Have I done something wrong?"

*

A few minutes later, in the office of the bank's head of security, Macaire was studying the footage from the security cameras at the entrance of the bank. A strange person had entered the bank, dressed in a long coat with the collar turned up, a cap pulled low over his head, and aviator sunglasses that hid much of his face. The entrance hall cameras showed him rapidly entering the bank and giving the letter to one of the tellers before hurrying back out again.

"He's a pro, that's for sure," said the head of security, who had watched the footage with Macaire.

"What kind of pro?"

"I don't know, but look how he avoids looking directly at the camera. You can't get a good picture of his face."

To prove this, the head of security froze the image and enlarged the visitor's face.

"You see, just like I said. He's a pro. Maybe a private detective. What's in the letter? Do you want to alert the police?"

"It's nothing important," Macaire assured the man – he had no intention of telling the talkative head of security anything.

Macaire returned to his office. He was pensive all morning, and kept looking out the window anxiously. He reread the message several times: "If you want to be named president of the bank, don't be late." Should he go? What if it was a trap? What if someone wanted to kill him? He was uneasy, his stomach knotted and taut.

He was roused from this listless state by Cristina, who kept coming into his office to ask how he was. "Are you sure you're alright, Monsieur Ebezner? You look a little strange. Do you want to tell me about the letter? Was it a threat? Can I get you some tea?" At noon, she became even more concerned when he didn't go out for his customary and seemingly endless lunch break. "I'm not in the mood," Macaire simply said.

Finally, at quarter past twelve, Levovitch came in.

"How's it going, old man? Cristina said you're a little out of sorts."

"No, no, I'm fine, Lev."

"I'm going to have lunch at Lipp with some friends. Why don't you join us? It might put you in a better mood."

"No, thanks, I'm not feeling up to it right now. I think I need to be alone for a while."

"You're sure?"

"Sure. I'm going to try to close my eyes for a bit."

Levovitch didn't insist and left. Macaire curled up in his armchair, feeling his eyelids droop. He put his feet up on his desk and leaned back. A small nap would do him good. He fell asleep without difficulty and had a few minutes of rest – until Tarnogol stepped into his office.

* * *

"Get up, for God's sake! You're sleeping at work?"

Macaire jumped and opened his eyes wide. Tarnogol was standing in front of him. Macaire sat straight up.

"Well, dear Sinior, you're here!" he stuttered, wiping the drool from the corner of his mouth.

"I came to see if you were working, but you're sleeping."

"No, I've been hard at work all morning," Macaire assured him, rummaging through the pile of letters on his desk.

"Still with this mail? You've done nothing since yesterday."

"I assure you, I have – quite a bit, in fact. But this morning, when I was just getting started, I had a bit of a setback."

"Always excuses!" Tarnogol shouted. "Enough! Enough!"

Without giving Macaire the time to explain, he left, making sure to slam the door on his way out, something that was becoming a habit with him. Macaire collapsed into his chair again, groaning. In need of sympathy, he phoned his wife.

Anastasia was crossing the carrefour de Rive when she received the call from her husband. From the sound of his voice, she immediately understood that something wasn't right.

"Everything alright, kitten?" she asked, knowing this would put him at ease.

"Yes, I just wanted to hear your voice. What have you been up to?"

"I've just arrived at Roberto's for lunch with my mother and my sister."

"Oh, right, the Wednesday lunch. I had forgotten. Say hello to everyone for me. Enjoy your lunch."

"Thanks, kitten. Call me if you need anything."

"Yes, yes, don't worry."

"Anything else you wanted to tell me?" she asked, suspecting there was another reason for the call.

There was a moment of silence. It was just dawning on Macaire that after Tarnogol's reaction, he had no choice but to go to the mysterious rendezvous that night at Parc Bertrand.

"I . . . I won't be home for dinner this evening. I'll be back late."

"Late?"

"Yes, I . . . I have to meet someone." Macaire hesitated, unsure whether to mention the anonymous letter, before deciding not to bring it up. "A client. He's arriving late from London and insists on seeing me before an investment meeting tomorrow morning."

"I'll see you later, then."

Before entering Roberto's, the elegant Italian restaurant in central Geneva where she had lunch every Wednesday with Olga, her mother, and Irina, her sister, Anastasia quickly checked her appearance in a pocket mirror. She didn't want them to see that she'd been crying all morning. When she awoke, she had hoped to hear from Lev, but there was nothing. No news. She had the impression he was playing with her and wondered whether it was because she had said she wanted to break up with him. She took a deep breath and walked in.

As always, Olga and Irina von Lacht were already there, having arrived early and settled into the banquette of a well-placed table, in their furs and jewels, sipping champagne. Anastasia was greeted with a dry "Ahh, you're finally here" from her mother, who never failed to point out when she was late. Irina smiled at her coldly, inspecting her from head to foot, trying to determine whether she had put on weight since the previous week.

"Is your bracelet new?" her sister asked, glancing at Anastasia's wrist.

"A trinket," Anastasia said, seating herself at the table.

"A gold trinket," her sister teased.

"Well, a gift," Anastasia replied, pretending to examine the menu to change the subject.

"A gift from whom?" her sister demanded. "Your husband?"

"Mind your own business!" Anastasia snapped.

"Calm down, both of you," their mother ordered, as if she were speaking to two little girls. "We are von Lachts, don't forget that. Descendants of the Habsburgs don't squabble in public."

"We're not Habsburgs," Anastasia sighed. "We're nothing."

"*Тишина*," her mother ordered, glaring at her.

There was dead silence at the table as Olga forced herself to smile to compose herself. Her two daughters remained silent and buried their faces in their menus. Ever since childhood, they had learned to remain silent whenever their mother raised her voice in Russian.

Olga adjusted her diamond necklace and then, waving a hand covered in tarnished jewels, signalled for more champagne. A waiter rushed over and filled the three glasses before taking their orders. Olga and Anastasia both selected the grilled sole. Irina ordered the pasta with white truffles.

"You're not eating pasta, dear," her mother declared. "You're not going to find a husband by stuffing yourself."

"But mamochka," Irina whined, "this is the season for white truffles!"

"You'll eat truffles when you've found a husband," Olga ordered peremptorily. "Meanwhile, you'll have grilled fish." She turned to the waiter. "Make that three soles. Thank you."

"Please don't humiliate me in public, mamochka," Irina murmured, her face a frozen mask.

"I didn't humiliate you; I'm helping you maintain your standing. We're Habsburgs, don't forget it."

Anastasia, seated opposite her mother and sister, observed them, wondering why she endured these weekly get-togethers.

They weren't real Habsburgs. They were merely a family of fallen aristocrats. Their mother was a White Russian whose great-grandfather, a very wealthy arms dealer, had been ennobled by the tsar, only to be stripped of his wealth by the revolution. Olga had been born into a poor family but constantly reminded her daughters of the family's standing during the Russian Empire, now long lost. Quite naturally, Olga's singular obsession had always been to rediscover that former glory and, during a trip to Vienna, she had become infatuated with one Stefan von Lacht, the man who would become her husband, for two reasons she believed were entirely valid: he was noble (the von Lachts were Austrian aristocrats stemming from a branch of the Habsburgs), and he was rich (his father had conveniently died shortly before Stefan met Olga, leaving him an immense fortune, amassed from oil trading and real estate).

Stefan and Olga's marriage was held with great pageantry in the St Charles Borromeo Church in Vienna. They settled into a large and luxurious apartment on Innere Stadt, the historic centre of the Austrian capital. Stefan didn't work, living on the income from his father's fortune. He and Olga spent their time shopping and dining at fashionable restaurants, where Olga always appeared wearing a different dress and jewels, explaining to anyone who would listen that Habsburgs never wore the same clothes twice. After a few years of marriage, Irina was born, followed by Anastasia two years later. In the salons of Vienna's high society, Olga claimed that the couple would marry their daughters into princely European families, but what Olga had failed to realise was that her husband, who had desperately wanted to win her hand when they first met, had slightly exaggerated his wealth. And since he didn't work and was generally rather bored, he spent the majority of his time at the casino. Their extremely high standard of living – and in particular the lavish expenditure on clothes and jewellery, the accumulation of gambling debts, and a hefty tax settlement – together with a weakening economy, ate up the last schillings available to the young von Lacht family.

Up to his ears in debt, Stefan von Lacht disappeared one day, abandoning his family. Upon discovering his absence, Olga fled Vienna with her two children, ages nine and eleven, to reinvent herself in Geneva. They ended up in a tiny apartment in the Pâquis neighbourhood. Of their former life, all that remained was their furs and jewels – and a bitter taste in Olga's mouth. She didn't leave Vienna to escape her creditors, as her cowardly husband had done, but because she couldn't bear the idea of being ostracised from high society. "There is no affliction, there is only acceptance," Olga decreed. She rolled up her sleeves. She found a job as a sales assistant at Bongénie, a large luxury store in Geneva. She managed the family budget with an iron fist. Their spending had been reduced to what was strictly necessary – no evenings out, no shopping sprees, canned goods for all their meals. She saved every franc she could to allow them to visit Geneva's upscale watering holes on the weekends.

On Saturdays, Olga and the girls would have lunch at a trendy restaurant, a tradition that would continue on Wednesdays once the girls were married. On Sundays, they took tea at the bars of the city's most fashionable hotels.

For those occasions, they made careful preparations. Olga wore her finest clothes and jewels. Her daughters wore their mother's creations. Olga had always had an innate talent for dressmaking and, taking her inspiration from the latest fashion catalogues from Paris, made dresses from inexpensive fabrics found at local markets.

Upon entering those large hotels, outfitted like reliquaries, one of

139

the girls, often Anastasia, would invariably experience a moment of apprehension.

"Don't we look a little ridiculous, the three of us, going for tea at the Beau-Rivage in evening wear?"

"What's ridiculous is to have been rich and become poor," Olga explained. "And now, ladies, *Kopf hoch*! Hold your heads high. Appearances are what counts."

They entered the dining rooms of hotels and restaurants with confidence. Everyone turned to observe these three, apparently wealthy, women, who were soon said to be descendants of the Habsburgs, although no-one really knew what exactly that meant.

Olga found it easy to integrate with Geneva's high society. She got to know the people who counted, and was soon a fixture at all the most exclusive events: the Spring Ball, the Red Cross Ball, cocktail parties held by local watchmakers, gallery openings. To avoid disclosing her address in Pâquis, she had invitations sent to the Beau-Rivage, where she pretended to rent a very large suite. "Living at a hotel is very Nabokov," she explained to her daughters. "And besides, it's the Beau-Rivage, people are impressed by that; it's where Empress Sisi passed away." She gave the head concierge large tips to hold her mail and help maintain the ruse. But who was going to check? No-one dared imagine that the flamboyant Olga of the Habsburgs was an imposter. Once she had to hide when one of her new acquaintances came to the Bongénie to do some shopping, but she was never found out.

When Anastasia and Irina were sixteen and eighteen, their mother had but one ambition: to seal her status as a great lady through her daughters and help them succeed where she had failed by marrying a man of wealth and importance. She was no longer as concerned with a noble title as she once was; what mattered most was money.

She decided, therefore, that every weekend in winter would be devoted to scouring the sites where Europe's golden youth took their holidays. The sons of the greatest European families customarily spent the ski season in Gstaad, Klosters, or Saint Moritz, where they arrived in private planes and spent money with abandon. Heirs of royal families and captains of industry, they were all there, like carp in a fish pond; all you had to do was dip your net. And with daughters as attractive and well educated as Irina and Anastasia . . .

The family's meagre savings, coupled with the proceeds from the sale of some jewellery, helped finance these trips to mountain destinations, to which the three von Lacht women travelled by train and bus from Geneva. When they arrived, they piled into a small hotel room, rented at a reasonable price, where they slept and prepared for the fashionable evenings to which Olga Habsburg, who appeared to have stepped out of a novel by Tolstoy, obtained invitations merely by mentioning her stage name.

For Irina and Anastasia, these trips were not holidays. "You're not here to have a good time or to rest," Olga constantly reminded them. "You're here to find a young man and get engaged." Under their mother's watchful eye, the daughters spent their evenings pursuing young men from good families, while lying about their actual social status.

If the girls complained, their mother exploded into a theatrical outpouring of recriminations. "After everything I've done for you, is this how you repay me? I've fought tooth and nail for you. I've sacrificed my own life to improve yours. I've become your servant, and it's still not enough for you! What more do you want?"

If such recriminations failed to have an effect, Olga immediately shifted into high gear and pleaded. "Look at my fingers, red and bleeding from the needles I use to sew your dresses. I've worn out my eyes staying up at night to make sure you look beautiful, to make sure you'll be noticed! You want to throw your mamochka in the garbage, is that what you want?" Olga then pretended to have a coughing fit, trying to convince her daughters that she was wearing herself out for them. In general, her theatrics were enough to convince the girls, who rushed to their mother and covered her with kisses. And when Olga held them in her arms and they called her their "mamochka love", she felt fulfilled, almost happy.

But sometimes Olga lost control. The painful repercussions were felt by poor Irina when she was caught flirting with a waiter in a fashionable café in Gstaad. On their way back to the hotel, Olga slapped her, hard. "All the money I've spent to get you out of the gutter, and you go screwing around with a servant," she cried, mad with rage.

Over the following years, the von Lacht daughters each experienced several somewhat forced love affairs but, to their mother's consternation, nothing conclusive. At the ages of twenty-one and twenty-three, Anastasia and Irina were still not engaged. It was then that Olga learned of the Ebezner Bank's Gala Weekend in Verbier. She immediately saw it as an excellent opportunity to show off her daughters to some of the most important executives at the most important private bank in Switzerland. For a long time, she congratulated herself on the initiative, whose success exceeded her expectations: the following year, Irina accepted a proposal of marriage from a wealth manager twelve years her senior, and the year after that, Anastasia got engaged to Macaire Ebezner, the heir to the bank.

But sixteen years later, Irina, now thirty-nine and the mother of two little girls, was divorced without a franc in maintenance. Her wealth manager husband had been arrested for embezzlement. He had landed a prison term and a fine that had ruined him. Irina, who had never worked in her life, had to accept a job in a supermarket. She had refused, out of misplaced pride, a position in the post room of the Ebezner Bank, which Macaire had found for her. But she managed to get Wednesdays off from twelve to two so she could have lunch at Roberto's as Anastasia's guest. Irina arrived dressed to the nines and desperate, got drunk on champagne, and smiled at any Adonis with deep pockets who crossed her gaze, praying that one of them would snatch her out of the miserable life that fate had dealt her.

The grilled sole was served, and the champagne glasses were refilled again.

"You know, Anastasia," Olga said, unable to spend more than five minutes without criticising one of her daughters, "you could at least help your sister find a husband. You know so many people."

"Mother, I've introduced her to half the town."

"They were all hideous," Irina whined. "Do you like seeing me broke?"

"You give yourself too much credit," Anastasia said to her sister. "Do you think I'm going to arrange the whole thing for you? I have my own problems."

"Rich people have no problems," Olga declared.

"There's more to life than money," Anastasia retorted.

"Easy to say when you're rich," Irina remarked, with some bitterness.

Anastasia, who had come to a slow boil, forgot herself for a moment and blurted out, "I'm going to leave Macaire."

The announcement was met by stupefied silence.

"What are you saying?" her sister murmured.

"It's very simple. I want to leave my husband," Anastasia repeated, suddenly relieved to have unburdened herself.

"A passing fancy," her mother snickered. "You read too many books, my daughter. It's out of the question that you should leave him. The matter is closed."

Anastasia, for once, decided to contradict her mother.

"It's not a passing fancy. I don't love Macaire any longer; I love Lev Levovitch. He's the one who gave me this bracelet."

Her mother looked horrified.

"Levovitch!" she choked out. "The clown from fifteen years ago at the Verbier?"

"He's not a clown, Mother. He's become a very important banker. He speaks to the heads of state from around the world. All Geneva is talking about him. You seem to be the only one who doesn't know who he is."

143

"Well, Geneva has got very Jewish, then."

"Stop it, Mother," Anastasia implored.

"No, you stop it, you insolent child. How dare you speak to your mother that way? Stop this idiocy at once and stay with Macaire. He's a charming man and a very good husband. Do you want to end up like your sister? I forbid you to see this Levovitch again, you hear me? And I forbid you to wear his gifts in public – you're not some cheap whore."

"But I'm happy with Lev. I feel good around him."

Olga, her eyes bright with anger, raised a threatening finger at her daughter.

"I don't want to ever hear that name again, you understand? He's not like us."

"He's Russian!"

"He's Jewish; we don't associate with such people. Have I entirely failed to educate you? You're going to promise me never to see him again. Do you want to see me dead? I've sacrificed everything, I've lived off canned goods my whole life so that you could find a decent husband. Now, let's eat in silence. I've heard enough from both of you."

Anastasia, struggling to hold back tears, had difficulty finishing her fish. No further words were spoken until the end of the meal. Then, Anastasia paid the bill. The three women said goodbye to one another curtly before each went her own way. "See you next week," Anastasia's mother said as she walked away.

17

Memories

That day, December 12, after lunch with her mother and sister, Anastasia went directly home. Ordinarily, she would spend Wednesday afternoons walking around central Geneva, but between her mother's accusations and Lev's silence, she didn't have the heart for a casual stroll. She felt deeply demoralised and spent the rest of the day locked in the bedroom. She wanted to call Lev, to hear his voice, be reassured. But she wanted him to take the initiative. He was the one who had stood her up last night. On edge, she began to cry and then fell into a deep sleep.

Evening was falling over Cologny when Arma, uneasy because of her employer's silence, went upstairs to find her. Arma's day hadn't gone at all as she had expected. That morning, after a sleepless, worry-filled night, she had gone to work with the firm intention of telling Macaire about Levovitch. But when she got there, Macaire had already left for the bank. Of all days, why did he have to choose this one to be so industrious? She then decided to let Madame see her sulking. She couldn't confront Anastasia directly – she admired her too much – but she wanted to at least hint at her deep-seated disapproval. When Anastasia came down to the kitchen for breakfast, however, Arma saw how unhappy Madame looked, and her red eyes betrayed her tears. If Arma had wondered whether Madame's sorrow had to do with Lev, the connection was now obvious. How foolish she had been, Arma thought, to have jumped to such hasty conclusions. She had forgotten one important thing: if Lev had phoned here on Monday, it was because Madame didn't want to talk to him on her mobile. She wanted to break it off! Besides, didn't she tell him during the call that it was all over, that she didn't want to hear from him? Arma was furious with herself. She deserved to be a servant for having such poor judgment. How could she overlook that fact? Of course, it was because of the bouquet of white roses, but if he had sent flowers it was to try to win her back after she had calmly broken it off with him the night before.

Yes, there had been the bath immediately after receiving the flowers, but baths, she took them all the time – and for hours. It didn't mean anything. If Madame had joined Lev the night before, it was to end their relationship! Yes, she had allowed her passions get the better of her, but she had quickly recovered her good sense and acted accordingly. She had broken it off, and she was now suffering for it. Indeed, there was something beautiful in her sorrow. It was proof that their affair had meant something.

Anastasia hadn't touched her breakfast. When she returned to the bedroom, Arma felt renewed admiration for her employer. She was strong, dignified, courageous. Arma hadn't been wrong about Madame; she was a great lady.

As she did every Wednesday, Madame had left the house in the late morning. But what was very unusual was that Monsieur had returned home for lunch. He came rushing in, looking very concerned. He went to the bedroom for a few minutes, before leaving as quickly as he had arrived. As he was leaving, he said to Arma, "You didn't see me."

Then Madame had returned in the early afternoon. She looked even worse than she had that morning. She again locked herself in the bedroom. Listening at the door, Arma could hear her crying. She felt bad for her. Madame didn't come out all afternoon. Now, Arma was worried.

Anastasia heard a gentle knocking on the door. She rose from the bed and saw Arma's face in the opening. A ray of light from the hall entered the darkened bedroom.

"Are you okay, Médéme?"

"Not very well."

Arma took the liberty of entering the room and sat on the edge of the bed. With an affectionate gesture, she caressed Anastasia's leg to comfort her.

"Anything I can do, Médéme?"

"No, thank you. That's very kind of you."

"I prepared some soup. Would you like me to bring you some?"

"Thank you, but I'm not hungry."

"You're not going to eat, Médéme?"

Anastasia shook her head.

"And Moussieu? He still hasn't returned."

"He has to see a client."

"I think that Moussieu isn't doing so well either."

"It's a difficult time, Arma."

"I would like very much to help you."

"You already do too much, Arma. You should go home; you must be tired."

"Are you sure? You don't want some company?"

"Don't worry about me. You can go. Thank you for everything."

Arma obeyed and left, feeling anxious. It wasn't going well for her employers, and she felt bad for them. And she was angry with herself for the anger she had felt about Madame the night before. Madame had always been kind to her – generous, attentive, considerate. For Arma's birthday, Madame had given her the day off and had taken her to lunch. "You're practically family, Arma," she often remarked.

Shortly after Arma left, the bell at the Ebezner home rang, which required Anastasia to leave the bedroom and open the door. There, to her surprise, stood Alfred Agostinelli, Lev's chauffeur.

"Pardon me, Madame, for showing up like this, but your husband's car wasn't here, and I thought . . ."

"You did well," she replied, eager to hear the news about Lev.

"Monsieur Levovitch sent me to apologise. He was kept at the office all night attending to government business. In fact, he's still at the United Nations with the secretary general to discuss economic sanctions. Unfortunately, I can't tell you anything more but, as you can imagine, it's a matter of the utmost importance."

Faced with these explanations, Anastasia felt ridiculous for having got so worked up. Relieved and happy, she felt her good mood return. Chiding herself for her adolescent behaviour, she said to the chauffeur:

"Please tell Monsieur Levovitch that I was very sad not to see him last night."

"Monsieur Levovitch also asked me to give you this note."

Agostinelli handed Anastasia an envelope. Taking it from him she couldn't suppress a brilliant smile. She clasped the letter to her heart.

"Thank you, Alfred."

Agostinelli bowed slightly and disappeared into the obscurity of the winter evening. Anastasia hurriedly opened the envelope. Joy had returned. Submerged in a very hot bath overflowing with foam, she read the note over and over again, being careful not to get it wet.

Let's go away together, far from Geneva.
Leave everything.
I love you.
Lev

Her head buzzed with a thousand questions. Where would they go? When? If they were ready to leave everything behind, should they take advantage of the Gala Weekend at the bank to escape? Macaire would go alone as he did every year; spouses were generally not invited. Knowing Lev, he had certainly taken care of everything.

Before her marriage to Macaire, Anastasia had attended two of the bank's Gala Weekends at the Hôtel de Verbier, to which she had been dragged by her mother. The first time, sixteen years ago, she was twenty-one and studying literature. It was there, at the hotel, that she had met Klaus, to whom she almost got engaged. She shivered when she thought about him.

* * *

Sixteen years earlier
Irina and Anastasia attend the Gala Weekend for the first time

"Let's go, girls!" Olga yelled, rushing into the narrow bedroom her daughters shared in the family apartment in Pâquis. "You'll never guess the good news. I've managed to get a room at the Auberge des Chamois in Verbier. Everything was full, but the owner just called to let me know. A last-minute cancellation. What luck!"

"It's Friday, mamochka," Irina noted. "We have class at the university."

"Trust me, you won't find a husband at school, but you will at Verbier this weekend."

"What's at Verbier?"

"The Ebezner Bank's Gala Weekend! The dream opportunity to find you a husband. We're done with those empty-headed youngsters from Klosters or Saint Moritz; you need a man, a real man, with a career and family ambitions. You need a banker!"

"I'm not sure I want to marry a banker," Irina remarked.

"You'll marry whomever I tell you to marry. Don't be an ingrate. As the queen of England put it, 'Never explain, never complain.' Go and get dressed – I'll prepare our bags. There's a train to Martigny in an hour. You'll thank me when you're rich and no longer have anything to worry about."

Several hours later, after the ride from Geneva to Martigny to Le Châble by train, and then by bus to Verbier, Olga, Irina, and Anastasia checked into their small, uncomfortable room at the Auberge des Chamois.

"There's a welcome cocktail reception for bank employees at four at the hotel," Olga explained to the girls. "Wear your blue dresses and your black heels. We'll make sure they get a good look at you."

"But we'll be thrown out!" Irina worried.

"Not if you're careful. Enter the room as if you owned the place. If a waiter asks questions, look him up and down and ask for a glass of champagne."

When Olga and her daughters entered the reception room of the hotel, all eyes turned to look at the two young women – beautiful, elegant, aristocratic. Conscious that Irina and Anastasia were attracting everyone's attention, Olga rejoiced.

"Look at that," she whispered, pointing to a group of men who were laughing together. "They're from the bank, the top executives. The old one, over there, is Auguste Ebezner, the president. The tall one next to him, who looks like an American actor, is his son, Abel Ebezner, the vice president. They say he's an amazing banker and makes all the decisions for his father. The young one, with the dark tie, is Macaire Ebezner, Abel's only son. The heir to the bank. He's twenty-five, and as soon as his grandfather passes the torch, he'll be named vice president – in a year, two years at most, given the way the old man looks. Vice president of a bank at twenty-six! Now, that's real class."

The three von Lachts asked for champagne and examined the small crowd of bankers. Suddenly, Olga started squirming like an eel.

"My dears, I think you're in God's good graces today. That's Klaus Van Der Brouck, an intern at the bank. He's directly connected to the Belgian royal family and he's filthy rich. His father is an important industrialist in Brussels. Go and introduce yourselves."

When the girls hesitated, Olga dragged them with her and greeted Klaus Van Der Brouck, deploying her genius for pretence.

"My dear Klaus," she exclaimed, rushing towards him.

The Klaus in question had no idea who she was but, after all, maybe they had once met.

"Olga von Lacht," she informed him, seeing that he had failed to place her.

"Of course, Madame." Klaus was courteous enough to pretend to recognise her. "Delighted to see you again."

"It seems you're on an internship programme in Geneva?" she enquired. This remark led Klaus to believe he had actually met her, though for the life of him he couldn't remember where.

"Yes, my father is good friends with Abel Ebezner. He thought I should acquire some banking experience so I could manage the family's money."

"Oh, how fascinating. Let me introduce my daughters, Irina and Anastasia."

The two sisters spoke for several minutes with Klaus, who couldn't take his eyes off Anastasia and flirted with her openly, which delighted Olga. When the cocktail hour was over, Klaus made Anastasia promise to come and find him after dinner. There was an orchestra at the hotel bar, which made for a wonderful atmosphere. Olga, delighted, accepted for her daughter. Anastasia felt like she was being smothered. She found a pretext and escaped through a service door, making her way outside. The fresh air felt good. Sheltered beneath an awning, she watched the snow falling in large flakes. She dreamed of escaping the world, especially from her mother. She wanted a cigarette but she hadn't dared bring a pack with her. Were Olga to find it, she would have slapped her daughter silly.

Anastasia noticed a man with his back to her, sitting on a wooden box and smoking. Although she couldn't see his face, she knew he was handsome. Wearing a black tweed coat, he had an indefinable appeal. Even his way of smoking seemed elegant. She imagined he was a prince or, more likely, a wealthy Genevan banker.

"Do you have a cigarette?" she asked.

The man turned. She noticed that he was about her age, maybe a little older, but also that he wore a name tag on his jacket. He was a hotel employee. He smiled and rose to bring her the cigarette. Anastasia felt drawn to the young man's magnetism. She read the name on the tag: Lev.

"You work for the Ebezner Bank?" he enquired.

"No, just visiting. I'm Anastasia; I'm a Habsburg."

She bit her tongue, feeling like an idiot. Why had she said such a thing? To impress him? The man smiled broadly.

"Lev Levovitch. I'm a baggage handler."

She consumed him with her eyes. Lightning had struck.

* * *

Anastasia remained in the bath for a long time, daydreaming. She was so happy to have Lev back in her life again, but angry with herself for the harm she would do to Macaire. To appease her conscience, she repeated that she had to put herself first. When she finally went to bed, it was eleven p.m. She had had no news from Macaire since the call at midday. On the phone, he'd sounded strange. She should have called him back, asked him what was going on. For the first time in longer than she could remember, she missed him.

Eleven thirty, Parc Bertrand. Macaire, frozen from the cold, paced back and forth before the pond. An icy wind whipped his face and caused the tree branches to crack. The place was dark and deserted. A handful of scattered street lamps gave off what little light there was. He felt that nothing good could come from this mysterious rendezvous. But he had no choice. He slipped his hand into his pocket and caressed the handle of his revolver, feeling reassured. During lunch, he had taken advantage of Anastasia's absence to return home and collect the gun. His wife did not know he owned a gun, but he had bought it – legally – a few years earlier. A Glock 26 9 mm semi-automatic, made in Austria, compact, light, and reliable. He kept it in the safe in the bedroom, to which only he had the combination. While working for P-30, he had felt he should be able to protect his home. Just in case. This evening, especially, he was glad he had bought the gun.

Suddenly, a silhouette appeared against the light. Macaire felt his heartbeat accelerate.

"Who's there?"

The silhouette remained silent; Macaire took out the revolver and pointed it in the direction of what might turn out to be a threat. Then, in the lamplight, he recognised the face of the man who approached him.

"You . . . !"

18

A Night in Geneva

Scarlett and I were preparing to leave Geneva to return to Verbier when Arma phoned. She was cleaning offices until late that evening, so we agreed to meet the following day at a café in Champel, where I knew that we could talk without being disturbed.

"I assume we're not going back to Verbier tonight," Scarlett said.

"You assume correctly."

Taking advantage of the fact that there was no traffic heading in the opposite direction, I made a U-turn in the middle of the road and headed for my apartment.

"Where are we going?" she asked.

"To my place."

"If there's a hotel nearby you could recommend . . ."

"I'm not abandoning you to a hotel. You can have my guest room. There's a bathroom and everything you need."

"You're too good to me, Writer."

"Do you need to stop in town to buy a toothbrush or pyjamas?"

She pointed over her shoulder to the small bag she had dropped into the boot of my car that morning.

"I've taken care of it. I've got a change of clothes and a toothbrush. I don't need pyjamas, I sleep in the nude."

"I see."

She smiled. And I couldn't help but smile in return. I parked the car in front of my building. Scarlett was delighted with the small one-way street, charming and tree-lined, with old houses on one side and Parc Bertrand on the other.

We met no-one inside the building. Once in my apartment, I made some coffee, which we drank at the kitchen counter. It felt good to be around her. We were seated side by side, and I could feel her body against mine. I wanted to hold her to me: I wanted something to happen. She was close, close enough to kiss, and I wanted her badly, but at the same time a thought ran through my head: what if Sloane showed up? I didn't know whether this thought reflected my anxiety or my desire to see her again. I felt drawn to Scarlett the way I missed Sloane.

I suggested that she see the rest of the apartment: "Can I show you around?"

"Sure."

I showed her the bedroom, then led her to my office.

"So, this is where you write your books!"

She walked around, examining the pictures and notes on the wall.

"Fascinating, absolutely fascinating!"

"What is? The office?"

"You," she replied, looking directly into my eyes and poking me in the chest with her finger. She went on, "I'm exhausted, Writer. I'm going to take a nap. Are we having dinner together?"

"That would be wonderful. There's an excellent restaurant not far from here."

"Marvellous! See you later. Rest a bit. It's been a long trip."

She left me alone in the room.

I sat at my desk, taking my notes and laptop from my bag. I began to work.

19

The Start of Things Unwanted

"You?" Macaire murmured, having discovered that the one meeting him at the mysterious rendezvous was none other than Wagner, his contact at P-30. "You scared the hell out of me."

"Good evening, Macaire. Sorry to have got in touch like this and for the late meeting, but I knew we'd be alone here at this hour."

"I nearly shot you."

"You have a gun?"

"A simple precaution," Macaire replied, slightly annoyed. "Between the message and the location, I thought it was a threat. Want to tell me what's going on? Why didn't you contact me through the usual channels?"

"I did! I sent you three invitations for the opera, but you never showed up. Don't you read your mail anymore?"

"Apologies. I've got way behind on my correspondence recently."

"Well, thanks to your lack of discipline I had to watch *The Barber of Seville* three times."

"Terribly sorry. What's so urgent that you had to see me in the middle of the night? Is it because of what happened in Madrid? Did Perez talk?"

"It's got nothing to do with Madrid. It's about the bank. The situation is critical. You're going to lose the presidency, and that's a real problem."

"What's that got to do with P-30?" Macaire asked, not understanding why his affairs were suddenly Wagner's concern.

"Everyone in Bern is worried," Wagner explained. "All the way up to the top ranks of the government. The Federal Council is demanding we provide a daily report on the situation for the intelligence services."

"But why?"

"Macaire! Sinior Tarnogol is about to become president of the most powerful private bank in Switzerland. I'm sure you can appreciate how that presents a problem for us."

"Tarnogol, president of the Ebezner Bank? No, not at all. You're mistaken. Levovitch is the one they have in mind."

"And who wants to install Levovitch as president? Tarnogol. Don't you find it odd that, back in January, the board agreed it would be you and then, suddenly, a few days before the election, Tarnogol declares that Levovitch is going to be appointed?"

Macaire was shocked to discover that Wagner knew everything that was going on at the bank.

"With Levovitch in charge, he'll defer to the vice president, and that will be Tarnogol."

"Why would Levovitch do that?

"For the money. Tarnogol will offer him a mountain of cash. He's got an extensive network; he's very powerful. Tarnogol is a devil. He's capable of anything. You should know that only too well, Macaire, after your little exchange fifteen years ago."

Macaire preferred not to respond to Wagner's last remark.

"In spite of your father's efforts, we never managed to counteract Tarnogol. It's time to employ stronger measures."

"My father!"

"Your father did a lot for us."

"My father worked for P-30?"

"An outstanding agent!"

Macaire stood there, stupefied and moved by the news. He and his father had shared the same destiny.

"The only reason your father didn't make you president, Macaire, was to get rid of Tarnogol."

"My father was planning to appoint me president?"

"Of course. He spoke about you often, you know. He was tough on you in public but, in reality, he admired you. So, naturally, he intended to name you president, but we talked him out of it. If you had been appointed you would have been stuck with Tarnogol as vice president, and, believe me, he would have stopped at nothing to get you out of the way and take your place. We had to find a way to break with three hundred years of tradition at the bank."

"So this whole business of the succession was a P-30 operation," Macaire murmured as he realised what Wagner was telling him.

Wagner nodded.

"It was the only way to undo Tarnogol's hold on the bank. By letting the board choose the president, while excluding its members as candidates, your father prevented Tarnogol from advancing, but also set a precedent for change. It was a perfect plan. We knew you would be elected, and we knew you would then be in a position to change the rules of the game and appoint someone you trusted as vice president. Tarnogol would have been out of the way. He would have remained a shareholder, of course, but he would have lost his power."

"So what went wrong?"

"Tarnogol was stronger than we thought. He beat us at our own game. He managed to turn Horace Hansen and convince him to back Levovitch. We're three days from the election. This is serious."

"But you have something in mind. Otherwise you wouldn't have asked to see me."

Wagner smiled coldly. "Very perceptive, Macaire. I expected nothing less of you. The truth is, we only recently realised that something was going on at the bank. In January, Tarnogol didn't dare to push his boy Levovitch on Horace and Jean-Bénédict Hansen. They were too attached to tradition. 'Only an Ebezner can run the Ebezner Bank,' they repeated. And now, a few days before the election, they've changed their minds. That's when we understood that there was a worm in the apple. There's a traitor in the bank who's working for Tarnogol and against us."

"A traitor? Do you know who it is?"

"Yes, Macaire," was all Wagner would say.

"So who, then? Who is it? Don't tell me it's Jean-Béné – I'd never believe that. I can't imagine that he's not loyal to the bank."

"It's not Jean-Bénédict," Wagner reassured him, laconically.

"Stop playing guessing games, Wagner. Spit it out, will you?"

Wagner stared at Macaire with an icy expression. After a moment of silence, he said to him, "Stop pretending, Macaire, it doesn't suit you. We know everything."

"What the hell are you talking about?"

"You're the traitor, Macaire."

"What! That's ridiculous."

"Is it? Your earnings this year have been terrible. Throughout your career, they've never been this bad. All your clients have lost money. You arrive hours late. You don't even answer your mail. You've sunk your own ship. And Tarnogol, after showing the Hansens your results, had little trouble convincing them not to appoint you president."

"But that's completely absurd! For the love of God, why would I do something like that?"

"For the money. God knows how much Tarnogol has promised you. Probably enough for you to buy an island in the Bahamas and spend the rest of your life there. You want nothing to do with being president; you proved that fifteen years ago by transferring your shares to Tarnogol. And you're getting ready to do it again by letting him become president. Tarnogol and you are working together. And you're also friends with Levovitch. It's a tight little circle. You three, you're the Bermuda triangle."

"But that's absolutely ridiculous. How can you doubt my loyalty after everything I've done for P-30? Yes, I've had a bad year, I admit it. But the circumstances explain that. I always had good results – until my father decided not to name me president; that broke me."

"Stop pretending, Macaire. We know all about your connection with Tarnogol. We know you're the only one he trusts."

"My connection? I must be dreaming. You're out of your mind, Wagner. Tarnogol hates me; he spends his time insulting me."

"Do you really think we're fools?" Wagner burst out, pulling an envelope from his pocket and handing it over.

Macaire opened it. Inside were photographs taken two days earlier, in the dead of night, in which he was seen entering Tarnogol's town house at 10 rue Saint-Léger.

"I have to say I was surprised, Macaire, when our surveillance of Tarnogol's house revealed your night-time visit with your dear friend."

"You're mistaken! Tarnogol asked me to do him a favour in exchange for his vote."

"What type of favour?"

"Well, on Monday night, a man phoned the restaurant where I was having dinner and gave me the following instructions: 'There's an envelope that needs to be collected. Take the road to Basel and go to the bar at the Hôtel Les Trois Rois. Ask to speak to Ivan – he's one of the waiters. Order a strong coffee and *everything that goes with it*. He'll understand.' I followed the instructions. Ivan handed me an envelope. I was told to bring it to 10 rue Saint-Léger, Geneva – Tarnogol's home."

"So you brought the envelope to him and . . . let me guess the rest. He welcomed you like a king – rare vodka, Iranian caviar, the works. Then he showed you a painting of Saint Petersburg and told you the sad story of his family, which made you want to cry. And before you left, he was calling you 'brother'. Isn't that right?"

"Yes. How did you know?"

"Because you're not the first to be duped by Tarnogol. For years we've suspected him of working for Russian intelligence. He has a talent for manipulation. And since we've been following him, we've compiled a file with information about everyone he's used. Oh, you must have been delighted when he called you 'my brother'. He always finds good-natured people, easy to mould, easy to exploit. He uses them and then disposes of them. There's a good chance the envelope you brought him contained secrets that will be delivered to Russia. Technically, you've collaborated with a foreign government, Macaire. That's high treason."

"I did it to become president!"

"Then explain why Tarnogol has no intention of voting for you."

"Because of the mess in my office," Macaire acknowledged.

"And you think I'm going to believe that?"

"It's the absolute truth."

Wagner shrugged as if the truth didn't have much importance for him.

"Macaire, I'm going to give you a chance to prove your loyalty to the bank and to the country."

"Tell me what I have to do."

"It's very simple. You're going to kill Tarnogol."

Macaire stared at Wagner.

"What? Murder? Are you out of your mind?"

"You have no choice, Macaire. It's time to put an end to this circus, and you're the one to do it. It'll be your last operation for P-30. The one we've been preparing you for all these years."

With those words, Macaire suddenly understood the cruel truth: he hadn't been recruited at random by P-30.

"You planned it all from day one, is that it? The very first mission, Operation Diamond Wedding, you could have asked anyone at the bank. You could have asked my father, since he was also working for P-30."

"But it was a very simple mission and a wonderful opportunity to test you and bring you in," Wagner replied. "What did you think? That we were simply going to let the crown jewel of Swiss banking pass into foreign hands? You turned out to be a very good agent. I have to admit, you surprised us all. But, in reality, we wanted you for a single purpose, if it turned out to be necessary: eliminating Tarnogol. And that's exactly what you're going to do."

Macaire turned pale. All these years he had allowed himself to be trapped like some gullible trainee. And now the trap was closing on him.

"Wagner, you've lost your mind. Intelligence, okay. But there was never a question of killing anyone."

"I suspected you might make a scene," Wagner said before handing Macaire a second envelope. Inside was a photo that gave Macaire a shock: the bank's retired computer expert and his wife, dead in their living room, each with a bullet wound to the head.

"Your last masterpiece." Wagner smiled cynically.

"You killed those poor people?"

"They were a threat to our banking system. We had no choice but to get rid of them."

"You used me. That's why Perez came with me. He was never pulled in by the Spanish, that was just a bit of theatre. You made sure I would remain in my apartment while he calmly went over and executed them."

"Get off your high horse, Macaire. You're responsible for their deaths."

"No, I had nothing to do with this mess, and you know that."

Wagner smiled again.

"Guess what, Macaire. The weapon used for the murder was a Glock 26, just like the one you've got in your pocket. What an amazing coincidence. I believe you're much more involved in this assassination than you think. For now, the Spanish police think it was a burglary that went wrong. But all we have to do is put Interpol on your tail."

"Then you knew I had a weapon?"

"Let's just say we prefer to stay informed about what our assets are doing."

Macaire was shocked. He felt his world falling apart. P-30, which he had served devotedly all these years, had turned against him. There was a long silence, during which the two men looked at each other. It suddenly began to pour.

"Listen carefully," said Wagner, whom the rain seemed not to touch.

A series of shots suddenly rang out, interrupting him. Then there was a short silence, broken by more shots.

Scarlett knocked on the door to my office.

I raised my eyes from my computer and, as soon as I interrupted my work, the rain stopped, the snow-covered ground in Parc Bertrand became a white blanket again, the bare and terrifying trees disappeared, and the room returned to its former cheeriness.

I got up to open the door. Scarlett stood before me, beautiful in a short dress, ready to go to dinner. She had put her hair up, which highlighted the diamonds in her ears above her bare shoulders. Seeing my face, weary after the hours I'd spent buried in my book, the radiant smile disappeared from hers. She seemed disappointed.

"Have you forgotten our dinner?"

"Not at all," I lied. "I was just finishing my chapter."

"You don't look like you're ready to leave," she noted.

"I hadn't noticed it was already eight o'clock."

"It's not important – let's forget about dinner. It's obvious you don't want to go out. I'm sorry to have interrupted your work. Good evening."

She was about to turn away when I grabbed her hand to stop her.

"Wait, Scarlett, give me ten minutes. I'll get ready and we can go."

20

Bernard and Me

It was early in the evening of Wednesday, June 27, 2018, and it felt good to be outside in Geneva. Scarlett and I walked along rue de Contamines to the Museum of Natural History, then down rue des Glacis-de-Rive. The air was soft and smelled of summer.

After a while we reached a small French restaurant I was fond of. The owner sat us out on the terrace at a small table lit by candles. Scarlett examined the menu.

"I'm going to have the John Dory."

"It was Bernard's favourite fish. When he took me for lunch at Le Dôme in Paris, he would say solemnly, 'John Dory is the king of fish.' We spent some wonderful moments together in that place. We would plan a thousand projects for the future."

I ordered a bottle of Burgundy (Bernard believed a light red was a perfect accompaniment for fish) and some sparkling water. The waiter brought us a bottle of Châteldon, and I remarked on the coincidence.

"Bernard's favourite water. It's really his evening. He loved sparkling water, but not too sparkling. This he found perfect; he said it was the water of kings, Louis XVI in this case."

"The water of collaborators, too," Scarlett pointed out. "Didn't Pierre Laval buy Châteldon?"

"Bernard mentioned that as well," I replied, laughing.

She smiled.

"Tell me more about Bernard – you started to mention him this morning."

"How far did I get?"

"You were talking about your first novel, which wasn't very successful."

"Oh, yes. In January 2012, my first novel was published, and it was a commercial failure. A couple of months later, Lydwine Helly called me."

"Lydwine Helly, she's your benefactress, isn't she? The one who put you in contact with Bernard?"

"Exactly. You have a good memory. She knew I had a finished manuscript and, as she was getting ready to go on holiday, she wanted to take it with her. I sent it and when she returned, two weeks later, she said to me, 'It's very good – Bernard has to read it.' Bernard read it and was immediately convinced. 'This has to be published quickly, between now and September.' The only one who wasn't convinced was me. After what I believed to be the failure of my first novel, I didn't see how my second, published only a few months later, would have a different fate. So I refused."

"You refused?"

"Yes. It didn't leave enough time to prepare for publication. Generally, publishers announce new books a year before they come out."

"So what happened?"

"I discovered how very persuasive Bernard could be."

* * *

Paris, June 29, 2012

I was passing through Paris, and Bernard had suggested we have lunch together. I suggested I stop by the office around eleven a.m. We had spoken on the phone several times, but this was the first time since January that we were meeting in person. When I arrived at Éditions de Fallois, 22 rue La Boétie, I was struck by how different Bernard looked. He seemed younger, in better shape, animated by a new force. Entering his office, I saw dummies of my novel printed in different sizes on a table.

165

"Because it's rather thick, I wanted to find the most practical format for the book: finer but heavier paper or thicker but lighter-weight paper."

"But Bernard, I told you I didn't want to publish the book now."

"I know, Joël. I simply wanted to run a few tests out of curiosity. I wanted to see you to thank you."

"Thank me for what?"

"For the excitement you've given me with this book. It's an extraordinary feeling."

For an hour he talked about the novel. He explained why the book might be immensely successful. Then we went to lunch at Divellec, one of the best fish restaurants in Paris. I was very surprised that he would take me to such a place, as if he were celebrating something. He immediately ordered champagne – something he didn't ordinarily do – and, lifting his glass, said to me, "Dear Joël, I want to toast the health of this novel, which I won't publish but which has given me more excitement than I've felt in a very long time. Thanks to you, I remembered why I stay in this business."

It didn't take anything more to convince me. Bernard in all his glory: that charisma; that voice; that ability, which great politicians have, of making you feel unique. And there was something wild and thrilling about this sudden and hurried publication. This eighty-six-year-old man had more ambition than I did.

The next day, after a night's sleep, I went to meet Bernard to tell him I agreed to publish the book in September.

"You're sure it's not too soon?" I asked him again. "It's June thirtieth and you're going to publish the book in early September?"

"The author doesn't determine the book's publication date, nor does the publisher. The book decides when it should be published."

He reassured me that the book would be an "immense success".

"How can you be so certain?" I asked.

"The success of a book can't be quantified by the number of copies sold but by the joy, the pleasure one gets from publishing it."

Once again, Bernard was right. For the next two months, we worked together in a state of inexpressible excitement, rereading the text, choosing the cover design, sending proofs to journalists and bookshops. The entire publishing house was in a state of ferment.

But those in the know in the world of Parisian publishing all predicted that the book would flop. They pointed out, "No-one has tried this before. You don't announce a book for September in June. Journalists are already on holiday, the bookshops have already made their selections." They had a point. Why would booksellers choose to promote the book of a young and totally unknown writer from among the six hundred new titles that were being published?

When I asked the question, Bernard replied without hesitation: "I'm going to make some phone calls."

"Phone calls? To whom?"

"To the bookshops. I'm going to call all the bookshops in France." Which is what he did. Bernard spent whole days phoning hundreds of bookshops. Each of them received several phone calls from him. The first call was to inform them that he was sending a book that he liked a great deal, and he wanted their advice as booksellers. The second was to remind the booksellers he had spoken to previously about the book and to make sure they had received it, among the hundreds of identical packages they were sent by publishing houses. "I'll call you back tomorrow to get your opinion," Bernard would say. And he called them back – and then called again. He arranged it so that my book was read all over France by booksellers eager to discover what kind of book was worthy of a phone call from the great Bernard de Fallois.

My book appeared at the same time as the new J. K. Rowling novel, her first book that was not part of the Harry Potter series, which everyone was curious about. The market was inundated with copies of Rowling's book; people spoke of nothing else. Readers' expectations were at a peak for the new work, spiked by a veil of secrecy imposed by the French publisher, who had spent a fortune to obtain the rights.

No-one had been able to read it in advance, and copies had been delivered to bookshops in sealed boxes transported by security guards, as if they were precious stones. I wondered, uneasily, what I could do to avoid being swallowed whole by such a beast.

But when readers, rushing to their local bookshop to buy a copy of the Rowling book, asked – as they often do – how it was, the booksellers replied, "I don't really know, I wasn't allowed to read it. However, I have read another book, by an unknown young author, which I liked very much . . ."

Bernard had the nose and the talent of a great publisher. Starting with an initial print run of six thousand copies, we had sold half a million three months later. Rights were sold to publishers from around the world. My novel would go on to sell millions of copies in forty languages.

Bernard was like a great man from another century, made of stuff that no longer exists today. In the forest of human beings, he was the most beautiful tree, stronger and taller than the others – a unique species, one that will never return.

That evening, in Geneva, I spoke about Bernard for hours. Scarlett never tired of my anecdotes, which traced the six years of happiness I had experienced with my publisher, though it felt more like twenty. I had the impression that my life would have been empty without Bernard, as if he had always been at my side.

I told her about our lunches at Le Dôme, where so many of our projects took shape.

I told her about Bernard's car, a blue Mercedes 230e from the 1980s. "My car is older than you, Joël," he would say, laughing. When he couldn't find a parking spot near his office, he simply left it on rue de Miromesnil, in front of the restaurant Le Mesnil, whose owner would call Bernard if anyone came by to impound it.

I told her about his erudition.

I told her about his passion for clowns.

I told her about his passion for cinema.

I told her about his passion for Proust, whose importance Bernard was one of the first to recognise, and whose unpublished writings he had discovered.

I told her about his kindness, his curiosity, his generosity, his spiritual greatness.

I told her how he joined me on my trips to Milan, Rome and Madrid – where he often stayed. And he hoped to accompany me one day to Buenos Aires, where his mother was born.

I told her how happy we had been, Bernard and I – the man who was my publisher, my teacher, and my friend.

After dinner, Scarlett and I went for a short walk near Lake Geneva. The city seemed more beautiful than it had ever been. We stopped at a bar for a drink, then another, and we continued our little tour of the city this way. It was late when we finally got back to avenue Alfred-Bertrand.

"Can I offer you one last drink?" I asked as we entered the apartment.

"I never refuse a last drink. But that's the third last glass you've offered me."

"You know what they say: never quit on an odd number!"

Scarlett burst out laughing and moved over to the living room couch. I selected a few bottles from the bar. When I had returned from the kitchen with the ice, Scarlett was asleep. I put a blanket over her legs, kissed her cheek, and gazed at her for a long while.

I went out to the balcony for a smoke. I couldn't stop myself from turning to the neighbouring balcony, where Sloane lived. Her apartment was dark. I wondered where she was, what had become of her. I looked at the park before me and felt the air suddenly grow heavy. The night, a few minutes earlier scattered with stars, was now filled with roiling clouds. A rumble tore through the sky, and it began to rain.

* * *

169

It began to rain.

"Listen carefully," said Wagner, whom the rain seemed to avoid. "You're going to prevent Tarnogol from taking power."

"Wait," Macaire said, desperate now, "I might have a way to get rid of him without having to do away with him."

"How?"

"I've got something going with my cousin, Jean-Bénédict Hansen. We're calling it Operation Turnaround. My wife and I will go to the Association of Bankers of Geneva reception tomorrow night instead of Jean-Bénédict. It's at the Hôtel des Bergues, and Tarnogol will be there. After the reception, I'll find a pretext to lead him out to the quay. We'll talk for a while. Then, my cousin will drive towards us in his car, I'll save Tarnogol, and, since he'll owe me his life, he'll be obligated to make me president. You see, no need for your shenanigans; everything will turn out for the best."

A nervous Macaire awaited Wagner's reaction. He didn't have to wait long.

"You're completely out of your mind! If the car hits him, you'll attract attention, and you'll be caught. The risk is even greater with your cousin mixed up in this. He'll crack the moment the police question him."

"No, because we're not going to run into him. That's the point."

"But you have to kill Tarnogol!"

"Then kill him yourself. I'm not a murderer."

"You don't understand, Macaire. You have no choice. If you refuse to do as I say, I'll destroy your life. Here's how it will go: Tarnogol will die, that's inevitable; he'll be shot. The weapon will be a Glock, like the one in your pocket. Eyewitnesses will identify you. You'll be trapped like a rat. When the police dig a little deeper, they'll discover the double murder in Madrid. You can tell them what you like, no-one will believe you. I fail to see how you can avoid getting life in prison – for crimes you didn't commit. Life is unfair, isn't it? To avoid all that mess, all I ask is that you do one little thing: get rid of

Tarnogol, the right way. There's a way to do this. It leaves no trace and it's been used by secret services the world over." Wagner pulled a vial of clear liquid from his pocket and handed it to Macaire. "Tomorrow at that big bankers' reception, you'll pour the entire vial into Tarnogol's glass. That's all you have to do. Nothing will happen right away. But that night, he'll have a fatal heart attack. It's the perfect crime. No-one will suspect a thing. No-one will ever know that Tarnogol was murdered."

21

Arma

It was Thursday, June 28, 2018. I opened one eye. It took me a while to realise that I was at home, in my bed, in Geneva. My head was still heavy from the previous night. Suddenly, a voice called out, and I jumped.

"Good morning, Writer. Did you sleep well?"

In the doorway stood Scarlett, a cup of coffee in her hand. Her hair was still wet from her shower, and she smelled awfully good. She looked at me, amused.

"Do you often watch people sleep?" I asked.

"I thought you were dead, so I came to see what was going on."

She offered me the cup.

"Thanks."

I took a sip of coffee, then asked, "Scarlett, why do you smell so good?"

"Because I took a shower. You should do the same, we're meeting Arma in a half hour."

We had agreed to meet Arma in a café at the corner of avenue Alfred-Bertrand and avenue Peschier, a few minutes from my apartment. She was the only customer out front when we arrived – a woman with a gentle face, who took good care of herself. I noticed at once that she was uncomfortable.

"Why did the neighbour talk about me?" she asked as we sat down.

"She told us you used to work for the Ebezners," Scarlett explained. "You were a privileged witness – you can help us a great deal."

"Help you how?"

"We're trying to find out what happened in room 622."

Arma's face fell.

"That's all been very difficult for me. I'd like to erase it from my memory. I was very fond of Macaire Ebezner, you know."

"The neighbour said you were in love with him."

"Yes, that's true." Arma lowered her head. "It was very hard to lose him. I was also a victim of everything that happened. I had to start again from the beginning – find a new job. I clean offices in the evening now. There isn't a day goes by that I don't think about him."

She stopped. Scarlett encouraged her to continue.

"Can you tell us about the day before the murder?"

In response, Arma pulled out an album into which she had glued newspaper clippings from the time. She said softly, as if uncomfortable: "I live a little in the past."

"We all do," I reassured her. "It's a good way to survive."

She looked thoughtful. Then she went on.

"It was crazy. The week before that big Gala Weekend, the paper said Macaire Ebezner would be named president but, in reality, I could see that things were going very badly. Macaire was under a lot of stress. He mentioned a man named Tarnogol who had wrecked his all plans."

"Did Ebezner talk often about Tarnogol?"

"The week before the murder, the name came up a lot. At the time, I didn't suspect anything. I learned the whole truth later, like everyone else, from the newspapers."

"The neighbour told us that Anastasia, Macaire's wife, had a lover at the time."

"Yes, it's true."

"Who was it?"

"Lev Levovitch. I eventually found out that they were planning to run away together."

"Did you talk to anyone about it?"

"I was planning to tell Macaire but I couldn't find the right moment. As I said, it was a very stressful time for him. And I had overheard a conversation between him and his cousin, Jean-Bénédict Hansen. They were planning to scare this Tarnogol to get him to name Macaire president."

"Scare him how?"

"Jean-Bénédict Hansen was supposed to pretend to run him over in his car. Obviously, nothing went as planned. It was Thursday, December thirteenth; I remember it very clearly."

22

Operation Turnaround (Part 1)

Thursday, December 13, three days before the murder
The door to Dr Kazan's office opened.

"Hello, Macaire," Kazan said to his patient, who was waiting in the hallway, inviting him into his office. Macaire greeted the doctor with a formal handshake and entered the room.

"Since our last Tuesday session, something has been unlocked in me," Macaire said, after he had seated himself in the chair facing Kazan.

"I'm glad to hear it. Can you tell me what it is?"

"I'm ready to show them who Macaire Ebezner really is. Tonight, they're going to discover my true face."

"What's going on tonight? And who are 'they'?"

Macaire put his hand in his pocket and toyed with the vial of poison. The previous night, returning from his meeting with Wagner, he had made a decision. He wasn't going to be Tarnogol's plaything or P-30's. He had decided to go through with Operation Turnaround as planned. He was giving himself a chance to stop Tarnogol and carry out the mission given him by P-30, but without violence. But if Operation Turnaround failed to convince Tarnogol to change his mind, if he insisted on being stubborn, then Macaire would use the vial. He would kill him. That was what Macaire had decided.

"I'm going to talk to Tarnogol tonight," he explained to Dr Kazan. "Jean-Béné gave me his tickets for the dinner of the Association of Bankers of Geneva. I feel everything is going to turn out well."

"So much the better."

175

"I've also prepared some notes," Macaire continued, trying to justify his optimism. "I want to be a hit at my table tonight. I'll start with a few subtle jokes to get their attention, followed by a list of hot news items and key events in the world of international finance from the past few months. I'm done with being the silent Macaire at these fancy dinners. The new Macaire, the man now before you, here in your office, will be Macaire Ebezner, the new president of the Ebezner Bank."

"I'm very happy to hear this."

"I've planned a little joke for the start of the meal to get their attention. Apparently, you should start every speech by making your audience laugh. Do you want to hear it?"

"Gladly."

"Okay. I read it in the *Tribune de Genève* the other day. There was an article on Picasso. A funny story about the value of things, which is good for a bankers' dinner, no?"

"I'll tell you once I've heard your story."

"Yes, well." Macaire inhaled deeply. "Picasso was eating in a restaurant. At the end of the meal, the owner said to him, 'Master, dinner is on the house.' Picasso, appreciating the gesture, grabbed a pen and made a small drawing on the paper tablecloth. But he didn't sign it. The owner then asked, 'Master, could you sign it for me?' Picasso replied, 'You offered me a dinner, not your restaurant.'"

Kazan burst out laughing. "That's really very good."

"And it's a classy joke, too. Cultivated. Not some filthy story."

"You'll do very well," Kazan predicted.

Energised by his psychoanalyst's reaction, Macaire then asked the doctor to test his knowledge of current events.

"Go ahead, ask me a question. Anything."

"I don't think that will be necessary," Kazan assured him. "I'm certain you're well prepared."

"Please," Macaire insisted, "just one question."

"Very well." Kazan took a moment to reflect before asking. "What was the resolution issued by the United Nations during the conference on refugees that took place at the beginning of the week?"

The psychoanalyst's question was followed by a long silence.

"Damn, I didn't expect that! Ask me another."

"There's no point," Kazan said. "I'm sure you're ready."

"Go ahead, Doctor. A financial question this time – that's my strong suit."

"Very well, very well. How did the Asian stock markets react yesterday to the announcement by the American president of a new free-trade agreement with Canada?"

"Oh, damn it, yesterday I was busy all day with something I had to take care of; my mind was elsewhere. I still have some time before dinner. I'm going to call in sick this afternoon and review my notes."

In Cologny, Anastasia, locked in the bedroom, sorted through the things that were important to her. Along with a few articles of clothing, she collected her best jewellery, her passport, some money she had hidden in a drawer, and her gold pistol – just in case. She put it all in a canvas travelling bag.

A half hour earlier, Alfred had brought her a new bouquet of white roses. Hidden in the bouquet was a note in Lev's handwriting.

Prepare a few things.
Only what's absolutely necessary.
We're leaving soon.
Lev

Why only what's absolutely necessary, she wondered. What was he planning? Didn't he say in his previous message that they were leaving for good? And why didn't he answer her calls?

She heard the hall floorboards creak. Had Macaire returned from work already? It was much too early for that. Uncertain, she quickly hid the bag at the bottom of a wardrobe and went to check the corridor. There was no-one there. It was very strange. She felt as if someone was spying on her.

As she returned to her bedroom, Arma appeared before her and cried out, face twisted with anger.

"How could you do this to Moussieu?"

"Do what, Alma?" Anastasia stammered.

"I know everything, Médéme."

"What? What are you talking about?" Anastasia said, trying to conceal her uneasiness.

"I know you've been having an affair with Lev Levovitch. He wants to take you away; he wants to be president of the bank. He wants to destroy Moussieu."

Anastasia replied sharply, "You don't know what you're saying. What's got into you? Get a hold of yourself!"

"I'm not stupid, Médéme. Flowers yesterday, flowers today. And the message you hid in your nightstand: '*Let's leave together, far from Geneva. Let's leave everything.*' That man wants to run away with you."

Anastasia, collecting herself, began to yell.

"You dared to look through my things!"

Arma understood from her employer's reaction that her intuition was correct.

"I'm ashamed for you, Médéme. You don't deserve Moussieu Ebezner."

"Arma, keep quiet now or I'll be forced to throw you out."

"Fire me if you want. I'm going to tell Moussieu everything!"

Arma rushed downstairs, pursued by Anastasia.

"Wait, Arma. Don't do that!"

"It's too late," Arma screamed, locking herself in the guest bathroom.

"Don't say anything, please. I'll give you money – a great deal of money."

"To hell with your money. You rich people, you think money can buy everything."

Anastasia banged on the door.

"Please, Arma, don't do this to me. Open the door, please. We have to talk, you and me."

"And you're a coward, Médéme. I'm going to tell Moussieu everything. As soon as he returns, I'm telling him everything."

Anastasia's voice grew desperate.

"You're going to ruin his evening, that's what you're going to do. We have a dinner tonight, an important dinner. If you upset him, he'll never convince Tarnogol to back him for president."

In the bathroom, Arma grew rigid. Overwhelmed by the proof of Madame's infidelity, she had forgotten that tonight was the night when Monsieur and his cousin were supposed to put their plan into action. If she upset Macaire by revealing that Anastasia was cheating on him, he might not be able to go through with it. He wouldn't be named president of the bank, and it would be Arma's fault.

There was a long silence on both sides of the door. Then, suddenly, Macaire appeared in the hallway, his arms full of newspapers he had bought on the way home.

"Hello, everyone," he greeted them exuberantly.

"Darling," Anastasia blurted out, "what are you doing back so early?"

"I have to read up a bit if I want to impress Tarnogol tonight. I can't afford to make any mistakes. I'm going to my office. I don't want to be disturbed."

With that, he walked into his office and buried himself in his reading.

Arma, having heard Macaire return, stepped out of the bathroom.

"Arma," Anastasia whispered, her hands joined in supplication, "I . . ."

"Don't say anything, Médéme," Arma interrupted, dryly. "I'll wait for your return tonight. I'm not setting foot outside this house, do you hear me? When you get back from your dinner, I'm telling Moussieu the truth. I'll tell him what's going on between you and Levovitch."

The office door opened. The two women fell silent as Macaire made a quick trip to the kitchen to look for something.

"You have to tell me if you're hungry, Moussieu, that's what I'm here for," Arma said, as he returned with a plate of cheese. His only response was to assume an air of great importance.

"Work well, kitten," Anastasia encouraged him before he closed the office door. "And don't worry about Tarnogol. You're going to skewer him."

"Stop calling him that," Arma whispered in a low voice. "You know how he feels when you say that word."

"I want him to succeed," Anastasia assured her.

"When you want your husband to succeed, you don't sleep with the first man that comes along."

"Oh, are you the couples police? You've never even been married!"

"And you're an ungrateful wife. Tonight I'm telling him everything, and he'll throw you out."

Arma returned to the kitchen, and Anastasia, greatly upset, rushed to the bedroom. She burst into tears. She had no idea what to do.

* * *

Sixteen years earlier
Anastasia's first Gala Weekend in Verbier

At ten p.m. on that Friday evening of the Gala Weekend, the bar at the Hôtel de Verbier was under attack by the employees of the Ebezner Bank. As she had promised Klaus, Olga brought her daughters. They were all sitting around a high table on which sat a bucket of champagne. Klaus was shackled to Macaire Ebezner, whom he had been unable to get rid of, and the two men were using every stratagem they knew to court Anastasia. They talked about the stock market and business, complacently describing their great responsibilities, while swilling champagne as if it were water.

Klaus was handsome and well built, elegant, but he exuded an air of malice. His gaze was dark, his intonations sometimes clipped, sharp – aggressive. But most of all, he was pretentious – satisfied with himself, boasting of his position and his wealth, which repulsed Anastasia but did not at all displease her mother.

Macaire, for his part, was a good-looking young man, cultured, pleasant; he seemed likable and kind but unsure of himself and a bit clingy. You could see he was attracted to Anastasia but also intimidated by her. Olga, who had no equal in getting her way with people, had little difficulty in convincing him to let her and her daughters attend the bank's grand ball the following evening.

Irina, overshadowed by her sister, stepped up her efforts to participate in the conversation, while Anastasia barely paid attention to the two men. She seemed nervous and kept looking at the big clock on the wall. Already ten thirty. Only thirty minutes more. She didn't want to be late.

Olga was in seventh heaven. Her two precious daughters were in the company of a wealthy aristocrat and the heir to a bank. When Klaus stepped away to order another bottle of champagne at the bar and Macaire stepped away "to satisfy a need", Olga could not hide her joy.

"You see, girls, how the Lord loves you," she said in Russian so no-one would understand. "Look at those two men just burning with desire."

"Especially for Anastasia," Irina whined. "Both of them are drooling all over her. Me, it's as if I don't exist. No-one's even noticed me."

"Everyone is looking at you, my dear," her mother reassured her. "You see that guy at the bar, over there? He's been staring at you for a while."

"He's old!" Irina interjected.

"No, he isn't, he's forty-five at the most. Come, come, daughter, when someone offers you a horse, you don't count its teeth."

Near the three women, a man who had been mingling with the bankers was listening to their conversation. Pretending to play distractedly with his empty glass of vodka, he didn't miss a scrap of their discussion, for they spoke his mother tongue. He was one of the hotel's biggest clients, one of the only ones able to remain at the hotel during the long weekend of the Ebezner Bank. His presence put the entire staff on high alert – one of those you didn't risk rubbing the wrong way.

A waiter approached the man.

"Another glass, Monsieur Tarnogol? Beluga vodka, on the rocks, isn't that it?"

Tarnogol refused with an annoyed wave of the hand, and the waiter immediately left his side.

At eleven, the miracle occurred. Olga, having discovered that the man who had been eyeing Irina was a prominent wealth manager who had achieved the best returns for the year, decided to take control of the situation and present him with her daughter.

At the same time, Klaus suggested that they leave the hotel and go to a club in Verbier. Macaire thought it was a good idea. Anastasia, sensing an opportunity to ditch them, said she would join them if her mother approved. They left the bar, and Anastasia went to find her mother.

"Mama, Klaus wants us to go out."

"So, go, hurry. Why are you still here?"

"I may get back late. I wanted to ask you first."

"Go, go. Have fun. And be careful. You'll tell me all about it tomorrow. Get going, go."

Anastasia's face brightened. She kissed her mother and quickly walked off. In her hurry, she failed to notice the shadow who was watching her.

She ran along the small corridor she had taken earlier, then pushed open the service door. She saw him there. He was still wearing his work clothes but retained that same princely allure. She couldn't help herself from calling his name. His beautiful, magnificent name.

"Lev!"

He turned and smiled with his perfect teeth. "Eleven on the dot!"

She ran to him and kissed him. A long, deep kiss. What she felt was indescribable: an explosion inside; a quivering that ran up and down her body – like thousands of brilliant butterflies escaping from her chest.

He led her to a service elevator that took them up to the top floor of the hotel, where the employees had rooms. He took her to his own. It was neat, filled with books, lit with candles that he had arranged around the room in anticipation of this moment. They undressed slowly, while they kissed, as if they couldn't let go of each other. And within the shelter of the room, away from the world and the cold, with a small mansard window giving a view of the Rhône Valley spread out before them, they made love.

She was not a virgin. She had given herself before, many times, in fact. Following her mother's advice, she had submitted to the embraces of certain insignificant cyphers who were part of the gilded youth of Klosters, Saint Moritz, and Gstaad. "Men have needs," her mother would say. "You have to satisfy them, otherwise they'll never choose you."

But what Anastasia felt that night with Lev she had never felt before. When the sun came up, they still hadn't slept. Wrapped in each other's arms, they observed the sun as it rose slowly behind the mountain peaks, colouring the sky with brilliant light. Lev held her in his wiry arms, sliding the tip of his finger along her naked back, and each caress made her shiver. She loved him. Over the past few hours, she had discovered what love meant.

Finally, she fell asleep. When she opened her eyes, he was no longer in bed but sitting beside her. He had dressed in his work uniform. He offered her a cup of coffee and a basket overflowing with warm croissants.

"I have to go to work. You can stay here as long as you want. Take the elevator to go downstairs. You know the way."

"When will we see each other again?"

Lev seemed surprised by the question.

"You want to see me again?"

"Of course, I want to see you again. Why would you think otherwise?"

"Can you really see yourself with someone like me?"

"What do you mean, 'someone like me'?" She seemed amused by the remark.

"I mean, a low-level hotel employee with no future. I live in a tiny room under the roof of the hotel where I work doing menial tasks. I depend on tips from the customers. I'm poor, Anastasia. I have nothing. I'm a miserable little hotel worker."

"And who do you think I am?"

"A Russian princess, filthy rich, who spends her winters in Switzerland and her summers on the Côte d'Azur, and has a legal residence in London or Monaco."

She burst out laughing and kissed him.

"I'm nothing at all like that," she said, delighted not to have to lie for once and feeling free to live her life. "I share a small room like this with my mother and sister. My mother works in a large department store in Geneva. We have nothing, nothing. We saved enough to rent a cheap room in the Auberge des Chamois for the weekend. My mother thinks we should circulate in society, marry a prince, a baron, or I don't know whom. We're poor, Lev, that's what we are. So, yes, I absolutely want to see you again. I never want to leave you."

He smiled extravagantly.

* * *

"Anastasia?"

Macaire stopped the car in front of the hotel, where a throng of Geneva's leading private bankers huddled. It was 7:25 p.m.

"Anastasia, are you alright?"

She wiped a tear from her cheek.

"Everything's fine."

"You're crying?"

"No, I've got a speck of dust in my eye."

"That's the kind of thing people say in novels. Dust never makes anyone cry."

"The dust of memories does."

Macaire didn't understand what she was talking about. Two valets opened the car doors and at once they were surrounded by the crowd and rushed into the hotel. In the entrance hall of white marble, a flotilla of triumphant bankers, with their wives at their sides, converged on the large ballroom on the first floor. They greeted one another, spoke loudly, tried to appear important – happy to be at the pinnacle, part of the elite, and excited by the annual bonuses that would come with the year's end.

Anastasia and Macaire entered the hall. They were handsome together, she in a long dress of black satin and he in his tux. In his pocket, he nervously fingered the vial of poison. Suddenly, Macaire saw Tarnogol as he made his way quickly down the staircase, against the crowd. Assuming he was coming over to say hello, Macaire stood still and smiled innocently.

"Hello, Sinior," he said, but he came off looking like a fool. Tarnogol walked right past him without even glancing his way, left the hotel at once and jumped into a taxi. Watching him go, Macaire suddenly noticed Levovitch in the middle of the staircase, infernally handsome in a three-piece suit.

"Shit, Levovitch. What the hell is he doing here?"

Anastasia raised her eyes to her lover; a broad smile illuminated her face. She felt her heart beat faster than ever before and felt even more in love. He stood out sharply from the other men around him – more handsome, straighter, more powerful. She felt alive in his presence and suddenly pictured him as he was sixteen years earlier, on the weekend of their first encounter.

*   *   *

Sixteen years earlier
Anastasia's first Gala Weekend in Verbier
Saturday evening

At the hotel, Anastasia, her sister, and her mother were alone in the elevator that was taking them to the first floor, where the ballroom was located.

"The bank gala, it's the best of the best!" Olga rejoiced, her eyes overflowing with happiness. "Girls, do you realise the opportunity you have?"

"Thanks to you, mamochka," Irina flattered her mother. She was quivering with joy at the idea of finding her wealth manager.

"It's thanks to the Ebezner boy, especially. He's really nice. Not the brightest bulb in the room, but he'd make a good husband. Isn't that right, Nastya?"

"If you say so, Mama," Anastasia replied, forcing herself to appear enthusiastic to avoid angering her mother. She could think only of Lev.

"I managed to get us seated at Macaire and Klaus's table," Olga announced proudly. "He's very nice, that Klaus. Good family and everything."

"And me, mamochka?" Irina asked, afraid that she was being ignored.

"Don't worry, once people get up to dance, you'll make a beeline for your nice wealth manager. Everything's taken care of, girls, everything. I think that tonight, your future will finally be settled as planned."

"Bravo, mamochka," Irina cried out, excited at the new life that awaited her with her wealth manager. He was older than she had imagined, yes. And not as handsome as she would have preferred. But he had a villa with a pool in Vésenaz.

The bell sounded, and the elevator doors opened. The three women saw a magnificent young man, dressed like a prince, who appeared to be waiting for them.

"Lev?" Anastasia couldn't keep herself from saying, as she smiled broadly.

"You know this young man?" Olga asked, impressed by his appearance.

Lev bowed to Olga.

"Good evening, Madame," he said as he kissed the old woman's hand. "Allow me to introduce myself: Lev, Count Romanov." He lied with aplomb.

At those words, Olga nearly fainted with joy. A Romanov! Praise the Lord, a Romanov – the imperial house of Russia. To make certain he was sincere, she asked him in Russian: "You mean *Romanov*?"

"Czars and emperors of Russia, czars of Kazan, of Astrakhan, of Siberia, of Kiev, of Vladimir and Novgorod, kings of Poland, and grand dukes of Finland, at your service, Madame."

Olga presented him with a compliant smile. Anastasia suppressed her laughter.

"My daughter, Anastasia, named in honour of the imperial court," Olga explained.

"May you bask in glory for perpetuating the greatness of my family!"

They continued in French.

"I didn't know there was a Romanov working at the Ebezner Bank," Olga remarked, for she had done her research carefully.

"Work?" Lev said teasingly. "Do you think I need to work? Are we trading insults already?"

Olga laughed, conquered by this young aristocrat with the sharp tongue.

"I'm in Verbier by chance," Lev explained. "The elder Monsieur Ebezner invited me to join tonight's dinner – perhaps out of friendship, perhaps because I'm one of the bank's biggest clients."

Olga was completely under his spell.

"Lev," she murmured, blinded by the young man's charisma. She'd never heard the name before. Surely that was proof it was the name of a king.

A short distance away, navigating the crowd of bankers to which he did not belong, Sinior Tarnogol, half amused, half curious, observed the young man, whom he knew to be an employee of the hotel.

23

Operation Turnaround (Part 2)

In the reception room of the Hôtel des Bergues, the night of the bankers' dinner, Macaire and Anastasia joined Lev on the large stone staircase.

"Hi, Lev," Macaire said coldly. "What are you doing here?"

Lev bowed politely to Anastasia as she approached.

"It seems that Tarnogol is sick as a dog," he informed them. Hearing this, Macaire wondered if P-30 hadn't gone ahead and poisoned him already. Lev went on: "He told me he wasn't well enough to stay for the dinner and wanted someone to replace him and represent the bank's interests."

"Oh," Macaire responded, annoyed by Levovitch's presence at the dinner. "Why you? He could have asked me."

"I guess it was more practical, given that I live here. He called me in my suite, and I came down at once. I didn't know you would be here. What a pleasant surprise."

Anastasia suppressed a smile.

"In fact, we're replacing Jean-Bénédict and Charlotte. They couldn't make it," Macaire explained.

He was now in a foul mood. Practical or not, it was a very bad sign that Tarnogol had called Levovitch to replace him at the dinner. The three of them walked up to the first floor. When they got to the entrance of the ballroom, Levovitch took Macaire aside, asking Anastasia to excuse them so they could talk business.

"Macaire," Lev said, when he was sure no-one was listening, "I need to talk to you about something very important."

Macaire put on his most serious face to signal to Levovitch that he had his complete attention, but, at that moment, they were interrupted by a hotel employee, who ran over holding Tarnogol's cane.

"Sorry to bother you, Monsieur Levovitch, but the gentleman who was just with you left his cane in the cloakroom."

"Thank you," Levovitch replied, as he took the cane with its diamond-studded handle. "I'll return it to him."

"Would you like me to bring it up to your suite?"

"No, thank you, I'll keep it with me. It'll be safer that way."

The hotel employee left, and Levovitch played with the cane.

"Do you want me to return it to him?" Macaire asked, seeing it as an opportunity to get together with Tarnogol.

"No, don't trouble yourself."

"I assure you, it's no trouble at all," Macaire insisted, trying to take the cane.

"Come, I don't want to be responsible for wasting your time," Levovitch said, holding the cane tightly. "You're not the lost property officer. Let's get back to our business."

"I'm listening." Macaire gave up on the cane idea and assumed a stately air.

"It's a bit complicated."

"You can speak freely."

"Well, before returning home, Tarnogol spoke to me about something. It concerns the presidency."

"Finally! Let's hear it," Macaire urged him on. "What's going on?"

After a moment's hesitation, Levovitch continued.

"Tarnogol wants to appoint me president. He said I have Horace Hansen's vote as well."

"Oh?" Macaire replied as his stomach began to tighten. He pretended to be surprised by the news to mask his panic. He put his hand in his pocket and played with the vial of poison. The idea of pouring it into Levovitch's glass that evening crossed his mind. A single gesture, and Levovitch would be eliminated once and for all. But

Levovitch assured his future well-being by adding, "Obviously, I refused."

"Oh," Macaire replied, letting go of the vial.

"Yes, obviously, the position should be yours. I'm surprised that Tarnogol thought of me at all."

"Well, I'm flattered that you think I'm the man for the job." Macaire's face brightened. "Thank you, Lev. And did Tarnogol agree with you?"

"No. He said it was out of the question. That's what's bothering me." Macaire turned pale.

"Oh, really?"

"He said that, if I refused, he would appoint someone else, but not you. Maybe Jandard. Apparently, he was Jean-Bénédict's second choice, and his father's, from the beginning."

"Jandard, the head of human resources?"

"Yes. Apparently, he's the senior director."

Macaire was gripped by panic. He was losing control of the situation. A hotel employee rang a bell, indicating to the guests that they could enter the ballroom and take their seats. Macaire left Levovitch to mingle with the crowd and stepped aside to call Jean-Bénédict. Macaire wanted to inform him of Tarnogol's departure and the cancellation of their operation. But there was no answer. Macaire tried his cousin at home, but there was no response there either.

Macaire then called Charlotte on her mobile in the hope that she was with her husband, but she told him that she had gone out with her sister. "He was in a terrible shape when I left. The poor dear was in bed. Did you try his mobile? Or call the house? But I don't think he'll get up to answer the phone."

"Shit! Shit!" Macaire fumed after disconnecting.

Jean-Bénédict had clearly lost his nerve. Macaire, uneasy after the evening's turn of events, took refuge in the toilet for some peace and quiet. While there, he reread his notes, which he'd kept safely in his jacket pocket. But the jokes he had written down now seemed flat, and he was getting the news items mixed up. An hour earlier, he could recite the notes by heart, but now he was confusing Iraq and Iran. He threw some water on his face to calm down but managed only to wet his tie, which he then had to dry by holding it under the hand dryer.

When Macaire finally entered the ballroom, the president of the Association of Bankers of Geneva had already completed his opening remarks. The appetisers were being served, and the guests were talking gaily among themselves.

Having forgotten to check the seating arrangements at the entrance of the ballroom and unable to find Anastasia among the guests, Macaire had to leave the room and examine the alphabetical list, on which his name didn't appear. He examined it again, still couldn't find it, and called an employee over, who was equally at a loss, before Macaire remembered that he was registered under the name of Jean-Bénédict Hansen. The employee pointed to table 18, at the very back of the ballroom, where the Ebezner executives would be seated with two senior associates of Pittout Bank, their wives, and the president of Bärne Bank.

When he reached the table, Macaire was met with an unpleasant surprise. All the guests were attentively listening to Levovitch, who, having warmed them up with his wit, was now telling them a joke. Macaire caught only the end of it.

"The owner of the restaurant then asked Picasso, 'Sir, could you sign it for me?' And the painter replied, 'You offered me dinner, not your restaurant.'"

The table burst out laughing.

"I've heard it before; it was in last week's paper," Macaire grumbled as he sat down next to Anastasia.

Dinner was hell for Macaire. Levovitch, majestic and more brilliant than ever, captured everyone's attention. Admired and admirable, radiant, he was superior in every way. Everyone wanted his advice. What did he think about this, and what did he think about that? As soon as he finished answering one question, another was proposed. And his insightful responses garnered ohs and ahs of wonder, as everyone praised the acuity of his intellect and welcomed his words with admiring nods, overcome by a man who poured forth such inexhaustible knowledge with such modesty.

Moving easily from one subject to another, Levovitch distilled his expertise with insolent mastery, sometimes serious, sometimes joking, his changes in tone holding the attention of his audience. Macaire couldn't get a word in – partly because of Levovitch but also because the woman to his right was deaf as a post and he had to report the exchanges to her as if he were an interpreter at the United Nations.

As the main course was served, the subject of the United Nations, in fact, came up, specifically the recent conference on the refugee question. Macaire, who was very familiar with the subject from his afternoon review, was getting ready to wow the crowd, but just as he was about to open his mouth, his neighbour moved closer and asked, "What are they talking about? I can't hear a thing."

"About the refugee conference at the United Nations," he whispered.

"*The what*?"

"The refugee conference at the United Nations," he repeated with annoyance.

Hearing Macaire utter the word *refugee*, Levovitch barked, "Who are you calling a refugee?"

The guests at the table scratched their heads.

The deaf woman, who this time had no trouble hearing what had been said, piped up: "Refugees are thieves and troublemakers."

"Chagall, Nabokov, Einstein, Freud were all refugees," Levovitch replied.

There were mutterings of approval.

"My father was a refugee," replied the president of the Bärne Bank, seconding Levovitch's comment. "He fled Tehran when the shah fell and came to Switzerland."

The discussion shifted to Iran.

Shit, Macaire said to himself. He had been unable to get a single word in about the conference on refugees and now they were talking about Iran, a country he knew nothing about. Say something fast! But what? He discreetly examined his notes, recalling that he had written down some statistics from the Organisation of Petroleum Exporting Countries. But the discussion had already moved on; now the president of the Bärne Bank was asking, "Levovitch – where is that name from?"

"It's Russian. My paternal grandparents were from Saint Petersburg."

"So you speak Russian?" one of the guests asked.

"Yes, although my grandparents usually spoke to me in Yiddish."

"And your mother is also Russian?"

"No, she was from Trieste."

"So, Italian?" concluded the president of the Bärne Bank.

"No, she was born in Trieste, but her mother was French and her father Hungarian. He was an ophthalmologist who left Hungary on foot to study medicine in Vienna before settling in Trieste, where my mother was born. They then moved to Smyrna, which was Greek at the time, because a rare eye disease had been spreading rapidly there."

"Didn't Smyrna become Izmir after it was annexed by Turkey?" asked one of the senior associates of Pittout Bank, who also wanted to shine a little.

"Exactly," Lev confirmed.

Turkey! Now, I've got it, Macaire rejoiced, shamelessly taking from his pocket his note on the devaluation of the Turkish lira so that he might regale the table. But before a single word could escape his lips, someone asked Levovitch, "So, you speak Italian, too?"

"Yes, my mother spoke to me only in Italian. My maternal grandparents decided to speak to me in Greek – I forget why. But, to answer your question about my origins," Levovitch recapitulated, sensing that

194

his listeners were losing their way, "my father was Russian and my mother French."

"And you, where were you born?" asked the president of Bärne Bank.

"In Geneva, obviously. That's where my parents met and I spent my childhood."

"Obviously," repeated Macaire, who, deprived of attention, was ready to do anything to ensure they heard the sound of his voice.

"Oh! So you're Swiss?" one of the Pittout associates piped up, as if there was something incongruous about the fact.

"Certainly," Lev said.

"Certainly," Macaire repeated as he again sought to enter the conversation, all the while thinking that his rival's family history was enough to put you to sleep on your feet.

"It's really not very practical to have a first name and a last name that sound alike when you're Swiss," lamented his neighbour after Macaire had repeated the exchange. "Everyone will think you're a foreigner!"

"We're all foreigners for someone, no?" Lev noted.

"And you've always lived in Geneva?" asked one of the Pittout associates.

"Until I was fourteen. Then we went to Zurich, then to Basel, before settling in Verbier. I came back to live in Geneva fifteen years ago."

"How many languages do you speak?" asked the deaf woman, admiringly. "Six at least."

"Ten," Lev acknowledged. "There's also English, Spanish, and Portuguese, which I learned at school, through my travels and my acquaintances."

"Through my acquaintances," Macaire interjected, now desperate for the group to take an interest in him.

"There's also Hebrew, which I learned when preparing for my bar mitzvah."

"Bar mitzvah!" Macaire the parrot cried out.

"And Farsi, which I learned from my clients."

"You speak Farsi?" exclaimed the president of Bärne Bank in Farsi, looking at Lev affectionately.

That damned Levovitch answered him in Farsi, and the two of them spoke for a while, as the rest of the table looked on dumbfounded.

"Where did you learn Farsi?" the Bärne Bank president asked.

"For several years I worked for a large Iranian family – in Verbier, in fact."

"You mean that you were their investment manager?" asked one of the Pittout bankers, who wasn't sure he had understood correctly.

"No," Levovitch replied, "I was their major-domo at the Hôtel de Verbier."

"Major-domo?" the husband of the deaf woman said with surprise.

"Yes. The English would say butler, it's more chic. In reality, I was a jack of all trades. I worked at the Hôtel de Verbier for ten years."

"Well, really, was that before your studies?" asked the other senior associate of the Pittout Bank.

"I didn't really go to school. I learned what I needed through reading and my interactions with people."

The last statement aroused the curiosity and enthusiasm of the table. In response to their prodding, Levovitch began to relate a bit more of his life story.

24

Lev Levovitch's Youth

Geneva, thirty-five years earlier

"Lev, Lev!"

When he heard his name, the young boy, as he left the school building, turned around and saw his mother. He ran towards her open arms.

"How's my little prince?" she asked him in Italian.

"I'm good, Mama," he said, hugging her.

Every day, his mother would take him to school in the morning and pick him up in the afternoon. The walks back and forth with her were the times of day he liked the most.

They walked hand in hand. Their apartment, at 55 route de Florissant, was only a few minutes away. They crossed Parc Bertrand, following the long pathway bordered with century-old trees, and they were home. When they arrived at their apartment on the sixth floor, Dora, Lev's mother, put some milk on the stove to warm. She took a small brioche, which she cut in two, buttered generously, and piled high with squares of chocolate. For Lev, bread and chocolate would always be associated with the memory of his mother.

Dora worked at the Italian Consulate in Geneva, located on rue Charles-Galland. Ten years earlier, while single, she lived in Eaux-Vives. She walked to work all year long and would stop at the Café Léo, on the carrefour de Rive, for a cappuccino and an almond croissant. That's where she met Sol Levovitch, who was a waiter and who became her husband and Lev's father.

When asked what he did for a living, Sol Levovitch replied that he was an actor and trying to make his name as a comic. Meanwhile, the job at the café was a way to earn some money and had allowed him to meet Dora.

Dora had quickly succumbed to the charms of the young, cultured waiter and his subtle sense of humour. He made her laugh so much that she had to ask him to wait so she could drink her cappuccino without choking.

"The man who can make you laugh can also make you live, for there is no finer feeling," Sol had said to her one morning.

"Why's that?" she enquired, amused.

"Because laughter is the strongest feeling of all, stronger than love and passion. Laughter is a form of perfection. We never regret it; we always experience it fully. When it's over, we're always satisfied – we want it to go on, but we do not ask for more. Even the memory of laughter is pleasant."

They soon became a couple. Dora knew she would enjoy her life with Sol. They would never be rich, but they would be happy. She laughed from morning till night. In the afternoon, when his shift at the café was over, he worked diligently on his material, perfecting his delivery, his gestures, his make-up. The absurd and burlesque characters he impersonated were irresistibly funny. On evenings and weekends, he toured the clubs in the region, acquiring a small reputation but not very much money. The couple would walk together down the elegant rue de Rhône, passing the windows of the Parisian designers; Sol promised her that one day he would be successful and be able to buy her such clothes.

"Oh, I don't care about that. You can't fill your life with scraps of fabric."

"But those, those are *beautiful* scraps of fabric," Sol exclaimed, assuming the voice of one of his characters, which made her laugh out loud. Then Lev was born, their only son.

A few years passed.

Bit by bit, the day-to-day worries and the unpaid bills accumulated. Sol became increasingly preoccupied with his shows, which were less and less successful because he never updated them and the public came away with the disagreeable impression that they had already seen his act. He convinced Dora to invest their household savings in a short tour of France, which was supposed to jump-start his career but turned out to be a complete failure. Dora felt less and less like laughing. Whenever she tried to discuss something serious, Sol replied with a joke.

Lev had had a happy childhood until he was eleven, for his parents never argued in front of him. When, at the end of the day, tensions rose in the small kitchen, Dora and Sol, who didn't want to settle things in front of their son, would say, "Papa and Mama are going to the restaurant." They left, leaving Lev in the care of their kind next-door neighbour, and went to the park to argue back and forth for hours.

At first, they didn't go to "the restaurant" very often.

Then they went more frequently.

Then they went nearly every evening.

And while Lev imagined his parents in love in a large restaurant, just like in the American movies his neighbour let him watch, in the darkness of the park, Dora and Sol argued.

"Maybe it's time to give up acting, at least for a while," Dora said, "and spend more time working and bringing a bit of money home."

"This career is my life!" Sol protested.

"No, Sol, your life is your wife and child, not locking yourself up all weekend rehearsing roles that you play to empty rooms rented at your own expense. Not to mention the money you spend on your costumes, your make-up, and your friends!"

"But it's my dream!"

"We no longer have the money for your dream."

"A life without dreams isn't a life."

"Look, Sol, I don't want this life any longer. We spend our time trying to catch up and pay our bills, we never go anywhere, and we skimp on food. I want to live! I want to exist!"

"Oh, Madame has wishes now, does she?" Sol jeered. "A far cry from the days when you lived for love and cool water."

"You know what your problem is, Sol? You love your comic characters more than you love me, more than yourself. You've lost touch with reality."

Because he had been spared their fights, Lev's parents were unable to prevent his complete incomprehension when they separated. His parents, who he believed to be in love just like in the movies and who spent their time at "the restaurant", now were tearing themselves apart. Dora was the one who moved out, leaving Lev with his father. She needed to get away, to find herself. She asked for a leave of absence from her job and left for Italy.

"I'll come back to get you," she promised Lev. "I'll pick you up from school like before. Mama just needs a bit of time for herself."

At school, the teacher and the other parents decided that it was highly unusual for Dora to go away and leave her child with his father. "In general, it's the father who meets another woman," the mothers whispered, casting sidelong glances at Sol as he waited for his son after school. When the boy came out, his father handed him a small bag from the bakery on avenue Alfred-Bertrand.

"What is it?" the boy asked.

"A pain au chocolat."

"No, Mama makes me bread with chocolate, not a pain au chocolat; it's not the same," Lev said as he nibbled on the pastry. And with each mouthful, he repeated, "With Mama, it's different. It's better when she makes it for me. When is she coming back?"

"Soon."

But Dora never returned to meet Lev when he got out of school.

Desperate for a bit of adventure, she thought she would leave for no more than a few weeks. At the consulate, she met a Milanese banker who took her on a tour of Tuscany. For the first two weeks, she felt terribly guilty and alone without Lev. Then the feeling of freedom took over. She would wake in the morning in a luxury hotel and drink her coffee as she watched the sun rise over some of the most beautiful countryside in the world. She felt alive. She had the impression that she was finally, finally living her life. She wanted that feeling to go on, and the trip was extended to Puglia and to Sicily. She wanted so much to see Mount Etna. The banker, trying to impress her, rented a helicopter. But the trip ended at the bottom of the Mediterranean. The Italian navy pulled up three corpses: the pilot, the banker, and Dora.

On Dora's finger, they found the engagement ring Sol had given her. She had kept it, as if the marriage wasn't definitely over yet. Sol gave the ring to his son. It was the only thing belonging to his mother he had kept.

* * *

When Lev was fourteen, his father decided to try to jump-start his career as a comic again, first moving to Zurich, where his act was equally unsuccessful, and then to Basel, where Sol found a decent-paying job at the bar of the Hôtel Les Trois Rois. In Basel, Lev finished his second year of secondary school two years early. Despite the encouragement of his teachers, all of whom were captivated by his gifts, his father persuaded him not to waste his time with pointless studies.

"My teachers say that I could become someone important and earn a lot of money," Lev explained.

"Son, the rich are rich because they're crooks, never forget that."

"Yes, Papa."

"They stole your mother from us, and she was the most precious thing we had."

"Yes, Papa."

"I'll teach you to be a comic. We'll put on an amazing show together. Mama would be proud of us."

That summer, hoping his son would become the great comic he had never been, Sol taught Lev everything he knew about the theatre, from posture to diction, costumes, and make-up. But one night, when he was working at the hotel bar, Sol met Monsieur Rose, the owner of the Hôtel de Verbier, who was passing through Basel on business. The bar was empty that evening, and Monsieur Rose, talkative by nature, began conversing with Sol. During their discussion, Sol, as he inevitably ended up doing, mentioned his career as a comic. That was all it took to convince Monsieur Rose that Sol was just the man he needed.

"Monsieur Levovitch, you are the rare pearl I've been searching for all these years. I'd like to offer you a job, an unusual one. Would you be willing to come to Verbier?"

The day after meeting Rose, Sol told Lev about the great opportunity that lay before them.

"I can't tell you what my job will be at the hotel; I've promised to keep it a secret. But it's very important – the best job I've been offered in my life."

"So you'd like to go to Verbier?" Lev asked him.

"Very much."

"And me, what will I do there?"

"Monsieur Rose said he could hire you as a baggage handler, and if you liked the work, you could move up the ladder. I'll have some free time – you will, too, of course – and I could continue to teach you everything I know. Passing on the family secrets, my son – it's very important. People never really die that way. Even when their body has been eaten by worms, their spirit survives through someone else. And so on and so on. You know, when I'm ready to retire, you'll be able to take my place at the hotel. And your son can take your place after you. All I can say is that we'll be a great line of comedians. We'll be the new Pitoëff family!"

Lev, without fully understanding what his father was implying, found the idea of going to live in the mountains appealing. And so the Levovitch family moved to the Valais, where the two of them began a new life at the Hôtel de Verbier.

For a long time, Sol's actual title at the hotel was kept secret. Officially, he was hired to help Monsieur Rose maintain the hotel's standing, and at first his duties were a mystery to the other employees. He was often locked in his small office in the bowels of the hotel; at other times he was off travelling. But from a brief slip of the tongue, it was discovered that Sol, whose familiarity with the hotel business and resourcefulness had impressed Monsieur Rose, was being sent across Switzerland and Europe to visit luxury hotels, where he passed himself off as a client, subsequently producing reports on the innovations and good practices of the competition, as well as any ideas that might help improve the quality of service at the Verbier. Of his new collaborator, Rose said that he "was exacting and had the right eye" for the job. And Sol, grateful for the confidence placed in him, appeared to shine in his new position. He was well paid and was able to move into a small but pleasant apartment in the centre of Verbier.

Lev was delighted by his new life in Verbier. Working as a baggage handler and bellboy at the hotel, he had discovered the joys of independence. All employees of his rank had the right to a comfortable room in the hotel attic, and Sol had allowed his son to move there. After all, his own apartment was no more than a few minutes away on foot, and they saw each other constantly. Lev spent most of his time at the hotel, where he ate, slept, and washed his clothes. Although his was a relatively cloistered existence, he experienced a sensation of freedom that he had not known before. The days were varied; he met a great many people, got on well with visitors from all over the world, and spent his winters skiing. He felt good in Verbier. He was happy, happier than he'd been since his parents were together in the house on the route de Florissant. And then there was Monsieur Rose, who was especially kind to Lev. Monsieur Rose had felt well disposed to the young man, a hard worker who was eager, elegant, polite, and unanimously praised by the hotel's clientele. Moreover, Monsieur Rose discovered that the boy had an almost encyclopedic knowledge and spoke an incredible number of languages.

It didn't take long for Lev to win over the hotel's regular customers. They all wanted him to serve them. Wealthy families who spent summers or winters at the hotel insisted on his presence and his company. Many of them offered to hire him as their private secretary for substantial salaries, but he always refused.

Monsieur Rose, believing that Lev didn't belong in a hotel, tried to convince him to continue his education. But Lev refused.

"You could do anything you want for a profession! I have contacts at several universities."

"I can't leave my father here alone," Lev explained.

"You'll come back to see him."

"People who promise to return never do, Monsieur Rose. They wouldn't have left if they had intended to come back."

"Sometimes life is more complicated than it seems, my boy. You could have an extraordinary career."

"What good would a career be?" Lev scornfully asked. "To get rich? The rich are thieves; they stole my mother from me."

"So you can do well for yourself, I should think," Monsieur Rose replied, somewhat embarrassed.

"I do very well carrying suitcases and providing services to the guests."

"You could become an important man."

"Importance isn't tangible. It exists in relation to other people, not within ourselves."

"Stop being so philosophical, please, Lev! You have only one life; you're not going to spend it carrying suitcases! You need an education."

"I've been training to be an actor. My father taught me everything he knows."

"Listen, Lev, if your father were a great actor, he'd be at the Comédie-Française, not at the Hôtel de Verbier."

"Don't be cruel, Monsieur Rose. My father thinks very highly of you."

"And it's reciprocal. But I'm worried about your future. I've half a mind to fire you, if only to force you to find a new path."

"Why would you want to fire me? I work hard; the guests like me."

"Listen, my boy, here's what I propose. I'll keep you on at the hotel, and I'll teach you everything I know."

"Everything you know about what?" Lev asked.

"About managing a hotel. That could always come in handy."

Lev accepted the offer – not only to keep his job at the hotel but also because he knew that Monsieur Rose's tutelage might be useful. As Lev's mother had always said, "You can never know too much." For the next few years, and in secret to avoid provoking the jealousy of the other employees, Monsieur Rose taught Lev about good manners and propriety, the art of refinement, good taste, elegance, wine, and food.

Monsieur Rose had never married and had no children, but if he had had a son, he would have wanted him to be like Lev. The day would arrive when he would no longer have the energy to run the hotel, and he felt that Lev would make an excellent replacement. "You never know," Monsieur Rose said to Lev, with almost paternal pride, one evening when they were doing a blind tasting of grand cru wines, "you might be running this hotel one day. You would make it the most sought after in Europe."

For a moment, Lev saw himself as the head of the business. The idea pleased him. He liked it there.

Every week, Lev spent long hours in his father's apartment. In the middle of the living room, his father kept an imposing trunk in which he stored all the paraphernalia from his past shows. Some of the costumes, attacked by moths and time, needed to be patched. The two men worked on the repairs together.

"You don't miss performing?" Lev asked his father one day.

"Life is one big comedy," Sol replied. "One day I'll go back."

He nodded towards a large leather-bound book on a table.

"I've got quite a number of characters in my head. I write everything down in the book so I don't forget it."

"Can I have a look?"

"Some other time," his father replied.

"So, it's for the theatre that you're keeping all this old stuff?"

"No, these things will all be yours one day."

"And what do you want me to do with them?"

"You'll give them to your children."

"But what will they do with them?"

"They'll give them to their children."

"And then?"

"And then they'll remember me."

The Levovitches, father and son, were happy at the Hôtel de Verbier. But since their arrival there, as they learned from the other employees, something had changed. Monsieur Rose suddenly began monitoring everything. Now he noticed the slightest infraction on the part of his staff. This didn't necessarily mean that Sol and Lev were informers, however; some of these events had taken place in private, and others had occurred at the bar, the pool, or the restaurant, and while the Levovitches were absent.

For years, the mystery remained unsolved.

25

Operation Turnaround (Part 3)

In the ballroom at the Hôtel des Bergues, the guests seated around the table had listened to Lev's story in devout silence.

"So you were trained to manage a hotel?" the president of Bärne Bank asked Levovitch.

"Perhaps. I would have liked to run the Hôtel de Verbier. But life had other plans. I stayed until I was twenty-six – until I met Abel Ebezner, Macaire's father. He's the one who gave me a start at the bank. Once I was in, I advanced through the ranks."

"And what an ascent!" one of the Pittout bankers remarked, clearly impressed.

The guests, quietly finishing their dessert, looked at Levovitch with admiration. He had talked throughout the meal. He was willing to listen, but every time he tried to be brief in his answers, he provoked an outcry from his listeners, who asked for more.

"In any case, your mother would be proud of you," said a woman at another table, as she wiped her eyes.

"And your father, does he still live in Verbier?"

"Papa is dead. He died because of me."

An uncomfortable silence settled around the table. Then the president of the Association of Bankers of Geneva took the microphone to announce that coffee and tea were being served in the Léman Room next door, so all the members could mingle. The guests rose and noisily headed for the large, quiet salon. Lev let himself be carried along with the crowd. In the Léman Room, he ordered an espresso, which he took out to the balcony to drink. He was alone in the frigid air. He looked out over the lake and the left bank of the city, which rose before him. He found Geneva more beautiful than ever.

Suddenly, I interrupted my novel. Alone in my room, in the calm of night, I began thinking of Geneva, my beloved city, and gave thanks.

City of peace and kind souls,
Which welcomed us and gave us a home.

On the balcony, Levovitch raised Tarnogol's cane in the air as if it were Moses's staff, and the diamonds glittered in the moonlight. He was filled with a sense of power he had never known. Then, remembering the past sixteen years, he allowed himself to be overcome with nostalgia.

* * *

Sixteen years earlier
Anastasia's first Gala Weekend in Verbier
Saturday evening

In the ballroom at the Hôtel de Verbier, among the guests at the Gala Weekend of the Ebezner Bank, they danced, superbly: two magnificent imposters. Anastasia, clinging to Lev's body, shut her eyes for a moment. She was in the arms of the love of her life, she knew it. Observing the crowd of bankers around him, Lev murmured in her ear.

"I'm going to become rich and powerful for you, Anastasia."

For the first time, he was dissatisfied with his station in life.

"I want you," she whispered.

"Meet me in fifteen minutes at the bottom of the service stairs."

Anastasia, her eyes bright with love, her heart beating rapidly, agreed. The song ended, and they separated for a while. Anastasia returned to her table, where her mother greeted her with a smile while Lev slipped out of the room. As he passed through the door, a hand grabbed him and drew him aside. It was Monsieur Bisnard, the hotel's banquet manager, built like a refrigerator. He was furious.

"What do you think you're doing, dancing with the guests, you little shit?"

Sinior Tarnogol appeared at that moment, a cruel smile on his face.

"It's him," he told Bisnard. "He's one of your employees, no? Could you explain to me why he's dancing with the guests?"

"I'm terribly sorry, Monsieur Tarnogol," Bisnard replied without letting go of Lev. "This fool is indeed an employee of the hotel. Don't worry, he'll be dealt with."

Lev didn't dare cause a scene, so he let Bisnard lead him, by way of the service stairs, to a scullery, where the sinks were overflowing with dirty dishes.

"Who do you think you are?" Bisnard screamed. "Just because you're Monsieur Rose's pet, you think you can do anything, is that it? Always trying to be clever, always picking up those big tips! Let's see what Monsieur Rose has to say when I tell him that you snuck into the Ebezner ball. Dancing in front of everyone. There's going to be hell to pay, believe me. Maybe I should call him right now."

Lev knew he had broken the hotel's rules.

"Please, Monsieur Bisnard, I'll do anything you want, but don't tell Monsieur Rose. Please. He'd be terribly upset by my behaviour."

"You should have thought of that earlier."

"Please, I'll do as you ask. I'll give you my December salary and my Christmas bonus if you keep it to yourself."

"I want three months' salary and your bonus," Bisnard demanded.

"Agreed."

Bisnard smiled with satisfaction.

"May I go now?" Lev asked, who thought only of rejoining Anastasia.

"Not before finishing the dishes," Bisnard ordered. He left the scullery and locked the door behind him.

*

Anastasia waited in vain for an hour and a half by the service stairs. She realised that he wasn't coming and went to find her mother before she grew impatient.

"Oh, there you are!" Olga said when Anastasia appeared in the room. "Come, it's late, let's go back. We leave for Geneva tomorrow morning early. Where is that Count Romanov? I would have liked to say goodbye."

"He disappeared."

"Do you have his address? His number?"

"No."

"Hmm. It's his loss. He loses a point. To tell you the truth, I thought he was pretentious. Not like Klaus, who is polished and elegant – high-class. He looked everywhere for you. He wanted to say goodnight properly. I told him that I would give you the message, and we both agreed to meet for lunch in Geneva next Wednesday, at the Beau-Rivage – his idea. The Beau-Rivage, imagine that. Just you and him and me. He invited us. Elegant, that Klaus."

Anastasia followed her mother submissively. They collected their fur coats at the cloakroom and left the hotel. She felt very sad – empty. Why had Lev disappeared? She wondered whether he loved her as much as he said he did.

Lev spent hours cleaning the dishes. When he had finished and finally returned to the ballroom, the party had been over for a long time. The place was dark and empty. The hotel was already asleep. Anastasia had vanished. They had lost each other.

* * *

Lev chased all that from his memory. Suddenly, the balcony door opened, and he saw Anastasia standing there. She came towards him. They didn't touch, fearing that someone might see them, but they seemed to embrace each other. Lev looked deep into her eyes.

"You never told me what happened to your father, Lev."

210

"What happens to all of us. He died."

He gently placed his hand on his heart.

"I want to heal your wounds, Lev."

Lev took out a pack of cigarettes and offered one to Anastasia. They smoked in silence. They felt at ease.

"When are we leaving?" she asked.

He leaned over to her ear and whispered his reply. Anastasia smiled radiantly and took his hand. They were alone in the world. Suddenly, the balcony door opened noisily, and Macaire rushed outside, his coat over his shoulders and Anastasia's under his arm.

"Oh, there you are!" he said, impatiently. "Are you smoking now? Terrific. Come on, we're leaving."

He was in a very bad mood. Nothing had gone as planned. He greeted Lev with a rapid wave of the hand and turned on his heels, taking his wife with him.

As the Ebezners descended the large marble staircase, Lev caught up with them, waving Tarnogol's cane in the air as if to signal them.

"Hold on, Macaire. I have to talk to you."

"What now?" Macaire asked, irritated.

"It's about the position, the presidency, but I want to do it where we can't be overheard."

"Let's go to the Dufour Room," Macaire suggested, nodding towards the comfortable couches in the room nearby.

"No, there are too many people milling about. Let's take a walk."

The two men walked out into the frigid air, away from the hotel and along the Rhône. Macaire, in spite of his thick coat, shivered. Lev pulled his jacket collar up around his neck to protect himself from the cold.

"I'm listening," Macaire said, as they walked along the deserted quay.

"Don't worry about Tarnogol," Lev assured him. "I'm going to talk to him."

"And if he refuses to listen to reason?"

"I'll hit him with his big cane," Lev joked.

Lev, extending the joke, bent forward and nervously waved the cane, as Tarnogol so often did.

"I'm Tarnogol!" he snickered, badly imitating the man's accent.

He didn't notice the car that had been parked on the esplanade for several hours and was now closing in behind him with its headlights off.

On the steps at the entrance of the Hôtel des Bergues, the valets suddenly heard the sound of screeching brakes, followed by shouts coming from the esplanade. They ran to see what the commotion was. A pedestrian had been hit by a car.

26

The Last Resort

Arma stared at the living-room clock anxiously. One in the morning. Where were they? Why hadn't they returned from their dinner at the Hôtel des Bergues? Suddenly, in a rush of noise, the front door opened. She ran to the hall.

"Oh, my little Arma," Macaire said, without the slightest surprise at seeing his maid in the house at that late hour. "Thank God, you're still here."

"Is everything alright, Moussieu?"

"It's Anastasia . . . something's happened."

Arma opened her eyes wide. She wondered whether Anastasia, out of fear for what Arma had said she would reveal to Macaire, had done something foolish. Had Madame killed herself? But then Anastasia entered the house, limping slightly, held up by Jean-Bénédict and his wife, Charlotte, who were followed by a third man, whom Arma ignored in her panic about what might have happened.

"Anastasia was hit by a car," Macaire said to her, leading everyone into the living room. "And Jean-Bénédict was driving."

"Fortunately, we mostly just got a fright, that's all," Charlotte interjected, happy to be able to get a word in. She had got the call from her husband as she was leaving the concert at Victoria Hall and had rushed to the hospital. Jean-Bénédict appeared to be in shock. His face was pale as death, and he continued to repeat the lie he had told to his wife when he called her.

"I was at the house . . . not feeling well . . . it's flu season, after all . . . then felt a bit better . . . wanted to stop by the Bergues for a drink . . . say hello . . . always good for networking . . . then changed my mind and decided not to . . . while leaving, forgot to turn on the headlights . . . how stupid . . . really stupid."

A few hours earlier, upon returning from the bank, Jean-Bénédict had complained to his wife that he was feeling feverish. When Charlotte left at around 6:45 to meet her sister, have dinner, and go to the concert, she had seen her husband under the sheets in bed. As soon as she walked out the door of their town house, Jean-Bénédict had leaped out of bed. He had several hours ahead of him. The concert would not end until 10:15, after which Charlotte and her sister would certainly share a pot of verbena tea at the Remor. His wife wouldn't be home before eleven and would find her husband sound asleep, as if he had never left his bed. Not for a moment would she suspect what had happened that evening. Jean-Bénédict felt it was the best possible alibi. If Operation Turnaround went badly, if the police questioned him, he could claim that he hadn't left his bed. His wife could confirm his story. And to corroborate his claim, he had been careful to leave his mobile at home. He had read in an article that the police could trace the movements of your phone by capturing data from relay antennas.

Around eight p.m., Jean-Bénédict was lying in wait at the wheel of his car on quai des Bergues, as planned. He had found the perfect spot for the car and the weather was in his favour: it was a dark night, and a heavy fog was rising from the Rhône. You couldn't see thirty feet ahead of you. No-one could make out his licence plate, which he had covered with snow just to be sure.

Finally, shortly after nine thirty, he noticed two silhouettes walking along the esplanade. He couldn't make them out too clearly, but he recognised Macaire, and the person at his side, with a cane in his hand, had to be Tarnogol. Jean-Bénédict felt a rush of adrenaline. It was time to act. He started the car without turning on the lights and without taking his eyes off the two silhouettes, half buried in the fog. When he felt the moment had arrived, he took off quickly. Suddenly, Anastasia appeared out of nowhere; he saw her too late and struck her.

"It's not your fault, Jean-Béné," Anastasia reassured him after they had settled her on the couch. "I wanted to join Macaire and Lev on their walk, and I crossed the esplanade without paying attention. I'm the one who should have been more cautious. It's totally my fault."

Anastasia forced a smile to try to lighten the mood and hide the fact that she wasn't telling the whole truth. When Lev had asked to speak to Macaire and they had started to leave, she grew fearful. Lev had already taken her husband aside before dinner. She was worried about what he might say. Was he going to tell Macaire about their affair?

When she saw them leave the hotel, she had followed, but when she stepped outside, they were nowhere to be seen. A valet pointed out which way they had gone, but she couldn't see anything. She walked along the pavement then suddenly seemed to notice, through the fog, two silhouettes in the middle of the esplanade. She ran towards them but, at the same moment, a car she had assumed was parked had quickly accelerated with its lights off and struck her.

"In any case, it was quite a drama!" Macaire remarked.

"Don't make a big deal out of it," Anastasia replied.

"It could have been much worse!" Macaire raised his voice, delighted to be part of an event that again made him seem important, after having been so diminished in the eyes of his peers throughout the dinner. Now he had the starring role. A shame Tarnogol hadn't been there to see it.

After the accident, Anastasia had got up, assuring her husband that it was nothing and that she had no need for an ambulance. But Macaire could see she wasn't alright; her leg was swollen where she had been struck. Everyone then returned to the warmth of the hotel, where they placed Anastasia in the Dufour Room, stretched out on a couch with her leg raised on a pile of cushions, while Macaire went to call the hospital. He spoke loudly on the phone, his face serious, while the hotel employees circled nervously. Because the accident had coincided with the first wave of departures that evening, a small crowd had quickly formed at the entrance to the room. "What happened?" the guests enquired. And the staff, assuming terrified expressions, replied, "An accident, almost directly in front of the hotel . . . a miracle it wasn't serious . . . the next time someone's going to die; the esplanade is very badly lit."

Reflecting on the scene, Macaire delighted in the fact that all the bankers assembled around them had been witnesses to his authority. They had all seen who he really was, how he had taken the situation in hand. He had called the head of the Geneva University Hospitals, a friend, and had demanded that they be seen at once by a leading practitioner. Macaire hadn't even been concerned by the late hour. It was an emergency, after all. "Get him out of bed if you have to!" he had shouted over the phone. The director had contacted his underlings at once. He must have made them tremble because, when the Ebezners arrived at the hospital, the staff were waiting for them. They had rolled out the red carpet. These were important people in Geneva, for God's sake! No need to sit around for hours in a waiting room filled with the walking wounded, certainly not. An examination at once and with one of the big shots – and some additional tests as well because, well, you just never know. The director was solid, the dear man!

Like a great commander, Macaire ordered Arma to bring ice for his wife's knee and to put some in a glass for everyone else: "We're going to have a drop of whiskey."

"Yes," Charlotte agreed, "something strong. Because I'm feeling a bit overwhelmed."

Macaire planted a wet kiss on his wife's forehead while Arma, trotting like a mule, arrived from the kitchen with the ice. She placed an ice bag on Anastasia's knee without daring to look at her. Then, as Macaire had ordered, she served whiskey to each of the guests. It was only when she reached the third man that she suddenly recognised him. It was the man from the paper. It was Lev Levovitch!

"Good evening, Madame." He greeted her with a generosity and consideration that no Ebezner guest had ever shown to her in her ten years of service in their home. The photo she had seen in the paper didn't do him justice. His beauty was absolute. His eyes. His features. Such elegance. Such hauteur. Arma began to feel faint. And then he began speaking with her, taking an interest in her. He asked where she came from. "I'm Albanian," she told him. And he suddenly started speaking Albanian!

Arma opened her eyes wide. The conquest was complete.

"Oh, Lev, you speak her language!" Macaire rejoiced, once again unable to conceal his admiration.

"My Albanian is rudimentary."

"Your Albanian is very good, Moussieu Levovitch," Arma insisted.

And he's modest as well, she thought.

"And where did you learn that gibberish?" Macaire asked.

"I had an Albanian fiancée years back, a niece of the former king. It didn't last. But I went to the Adriatic coast of Albania several times, mostly from Corfu. It's absolutely magnificent. The sea is turquoise; the people are very nice."

Arma's face lit up, deeply moved by the sudden interest in her and her birthplace.

"I was crazy about their tres leches," Lev said to Arma.

"The what?" Macaire asked.

"A cake with three milks," Arma explained. "I could make one for you, but you have to let it rest for several hours. But we have the makings in the kitchen for revani."

"Revani," Lev explained, "is a cake made with yoghurt. Very creamy. But more Turkish than Albanian, no?"

Arma smiled because Lev was right. He had won her over. But she was supposed to hate this man. How could that be? Unsure of herself, she declared she was going to prepare some revani and disappeared into the kitchen. She was troubled. She understood Anastasia's passion. Monsieur was certainly a wonderful person, but Lev was the kind of man you meet only once in your life. Still, Arma couldn't imagine that he would seek to take Monsieur's place at the bank. And when Lev appeared in the kitchen, a short while later, to get some water, she took advantage of the situation to speak to him.

"I have a question for you, Moussieu Levovitch."

"Please."

"It's delicate."

"No need to use kid gloves with me, Arma."

And so she began.

"Is it true that you want to steal the presidency of the bank from Moussieu?"

"No!" Lev replied, opening his eyes wide in anger. "Of course not. Who told you such a thing?"

"That's what I heard."

"Sinior Tarnogol, the bank's vice president, wanted to appoint me president. But I simply told him no. I think I made him see reason. Macaire should be president."

An hour later, everyone was gathered in the kitchen, marvelling at the sight of the beautiful round cake that Arma had taken from the oven and cut into small pieces. It was two thirty in the morning when Jean-Bénédict, Charlotte, and Lev finally left, celebrating Albania, thanking Arma with their hands on their hearts, promising to return to eat revani again together.

Macaire was profoundly out of sorts. He had come to understand that Levovitch had won them all over. From the bankers at the dinner to Arma, they all adored him. He was irresistible. He was made to be president of the bank. That was obvious. He was the best choice. Macaire was resigned. He should give up. Just then, he felt his phone vibrate in his pocket. Who could be calling him at this hour? Seeing the name that flashed on the screen, he stood there, frozen, for a moment. And then he walked off to take the call in private.

Now that they were alone in the kitchen, Arma whispered to her employer, "Médéme, this Moussieu Lev is extraordinary. I've never met anyone like him."

"You need to understand, Arma, that Lev and I, this isn't a passing thing or some sudden infatuation. We're made for each other. We should have been together from the first day we met. But nothing went as planned."

* * *

Geneva, fifteen years earlier
April, three months after the Gala Weekend

"Oh my God!" Olga exclaimed, as if she had just had an orgasm, when she saw the ring on Anastasia's finger. "That diamond is huge!"

Hearing the word *diamond*, Irina ran over.

"Did Klaus ask you to marry him already?" she choked. "You've only been together a few months."

"Don't worry," Anastasia reassured her, "it's not an engagement ring."

Irina sighed. Her wealth manager had asked her to marry him two weeks earlier, and she didn't want her sister stealing the limelight. Irina hadn't expected him to propose so quickly but, as he himself said, he wasn't getting any younger. The marriage was planned for the autumn, at the Hôtel Beau-Rivage – nothing less!

"That Klaus is something," Olga marvelled. "First the earrings, then the necklace, now a ring. He offers you diamonds as if they were nothing. Just to make his sweetheart happy. Keep your eye on him. Don't let him get away."

Anastasia forced a smile. She wanted to explain that the more he hurt her, the more extravagant the gifts became. She wanted to unbutton her blouse and show her mother the marks on her body. But she didn't dare. She was ashamed. Afraid that she wouldn't be taken seriously. Besides, he had promised that it wouldn't happen again; promised to get help for his outbursts of anger. When he got carried away, he regretted it at once and asked her forgiveness, kneeled before her, called her his princess. She no longer knew what to think.

Then Olga remarked, "What luck to have met him, that Klaus. I'm happy for you, Nastya, and not just because of the gifts. He's a good man, you can feel it. Good-natured, generous. And you make such a handsome couple."

"We have problems," Anastasia confided.

"But all couples have problems, my daughter. It's a good sign. That means that you are coming together, growing stronger. A bond has to be forged. Never forget that there are no problems that can't be solved."

"Klaus has to return to Brussels for good in a month. He wants me to come with him."

"That's wonderful. You can move in together. That means it's serious."

"I haven't even finished school."

"You can finish in Brussels, no? And frankly, do you really think you're going to get ahead in life by studying literature? You've got this nice young man from a very good family who's crazy about you, who wants to take you with him. I've had far harder decisions to make in my life."

With Klaus, everything had to be done quickly. Anastasia no longer knew how or why.

After Lev had skipped out the night of the ball, she had spent a lot of time thinking about things. Did she really want to live in a maid's room all her life? She didn't want to end up bitter, like her mother. She had convinced herself that any relationship with Lev would end badly. So she had gone back to Klaus; she had allowed herself to be seduced. He offered her the promise of a different life, far from all the difficulties she had known. But he didn't like to be contradicted and was quick to anger. She felt terribly alone.

Her only real friend was Macaire Ebezner. She hadn't known him very long, of course, but he was kind and attentive. Since the Gala Weekend, she had seen him regularly. They would meet for tea at the Remor, the slightly highbrow café on the Place du Cirque, and would spend hours there. He invited her to visit his parents, who lived on a magnificent estate in Collonge-Bellerive.

Anastasia wasn't attracted to Macaire, but she felt good around him. She could be herself and confide in him. He knew everything: her family history, the little apartment in Pâquis, her mother's job as a saleswoman at Bongénie.

When Anastasia told Macaire she was leaving for Brussels, he responded that he would miss her a great deal, that he would come to Belgium to visit her, and that they would write to each other. In front of the Remor, when it came time to say goodbye, she kissed him warmly on the cheek. That day, she realised that the only man she had ever truly loved was Lev, the young hotel employee.

They too had stayed in touch. Every Sunday, she would go to a phone box and call the hotel's restaurant. She asked to speak to Lev. They knew her now. The maître'd would go to find him, and soon he would be on the other end of the line. It made her happy to hear the sound of his voice, and an indescribable feeling came over her. But why had he disappeared on the night of the ball? He had never wanted to tell her the real reason, saying only that something had come up at work. He had promised, several times, that he would take the train to Geneva to see her, but he never did; there was always some excuse. If he really cared about her, he would have kept his word. From his behaviour, she concluded that Lev didn't feel that strongly about her, although she thought about him constantly. During their many calls, she had never dared reveal her relationship with Klaus. Was this the proof that she loved him?

Anastasia left for Brussels on the first Sunday in April. It was on that day, from a phone box at Geneva Airport, that she found the courage to call Lev to tell him she was leaving.

"Anastasia?" he said excitedly as he picked up the receiver.

"I've met someone," she told him. "His name is Klaus."

Lev, deeply affected, tried to hide his sorrow.

"You have the right to do as you please," he replied stiffly. "We aren't really together, in any case. Is that why you called?"

"I'm going with him to Brussels."

"When?"

"Today."

There was a long silence; she felt she had to explain.

"That Saturday night at the ball, where were you? I waited for you – I was desperate."

He remained silent. How could he admit that he had been humiliated by Bisnard and forced to wash the dishes?

"It doesn't matter. Who is this Karl?"

"Klaus," she corrected. "His father is an industrialist."

"Is he rich?"

"Very, but . . ."

She stopped herself, then went on.

"It's not because he's rich, Lev. That has nothing to do with it. Besides, what difference does it make to you? You want nothing to do with me!"

"That's not true!" Lev protested.

"Yes, it's true, otherwise you would have come to Geneva as you promised."

Lev remained silent. He held the receiver in his hand, and with the other he played with the ring he kept in his pocket: his mother's ring, the only thing of hers he still had. It was for Anastasia; he had known it from their first night together. Since December, he'd had only one thing in mind: to come to Geneva and offer her the ring. But right now, he didn't have a single franc to pay for his train ticket. His past three pay cheques and his Christmas bonus had been held ransom by Bisnard in exchange for his silence. And it had all been for nothing, because while Bisnard had kept silent, the other employees had taken it upon themselves to tell

Monsieur Rose about what Lev had done. He had been furious. To avoid having to fire Lev, Monsieur Rose had been forced to make an example of him. Monsieur Rose withheld a month's salary and gave Lev a final warning.

For Lev, that meant no money until May. Following the reprimand, it would have been unthinkable to ask Monsieur Rose to advance him his salary. As for Lev's father, he had refused to lend his son anything. "You should save your money," Sol told Lev, trying to teach him a lesson. He had tried to sneak on the train to Geneva but had been caught by a conductor in Montreux. Lev was forcibly removed from the train and given a fine. Of course, he was much too proud to mention any of this to Anastasia. What would she think of him? That he was a bum, a good-for-nothing.

"Goodbye, Lev," she said, the final blow.

A tear of rage slid down his cheek.

"Goodbye, Anastasia," he said as he hung up the receiver abruptly. An hour later, in tears as her plane took off, Anastasia thought about Lev and Switzerland receding beneath her and about the error she had just made.

* * *

In the Ebezner kitchen, Anastasia told Arma that from the very first, she and Lev knew they were made for each other. But life had continued to keep them apart. Arma was stunned by the revelation.

"I won't tell Moussieu, I promise. Leave with Lev. It's your destiny."

At that very moment, Macaire, following the information he had received over the phone, was walking along chemin de Ruth. Suddenly, before him, Sinior Tarnogol emerged from the darkness. He appeared to be very nervous.

"I'm in danger, Macaire. Swiss counter-espionage is on my heels. The situation is serious."

Macaire pretended to be surprised by the news. He felt it was the moment to inform Tarnogol of his proposal: to fake Tarnogol's death in exchange for the presidency and Tarnogol's shares. But Tarnogol continued.

"The Swiss government wants to prevent me from taking control of the bank."

"Is that your intention?" Macaire asked.

Tarnogol responded with a sly smile.

"You never had the look of a president, Macaire. So don't expect me to appoint you and abandon my plans just to appease my enemies. I have more courage than that."

"You're a devil!" Macaire yelled.

"But that you've known for fifteen years," Tarnogol cynically reminded him.

"What do you want from me?"

"I'm offering you a new arrangement. One that suits us both."

"Meaning?"

"We cancel our agreement from fifteen years ago. I return your shares and you can become president. In return, you give me what I gave you back then."

"What do you mean?" Macaire blurted out.

"I'm ready to turn back the clock!" Tarnogol hissed. "You give up what you gained fifteen years ago and you become president of this damn bank."

"You mean . . . ?" Macaire said, unable to complete his sentence.

"What I mean is that you lose Anastasia," Tarnogol replied. "Those are my terms."

"If you dare touch a hair on her head . . ." Macaire threatened.

"You will lose Anastasia. You'll become president of the bank, but you'll be alone."

PART TWO

The Weekend of the Murder

Friday, December 14, to Sunday, December 16

27

Initial Leads

It was early morning on Friday, June 29, 2018, and I was in my room at the hotel in Verbier. Scarlett and I had returned from Geneva the night before. I have to admit that our little escapade had pleased me a great deal – especially because she had helped advance our investigation. Early that morning, at dawn, I had gathered my notes and compared them to the different articles that Scarlett had found and arranged on the wall of my suite.

What did we know?

That the victim was someone well known who had no identifiable enemies.

That, according to the teller, the current bank president, appointed after the murder, was no longer the same man after the murder.

That the Ebezners' neighbour knew quite a lot. She was president of the Swiss Foundation for Aid to Orphans, a charitable organisation prominent in Geneva. For years, the honorary president had been Horace Hansen, who had taken a great interest in the foundation's work. Every year, in a large hotel in Geneva, the foundation organised a gala evening to raise money. Horace Hansen always invited prominent names in the banking world. In this way, the neighbour had met, over the course of several years, Abel Ebezner, Sinior Tarnogol, Jean-Bénédict Hansen, Macaire Ebezner, and Lev Levovitch.

"It was no secret Abel Ebezner was angry with his son for what he did with the shares. He talked about it openly. This hurt Macaire, of course. But when he moved next door with his wife, I realised that he was nothing like the way his father had described him," the neighbour had said.

"And Levovitch?" I had asked.

"An extraordinary man. When he walked into a room, he became the centre of attention. It was clear that Abel Ebezner was deeply attached to him. People said that he was the old man's right hand."

Scarlett and I had learned that the neighbour was a bit of a busy-body, which did not displease us, since it would likely prove useful. After the events of the Gala Weekend, she had got her hooks into Arma to try to learn more. "Arma said that she had seen it all coming – she knew that Anastasia planned to run away with her lover."

Someone knocking at the door to my suite tore me from my reading. It was Scarlett.

"Is the writer already at work?" she asked, seeing the pages spread across my work table.

"I was rereading some notes."

"Will you join me for breakfast?"

"Gladly."

We went down to the hotel terrace and sat at a table in the sun.

"So, how's the book going?"

"Rather well. I'm putting together everything we found."

"When can I read what you've already written?"

"Soon," I promised her.

A waiter brought us a pot of coffee and a basket of pastries. Delicately, she reached for a croissant and took a bite. Then she asked, "Do you have any leads?"

"About the murderer? No, not yet. I'm still at our conversation with the neighbour."

"And . . . ?"

"I don't think what happened at the Ebezners on the Friday morning of the Gala Weekend can be a coincidence. It must be connected to what happened later."

While talking, I had prepared some bread, butter, and jam, which I dipped into my coffee with a mechanical gesture. This amused me. It was one of Bernard's habits. Every morning, before meeting me at the office on rue La Boétie, he stopped at the Mesnil, the restaurant on the ground floor of the building. He would order bread and butter with jam, which he dunked into his coffee.

"Connected how?" Scarlett asked.

"That's up to us to find out."

Having finished my bread and coffee, I rose from the table.

"You're leaving already?" Scarlett asked, surprised.

"I have to get back to work. You know, that book I started because of you."

She smiled.

"Writer, since I'm not going to see you all day, we should have dinner together. Apparently, the Italian restaurant at the hotel is excellent."

"Italian is always a good idea," I agreed.

"This evening, then. Work well!"

I walked back to my room. I sat at my table and reread the neighbour's comments. Thanks to her, we knew what had happened on Friday, December 14, at the Ebezner home.

28

False Starts (Part 1)

Friday, December 14, two days before the murder

Day was breaking.

In the winter night, the front of the large Ebezner home was dark except for a solitary window – the one in the office just off the bedroom. Enclosed in this small room, wrapped in a bathrobe, Macaire was bent over his notebook.

> *My final mission will take place at the bank's Gala Weekend in Verbier.*
>
> *P-30 has asked me to prevent Sinior Tarnogol from taking control of the Ebezner Bank.*
>
> *I have very little leeway in the matter. Either I convince Tarnogol to appoint me president, or I will have to kill him. I know that, should I fail, P-30 will accuse me of the double homicide in which I indirectly participated.*
>
> *I would never have believed a day like this would come. But I can't feel sorry for myself because I'm responsible for the situation. I am the one who enabled Tarnogol to get where he is by transferring my shares to him.*
>
> *And because this document is my confession, there remains one secret that I have to reveal here. I must reveal to you what Sinior Tarnogol gave me in exchange for my shares.*

And for the first time, Macaire recorded in detail everything that had happened fifteen years earlier at the Hôtel de Verbier.

When he had finished his report, it was almost seven in the morning. Day was slowly dawning. Closing his notebook, he looked at the small pile of paper that harboured his secrets. He decided not to place it, as he always had, in the safe to which he alone had the combination. This time he hid it on a shelf in the bookcase, behind a row of books – just in case something happened to him that weekend. That way the entire truth would be revealed.

In the empty kitchen, he wolfed down his breakfast. Arma was off until Monday. He suddenly missed her reassuring presence by the stove. He liked seeing her there when he got up in the morning and when he returned in the evening. "Bonjour, Moussieu," Macaire muttered to himself.

It was almost time to hit the road for Verbier. He returned to the bedroom, where Anastasia was still sleeping, crossed the room silently, and entered the bathroom. He showered and dressed with care, shaved himself attentively. His bag had been packed the night before and was already in the boot of the car.

As he was about to leave, he delicately kissed his wife on the cheek, making sure not to wake her. Anastasia hadn't been asleep for a while but had kept her eyes closed; she didn't have the courage to confront her husband. Today, she was going to leave him once and for all.

"See you, chouchou," Macaire whispered, whistling annoyingly in her ear as he did so. "I'm leaving for Verbier; on Sunday I'll be president. You'll see – it'll all turn out okay. Don't forget, Arma is off today; I hope you're not angry with me for leaving you all alone here."

Anastasia, maintaining her posture as a sleeping virgin, thought that Arma's absence would suit her just fine. Macaire kissed her once more, then left.

When Anastasia heard the front door close, she jumped out of bed. She was angry with herself for the way she was going to leave, like a coward. But there was nothing else she could do.

From the wardrobe, she pulled out the luggage she had hidden. The night before, on the balcony of the Hôtel des Bergues, when she had asked Lev when they were leaving, he had whispered in her ear: "Tomorrow morning. Meet me at eleven a.m. in front of the ticket windows at Cornavin station." She didn't want to wait a second longer to get going. She didn't care if it was early. She would go somewhere and have a cup of coffee as she waited for eleven a.m. to arrive.

At the wheel of his car, Macaire passed the gate of his property. He had just turned on to chemin de Ruth when a figure rose from the rear seat and loudly exclaimed, "Hello, Macaire!"

Macaire, on the verge of a heart attack, stomped on the brake pedal and turned around. It was Wagner.

"You're completely out of your mind!" Macaire shouted.

"And you, that wasn't very smart, leaving your car unlocked," Wagner noted.

"What are you doing here?"

"This is a big day for you, Macaire. I want to make sure that you're ready."

"In twelve years of working for P-30, I have never failed any of my missions. Calm yourself."

"Delighted to hear it. So you're determined to eliminate Tarnogol?"

"I'm determined not to let him get his claws into my bank. How I do that is my business. You've never interfered with the way I work before. And the results have always been as planned."

"As you wish, Macaire. But it is in your interests to be appointed president tomorrow evening. Otherwise, the consequences could be disastrous for everyone, beginning with you."

"Everything will be fine – don't you worry, Wagner. I'm really disgusted by the fact that you felt it was necessary to threaten me after I've served the country without fail for twelve years."

"Macaire, the only thing I want is for you to end your career in P-30 with a flourish. You have the vial of poison, just in case?"

In reply, Macaire pulled the vial from his pocket and waved it in front of Wagner, who expressed his satisfaction.

"Don't forget that it takes eight to twelve hours to take effect," he reminded Macaire before stepping out of the car.

Macaire started the car again and headed down chemin de Ruth towards Verbier.

At eleven a.m., Anastasia crossed the large hall at Cornavin station, her small bag in her hand. It had been hard to leave the house in Cologny. She'd been overcome with nostalgia, making a final pilgrimage through the rooms, overwhelmed by emotion. She cried for a long time. She was leaving a life she had enjoyed in spite of everything. She was leaving a man who had always been good to her. Macaire had been the only person who had never hurt her, and she was about to betray him and break his heart. She'd left a note on the bed, a few lines to tell him that she was leaving, that she was leaving for good, that he shouldn't try to look for her. To mark the importance of her decision, she had even thought of leaving her engagement ring with the message. A sapphire that Macaire had offered her when he asked her to marry him. She hadn't worn it often: the sapphire was soon replaced by a large solitaire. As she was about to leave the ring, she looked at the blue stone and, finally, without knowing why, had decided to take it with her. Maybe as a memento of the life she was leaving behind. She put it in her pocket and left for the station. She wondered where Lev was planning to go. Milan? Venice? She had always dreamed of living in Italy.

When she arrived at the ticket windows, she saw him. She ran towards his arms.

"Lev, I thought this day would never come!"

"Anastasia," he began, in a voice that betrayed his concern.

She understood that something was wrong. She noticed that he hadn't brought any luggage.

"What is it, Lev?"

"I have to go to Verbier."

"For the Gala Weekend? But why?"

"It's better that you don't know. Trust me, everything will be alright. We'll have to postpone our departure for two days, that's all."

"I want to know what's going on."

Lev sighed.

"It's Macaire . . ."

"What do you mean?"

"He's not going to be named president."

Anastasia was shocked. If Macaire wasn't named president and she left him, it would be too much for him. There was a risk he would end it all, and she knew it.

"I shouldn't get you involved in all this," Lev continued. "I received a call from Jean-Bénédict Hansen. Apparently, Tarnogol is ready to back anyone except Macaire. I think it's personal with Tarnogol: he wants to push Macaire as far as he can or put pressure on him, but I don't know why. Something's brewing this Gala Weekend, I can feel it. I'm afraid something bad is going to happen."

She was stunned.

"I can't leave him . . ." She sighed. "If Macaire isn't named president, I can't leave him."

She suddenly felt like a prisoner – a prisoner of a man, a prisoner of her life. A tear slid down her cheek. Lev wiped it away with his thumb, then embraced her.

"I'll take care of everything. I promise you that by the end of the weekend, everything will work out. On Sunday, we can leave for good, far from Geneva, far from everything. On Sunday, we'll be free at last! I promise you."

*

Anastasia returned to Cologny feeling anxious. She now regretted that Arma hadn't been able to stay for the weekend. Anastasia had no desire to find herself alone in that immense house for two days. When the taxi dropped her before the gate, she was weighed down by a sense of tremendous disappointment. She couldn't help herself thinking what might happen if Macaire wasn't named president. Just thinking of it turned her stomach into a knot.

Unlocking the heavy front door, she tried to convince herself that everything would be alright; she'd make the best of it. At least she'd have the time to think calmly about what she wanted to take with her and exchange her small bag for a larger suitcase. A few more pieces of clothing and a few things that meant something to her. Yes, even two suitcases. She could also take a few books.

Walking down the hallway, Anastasia heard a noise coming from the bedroom. She automatically thought it was Arma and walked towards the room. But she stopped short, realising that Arma was off and that if it was Arma, the front door wouldn't have been locked. Suddenly, she felt afraid. She wanted to flee, but it was too late. The bedroom door opened violently, and a man dressed in black appeared, gloves on his hands, his face covered with a mask, ready to pounce.

29

False Starts (Part 2)

Fifteen years earlier
April, three weeks after Anastasia's departure for Brussels with Klaus

At nine in the morning, a black sedan arrived in front of the Hôtel de Verbier. The hotel employees, standing at attention, were waiting for a celebrity guest who regularly stayed at the hotel. The driver hurried to open the door and, with due ceremony, Sinior Tarnogol exited the vehicle.

Tarnogol was one of the hotel's most demanding guests – and certainly the most feared. Monsieur Rose warned that he could use his influence to ruin the hotel's reputation. Instructions had been given to all the hotel staff to be particularly attentive to his needs.

Each of the employees, standing in a row, greeted the new arrival. "Good day, Monsieur Tarnogol." "Welcome to the Hôtel de Verbier, Monsieur Tarnogol." In response, Tarnogol simply coughed with indifference and walked up the steps that led to the large entrance door, where Monsieur Rose waited nervously, as he always did when Tarnogol arrived. Monsieur Rose cast a quick glance at the small sheet of paper in his hands on which Lev had written, phonetically, a Russian sentence.

"Welcome," Monsieur Rose articulated with difficulty.

Tarnogol stared at him, intrigued, before replying in French, evidently in a bad mood, "Your Russian is pathetic, my friend. You sound like you're trying to tame a monkey."

Monsieur Rose tried to smile.

"Did you have a good trip?"

"Terrible."

"I'm ever so sorry. Your room is ready if you'd like to rest."

"I'm hungry. Take me to the restaurant. A table off to the side, with a view of the mountains. And get me the banquet manager; I want him to serve me."

"Very well, Monsieur Tarnogol," Monsieur Rose mumbled. He snapped his fingers, and a cloud of employees gathered around him, while someone rushed off to find Bisnard, the banquet manager.

A few moments later, Tarnogol was seated at a table in the restaurant, where, satisfied with the magnificent view of the Alps and, especially, by the well-oiled movements of the corps de ballet around him, he had Monsieur Bisnard serve him two soft-boiled eggs and a small glass of Beluga vodka.

"Thank you, Bisnard." Tarnogol always called the manager by his family name as if it were a nickname. The other employees of the hotel greatly enjoyed seeing the feared Monsieur Bisnard treated with disdain by this powerful client.

"Would you like anything else?" Monsieur Bisnard asked.

"A black tea with a hint of milk."

Bisnard clicked his heels and returned in a short while with a platter laden with a steaming teapot and a Chinese porcelain teacup. With a ceremonial flourish, he lifted the lid of the teapot and removed the metal tea caddy.

"Do you like your tea strong, Monsieur Tarnogol?" he asked.

Tarnogol looked as if he were about to throw up.

"You infuse the tea with a metal ball?"

"Excuse me, Monsieur Tarnogol?"

"You should never infuse tea in a tea caddy or in metal."

"I was unaware of that, Monsieur Tarnogol. Please excuse me."

"How do you expect the tea leaves to release their flavour if they're compressed like that. And the metal kills the taste. And the water? What kind of hot water?"

"Boiling water," Bisnard mumbled.

"Black tea has to be infused at ninety degrees centigrade. We're at approximately two thousand metres above sea level here; water boils at . . . ?"

"Slightly less than one hundred degrees?"

Tarnogol took out a pen and wrote some calculations directly on the tablecloth.

"Roughly ninety-three degrees. Therefore, the temperature is approximately correct," Tarnogol declared, looking satisfied. "Well done, Bisnard!"

Bisnard looked relieved and wiped a few drops of sweat from his brow.

"Now, serve the tea and add the milk."

Bisnard nodded. He filled the cup. Then he took the pitcher of milk and poured a small amount into the beverage.

"I said a hint, not a dash," Tarnogol ordered, peering into his cup, implying that there wasn't enough milk. Bisnard added a bit more.

"That's a small hint," Tarnogol decreed. "Is there a milk shortage? Should I have some delivered to the hotel? Should I present my ration card?"

Bisnard, realising that he had to pour more milk, emptied half the pitcher into the cup. Tarnogol began to scream.

"I said 'a hint' and you've dumped a bucket in there. There's more milk than tea now."

Tarnogol swept the cup away with his hand, spilling it across the table. Bisnard rushed to clean it up. The other employees laughed silently.

"Go get Monsieur Rose, and tell him to send me the little Russian," Tarnogol demanded. "He's the only one who knows how to serve me correctly."

The "little Russian" was Lev.

A few moments later, Lev appeared in the restaurant. He looked thinner and preoccupied, sad even.

"Hello, Monsieur Tarnogol," he said in Russian.

"Hello, young Levovitch."

"How may I help you?"

"A black tea with a hint of milk."

Lev excused himself and returned with a teapot in which he had let some tea leaves infuse inside a paper filter. He served a cup and added a bit of milk. Lev did all this without batting an eye and with complete assurance, as if it were perfectly obvious. Tarnogol watched Lev at work, marvelling. Tarnogol then tasted the tea and found it perfect. He said to Lev, again in Russian, "You know, young man, you're better off here than in the ballroom playing the stud."

"I got into a great deal of trouble because of you. They withheld my salary and gave me a final warning."

"Monsieur Rose was right to do so. One must punish low-level employees. You had no business being there."

"Neither did you have any business being in the ballroom," Lev retorted.

Tarnogol, amused, stared at the impertinent and confident young man who spoke an elegant Russian from another era, inherited from his ancestors – the language of Tolstoy.

"Well, I was invited by Abel Ebezner. I think that he wants me as a client for his bank. Still, I regret that Bisnard grabbed you the way he did. It was unworthy of a man of his position."

"How do you know what happened?"

"Every employee at the hotel was talking about it. There are ears everywhere. I hate cowards. Bisnard is a coward. I did what I had to do."

"It seems like you've been giving him a hard time for the past fifteen minutes," Lev remarked.

Tarnogol smiled.

"You know why I like you, Lev? You're the only one who talks back to me here."

"Allow me to say that I don't really like you very much."

Tarnogol burst out laughing.

"Exactly my point. So, it's because of me that you're in such a bad mood? You look terrible. Sad, depressed, a bit frail, even."

"No, that has nothing to do with it."

"Then what is it?"

"I'm heartbroken."

"What, the girl at the ball you were dancing with?"

Lev nodded in agreement as he stared into the distance. For the past three weeks, ever since Anastasia had left for Brussels, he had been miserable. He imagined her there, happy with Klaus, walking the streets of the Belgian capital, kissing, making love. The worse he felt, the more he thought about it, and the more he thought about it, the worse he felt. He had the impression that the pain would never go away.

"Come, come," Tarnogol replied, "your conquests must be legion."

"It's not the same. When you're in love, you're in love."

"At your age, you like girls the way you like pizza. A slice here, a slice there."

"Because of you, I've lost her."

"Because of you!" Tarnogol objected. "I heard you mention the name Romanov, pretending you were one of them."

"You've never lied to make a woman happy?"

"I've never betrayed my identity. Tell me who you are?"

"Lev."

Tarnogol smiled.

"That I know, idiot. I asked you who you really are. What are you doing this evening?"

"I'm working."

"Then you're at my service, and I want to have dinner with you."

"With all due respect, Monsieur Tarnogol, I can't accept your invitation. The other hotel employees would be very angry to see me dining here with you. And Monsieur Rose told me to stay out of sight. The other staff members didn't appreciate my little escapade during the Ebezner Bank ball."

"Very well, then, we'll dine elsewhere," Tarnogol declared. "Monsieur Rose can't refuse me. Otherwise, I'll buy his hotel, raze it to the ground, and turn it into a car park. I'm taking you to the Alpina, one of the best restaurants in Verbier, one of the best in the country, in my opinion. Have you been there?"

"No, sir. It's a bit out of my reach. Especially now."

"That works out well, then, since I'm inviting you. Eight p.m. at the restaurant. I'll tell Monsieur Rose."

That evening, as he was about to meet Tarnogol, Lev ran into his father in the hotel reception area. Sol was surprised to find Lev out of uniform.

"You're not working? I thought you were on shift tonight?"

"I am. Special service – I am supposed to have supper with Tarnogol."

Sol Levovitch frowned when he heard the name.

"Tarnogol? What does he want with you?"

"I have no idea."

"Be careful with him."

"He doesn't scare me."

Lev continued on his way, but when he got to the reception desk, an employee indicated that Monsieur Rose wanted to see him. Lev at once went into Monsieur Rose's office. Lev found his employer looking out the window, contemplating the night. He seemed preoccupied.

"You wanted to see me, Monsieur Rose?"

"Come in for a moment, my son."

"I'm going to be late for my dinner with Tarnogol."

Rose smiled. Punctuality was one of the first values he had impressed on Lev. "Punctuality is the politeness of kings," he liked to say.

"Tarnogol can wait a few minutes. I wanted to tell you that I had no choice but to authorise this supper. We can't refuse Tarnogol. But be careful. That man is a snake. He wraps himself around people like a boa constrictor and doesn't let go. And then he suffocates them."

"I'll be careful."

"He's not who you think he is," Rose said with considerable gravity. "Be very careful. Whatever he tells you, believe nothing."

The warning rang in his head as Lev walked along Verbier's main street, where the Alpina was located. He wondered what Monsieur Rose had meant by what he said.

When Lev entered the restaurant, Tarnogol was waiting at a table. He forced a smile, but Lev noticed that it did nothing to alter the sense of duplicity he gave off – as if he was always planning something disagreeable.

The meal was very enjoyable, though, and the conversation lively. No matter the subject, young Lev was never without something to say. Tarnogol was surprised by the depth and soundness of Lev's knowledge. At the table, he behaved like a prince; he was even able to blindly identify the wines they were served.

"Who taught you that?" Tarnogol asked, amazed. "That's astonishing, for . . ."

He interrupted himself, and Lev completed the sentence for him:

"For a hotel employee?"

Tarnogol smiled.

"Monsieur Rose taught me about wine, among other things. Since I arrived here, he's taught me propriety and table manners."

"Young Levovitch, you're wasted at the hotel."

Lev shrugged.

"I'm fine at the Verbier."

"Doing what? Thinking about that girl?"

"She's one of a kind," Lev replied in his defence.

"Because you live locked in this hotel in the mountains. I can assure you that big cities are swarming with so-called one-of-a-kind people. If you want some advice, leave here. Build your life somewhere else. You have no future in Verbier."

"I feel at home here. The guests like me."

"Were you born in Verbier?" Tarnogol then asked.

"In Geneva."

"You don't miss Geneva?"

"Yes."

"What do you miss most about it?"

"My mother."

"Where is she?"

"She died when I was small. I have my childhood memories of her: the memory of eternal life. The sensation that nothing can happen to you. And for me, that feeling has the flavour of bread with chocolate, which she prepared for me every day when I got back from school."

"What did it taste like?"

"Like butter and tenderness. Every mouthful was a mouthful of life and happiness."

Tarnogol stared at the young man and then said to him, with a hint of softness in his voice, "I experienced the exact same taste. Long ago. With my wife."

"Is she dead?"

Tarnogol nodded.

"I'm a widower, alone and unhappy. I haven't always been as subdued and caustic as this. There was a time when I was light itself. But ever since my wife died, I've lived in the shadows. It's like someone tearing out your heart and telling you to go on living. Since her death, I've wandered around like a shade. I play out this farce to survive. I hold my nose when I go to the Hôtel de Verbier. I scream at everyone, but it's only a masquerade. It's the only way to forget who I am."

He remained silent for a moment.

"Can I give you some advice, young Levovitch?"

"Please."

"Leave if you want. Live your life. And if I can help in any way, you can count on me."

"Why would you want to help me?"

"You know, I have a reputation I don't deserve. I'm hard, it's true. But I'm fair. Just as you didn't belong at that ball, you don't belong in this hotel."

The next day, as they always did on Sundays, Lev and his father had breakfast on a terrace at the Verbier. It was a sunny morning with a blue sky. Lev kept thinking about his discussion with Tarnogol the night before. Looking out at the mountains, he said to his father, "I like Verbier. I like the way people treat me. I feel appreciated here."

"That's good," his father said.

"But sometimes I get the feeling I've seen everything there is to see at this hotel; the guests always seem the same, and I know every little corner of this village. Sometimes I want to leave."

"Leave? Why? You just told me you like it here."

"Yes, but a person has to break out of his shell. I tell myself that if I had left for Geneva at the beginning of the year, maybe I would be with Anastasia today."

"Oh, son, stop worrying about that girl. It was just a momentary thing. You're dramatising. You get that from me. It's the proof that my theatre training wasn't entirely useless. But tell me about your dinner with Tarnogol. What did that crook want from you?"

"He just wanted to talk. Deep down, he's not so bad – just a lonely man. Life has made him bitter."

"He's the devil."

"His wife is dead," Lev said to try to arouse a hint of compassion in his father.

"You're defending him! My wife is dead, too, but I didn't become Satan's brother as a result."

"We talked about her."

With the mention of Dora, Sol broke into a warm smile.

"I loved your mother very much, Lev. I still love her. Death prevents us from being together, but it can't interrupt our love. She's with me – forever. You have her ring, don't you? The one I gave you after she died?"

"Yes, of course."

"Don't lose it. One day you'll offer it to your wife, someone you'll love the way I loved your mother."

"How do we know whom we'll love?"

"Love is the feeling that life means something."

"I think I feel that for Anastasia."

"Come on, Lev, don't be so easily swayed. She's a little tease, taking off with the first guy who showed up – another rich idiot. The rich take everything."

"Still, I feel it was real between us."

"If it were real, you'd be together."

Lev couldn't find anything to say in response.

That evening at the hotel, Sol Levovitch worked late, locked in his office. He had no desire to return home. No desire to be alone in his apartment. He ended up wandering around the hotel, consumed by his thoughts. His steps led him to the bar. The place was empty. Aside from the man behind the counter, only Monsieur Rose was there, sitting in an armchair drinking tea. Sol greeted him, and Rose suggested he join him.

"I thought you had gone home," Sol said, surprised to see him there.

"I thought you had gone home, too," Rose replied.

"My damned insomnia. What's the point in going to bed if I know I'm not going to fall asleep?"

Monsieur Rose took a sip of tea.

"Have you spoken to Lev?"

"Not yet."

"Sol, really, you must."

"I don't know how to tell him. I'm a man of the theatre, but I simply cannot say those words. And I don't want to ruin our time together. He's a terrific young man. You know, I've taught him the secrets of my art, so they stay in the family. Even if he doesn't want to become an actor, they won't disappear. All the same, it would be a waste if he didn't follow in my footsteps. He's so talented. He could be an amazing actor – the actor I could never be."

With those words, Monsieur Rose couldn't help but laugh softly.

"Why are you laughing?"

"I have to tell you something. Ever since you arrived in Verbier, I've been teaching Lev how to run a hotel. I hope you're not upset with me."

"Not at all. Besides, Lev told me about it."

"But we have to let him find his own path."

"I know. Live and let live – it's a difficult maxim to apply when you're a parent, though."

"Live and let live," Rose agreed. And he thought: the son I never had.

And the father thought: the only son I have.

There was a long silence.

"You have to tell him, Sol. You absolutely have to tell Lev before it's too late."

"He wants to leave Verbier. I'm afraid it will interfere with his plans."

"Sol," Rose insisted, "you don't have much time left."

"A year," Sol added. "The doctor said I could hold on for another year. That gives us a little time."

* * *

Two months later

It was early evening in Verbier, the end of June, the air was warm and smelled of summer. The sky was a deep blue, and in the fields, the insects had already begun to sing.

The bar at the Hôtel de Verbier was empty. The start of the summer season had been rather quiet. The phone on the counter rang suddenly, and the employee rushed to the receiver, eager to take a booking. He was disappointed to learn that the call wasn't from a customer.

"One moment, please," he said to the voice on the other end of the line, before leaving his post to find Lev, who was working as a porter at the hotel's entrance.

"Telephone for you, Lev," the bartender said.

"For me?" Lev looked surprised.

He quietly followed his colleague to the bar and picked up the receiver placed on the counter.

"Hello?"

The only thing Lev heard was a muffled cry.

"Hello? Who's there?"

A voice, one he recognised right away, said, "Come and get me, I beg you. Come and get me."

"Anastasia?"

"Lev, you have to help me. He's going to end up killing me."

"Anastasia, what's going on?"

"I beg you, come! I have no-one but you."

"Where are you?"

"Brussels."

Without realising what he was getting into, Lev understood that the situation was serious. He quickly estimated the distance separating him from the Belgian capital.

"I can find a car and leave immediately. If I travel fast, I should get there by daybreak."

They agreed to meet at six a.m. outside the house she shared with Klaus – no later. They had to get far away before Klaus woke up.

"Leave now," Lev insisted. "Find a place to stay, and I'll join you there."

"And go where? I have nothing, I have no money. I can't even rent a cheap hotel room."

"I'll be there. Don't worry; I'll be there."

He wrote down the address, a street in Ixelles. After hanging up, he rushed into Monsieur Rose's office, where he was going over the books. Lev quickly explained the situation. His friend was in great danger. He needed a car to go and get her.

"The girl from the ball?"

"Yes, sir."

"Where is she?"

"Brussels."

"If I understand correctly, you want me to lend you a car and give you a day off so that you can leave in the middle of the night to go to Belgium?"

"Exactly, Monsieur Rose."

The hotel manager was amused by Lev's nonchalance. Nonetheless, he forced himself to maintain his air of severity.

"You realise that I can't allow something like that. Especially after your escapade at the bank ball."

Lev lowered his head.

"I know that I'm not exactly a saint, but this is very serious."

Monsieur Rose opened the middle drawer of his desk. He pulled out a sheet of headed notepaper and wrote something.

"I'm leaving this note for the head of personnel; he'll find it tomorrow morning when he gets here. I told him that, given how few customers we have, I've requisitioned you for forty-eight hours to help me with something important."

His note completed, Rose got up from his chair with the paper in his hand. He grabbed his briefcase and turned off the light in the room.

"As for me, I'm leaving. I've forgotten the keys to my car in the desk drawer. In forty-eight hours, day after tomorrow, in the evening, my car will be here and you with it. I don't want any arguments, no little girl-friend in your room; you're familiar with the rules."

"Thank you, Monsieur Rose," Lev said, his eyes soft. "I don't know how to thank you."

"If you want to thank me, think about my proposal to train you to become manager of this hotel. Time is passing, and there'll come a day when I have to appoint a successor. I would like to pass the hotel on, rather than sell it to the first person who shows up, who'll turn it into something ordinary. With you, I know that the soul of the place will live on."

"I'll think about it," Lev promised.

Before leaving, Lev stopped by his father's apartment, in the centre of the village of Verbier, to let him know.

"Go, my brave boy. Be careful and be prudent."

"Don't worry. I'll be back in two days at most. I'll call you from Brussels."

Sol looked admiringly at his son.

"What is it?" Lev asked, seeing a strange light in his father's eyes.

"Nothing. It's just that, seeing your face, your charisma, the way you hold yourself, you could be a great actor – a much greater artist than I could ever be. I taught you all I know. Why not make a go of it?"

After a moment's hesitation, Lev replied, "Monsieur Rose says that I could become the manager of the hotel, have a career."

Sol frowned.

"Tsk, *manager*! What a ridiculous idea."

"I'd like to get to the other side. I want to be on the side of the served, not the servants."

"Tsk, *manager*," his father continued to harrumph. "We're artists! You come from a great line of artists."

"Not really, Papa."

"*Not a great line of artists*?"

"You don't even act anymore. You taught me everything you know, true. But you never go on stage. You're not an artist anymore."

"Once an artist, always an artist. It's in your blood, whether you like it or not. Go now. And I hope you've changed your mind by the time you get back. First your mother leaves; then you want to turn your back on me. What have I done to be treated this way? *Manager*! What a strange idea. Really. Don't let them dazzle you."

Lev drove all night and got to Brussels at six in the morning. He found the address without much trouble. Anastasia was waiting in front of the building, her only luggage a cheap canvas bag. She was leaving everything behind. He got out of the car, and she rushed to his arms. She held him tightly. She had grown thin.

"What's going on?"

"Let's get out of here!"

"I want to know what's going on."

"He hits me, Lev. He hits me all the time. He hits me no matter what I say. I can't take it any longer."

Lev looked at the magnificent woman with the sad eyes. He decided that Klaus wouldn't get off so easily.

"Wait for me, here. I'll be back."

"No, Lev, don't!"

But Lev wasn't listening and rushed inside the house. She ran after him into the elevator.

"Don't do it, please, Lev. Klaus is going to tear you apart."

Lev paid no attention and ascended. Examining the names on the doors, he easily found the one he was looking for: Klaus Van Der Brouck. He banged furiously on the door until Klaus opened it, in his socks, his eyes still half closed, wrapped in sleep. He didn't recognise the young visitor who punched him hard in the face. Klaus flew back across the entrance hall of his apartment before falling to the floor. Lev stood over him threateningly.

"Do you enjoy beating women, Klaus? I'm going to give you some advice. If you want to go on living, stay away from Anastasia. Don't try to get in touch with her; erase her from your memory. If I see you again, I'm going to kill you."

That morning, as day was breaking, Lev and Anastasia rediscovered each other. He took her to breakfast at a small café in central Brussels and watched her wolf down thick slices of buttered bread and gradually come back to life.

She told him about the weeks of hell with Klaus, the fits of jealousy, the bullying, the violence. Klaus, always so kind when in society, attentive and smiling around other people, was cruel and callous in private. He had forbidden her to travel and told her how to behave. He controlled her completely. "I was a prisoner even though the door was wide open," she explained, sobbing. "I wanted to get away so badly but didn't know how."

She had first tried talking to her sister, Irina, but she was too busy with her new life – marriage, the house, the summer, two weeks in a palace in Sardinia. She wanted to have children quickly. She had no time for chit-chat.

Anastasia had wanted to open up to her mother when she had come to spend Pentecost weekend at the Klaus family estate in the Belgian countryside.

"I want to go back to Geneva with you, Mama," Anastasia confided during their walk.

Olga was offended.

"You're not going to leave Klaus."

"I don't want to be with him. I feel trapped in Brussels. It's not the life I wanted."

"*Not the life you wanted*? What more do you want, then?"

"To be loved."

"Come, come, my daughter, Klaus loves you very much. Fight for your relationship. Do you want to drop everything, just like that? You're not going to shame me in front of his parents, are you? Go on! *Kopf hoch*! Give yourself the summer to make things right."

In the small, empty café in Brussels, having regained her confidence, Lev said, "So, you called me because no-one else wanted to help you."

"I called you because you're the only person I want to be with, Lev. We're made for each other."

Hearing those words, his eyes grew bright for a moment, but they quickly darkened.

"If you really thought that, you wouldn't have left with Klaus," he said, coldly.

"I was wrong. I needed to get out of my mother's apartment. I was attracted to the idea of freedom."

"You're mostly attracted by money."

"How can you say such a thing? You don't really know me, then. All I want is to be with you."

"I have nothing to offer you, Anastasia. I'm a hotel employee."

"Take me to Verbier! We'll be happy there."

"Impossible. I promised the manager that I wouldn't let you stay in my room at the hotel. The regulations don't allow it."

"So, let him hire me as a maid!"

"You wouldn't be happy."

"I would be very happy. I want to spend the rest of my life with you. With you, I'd be very happy. Nothing else matters."

After hesitating, Lev confided to her, "Monsieur Rose, the manager of the Hôtel de Verbier, says that I could take his place one day. You could run the hotel with me."

Anastasia's face brightened.

"Oh, Lev, that would be wonderful. I can see us managing the hotel together. Promise me that we'll do that. That's exactly the life I've been dreaming of. Promise me, Lev!"

"I promise."

At the table of that small café in Brussels, they dreamed of their future life. They imagined the changes they would make to the hotel and promised each other a peaceful life in the mountains, away from everything, amid those beautiful pastures – green in the summer and snow-covered in winter.

Believing their destinies to be sealed, they left Brussels, their heads filled with plans for the future. They drove towards Geneva. Anastasia didn't want to return to her mother and decided to move in for a while with the Ebezners. "You'll see," she said to Lev. "Macaire, their son, is very nice. His parents' house is immense, and he always told me I could stay there if I needed to." They alerted Macaire while they were on the road. After dropping her off, Lev would return to Verbier and inform Monsieur Rose that he had decided to accept his proposal. Lev would then ask Monsieur Rose to hire Anastasia, so she could be trained in all the jobs at the hotel: kitchen assistant, server, head waiter, concierge, chambermaid, housekeeper. "There's nothing better than on-the-job training," as Monsieur Rose often proclaimed.

It was late afternoon when Lev and Anastasia reached Collonge-Bellerive, in the Genevan countryside, where the Ebezners lived. Until then, Lev knew the Ebezners only because he had served them at the hotel. Passing the gate of their property along Lake Geneva, he was intimidated at first. A long row of century-old lindens led to a large house overlooking a garden with a perfectly manicured lawn, which ended at a small private beach.

Macaire welcomed them warmly, and Lev felt sympathy for the charming young man into whose hands he was entrusting Anastasia. Lev was getting ready to leave for Verbier, but Macaire retained him.

"You look exhausted, Lev."

"I haven't slept in thirty-six hours."

"Don't drive; spend the night."

Lev accepted. In that way, that evening, he made the acquaintance of Abel and Marianne Ebezner, Macaire's parents. They dined together on the broad terrace in front of the house. Lev found Abel Ebezner to be less severe and more affable than the image Lev had retained of the man from his presence at the hotel. Anastasia seemed to know Macaire's parents well. She told them what had happened in Brussels. Abel remained angry all evening after hearing how she had been treated.

"I know Klaus's father well. I'm going to tell him everything."

"No, please, Monsieur Ebezner. I want to forget; I want to leave all that behind me."

"Still, you're lucky that Lev was able to come to your rescue. The first time he slapped you, you should have called the police and got out of there."

"In the beginning, Klaus swore to me that it wouldn't happen again. He kept telling me he loved me."

"If you love someone, you don't beat them," Abel objected.

"My mother loves me, and she still hits me," Anastasia remarked.

Marianne Ebezner was alarmed by the comment but simply said, "In any case, dear, you can stay here for as long as you like. You have nothing to worry about."

Anastasia smiled sadly. "Thank you."

Abel Ebezner, already impressed by the way Lev had driven to Brussels to save Anastasia from Klaus, was struck by the young man's intelligence. Abel was accustomed to dull conversations with his son, Macaire, who worked at the bank without enthusiasm, or to the insufferable chattering of his imbecile cousin, Jean-Bénédict, who was always visiting them and whose admission, sooner or later, to the bank's board of directors by hereditary right left Abel with a bad taste in his mouth. And he was forever surrounded by the bank's ambitious young executives, who were just as ready to lick your boots as stick a knife in your back. Lev was unlike anyone Abel had ever known: brilliant and easy-going, genuinely cultured, with the backbone of a true banker. And this was confirmed when Abel left the table to make a phone call.

"If you'll excuse me a moment, the market is going to close soon, and I'd like to know where the dollar is."

"Whatever you do, don't sell dollars," Lev suggested. "The rate has probably risen against all the other currencies. The American Federal Reserve isn't planning to inject additional liquidity into the market."

"On the contrary," Macaire intervened, "it's more than likely that they will. We have advised our clients to sell their dollars before the exchange rate drops."

"Probably not a bad move for them," Lev considered. "But they would have made money by staying invested in dollars."

"I'm telling you that the rate has dropped," Macaire repeated, slightly annoyed. "It's the unanimous opinion of our analysts. They weren't born yesterday, believe me."

Lev shrugged.

"If you say so. You're the banker, after all."

When Abel Ebezner returned from his phone call, he stared at Lev with amazement.

"How did you know what was going to happen?"

"It seemed logical. Clients at the hotel asked me my advice on the subject. So I analysed the economic indicators for the United States the last time the Federal Reserve injected additional liquidity into the market. At that time, the macroeconomic data were completely different. I felt it was highly unlikely that the Fed would decide to intervene in the current climate."

"You advise the hotel's guests?" Abel Ebezner asked with surprise.

"Yes. Well, they ask for my advice with their investments. And they often listen to me."

"Your name is Levovitch, you said, right? You speak Russian?"

"Yes."

"And some English?"

"He speaks at least ten languages fluently," Anastasia interjected.

Abel Ebezner stared at Lev with admiration.

"I could use someone like you at the bank."

"Thank you, Monsieur Ebezner, but I'm not sure I want to work in a bank."

He wanted to talk about Verbier and the hotel, about the plans they had for Anastasia, but he decided to say nothing. After dinner, he and Anastasia went for a walk around the property. It was late, but it seemed as if the night would never arrive. The sky was still blue, the air soft.

"What an amazing place," Anastasia marvelled. "I've never seen anything like it. The house, the garden, the private dock. It's paradise."

"Verbier is our paradise, isn't it?"

"Yes, but it could be Geneva. And who knows, perhaps in a house like this. You made quite an impression on Abel Ebezner. You could have a great career at the bank."

She continued walking without noticing the disappointment on Lev's face. As they were entering the house, he stayed outside, alone, claiming he wanted a cigarette. He stood there on the terrace, the glowing tip of his cigarette the only sign of his presence. Abel Ebezner appeared then, a glass of Scotch in each hand. He offered one to Lev.

"Here's to your health, Lev," Abel said, "and the pleasure of having met you."

"Thank you, Monsieur Ebezner."

"Call me Abel."

Lev agreed and sipped his Scotch.

"What would you like to do for a career, Lev? You're not going to carry suitcases all your life?"

"I would like to make an impression on Anastasia."

"And what impresses her?"

"I don't know. Money, I guess. She dreams of living in a house like yours. And I'm prepared to do whatever it takes to make her dreams come true."

Abel smiled.

"You have the potential to make a great banker, Lev. Trust me, I see them all the time and I don't remember ever having met someone like you. Look, I have an idea. Why not come in for an internship at the bank? That way, you could see if you liked it."

"I would have to speak to my father," Lev replied after some hesitation.

"I can ask him myself, if you want."

"Better not, Abel. My father doesn't like bankers. Mother ran off with a banker, and she died in a helicopter accident while they were touring Italy."

"I'm sorry to hear that. Your father's sounds like a good man. What does he do?"

"He was an actor. Now, he works at the Hôtel de Verbier. He would like me to follow in his footsteps. He says we're part of a long line of actors but I've never seen such an unsuccessful line."

Abel burst out laughing.

"Talk to your father. Convince him to let you work in Geneva."

30

The Secret Notebook

In Cologny that Friday morning, several police cars were parked outside the Ebezner property. The neighbours, alerted by the sirens, had come out in force and had massed before the open gate. Fascinated, they watched the comings and goings of the police, accompanied by two dogs who scoured the garden, while gravely discussing the event animating their day: Anastasia Ebezner, upon returning home, had come face to face with a burglar.

"Apparently, she has nothing to steal," offered one neighbour, who had this information from another curious bystander, who had questioned a policeman. Upon seeing her, the burglar had fled.

"All the same, a break-in in broad daylight!"

"A break-in in broad daylight," a retired man said on the phone to his wife, to whom he carefully repeated everything he heard (the poor woman regretted having gone shopping, for she was missing the show). "But it seems that Anastasia is okay; the burglar fled when she arrived."

Another neighbour with a dog piped up, "And what if he hasn't fled? After all, we live around here!"

Small flakes of snow began to fall slowly, landing on the heads of the curious, who followed the movements of the police entering and leaving the house.

Inside, in the living room, Anastasia, still suffering from the shock of the event, told Inspector Philippe Sagamore, a lieutenant with the crime squad of the Geneva Judicial Police, what had happened.

"As I was telling the other officers, I came in by the front door. I heard a noise, and all of a sudden, a man rushed out of the bedroom. He wore a mask and was dressed in black. He wore gloves. He looked at me very calmly. I screamed, and he put a finger to his mouth – a sign for me to be quiet. I obeyed. Then he ran back into the bedroom and went out through the window. I lost sight of him in the garden."

"And then?" Lieutenant Sagamore asked.

"Then I called the police."

Lieutenant Sagamore rose from the armchair in which he was seated and went to look at the garden through the tall French window. He stood there for a moment, pensive. He was interrupted by a member of the forensic team.

"Did you find anything?" Sagamore asked.

"We found footsteps in the snow, but they disappear among the bushes along the edge of the property. The wall isn't very high there. The thief must have climbed over and fled down chemin de Ruth. The dogs followed a track for a while, but it stops abruptly. He must have got into a car. Unfortunately, what with the autoroute traffic, the hikers, and all the neighbours asking questions, whatever useful evidence there was has already been contaminated."

Sagamore made a face. He kept looking at the garden. He seemed intrigued. He opened the French windows and walked outside, like a tracker. He examined the immaculate snow and the footsteps around the broken bedroom window. Then he returned to the living room, where his colleague asked, as soon as he entered, "Did you see anything?"

"The footsteps go directly towards the bedroom window," Sagamore replied.

"And so?"

"Most of the time, a thief walks around the house he's planning to enter – if only to make sure no-one's home. Then, he'll enter by a French window rather than just an ordinary window. It's easier that way. But if I'm to believe the tracks, he headed directly for this window. He knew the house was empty and headed straight for this room."

"How could he know that there was no-one home?" Anastasia asked.

"He waited a long time. He was there, on the road, near your front gate. You said that your husband left early this morning?"

"Yes, around seven. I left around eight."

"He would have seen you both leave. And then he would have made his move."

Sagamore took out a notebook from his pocket and wrote something down.

"Madame Ebezner, you left here at eight in the morning and you returned at eleven thirty."

"Yes, that's correct."

"I'm curious. I'm wondering what this man did in your house for more than three hours. It seems that he didn't even leave the room where you walked in on him."

"There are no signs that he was in the rest of the house," his colleague from forensics added. "There's no sign of searching, no open drawers. And there are no footprints elsewhere in the house. The thief's shoes were wet from the snow; we should have found water on the floor or dirt on the rugs. Yet we found tracks only in the bedroom."

"And nothing is missing," Anastasia confirmed, having inspected the premises with the police. "There are a lot of expensive objects that my husband inherited, especially the paintings. Everything is here."

"That confirms my hypothesis," Sagamore remarked. "Our man targeted the bedroom. Let's take another look."

Aside from the broken glass and the open safe, the bedroom was intact.

"The safe doesn't look like it was broken into," the forensics officer explained.

"So you're saying our man knew the combination?" Sagamore asked.

"If he spent three hours in the room, I think he would have discovered the combination – probably the old way, with a stethoscope. It's a mechanical combination lock, so it would have been entirely possible."

"Why break a window to enter the house but then spend three hours figuring out the combination to the safe?" Anastasia asked.

"He broke the glass so he could enter quickly," Sagamore concluded. "It's daytime, and it looks like the neighbours keep their eyes on everything around here. There was no time to force the lock and risk being seen. But once inside the house, he could afford to take more time. What was in the safe?"

"I haven't the slightest idea," Anastasia admitted.

"Where do you keep your jewels?" Sagamore asked, surprised.

"In the other safe in the bedroom. My husband uses this small boudoir as an office. I think he keeps bank documents in the safe."

"And his watches?" Sagamore suggested, seeking a motive for the break-in.

"No, his watches are in the safe in the bedroom as well."

"Madame Ebezner," Lieutenant Sagamore went on, "have you received any threats lately?"

"Threats?" Anastasia said, surprised. "No, why?"

"Because I have the feeling this wasn't a simple robbery. Let me share something with you, speaking as a cop. You know why some people have two safes in their house? One is for their jewellery, the other for their secrets. I really need to talk to your husband, Madame Ebezner."

"I'd like to talk to him, too. But I can't reach him on his phone or in his hotel room. He's probably in a meeting. As I said, he's in Verbier for an important weekend with his bank."

"I read that in the paper. Your husband is going to be appointed president of the bank this weekend, isn't that right?"

"Yes."

Sagamore looked around the room once more.

"You said that it was a man. But his face was covered. Could it have been a woman?"

"He had the body of a man. I didn't get the impression a woman was standing in front of me. And his eyes . . . there was something special about his eyes."

"What do you mean, 'special'?" Sagamore asked, opening his notebook.

"For a fraction of a second, I thought I recognised him, and I think he felt the same. We looked at each other, and something happened – as if we had met before. The eyes, Lieutenant – the eyes don't lie."

"Does anyone else live or work here?"

"A household employee. She's off today."

"Write down her name, please." Sagamore offered his notebook to Anastasia.

She wrote something down.

"Anyone else? A gardener, maybe?"

"We have a company that takes care of the property. But most of the time they send the same people."

"I'll need the name of the landscaping company as well."

At that very moment in Verbier, the employees of the Ebezner Bank were arriving at the hotel in small groups. Everyone was in a good mood, excited by the prospect of a lavish Gala Weekend. As in other years, after checking in with reception and going to their rooms, most of them headed to the hotel shuttle, which took them to the foot of the ski slopes. A small minority preferred to take advantage of the hotel's amenities and relax in the heated outdoor pool, where steam was rising as the snow fell, or in one of the hot tubs.

The hotel was bubbling with activity. The staff were on their best behaviour. For the majority of the employees of the bank, the Gala Weekend was the event of the year. But for Cristina, who was attending for the first time, it had an entirely different meaning. She knew there wouldn't be any others after this one. She also knew that time was against her. She first had to find out where the bank board would be meeting. Then she would use whatever was at hand. By accident, she walked through a service door and wandered among the hotel's corridors. She reached the kitchen, but no-one paid any attention to her. There she saw, displayed on a wall, a service memo about the Gala Weekend. She moved closer to read it. Suddenly, she felt a heavy hand on her shoulder.

"Can I help you, Mademoiselle?"

It was Monsieur Bisnard, the banquet manager.

At the same moment, in the muffled comfort of his ground-floor office, Monsieur Rose was drinking coffee with Lev.

"So, finally, you've come for the Gala Weekend?" Monsieur Rose asked, surprised. "I get the impression you've never been to one."

"Never," Lev replied. Too many unpleasant memories.

"I put you in your usual room, as you requested."

"Thank you, Monsieur Rose."

"Lev, maybe one day you can stop calling me Monsieur Rose and just call me Edmond."

"You've always been Monsieur Rose to me."

Lev observed the painting hanging over the fireplace, displaying Monsieur Rose, a lieutenant colonel in the Swiss army reserves, in his uniform.

"I've always admired you, more than my own father."

"Don't say that."

Lev looked kindly upon the old man who stood before him. Monsieur Rose must have been around eighty. Although his body bore the marks of passing time, his mind was as alert as ever.

"You don't want to retire?" Lev asked him.

"I haven't found a replacement yet. The people who want to buy the hotel from me are just dreary hotel groups. I don't want this place to end up in the hands of some large chain. Independence is a beautiful thing."

Lev smiled, but he was unable to hide his nostalgia.

"I regret having let you down fifteen years ago, Monsieur Rose."

"Come, come, Lev, you're not going to rehash that old story again. You were right to accept Abel Ebezner's offer. Look what an amazing career you've made for yourself."

"I never really liked the bank, Monsieur Rose. Frankly, I would have preferred to stay here and work with you."

"It's not too late," Rose replied jokingly.

"Unfortunately, it is."

Monsieur Rose's expression darkened.

"What's going on, Lev? You look strange. Your father would be so proud of you. If he could only see what you've accomplished."

Lev rose from the armchair in which he had been sitting and moved to the window. He watched the snow falling on the pine trees.

"My father died because of me."

"Lev, please, you know that's not true."

Lev didn't seem to hear him. He went on. There was a darker timbre to his voice.

"Monsieur Rose, I'm going to disappear. I stopped by this weekend to say goodbye to you. I owe you a great deal."

"Disappear? What do you mean, *disappear*? What are you saying, Lev?"

"You may have heard some disturbing things about me. But you know what I am. You know that I'm not a bad person. You know why I did what I did."

On the sixth floor of the hotel, Macaire was pacing outside Tarnogol's suite. He absolutely had to talk with him. Since his arrival at the hotel, he had looked for Tarnogol everywhere, without success. He was not in the main hall, not in the reception rooms, not at the bar. For the past half hour, Macaire had been walking back and forth in front of Tarnogol's door as if doing so would make him appear.

"Macaire?" Tarnogol said, surprised to see him outside his door.

"I need to talk to you, Sinior."

Tarnogol looked around him, like a hunted animal, then opened the door.

The suite was dark. All the shades were down. After turning on the lights, Tarnogol opened all the wardrobes and walked around the room to make sure no-one was hiding there.

"Given the situation, I'm obliged to take a few precautions," he explained to Macaire before pointing to an armchair.

Macaire sat down, and Tarnogol, after settling into a couch opposite, began.

"Both of us know this is my last Gala Weekend, Macaire. The question is whether it's also yours."

"Why should it be my last?" Macaire asked, without hiding his nervousness.

"Because P-30 is on my back and yours, too."

Macaire blanched.

"Who . . . who told you about P-30?"

"Come now, Macaire, the Russian secret service has known for a long time. You've been under surveillance just as I have. You know, unlike many others, I have never taken you for an idiot – on the contrary. All in all, you made only one mistake: suspecting the foreigner when the danger comes from those closest to you."

"Danger? What are you saying?"

"Is Anastasia okay?" Tarnogol asked, slyly.

"Anastasia? What's my wife got to do with any of this?" Macaire shouted, digging in his pockets reflexively to find his phone.

He realised he had left it in his hotel room. Jumping up from his chair, he ran to his room and pounced on the phone, which he had left on the dresser by the entrance. The screen showed that he had missed several calls from his wife. He understood then that he had made a serious error. He felt as if his heart would explode. He phoned Anastasia at once.

"Macaire, finally!"

She was in the entrance hall of the house with Lieutenant Sagamore.

"What's going on, chouchou?" Macaire mumbled, panic-stricken.

"A man, in the house. He broke in . . . the bedroom window. I went out to do some shopping, and I surprised him when I got back."

"You weren't hurt?"

"No, he ran away. He opened the safe in your office. He emptied it. The police want to know what was inside."

Macaire remained silent. He was terrified. Tarnogol was preparing the trade: the presidency for Anastasia. He had to make sure she was safe, and quickly.

She repeated her question.

"What was in the safe? The police are here with me, they want to know."

"D . . . d . . . documents," he stammered, completely out of sorts. "Important bank documents; I took them with me. The safe was empty."

Anastasia sensed the fear in her husband's voice. She grew pale, which aroused the suspicions of Lieutenant Sagamore, who hadn't taken his eyes off her. He asked to speak to Macaire and grabbed the phone.

"Monsieur Ebezner? Lieutenant Sagamore, from the crime squad."

"Crime squad? I thought it was a robbery?"

"I think it's much more serious than a robbery. Your wife could have been harmed. What was in your safe on the ground floor?"

"Nothing but documents," Macaire assured him. "Documents for the bank that I took with me."

"What type of documents?"

"Oh, nothing special," Macaire said somewhat casually. "Administrative paperwork. Nothing of any interest. The thief must have thought he'd find some expensive jewellery."

"When you get back from Verbier, can you stop by to see me, please? I have a few routine questions I'd like to ask you."

"Of course, Lieutenant. And thank you and your men for being so prompt. May I speak to my wife?"

Lieutenant Sagamore handed the phone back to Anastasia, who stepped away to resume the call.

"You're in danger, Anastasia," Macaire whispered, his voice breaking. "In the bedroom library, you'll find, on the second shelf, hidden behind a row of books, a small notebook. Destroy it! Burn it in the fireplace. Nothing can remain. Do you understand what I'm saying?"

While listening to Macaire, Anastasia smiled, hoping Lieutenant Sagamore wouldn't catch on, then she assumed her most relaxed voice to reply to her husband.

"Absolutely, my darling. And don't worry about a thing. Everything will be fine."

She hung up.

Macaire, extremely worried, opened the small safe in his hotel room and took out his revolver, which he had brought with him. He ran to Tarnogol's suite, where the door had remained open. Tarnogol hadn't moved from the couch. Macaire pointed the weapon at him.

"I'm going to kill you, Tarnogol, and it'll all be over," Macaire yelled.

"Calm down," Tarnogol said, seemingly unconcerned by the gun pointed at him.

"You don't think I can do it?"

"On the contrary, I know you can do it. I know what happened in Madrid."

"What happened . . ."

"Lower your weapon, Macaire."

He complied but kept the pressure on Tarnogol.

"I'm warning you, Sinior, if you touch a single hair on her head . . ."

"It's not me, Macaire!" Tarnogol said, exasperated. "It's not me; it's P-30."

"What? Why would they do a thing like that?"

"Because they want to put pressure on you to kill me."

Macaire stared at Tarnogol, not knowing what to believe.

"You're worried about your wife right now. Yet, that's the agreement, isn't it? I make you president, you give me Anastasia."

"I've changed my mind. I want my wife and the presidency. All I have to do is kill you now, and everything will be taken care of."

"Except that you can't kill me," Tarnogol explained calmly.

"And why not?"

In reply, Tarnogol took an envelope from his inside jacket pocket. He held the envelope out to Macaire, who recognised it at once.

"That's the envelope I brought you from Basel on Monday night."

"Precisely. And I'm sure you're curious to know what's inside. Open it."

Macaire obeyed. Inside were a series of photographs. He stood there, stunned. His hands began to shake. He was finished.

"You see, Macaire, those pictures are my life insurance."

In the entrance hall of the Ebezner home in Geneva, Lieutenant Sagamore continued to question Anastasia.

"Madame Ebezner, I noticed the bag near the front door. Were you planning to go somewhere?"

Her heart started beating faster, but her face remained impassive.

"No, the bag has been there for a few days; I should unpack. Please excuse the mess."

Sagamore continued.

"You told your husband you had gone out this morning to go shopping. I don't see any shopping bags in the front hall, though."

"I didn't find anything. I was looking for a winter hat, but I didn't find anything I liked."

"Which shops?" Sagamore asked at once. Anastasia was caught off guard.

"I . . . I walked around the centre. I went to Bongénie and a few places nearby."

"Madame Ebezner," Sagamore interjected in an empathetic voice, "my team found a note in the bedroom. I don't think it has any connection to the investigation. Here."

He handed her the note she had left for Macaire earlier, telling him she was leaving. She crumpled it up and put it in her pocket. She felt she had to justify herself.

"I plan to leave my husband."

"That doesn't concern me, Madame," Sagamore replied before heading for the front door. "It's strange. Your husband didn't ask what the thief had taken from the house. Most of the time, when someone breaks into a house, the owner asks what was stolen and whether the house was damaged by the intruders. But your husband didn't – as if he had anticipated that someone might take an interest in his office and whatever was in that safe."

Anastasia shrugged.

"The shock of the news, I assume. He wanted to make sure I was okay. There's more to life than money, Lieutenant."

At the hotel, in Tarnogol's suite, plunged in shadow, Macaire couldn't take his eyes off the photos. There were pictures of him in Madrid, a week earlier. A series of images, each taken in different situations, which showed him leaving the airport, in the street with Perez, outside of the computer technician's building, then walking quickly away from it.

"I have nothing against you, Macaire," Tarnogol assured him. "But I'm forced to protect myself. So I've taken some precautions. If you've got it into your head to get back at me, if something happens to me this weekend, these pictures will be sent to the Spanish papers and the police."

"You're the devil!" Macaire screamed.

"I'm worse than the devil, because I exist."

The two men stared at each other like two lions ready to fight.

"There's no reason for us to be enemies, Macaire. Let me remind you that in the beginning, I obtained your shares legally. We made an exchange. If you want them back, then you'll have to give me what belongs to me."

"Anastasia is not yours!"

"Nor is she yours. You know that, at the time, she was in love with Lev. She told you that, didn't she? So, by what miracle would she have fallen in love with you if it hadn't been for me?"

"Give me the presidency and disappear forever," Macaire suggested. "I promise you'll be left alone."

"I know that my position is untenable. If you don't kill me, someone else will. I'm a condemned man – my only hope is to disappear. However, I can still block your appointment. Unless, of course . . ."

"Unless what?"

"Unless you exchange Anastasia for the presidency. It's time to decide which of the two you're ready to give up."

In Cologny, when the police had left, Anastasia rushed to the office. She found the notebook where Macaire said it would be. It was empty, except for a few lines of numbers on the first page. Inside was a letter. She was too nervous to read it at that moment. She shoved the notebook and letter into her travel bag and called Lev to warn him. Less than twenty minutes later, the black limousine driven by Alfred passed through the gates of the property. Anastasia left the house, her bag in her hand, and quickly stepped into the car, which left at once and drove down chemin de Ruth, heading for central Geneva.

The limousine reached Geneva from quai du Général-Guisan and crossed the Mont Blanc Bridge before arriving at the Hôtel des Bergues. They entered the hotel through a back entrance, used for deliveries, so that no-one would see Anastasia.

"Monsieur asked me to take precautions," he explained, entering the underground parking area. "You'll be safe here."

"Thank you, Alfred. I was very afraid – you have no idea. I'm still shaking."

"I'm very sorry you had to go through that, Madame."

"You know, it's not so much the robbery that frightens me; it's the context. My husband was very disturbed. He talked to me about some banking documents. And, even though the man wore a hood, I thought I recognised him."

"Was it someone from the bank?"

"I don't know. He seemed very nervous. It was all very strange."

Finding herself in Lev's suite, Anastasia felt better at once. She closed the door and locked it, served herself a glass of wine to calm down, and drank it while enjoying the spectacular views of Lake Geneva. She walked to the fireplace and lit a fire, then picked up the notebook she had taken from the office. She read the letter. It was signed by the president of the Swiss Confederation and thanked Macaire for his service. What service? What could it mean? She decided to follow her husband's instructions. She threw the letter into the fire and watched it burn. She began to do the same with the notebook, but as she was about to consign it to the flames, she noticed some shadowy lines on the pages she had thought were blank.

Feverishly, she exposed the paper to the heat. Suddenly, writing appeared. She began to read, her heart beating wildly.

Switzerland, this harbour of tranquility, with its green pastures and blue lakes, is also a country that protects its banks like a mother bear: fiercely. You have no need to know more than that. Myself, I hardly know anything more. "Order and symmetry" is our motto; silence and prudence our children. Twelve years ago, I was recruited by a special branch of the Swiss intelligence services. This clandestine unit is called P-30; it's financed by a hidden government fund and is not under the control of Parliament's Intelligence Committee.

Anastasia was stunned to learn of the double life her husband had been leading all these years. Feverishly she read his account of the missions he had undertaken for P-30. Macaire, her kind Macaire, her somewhat clumsy and awkward husband, had been an agent of the intelligence services. She would have been almost impressed and amused if the narrative hadn't taken a tragic turn.

> *I have to confess here and now: I have several deaths on my conscience. Reluctantly, I participated indirectly in the elimination of a former bank computer technician and his wife, who had attempted to send client lists to the Spanish tax authorities.*
>
> *[...]*
>
> *I regret the blood that has been spilled because of me. I didn't want that – ever. If someone is reading these lines, it's because things turned out badly. Whoever you are reading this now, you must believe me: I have never wanted to see anyone die. I was unaware of P-30's dark plans. I was raised to believe in Christian love and I hope that one day these sins will be washed away. May God forgive me!*

Anastasia interrupted her reading. She was terrified. She was shaking. She now understood the president's letter thanking Macaire for his service to the country. She continued reading.

> *My final mission will take place at the bank's Gala Weekend in Verbier.*
>
> *P-30 has asked me to prevent Sinior Tarnogol from taking control of the Ebezner Bank.*
>
> *I have very little leeway in the matter. Either I convince Tarnogol to appoint me president, or I will have to kill him. I know that, should I fail, P-30 will accuse me of the double homicide in which I indirectly participated.*
>
> *I would never have believed a day like this would come. But I can't feel sorry for myself because I'm responsible for the situation. I am the one who enabled Tarnogol to get where he is by transferring my shares to him.*

And because this document is my confession, there remains one secret that I have to reveal here. I must reveal to you what Sinior Tarnogol gave me in exchange for my shares.

Anastasia put her hands over her mouth as if she were going to scream. It was impossible. What she was reading couldn't be the truth. Tarnogol couldn't have done that. She felt the tears well up. She tried to remember what had happened, how she had broken it off with Lev fifteen years earlier, but her memories were suddenly hazy.

She again read what Macaire had written. How could Tarnogol have done such a thing? The man was evil incarnate. She grabbed her phone and dialled Macaire's number.

"Hello, dear, is everything okay?"

"Macaire, I . . . I . . ."

She began to cry. He understood then that she had read the notebook.

"Please don't say anything. These calls are not secure."

"What now, Macaire?"

"I can't tell you. But what I'm going to do, I'm going to do for you – for love. Hang up the phone now; I don't want *them* to know where you are."

She hung up and burst into tears. She sensed that something terrible was about to happen.

31

The Lucky Star

On Saturday, June 30, 2018, at eleven in the morning, as I was sleeping soundly in my suite at the Verbier, recovering from a night spent writing, I was awakened by a series of knocks on the door. At first I assumed it was the cleaning lady and decided to stay in bed. But when my visitor insisted, I went to the door, half asleep. It was Scarlett.

"Everything okay?" Her tone of voice was annoyed rather than concerned.

"I'm fine, thanks. Why?"

"We were supposed to have dinner last night. But no doubt you had better things to do."

"Damn, I completely forgot. I'm really sorry."

"I'm sorry, too. I waited for an hour at the restaurant like an idiot."

"Why didn't you call my room? I would have come at once!"

"Well, that's exactly what I did. It was busy. The reception desk said you had probably left the receiver off the hook. So I came up here and knocked on the door. Nothing. I'm sure you were out enjoying yourself somewhere."

"No, I was definitely here in my room last night."

"Stop with the stories!" Scarlett interrupted. "Do what you want at night, but don't take me for a fool."

"I'm telling you I didn't intentionally stand you up. I was writing, I got completely carried away."

"To the point that you couldn't hear me knocking at the door?"

"You know, when I'm living the story, I'm completely consumed. It's as if I was inside the book, part of the background. And there were all these characters around me."

"What are you talking about?" she said with exasperation.

"But it's the truth. It's as if I'm in another world. Listen, let me make it up to you. Let's have dinner tonight. Please."

She seemed to hesitate.

"Please, it would make me very happy."

"Alright. But I'm warning you, the book excuse will work only once."

"I promise."

That evening, after writing all day, I met Scarlett at the Italian restaurant in the hotel.

"Thanks for meeting me," I told her.

"Did you think I was going to stand you up?"

"I would have deserved it."

"I get the feeling that the more progress you make with that book, the less I see of you."

"I let myself get carried away."

"Does this happen often?"

"Every time I write a book."

"I don't like feeling that I'm losing the battle against your book."

"Please accept my apologies."

To change the subject, I offered Scarlett a small package. I had gone to the village bookshop to buy her a gift.

"About the book – I brought you something to read."

She opened the package. It was a copy of *Gone with the Wind*.

"It was one of Bernard's favourite books. He told me he read it during the war. He must have been thirteen or fourteen, escaping in a car with his mother and brother. He read it in the back seat as they drove. Word was going around that Italian planes were bombing civilian convoys, and Bernard, deep in his reading, hoped that the planes wouldn't kill him before he finished the book. He said it was a great novel."

275

"What *is* a great novel?"

"According to Bernard, a great novel is a painting – a world offered to the reader who allows herself to be wrapped up in the immense illusion created by the author's brushstrokes. The picture shows rain: you feel wet. A cold, snow-covered landscape? You start to shiver. Bernard would say, 'You know what a great writer is? A painter. In the museum of great writers, to which all bookshops have a key, thousands of paintings await you. If you enter once, you'll keep going back.'"

She smiled.

"I talk a bit about Bernard in the book," I said.

"What would he have thought about that?"

"He would have been flattered – and bothered by it. He would have said to me, 'If it makes you happy.' Like all great men, he was modest. He didn't like to be the centre of attention. He never liked to celebrate his birthday, which was May ninth. Of course, I always called him to wish him well. To tell the truth, I think he didn't like to celebrate because it reminded him of his age. It reminded him that he was born in 1926. When the papers referred to him as an 'old publisher', it drove him crazy. One day, boarding a plane that was going to take him back to Paris from Milan, where he had accompanied me to celebrate the Italian edition of one of my books, the steward asked him to change seats with a young woman. 'Why?' he asked. The answer came back, 'Because you're sitting next to an emergency exit and you're too old. The rules forbid it. You need to have the strength to open the emergency exit.' Bernard said, 'I'm stronger than this young woman.' The steward insisted, 'You have to change seats, Monsieur.' 'Then she and I can arm wrestle,' Bernard insisted. 'The winner can sit here.' The steward refused, obviously, and forced Bernard to change his seat. He was furious for a week. 'Can you imagine!' he said. But I didn't want to imagine. I wanted to believe that Bernard would live forever. I wanted to believe he was invincible."

After a brief moment of silence, I continued.

"I remember his last birthday – last May. Eight months before he died. I called him to wish him well, and this time, he didn't get angry. In fact, he said to me, sort of amused, 'You know, Joël, I tell myself that if the police inspect my identification card in the street, they'll be so surprised when they see my birth date, they'll say to me, *But why are you still here?*'"

"And what did you say?" Scarlett asked.

"I laughed. I told him he'd bury us all – not to reassure him but because I truly believed it. In spite of the sixty years between us, in spite of his age, I had the impression that he was eternal. And since I was convinced that Bernard would always be there, I told myself that he would be my only publisher."

"What do you mean?"

"Publishing is like love. You can really love only once. After Bernard, there won't be anyone else. After the success of my second novel, everyone believed I was going to leave Éditions de Fallois and sign up with a more prestigious publisher. 'What are you going to do now?' people would ask me. 'You'll certainly have offers from the biggest names in French publishing.' But the people who asked the question hadn't understood that the greatest name in French publishing was Bernard."

* * *

Paris, May, eight months after the immense success of my second novel.

A journalist came to interview Bernard at the offices of Éditions de Fallois at 22 rue La Boétie. Bernard didn't really like interviews, but he sometimes agreed to play the game when I asked him. I was present in the room as well. After a few painfully banal questions, the journalist looked at Bernard slyly and asked him, implying that I would yield to the siren call of the great names along Saint-Germain-des-Prés:

"Do you think you'll publish Joël's next novel?"

I became purple with rage and had to stop myself from kicking the journalist in the arse and throwing him out. Bernard simply smiled maliciously and replied, "If Joël's next novel isn't good, I won't publish it."

I'll never forget that line, which summarises my relationship with Bernard all these years. Bernard had written a contract that didn't require I publish my next book with him.

"One book at a time," he explained. "If you no longer want to work with me, I don't want to force you."

"And I'm not asking for an advance. You'll pay me as the book sells. If it's successful, we'll both be better off; if not, at least we'll have had a good time."

"Success is the pleasure of working together," Bernard reminded me, enthusiastically.

Not being our primary concern, our contracts were always signed at the last minute, often as the new novel was being printed.

Not only was he able to make me successful, Bernard taught me how to manage success, mostly through the constant reminder that everything remained to be done. He was a little like a boxing trainer who tells his protégé after the first round, "That was just the first round. There's eleven more to go."

Exactly a year after my second book came out, he wrote the following email to me:

Today is an anniversary. On September 19, 2012, Harry Quebert made its way into bookshops in France, Belgium, and Switzerland. I'm not fond of birthdays, but this one I enjoy because it shows the extent to which everything in life holds together, is connected, and assumes greater significance.

On that September 19, I recall going to the Libraire Fontaine to see whether the book was in the window. It was. Of course, it wouldn't be in every window, because we had broken every rule and convention to prepare this launch, but in this bookshop – they're friends, whom we contacted – it was.

Looking happily in the window, I remembered that beautiful passage in Proust where he describes the death of Bergotte:

"They buried him. But throughout the solemn night, in the illuminated displays, his books, arranged three by three, stood watch, like angels with their wings unfurled, and appeared to be, for the one who was no longer, the symbol of resurrection."

What lesson can be drawn from this? That you have published only two books, and if you wish to one day catch sight of them, arranged three by three, in bookshop windows, you will have to write many more.

I hope we can look at them together and that we'll remember Proust's apt words of caution.

My dear Joël, I'm sure you share my belief that we should never be too confident or let ephemeral success make us complacent, but all the same, thinking of the year that has passed, it seems that it wasn't bad at all.

Bernard

* * *

I raised my eyes from the screen of my phone, where I had gone to search for Bernard's email so I could read it to Scarlett. "Bernard will always live in me."

"What would you say to him if he were here, at the table, opposite you?" she asked.

"I'd tell him, 'I miss you, Bernard. Paris isn't the same now that you're not there. You changed my life, Bernard. I've never been able to thank you.' He would have laughed and said to me, warmly, 'You did it,

Joël. Don't worry about it.' And I would have replied, 'You know I don't think I want to publish novels if you're not around.' He would have laughed again and said, 'But you wrote before you met me, and you'll write after. Besides, you're already in the middle of a book.'"

I thought about how difficult it is to praise extraordinary men. We don't know where to begin. Bernard gave meaning to my life. He always looked out for me. He was my lucky star. But stars fall.

I was moved, and I felt that Scarlett was too. She put her hand on mine, looked deep into my eyes. From either side of the table, our faces drew closer and our lips as well. Suddenly, a voice interrupted us.

"Madame Leonas?"

We turned. A small man in a suit was smiling at us.

"Excuse me for disturbing you, Madame. I'm the assistant manager of the hotel. I was told you wanted to speak to someone in management, and I wanted to make sure that your stay has been satisfactory. I was told it had something to do with your room."

Scarlett reassured the assistant manager by explaining to him that she simply wanted to ask some questions about the events that had taken place in room 622.

"If you like, and even though it's not exactly confidential, I would prefer that we discuss the matter in a more secure location. Why don't we meet later and discuss this calmly?"

After our dinner (of absolutely exquisite pasta, with fresh tomato and basil sauce for Scarlett and butter and sage sauce for me), the assistant manager invited us for a nightcap in private. He met us in the manager's office, a comfortable room, with traditional furnishings. In front of the fireplace were four armchairs facing one another, highly suitable for conversation.

"I know that you questioned the concierge about room 622," the assistant manager told us. "We are trying to forget that tragic episode. As I was telling you, the murder is not a secret, but, in general, we feel a harmless lie is preferable to the truth so we don't frighten the clientele."

"Now that we're speaking honestly, what can you tell us about the murder?" Scarlett asked him.

"Unfortunately, I can't really help you. I wasn't working at the hotel at the time."

"Who was the manager at the time, then?"

"Edmond Rose," he replied. "The original owner. It was he who built the hotel. He ran it and was its embodiment for decades."

While speaking, he pointed to a painting that hung above the fire-place representing a man in a military uniform.

"Is that a portrait of Monsieur Rose?" Scarlett asked.

"Absolutely. From what I have been told, Monsieur Rose was an extraordinary man. Lieutenant colonel in the Swiss army reserves. He had natural charisma and he knew how to command, but he was also a man of great tenderness."

"Would you know how we might reach Monsieur Rose?" I asked.

"Unfortunately, he passed away several years ago."

"We would really like to speak to an employee of the hotel who was present the weekend of the murder," Scarlett added.

The assistant manager thought for a moment before replying.

"You know, the staff turnover is quite high. But I think that Monsieur Bisnard should be able to help you. He's our former banquet manager; he spent his entire career here at the hotel. He retired a year ago, but he still lives in Verbier. I often see him in the morning at the café next to the post office. You're sure to find him there."

32

Last Chance

Saturday, December 15, the day before the murder

It was dawn, and the great day had arrived.

At six in the morning, Cristina left her room at the Hôtel de Verbier and walked down the corridor, her steps muffled by the thick carpet. The sixth floor was unique in that all the rooms were suites, which were always assigned to bank bigwigs. Cristina had arranged it with Jean-Bénédict Hansen so she could reserve a room on what the other employees of the bank called "the floor of the chosen". In truth, she hadn't really given him a choice.

To reach the elevator, she had to make her way down the entire hall-way, passing before the doors to the suites. These were all on the same side of the hallway. The opposite wall was the front of the hotel, with alternating bands of broad windows and thick velvet drapes. The suites were assigned to the various department managers and then, in the fol-lowing order, to Horace Hansen, Jean-Bénédict Hansen, Sinior Tarnogol, Lev Levovitch, and Macaire Ebezner.

Cristina descended to the ground floor. Everything was silent; the lobby was deserted. The hotel appeared to still be sleeping. Most of the bank's employees were taking advantage of the comfort of their rooms, away from their families, to sleep late and relax.

But the apparent quiet of the hotel was merely a façade. In the kitchens and corridors, the hotel's staff were already on a war footing. They only had a few hours to get everything ready. At six p.m., the bank's employees would be waiting in the ballroom for cocktails. At seven, everyone would be invited to approach the large dais. Then the bank's board of directors would appear and officially open the evening's ceremonies by announcing the name of the new president. The guests would then be seated, and dinner would be served. The ball would start at ten.

At that early hour, in the hotel bar, still closed to guests, Monsieur Bisnard, the banquet manager, paced back and forth. He was very nervous. Suddenly, loud knocking on the bar's glass door caused him to jump: it was Cristina. He hurried to open the door.

"I don't like this," he said to her as she entered the bar.

She closed the door behind her.

"If it's any consolation, neither do I."

"I could get in trouble!" Bisnard protested.

"Me, too!"

She was taking a big risk. What if Bisnard talked? She knew she was crossing a line but so what – she had to know. Since Monday, when she had overheard the conversation between Tarnogol and Jean-Bénédict Hansen, she had been convinced there was something suspect about the election. It seemed that Macaire was willing to pay any price to become president. She was determined to discover the truth.

"Here's the list of all the bank employees here this weekend and their room numbers."

"Who's in charge of assigning the rooms?" she asked.

"Jean-Bénédict Hansen gave us the general outline."

"Was Macaire Ebezner involved? Did he contact you at the last minute, this week, to ask you to make any changes?"

"No, not at all. Why?"

Cristina, failing to reply, continued questioning Bisnard. "So, as far as you're concerned, everything is as normal?"

"Perfectly normal. I also spoke to the hotel's head of security last night. Everything appears to be completely calm. I think you're overreacting."

"Maybe," she admitted.

"You should enjoy your weekend," Bisnard advised, turning his back on her as he hurried out of the room.

After leaving the bar, Cristina went to the restaurant, where breakfast was already being served. Unsurprisingly, the tables were empty. She sat down, ordered a coffee, opened a newspaper, and waited.

Macaire got to the restaurant at seven. Cristina noted that he looked tired and stressed. Seeing his secretary, he forced himself to smile.

"Hello, hello, Cristina!" he greeted her with feigned enthusiasm.

"Hello, Monsieur Ebezner. Everything okay? You don't look well."

"To tell the truth, I'm a bit worried. I'm in deep shit, as they say."

"Because of the presidency?"

"No. Well, yes. I'm not going to lie – I'm very nervous. I barely slept last night."

"Oh, don't worry, Monsieur Ebezner, I never spoke to anyone about what I heard the other day at the bank."

"That was a misunderstanding. It's out of the question that Lev will become president. I'm the one who's going to be appointed."

"If you say so."

Macaire sat down at a table, alone. This behaviour was not at all typical. Usually, he would have sat down with Cristina to chat. Something out of the ordinary was going on.

Six floors above them, in his room, Lev was pacing, his phone in his hand. Since the night before, he had had no news of Anastasia. She hadn't replied to his messages or his calls. And no-one answered the phone in his suite at the Hôtel des Bergues. He was starting to worry. Although it was early, he decided to contact Alfred, even if it meant waking him up. Someone would have to find out what was going on. The situation might be serious.

*

At seven fifteen, Tarnogol arrived in the restaurant. He sat alone at a table off to the side reserved for members of the board. He ordered soft-boiled eggs, caviar, a small glass of Beluga, and black tea with a hint of milk. Macaire couldn't take his eyes off Tarnogol. There were less than twelve hours before the election. Macaire was losing control of the situation.

When Tarnogol had finished eating, he left. Around eight fifteen, Jean-Bénédict appeared, as if he were looking for someone. As soon as he saw Macaire, Jean-Bénédict rushed over to his cousin's table.

"You're here! I have to talk to you. Come with me."

The two men walked towards the hallway.

"What's going on?" Macaire asked his cousin.

Without replying, Jean-Bénédict led him to a private room. Horace Hansen was there, waiting, seated in an armchair as if on a throne. He examined Macaire with an air of superiority and announced, as if he were Caesar preparing to save a gladiator, "I'm going to give you my vote for president. I've spoken with Jean-Bénédict at length about this, and we agreed. It's you, and only you, who should be president."

Macaire's eyes glowed.

"Thank you, Horace. I appreciate your support."

"My support has a price. Here are my terms."

In Geneva, at the Hôtel des Bergues, Alfred Agostinelli paced back and forth in Lev Levovitch's suite. Anastasia had disappeared. He had knocked on the door for a long time, without a response. He finally entered the room with his duplicate key. The place was empty, the bed unmade. Her belongings were no longer there. In the fireplace, he found the cold embers of a fire. He poked around the ashes and in the chimney flue. There, stuck to the stone wall, he found a piece of scorched paper that had risen from the fire before it had been completely consumed. There were traces of handwriting on it, but he was unable to decipher what had been written. He phoned his boss at once.

Lev got Alfred's call as he was getting ready to leave the room. Lev listened, uneasy, to his chauffeur's remarks.

"If the bed was unmade, that means she slept there," Levovitch concluded. "No sign of a struggle?"

"No, Monsieur. No disorder. I think she left. She took her things. You don't take your toothbrush when you've been kidnapped."

Lev found Alfred's reasoning reassuring.

"Ask around the hotel. Maybe they saw something."

"Good idea, Monsieur. I'll get in touch the moment I hear anything."

Lev hung up. Anastasia's disappearance worried him, and he needed to think about this calmly. He decided to go to the bar for a coffee; he would have some peace and quiet there.

In the private room at the Hôtel de Verbier where they had gathered, Macaire listened attentively to Horace Hansen's demands.

"I want you to appoint Jean-Bénédict vice president of the renamed Ebezner-Hansen Bank. I also want you to agree to retire in fifteen years and transfer the presidency to my son. You'll have had a fine career; you'll be able to take a well-deserved rest. And Jean-Bénédict will have a few good years ahead of him to take control of the bank."

After a silence, Macaire agreed. It suited his needs to a tee. Fifteen years of power, after which he would depart from the summit. Everyone at the bank would miss him. The weeks prior to his departure, everyone would be crying, "What will we do without Macaire?" Fifteen years of being an exceptional leader. Adored by his employees, admired by the wider profession, and then he would leave. He would make a moving speech, and everyone would be in tears. And then he would be replaced by the incapable Jean-Bénédict, who would be the laughing stock of the entire industry. Oh, how he would get back at this frog who wanted to puff himself up to be as big as an ox! No-one could fail to make the comparison between them, and Jean-Bénédict as president would be forever in the shadow of his cousin and predecessor. Macaire thought how his father and grandfather should have done the same: quit their jobs while at their peak, leaving their mark on those who came after, rather than hanging on through old age and illness.

"Okay. You have my word."

Jean-Bénédict, bursting with joy, praised his cousin.

"I was afraid you would refuse."

"How could I refuse? I know what I owe you, Jean-Bénédict. You've always been loyal. And we're family, after all. We're like brothers."

Seated at the counter of the bar at the Hôtel de Verbier, Levovitch ordered a strong coffee. The bar had just opened, and as he had hoped, he was the only client. Levovitch observed with nostalgia the red velvet armchairs and low ebony tables. He allowed himself to be overcome with emotion: it had been fifteen years, and nothing had changed.

* * *

Fifteen years earlier

It was an afternoon in early August, one month after Lev had brought Anastasia from Brussels to Geneva. The summer had been scorching on the plain, and people were flocking to the mountains for the cooler air. The hotel was fully booked, and several very important and demanding clients had come to take the air in Verbier. But, as the summer season had begun quietly, Monsieur Rose hadn't anticipated the sudden influx of customers, and the hotel was not adequately staffed.

Sol helped out at the reception desk and assisted in greeting the new arrivals. That morning, he was behind the desk with Lev. Lately, Sol had noticed that Lev was irritable.

"You okay, son?" Sol asked between guests.

"I'm fine, Dad," Lev replied laconically.

"You look worried."

"Too much work at the hotel. We're overloaded."

But that was not the reason for Lev's concern. When he had returned to Geneva a month earlier, he had spoken to his father about Abel Ebezner's proposal. The man was furious.

"Geneva? Why?" Sol assumed an air of disgust. "We have only bad memories of the place."

"No," Lev protested. "I have good memories – with Mother, when she came to get me at school, our walks by the lake."

"Geneva took your mother! Geneva and the bankers! And you, you come here to tell me that you want to work in a bank in Geneva! What a betrayal. I didn't expect to be treated like this, especially by my son."

"We're not going to stay in Verbier all our lives," Lev shouted.

"And why not? Our acting careers are here now. And don't tell me you're not an actor; you have extraordinary talent. That's your problem, in fact – you're talented at everything. I can't believe you want to leave. And to surprise me like this. It's because of that girl, that Kamouraska, isn't it?"

"Anastasia," Lev corrected.

"Anastasia, whatever. It doesn't matter. You always said you were happy, and as soon as you meet this girl, you run off to Brussels in the middle of the night, and now you want to go and live in Geneva. You know, Lev, girls come and go."

"She's different. Papa, I want to marry Anastasia."

Sol sniggered.

"Marry! You see why you're such a great comic, my son. You really are a romantic – like your mother. Why do you want to tie yourself down with the first one who comes along? Whatever. Go if you want to go. Betray me, drop me like an old sock, I understand. You're ashamed of where you come from, right? Do you want to be like Abel Ebezner, like all those smart guys who parade around during the Gala Weekend?"

"That's not it, Papa."

"Then what is it? If you're going to go, at least give me a good reason."

"Look, Papa, the bank was just an idea. Nothing's been decided."

"So decide not to leave. It's as simple as that."

That's what Lev did. He called Abel Ebezner to decline his offer. But, hanging up the phone, he promised himself he would soon leave Verbier and get far away from his father. That also meant giving up becoming manager of the hotel. It would be impossible for Lev to run the hotel with his father looking over his shoulder all the time. Lev had to leave for good.

Anastasia was very disappointed that neither the Verbier prospect nor the one in Geneva would come to be. But Lev promised her that this was only a partial setback – a matter of a few months, no more. Meanwhile, she had gone back to living with her mother. Thanks to Macaire, she had secured a job as a secretary at the Ebezner Bank. The job allowed her to earn a living; she put all her money aside for a future project with Lev. Even if she didn't love what she was doing, it meant working with Macaire, whose company she enjoyed.

Every evening Anastasia and Lev called each other.

"When are we going to be together?" Anastasia always asked.

"Soon."

"When is soon?"

"I'm waiting for a sign. Life is full of signs."

And while waiting for a sign from destiny that never arrived, he had resumed his job at the hotel.

Behind the reception desk, Sol's voice tore Lev from his thoughts.

"My son, I have to tell you something."

"Go ahead, Papa."

"When I asked you not to go to Geneva and to remain here, it was for a very good reason."

"I know, bankers killed Mama."

"No, no, it has nothing to do with that. It's true that I keep going on about it, but don't forget that I'm an actor, and I sometimes overdo it. No, there's something very important I have to tell you. I should have told you a while ago."

Sol's voice trembled and he looked serious.

"I'm listening," Lev said, suddenly uneasy. "What's going on?"

Sol hesitated. At that moment, an employee appeared at the door that led to the hotel's back corridors.

"Lev, Monsieur Rose wants to see you in his office."

"Go, son. Don't keep him waiting. What I have to say isn't that important."

Lev acquiesced and walked off to find Monsieur Rose.

"What's going on, Lev?" Monsieur Rose asked, after the younger man had taken a seat in the armchair opposite his own. "For a month, ever since you've got back from Brussels, you haven't been yourself."

"I'm very sorry, Monsieur Rose."

"I don't care if you're sorry. I want to know what's bothering you."

"Nothing."

"Nothing?"

"Nothing."

Lev's silence irritated Monsieur Rose.

"Look, Lev, I don't know whether this girl has turned your head, but I need to make sure that all my employees are up to the job. Right now, there are some very important guests staying at the hotel, and I want to be sure that I can count on you whatever you're doing."

"Of course, Monsieur Rose. You can count on me. I won't disappoint you."

"Then go to the bar. It's going to be busy soon. I want to see outstanding service."

Lev obeyed and went to the bar. He had barely walked into the room when he ran into Tarnogol, seated in an armchair, who collared him.

"Young Levovitch, perfect timing. I'd like my black tea with a hint of milk, and you're the only one who knows how to do it."

Lev acquiesced and prepared the tea as he had always done. But this time, Tarnogol didn't find it to his liking.

"Not good. Too bitter. Make me another."

Lev did as he asked. But the next cup was judged to be too hot.

"I want to drink the tea now," he whined. "I don't want to wait hours for it to cool. Make me another."

Lev prepared him a new cup of tea, adding some water to cool it. But this time, it was too cold.

"Hot tea has to be hot! Not tepid, not cold. Otherwise I would have asked you for a tepid tea or a cold tea. What's going on with you?"

That was all it took for Lev, who had been on edge all day long, to lose patience.

"Listen, Monsieur Tarnogol, if you're not happy, make your own tea instead of wasting my time."

Tarnogol opened his eyes very wide. There was a brief silence, long enough for Lev's insolence to register. Then he began to yell. "What did you say? You impertinent little wretch. How dare you speak to me in that tone of voice."

Everyone in the bar froze. Lev immediately regretted his lapse, but it was too late.

In a state of rage, Tarnogol screamed, "Get me the manager! Get me the manager at once!"

A few minutes later, Lev was in Monsieur Rose's office.

"I can't get over it. How could you do this to me?"

"I can explain."

"I don't want your explanations!" Rose replied, deeply affected by the situation. "You always have a good explanation. Look, Lev, I warned you not to step out of line."

"I'm sorry . . ."

"It's too late for being sorry, Lev. Unfortunately, I don't see any other way out of this: I have to let you go."

"What? But why? You know that Tarnogol is unreasonable."

"Why? Because you must never lose your cool with a client. It's one

291

of the fundamental rules I taught you. I overlooked the hullabaloo after that business at the ball, but no-one here would accept it if I kept you on after a second incident. I have no choice, Lev. It's time for you to leave. I think that letting you go is probably the best thing I can do for you."

Shocked, feeling tears of rage well up in his eyes, Lev left without asking for his pay. He crossed the great hall at a run in order to reach the main entrance of the hotel. He tore off his name tag and threw it on the ground. He wanted to leave at once and forever. As he walked down the hotel's front steps, a taxi pulled up. The rear door opened and Lev heard someone call his name. He froze. It was Anastasia. Not believing his eyes, Lev ran to her. She threw herself into his arms.

"What are you doing here?" he asked.

"Life is too short to waste it waiting around. Come to Geneva with me, Lev. Let's be happy together."

He held her against him as tightly as he could and kissed her. He felt his heart come alive with a feeling of wild happiness.

"Yes, let's go."

That very day Lev left Verbier with his belongings to settle in Geneva. Monsieur Rose, standing at the window of his office as he watched Lev walk away, his luggage in his hand, murmured, "Goodbye, my son." A tear rolled down his cheek.

* * *

Twenty years earlier

Verbier was in a state of feverish animation. Every government official, every noteworthy person in the region had rushed there to be present for the inauguration of the majestic building that just been completed. It was not yet open, but everyone said it would be one of the jewels of the Swiss hotel industry. Journalists and guests were all focused only on the project's promoter, Edmond Rose, a businessman, barely forty years old, who, starting from nothing, had amassed an immense real estate fortune. A radio journalist, brandishing his microphone, asked him, "Monsieur Rose, when you've built something as ambitious as this hotel, would you say that your life has been a success?"

Edmond Rose thought about the question for a long time. Everything he had ever done had been met with success. While at school, he had been an outstanding student. He had completed his required military service and left the Swiss army reserves as a lieutenant colonel. He had started a business career and was now the head of a small empire. But he was alone. He had spent too much time running around the world in search of money and had never had a serious relationship. For now, all he wanted was to start a family. That was why he had built the hotel. He wanted to settle in Verbier, step back from his businesses, and assume the management of the hotel. Meet a woman, start a family. Lead a normal life.

* * *

Twenty years later, Monsieur Rose, at the window in his office, watched Lev's silhouette disappear in the distance. He would miss him terribly. Lev's presence at the hotel had been a daily source of joy ever since his arrival. But it was time for Lev to strike out on his own. The hotel, as large as it was, had become too small for a man of such ambition.

To console himself, Monsieur Rose told himself that, for the first time, he had come close to what he really wanted from life. He had never known love. He had no children. But he had Lev. He had loved and been loved.

One day Lev would have children. And he would be like a grandfather to them. Monsieur Rose, examining his reflection in the mirror, smiled. He would leave a small mark upon this earth.

33

Betrayals

In Verbier, the day of the Gala Weekend, it was three p.m. when Macaire, having just finished lunch, returned to the hotel. In two hours, the board would meet for the final vote.

Macaire had left the hotel in the late morning; he had felt the need to clear his head and find some peace and quiet. He could no longer bear running into bank employees, all of whom flattered him, calling him "Mr President" and smiling complicitly. It all made him nervous. He needed to calm down, so he had gone for lunch at the Dany, a small restaurant he liked, which was located at the bottom of the ski slopes, within walking distance. The walk had done him good, improving his appetite, and he had ordered a croque-monsieur followed by a fondue.

As Macaire passed the reception desk at the hotel, an employee who recognised him called out.

"Monsieur Ebezner, I wanted to let you know that your wife is here."

"My wife?"

"Yes, I'd never had the pleasure of meeting her before, Anastasia Ebezner. That is your wife, correct?"

"Yes, absolutely."

"Madame Ebezner asked me for a key to your room and, since you were out, I took it upon myself to provide her with one."

"That's fine."

Macaire hurried to his room. But once inside he was disappointed to find that Anastasia was not there. However, she had left on the bathroom mirror a note in red lipstick.

I'm here, my love.

A.

Her tube of red lipstick rested on the edge of the sink. Macaire picked it up and kissed it. She exclusively wore lipstick from a small boutique in Paris, and Macaire often complained when he travelled to the French capital for P-30 and had to cross the crowded city to get it for her. Right now he adored that lipstick – venerated it. Anastasia was here. She had come to support him. They would get through this struggle together; they would get through it together and more in love than ever before. Macaire was overcome by a powerful feeling of joy. That small tube of red lipstick, and everything it symbolised, suddenly made him feel strong and happy – ready to face Tarnogol and secure the presidency that was rightfully his. Macaire wanted to see her, to hold her close to him. Where was she?

She was in the wardrobe, a few feet away from him, watching through the crack between the doors but not daring to show herself. At first she had hesitated about coming to Verbier. Then, when she got there, she had hesitated about going to the hotel. How would he react to seeing her there? What would they say to each other? She had carefully prepared for this moment but felt so feverish that she no longer knew what to do. She didn't even know why she had come. To support him and be by his side for the most important day of his career? Or to tell him the terrible news – that it was all over and that, back in Geneva, he would come home to an empty house? Maybe it would be better to say nothing rather than risk spoiling his big moment. Most of all, she wanted to know how he would react to seeing her there.

As she was getting ready to reveal her presence, she suddenly heard a series of dull sounds. As if someone were knocking at a window.

Macaire jumped and turned in the direction of the French windows leading to the balcony.

"Wagner!" he yelled, when he caught sight of his case officer on the balcony.

She remained hidden. Wagner? Who was that? She heard Macaire open the window and go out to the balcony, closing it behind him to prevent the cold air from filling the room. She was unable to hear what the two men were discussing.

"Wagner! In heaven's name what the hell are you doing here? You scared the crap out of me."

"I've been standing out here for hours, freezing my arse off, waiting for you," Wagner complained. "Where did you disappear to?"

"I went to get some air, if you don't mind."

"You think this is the time to get some air? We're only a few hours from the announcement. Can you explain why Tarnogol is still alive?"

"Don't worry, everything is under control. Horace and Jean-Bénédict Hansen are voting for me. They gave their word that I'll become president."

"How can you suddenly be so certain?"

"We made a deal. In exchange for their votes, I'll name the bank the Ebezner-Hansen Bank and, in fifteen years, I'll turn it over to Jean-Bénédict. It's in the bag."

Wagner made a face. "I don't understand your procrastination, Macaire. It would have been so much simpler to eliminate Tarnogol. Well, do what you want so long as you become president. But I don't think it's very wise to have placed your fate in the hands of the Hansens. All it would take is for Tarnogol to turn them . . ."

"If Tarnogol steps out of line, I'll kill him." Macaire interrupted, waving the vial of poison that had been in his pocket.

At those words, Wagner stared at him as if he were an idiot.

"You really are an amateur, Macaire. It's already too late. The poison takes twelve hours to act! I did warn you about that. You should have done it last night. What are you going to do if he dies after securing Lev the presidency?"

"Shit."

"No, I must be dreaming. You have continued to disobey my orders. If you had followed our plan from the start, we wouldn't be where we are now. Sometimes, there's no other choice, Macaire. Have you learned nothing from your twelve years with P-30?"

"So what am I supposed to do to get rid of Tarnogol?" Macaire asked, suddenly unsettled by the fact that he had no contingency plan.

There was a paper bag at Wagner's feet. He took out a bottle of Beluga vodka.

"This bottle is your last chance, Macaire. Its contents are poisoned. Get Tarnogol to drink a glass; he'll be dead in fifteen minutes. Convulsions, cardiac arrest, and the job is done. In principle, it can't be detected during an autopsy."

"In principle?"

"It's not undetectable, unlike the other poison, which acts slowly. But there's little chance that a medical examiner would perform the tests needed to detect its presence in Tarnogol's body. Try not to let people see you walking around with the bottle and giving it to Tarnogol before he croaks on the hotel carpet. That could attract suspicion, if you see what I'm driving at."

"But what if there's an investigation, if they perform tests, what if . . ."

"Calm down, Macaire. It'll be alright. Just have him drink a glass of this vodka, and everything will be taken care of."

"And how am I supposed to do that?"

"Based on my information, the bank's board will hold its final meeting at five p.m. I know this because the Alpes Room, where they met last night, has been reserved for them at that time. The board will have the room until seven p.m., when they'll go directly to the ballroom to announce the name of the new president. Therefore, we know that Tarnogol is going to order a vodka, in the room, around six thirty p.m. It's an old ritual with him: every day, in the morning and late afternoon, wherever he is, he orders a glass of vodka. And he drinks only Beluga."

"So, am I supposed to bring it to him myself, and then he drops dead immediately after?"

"Let me finish, Macaire, and listen carefully to what I'm telling you. Do you think P-30 works with amateurs? Orders given in the meeting rooms are not handled by the hotel bar but directly by the employee in charge of the rooms. He has a small work space next to the Alpes Room. You'll see, there's an alcove with a small counter and, behind that, an ebony cabinet with a selection of spirits inside. The employee will prepare Tarnogol's drink using the alcohol in that cabinet. You'll replace the bottle of Beluga in there with this one. You'll find some plastic gloves in the bag, wear them so you don't leave any fingerprints. To avoid any confusion, there's a red cross on the rear label of the poisoned bottle. Place the bottle in the bar. That's all you have to do."

"And if someone else orders a vodka?"

"Only the board will be meeting in that room. And there's no risk that Jean-Bénédict Hansen or his father are going to drink it – they hate vodka."

Macaire stared into space.

"I would have preferred to arrange things using my own methods, to avoid having to resort to this. I'm no murderer."

"You're acting on behalf of your country, Macaire. It's not murder, it's a patriotic gesture. Switzerland will always be grateful to you for this. Now hurry up and put the bottle in the bar by the first-floor meeting rooms. It's your last chance. You can't make any more mistakes; I hope you understand that."

Hidden in the wardrobe, she heard the balcony door open. Through the crack between the doors, she saw Macaire and another man – probably Wagner – cross the room. Macaire was holding a paper bag in his hand. Before they left the room together, she could hear Wagner say, "Your aversion to assassination is an honourable trait, Macaire. But it's time to get rid of Tarnogol. Kill him before he ruins your weekend and destroys your life."

The door closed. They had left. She stood there, frozen with fear.

In the corridor, Wagner escorted Macaire to the elevator. When the doors opened, he said to him, "Good luck, Macaire. This is probably the last time we'll see each other. Complete your mission. It's better that I don't hang around. Once you're president, it will seem as if none of this had ever happened. Not P-30, not your missions, nothing. So, goodbye. And thank you for your twelve years of impeccable service."

Macaire, in that moment, thought about mentioning the photos Tarnogol had showed him. But he decided against it. Better not to add fuel to the fire. Wagner disappeared through a service door, and Macaire rode the elevator to the first floor. He followed a corridor that led to a series of private rooms. He saw the Alpes Room. Immediately adjacent to it was an alcove, just as Wagner had described, with a counter and an ebony cabinet with a small bar.

After making sure no-one was around, Macaire put on the gloves and placed the bottle of marked Beluga among the bottles of spirits, replacing another bottle of the same brand, which he hurried to dispose of in the nearest restroom. Nervous at the idea of leaving a bottle filled with poison in an accessible place, he decided to remain near the bar and keep an eye on it, at least for a while. He noticed an armchair nearby and sat down. It was a perfect observation post. He could monitor the cabinet with the spirits and the door to the Alpes Room, where in ninety minutes the bank's board of directors would meet for their final deliberations. All he had to do was wait. If he was elected president, Macaire would recover the bottle of vodka before a hotel employee could serve it to Tarnogol. But if the Hansens did not keep their word, then Macaire would let events follow their course as planned. Tarnogol would be struck down by the poison. He would die almost instantly, overcome with convulsions. The Hansens would get the message. At that moment, Macaire realised that there would be no way to know the result of the election before the public announcement. Tarnogol had to be neutralised while he was in the Alpes Room. Macaire needed an accomplice. He grabbed his phone and called Jean-Bénédict, who was resting in his room, five floors above. Macaire asked his cousin to join him in the Alpes Room. Jean-Bénédict did as he was asked.

"Is everything alright, cousin?" Jean-Bénédict asked, looking concerned.

"Everything's fine, but I'm going to need your help."

"Of course. What can I do?"

"As soon as you know that the board is in agreement about my appointment, send me a text message to alert me."

"You can't bring phones into board meetings. Those are the rules."

"Then pretend you have to make an urgent call, and leave the room. I'll be here."

"But why do you want me to alert you? You'll be president; there, now you've been alerted."

"Just do it. Don't ask questions, do it. It's very important."

34

The Final Vote

Saturday, December 15, the day before the murder

It was four thirty in the afternoon. Lev, after a walk around the village, had returned to the sixth floor of the Hôtel de Verbier. He followed the long corridor decorated with draperies to return to his room, when suddenly, emerging from between the thick drapes, a hand grabbed him by the shoulder. He turned with a start.

"Anastasia?"

She kissed him and held him close.

"Anastasia, what's going on? I was sick with worry. What are you doing at the Verbier?"

"I had to see Macaire. He's in grave danger, he . . ."

Lev placed a finger on his lips and led her into his suite before they were seen.

"Macaire is getting ready to do something terribly stupid," she said to him after Lev closed the door to the room.

"What sort of stupid thing?"

"I think he wants to kill Tarnogol."

"What?"

"Lev, it's very serious. Macaire has been working as a spy for the Swiss government."

Lev burst out laughing.

"Is this a joke?" he asked.

"No. He's been involved in several operations to protect the interests of Swiss financial institutions. He may be indirectly tied to a double murder, of a former computer technician for the bank and his wife, who

301

were trying to turn over the names of clients to the Spanish tax authorities."

"Alfred found the remains of a notebook in the fireplace of my suite at the Hôtel des Bergues, but the contents were illegible."

"It was Macaire's confession. I burned it to protect him. Oh, Lev, if you only knew . . ."

She was unable to finish; it was too hard. Lev, who sensed she was about to collapse, held her.

"I absolutely must speak to Macaire," she said after a lengthy sob. "I just saw him. I was hiding, but he wasn't alone."

"It's better if you don't see him," he advised.

"Why?"

"Because I'm afraid that you'll abandon our plan to leave together and stay here with him. I'm afraid of losing you, as I did fifteen years ago."

"No, Lev. You're the one I want to be with. But I don't want to see him hurt. I want him to be okay."

"I'll take care of it, I promise. Macaire will be president. It'll all go well for him. You have to trust me. But don't leave this room for any reason."

Shortly after five o'clock, in the Alpes Room, the board gathered for its meeting. As the senior member of the group, Horace Hansen had been presiding over their deliberations since Abel Ebezner's demise. He decided there would be no lengthy discussions.

"It's been a year now that we've been exchanging our views about the candidates. I think that everything has been said and that everyone has had enough time to make their decision. We can move directly to a vote. I'm voting for Macaire Ebezner."

Tarnogol struggled to conceal his surprise.

"I'm voting for Macaire Ebezner as well," Jean-Bénédict announced to the group.

"Two votes for Macaire," Horace remarked, eager to finish as soon as possible. "The matter is settled."

Tarnogol, opening a leather portfolio from which he took a laptop, then said, "I have some information to share with you. I received an anonymous email about an hour ago."

It was six fifteen. Macaire, still in the corridor facing the room, was waiting nervously for a sign from his cousin. Through the wall, he could hear the sounds of an animated discussion but couldn't make out what was being said. Suddenly, the door was thrust open, and Jean-Bénédict appeared. He seemed to be in shock.

"So?" Macaire asked.

"So you've lost," Jean-Bénédict managed to gasp. "Levovitch was appointed."

"What?"

"I couldn't do anything. We went to a vote. It's over. Levovitch has been named president."

35

Happy Days

Fifteen years earlier

It was early September. Geneva was slowly taking on the colours of autumn. Olga von Lacht, appropriately attired, her head held high, entered the Beau-Rivage along quai du Mont-Blanc, followed by Anastasia.

As they did every Sunday, the two women were taking tea at the hotel along the banks of Lake Geneva. As they did every Sunday, they sat in the same chairs, and as they did every Sunday, Olga ordered for them: "A samovar of black tea and a slice of carrot cake to share." She used the word *samovar* to appear distinguished. Anastasia was now the only one required to attend the tea ceremony; Irina had been freed from these family obligations ever since her marriage to the wealth manager at the Ebezner Bank. Her mother now required that Irina devote herself to the fecundity of the couple, insisting she become pregnant "as soon as possible".

Olga was very disappointed that Anastasia had left Klaus. But she didn't know the entire story. Klaus had been careful not to mention that he had been punched in his own apartment. Officially, the couple had broken up. Olga had called Klaus's parents to ask their forgiveness: "You have to understand that I deplore my daughter's behaviour – your Klaus is solid gold."

Klaus's mother was more philosophical. "They're young, sometimes these things don't work out. Better that they find out now and avoid an unhappy marriage." Olga didn't agree, of course, but she wasn't about to say so.

That Sunday, in the salon of the Beau-Rivage, Olga told her daughter, "You had a chance to make a dream marriage, and you let your temperament get the better of you."

"I'm happier without him."

Olga mocked her daughter, imitating her voice.

"*I'm happier without him*! Look how your sister has managed – your sister! Follow her example."

"She married some bald, fat guy," Anastasia dared to remark.

"Hold your tongue, daughter. He may be bald, but he's rich. And right now, your sister lives in a villa with a pool. And you, you're back to square one. Working as a secretary. Tss! Nobody dreams about becoming a secretary."

"At least I'm earning a living. That's the start of my independence."

"Independence from nothing. My daughter, my life, you'll leave my apartment only when you're married, and well married. There, I've said it. I don't want to hear you quibble about it."

Anastasia lowered her head, and Olga reached for the teapot that was now before them. Suddenly, she heard an employee address a customer seated behind them.

"Look, here's Count Romanov."

Olga, opening her eyes wide, turned around. It was him! Oh my, what an extraordinary coincidence. She bent towards her daughter and whispered in her ear, "Count Romanov is here."

"Who's that?" Anastasia asked, pretending not to know whom her mother was talking about.

"Lev Levovitch, Count Romanov! The handsome White Russian from the Gala Weekend at Verbier."

"Oh, him!" Anastasia feigned complete ignorance. Olga rose from her chair and grabbed her daughter by the arm, dragging her along.

"Why, Lev Levovitch, Count Romanov!" Olga shouted. "What a happy surprise!"

"Dear Madame von Lacht!" He bowed deferentially.

"Do you remember my daughter, Anastasia?" Olga asked.

"How could I forget such a face?" he replied, kissing her hand.

Anastasia shivered. She wanted to throw herself at him, to kiss him hard. But she restrained herself so as not to reveal their collusion.

"What are you doing in Geneva, dear friend?" Olga enquired.

"I just gave in to a request from my friend Abel Ebezner. He's been begging me to join the bank, and I finally agreed. I would prefer to maintain my position as a man of independent means," he added with a smile, "but what can you do? I'm unable to say no to a friend. And it will keep me busy. Don't they say that idleness is the mother of all vices?"

"In any case, loyalty in friendship is the most noble of virtues," Olga added, congratulating him.

"Here I am, a Genevan, for a while at least."

"And where are you staying?"

"I've taken a suite at the Hôtel des Bergues. It's practical."

"The finest hotel in Geneva," Olga gushed.

"Yes, it really is comfortable. But from time to time, I like coming to the Beau-Rivage for tea . . . Empress Sisi, right?"

"Indeed." Olga quivered, sensing she had found her soulmate. "Young people with your good taste are rare these days. If you need a guide to help you discover Geneva, don't hesitate to ask Anastasia. She'd be delighted to show you around town. Maybe you'd like to agree to a time?"

"I don't want to take advantage of your charming daughter."

"Oh, yes – take advantage, I insist."

"It happens that I have to attend a dinner tonight with the English ambassador, and I don't have a partner."

"Anastasia is free!" Olga declared.

"I'm afraid it may be terribly boring."

"At what time should she be ready?"

*

On that soft September night on Rousseau Island in the middle of Lake Geneva, as its waters flowed into the Rhône, Lev and Anastasia laughed happily, wrapped in each other's arms on the blanket where they were picnicking.

"Dinner with the English ambassador. I can't believe she swallowed that," Lev said, laughing.

They observed the majestic façade of the Hôtel des Bergues, which rose before them.

"My mother told me that if you asked me to spend the night in your suite, I should accept. She said, 'He's handsome, he's rich; there'll be no dithering.'"

"You can spend the night in the studio I'm renting on rue des Eaux-Vives."

"That's what I want."

"One day, I'll offer you something better, I promise. You'll have the life you've always dreamed about."

She kissed him passionately to silence his talking.

"I don't give a damn about a suite at the Hôtel des Bergues, idiot. It's someone like you I've always dreamed about. The rest doesn't matter to me. Besides, why a suite at the Hôtel des Bergues? Living in a hotel makes you feel alone and without friends."

"Where would you like to live?"

"I don't know – but not in a hotel."

"Come on, there must be some place that you dream about."

"There's a house in Cologny, on chemin Byron. They say that it has an extraordinary view of the entire city. I walk by the property every time I go to the Ebezners. You can just catch sight of the house through a large gate, but sometimes I imagine living there, having my coffee in the morning on a terrace overlooking Lake Geneva."

"So let's go take a look at the house," he suggested.

"What? Now? It's almost ten p.m."

"Let's go. You can dream at any time of day."

They took a taxi and stopped in front of the property. She found herself on top of the hillside of Cologny, near the Promenade Byron, with its breathtaking view of Geneva and the lake. Lev led Anastasia to a bench, and they admired the panorama.

"Pretend we're on the terrace of that house, and this is our view."

"It is ours, even without the house."

Lev held Anastasia tightly against him. They admired the glittering lake and the lights of Geneva emerging from the darkness.

"One day I'll get you that house. One day I'll have enough to place the most beautiful treasures at your feet. Abel Ebezner is very satisfied with me. He told me he's going to give me a raise by Christmas, with an additional year-end bonus. If I stay with the bank, it shouldn't be long before I'm earning a good living."

"I don't care about money, Lev – how many times do I have to tell you? Are you happy at the bank?"

"I think so, why?"

"I was prepared to become a chambermaid at the Hôtel de Verbier so I could be with you. Don't forget that."

At the bank, Lev had been installed in the office that Macaire and his cousin Jean-Bénédict shared. A small table had been added in a corner to serve as a desk. From their handsome ebony pulpits, the two cousins, future members of the board by birthright, had accepted the presence of the newcomer – familiarly referred to as the "intern" – whom Abel Ebezner had tasked them with training.

Anastasia was working as a secretary in the legal department one floor below. She stopped by to visit them during her coffee break and sometimes for lunch. In the bank's hallways, everyone had eyes for Anastasia and Anastasia alone, whose beauty and intelligence turned heads, beginning with those of the two cousins. For the sake of discretion, she had asked Lev not to reveal their relationship. Initially, he didn't understand why they had to conceal what was going on between them.

"There's nothing wrong with being in love."

"The wrong doesn't come from us but from the others. I think it's better if we protect ourselves."

"Protect ourselves? From what?"

"From the others! You may not realise it, Lev, but they're jealous of you."

"Why would they be jealous of an intern?"

As he said that, she threw herself into his arms in an outburst of infinite love. She held his face in her hands and looked deep into his eyes.

"Lev Levovitch, you're the only one who doesn't see what's so obvious."

At work, Anastasia observed Lev's rise day by day. In a matter of weeks, Lev had become the bank's new star.

Initially tasked with accompanying more experienced bankers to meetings as an observer so that he would be initiated into the subtleties of the business, Lev found himself in the company of new clients, often foreigners, whose language and culture he understood better than anyone else at the bank. Additionally, his experience at the hotel had familiarised Lev with the habits of wealthy clients, whose demands and self-indulgence he never found shocking. He was soon the one leading the conversations. The meetings grew longer and often veered off into matters of politics and culture, even matters of existence, to the alarm of the banker who accompanied Lev.

Soon, everyone was talking about him. Colleagues, managers, and clients were unanimous: the young man was extremely talented.

Obviously, there were discordant voices. Some were offended by the arrival of this young star, who was rumoured to have been last employed at a hotel in the mountains, without any experience at all. The disquiet made its way to the board of directors, where, at that time, Abel Ebezner was only the vice chairman. His father, Auguste, was the chairman at the time. Auguste Ebezner was a man of a certain age and got around with difficulty, but he was still quite lucid and deeply attached to tradition. He came to the bank only on Wednesdays now, when the board held its meetings, but he retained the title and the aura of president, even though Abel was responsible for the day-to-day management.

"I've been hearing strange rumours," Auguste said to his son during a meeting of the board that had become particularly raucous. "I've been told about a young intern, a man without experience – apparently, some cretin from the mountains – who's been here no more than a few weeks and has already been given important responsibilities."

"His name is Lev Levovitch," Abel interjected. "And he is far from being an Alpine cretin. He's one of the most brilliant young men I've ever met."

"Levovitch?" Auguste said with surprise. "Which ghetto did he come from?"

The remark triggered laughter from the two other members of the board, who, at the time, were Horace Hansen and his father, Jacques-Édouard Hansen.

"Look," Abel continued, disturbed by their laughter, "Lev is a young man of exceptional intelligence. If he's already been given responsibilities, it's because he's very gifted. I don't see the problem."

"The problem is that he was a bellboy!" Horace Hansen objected, visibly annoyed. "You've saddled us with a hotel bellboy in wealth management. Is this a bank or a circus?"

"For your information," Abel replied, "last June, when Lev was still a 'bellboy', as you call him, he predicted the movement of the American Federal Reserve while our own experts got it wrong. All of our clients lost money that day."

"Pure chance!" Horace exclaimed, sweeping away the argument with a scowl. "He had a fifty-fifty chance. And all the local banks got it wrong – it wasn't just us."

"Everyone but him!" Abel noted.

"In any case," Horace grumbled, "I find it disturbing that Levovitch is in direct contact with our large clients."

"It's the clients who've been asking for him," Abel reminded his cousin. "You'll see, it won't be long before our competitors are trying to hire him. They're all going to try to grab him. If he leaves here, we risk losing a portion of our clientele. As for you, Horace, I don't see why you're so upset about him."

"Because he just got here and he's already been given more responsibilities than our own sons, Macaire and Jean-Bénédict, who already have a few years under their belts."

"Is that true?" Auguste enquired.

"Our sons are worthless," Abel replied. "What should I do? One is as bad as the other."

"Your son is worthless!" Horace responded, deeply offended. "Mine has done very well."

"He's done well since he started asking Lev's advice," Abel noted. "He's been running around behind him, saying 'Tell me, intern, could you give me a hand with this account?' You should see them, the two idiots, at the restaurant every day for lunch while Lev manages with a sandwich in his office, studying his accounts."

"I can't allow you to call my son an idiot!" Horace huffed.

"Calm down!" Auguste yelled. "I'm the president, and I'm the one who decides here. I don't want this Lev character to have more responsibilities than two future members of the board. Abel, I'm telling you to follow my orders and limit him to an intern's duties: photocopies, coffee, correspondence."

"Papa," Abel Ebezner retorted, "that's absolutely ridiculous."

"It's not ridiculous! Based on the bank's requirements instituted by your grandfather . . ."

"Oh, please, don't quote that old rubbish. It's a joke. Is that all you have to justify your decision?"

"Silence!" Auguste said with irritation. "I'm fed up with your insolence. As the requirement states: 'Other than by heredity, only those may become bankers who have brought in their own clients.'"

"The law of heredity is ridiculous, and so is the requirement."

"Without the law of heredity, you wouldn't be where you are today." This remark was followed by a long silence. "When this intern brings in his first real client, he can become a banker."

"But that's insane," Abel shouted. "How can he find a client if he's not an accredited banker? That's putting the cart before the horse."

"Those are my orders," Auguste replied, cutting short all further arguments, as Horace and his father, Jacques-Édouard Hansen, smirked.

Abel was forced to comply with the board's decision, and Lev was reduced to carrying out simple administrative tasks. Macaire and Jean-Bénédict were delighted with the change and made sure Lev was kept busy. To avoid causing Lev further trouble, Abel had his protégé come secretly to his office after business hours. There he taught Lev what he could never have learned in any book: the codes of Geneva's high society, the inner workings of private banks, and the behaviour appropriate to this idiosyncratic universe.

"You'll eventually make your way in this bank, Lev," Abel confided in the secrecy of his office.

"I have the impression that some people don't want me here. I'm not part of the club."

"It's because you're not part of the club that you'll get ahead. You'll become someone important."

"A great banker?"

"A great man. One day you'll shape the future of this bank."

One November afternoon, as Macaire was looking for his father in his office, he stopped on the threshold. The door was slightly ajar. Hearing voices, he peered through the opening and saw Levovitch in the room, speaking animatedly with Abel. He heard his father say, "To tell the truth, Lev, I would very much like to have had a son like you."

*

"'A son like you'," Macaire fumed a short while later at a table in the Café Remor, where he had come to meet Anastasia. "He forgets that he already has a son!"

"I'm certain that's not what he meant to say," she replied, trying to soften the blow.

"I heard him clearly."

"And what did you do after that? Did your father see you?"

"No, I didn't go into the office, obviously. I didn't want to disturb father and 'son'. I just left and came here to meet you."

Every day, just about, after office hours, Anastasia and Macaire went to the Remor, a short walk from the bank, for a drink. Macaire especially enjoyed these special moments with her. They talked and talked; she didn't seem to be in any hurry. He gazed at her, completely subjugated. He was madly in love with her and couldn't help but think that their late afternoon meetings might be the sign of shared feelings. That afternoon in the Remor, Macaire asked Anastasia, "Tell me, what do you think of Lev?"

"He's nice."

"In what sense?"

"He's just nice! I don't understand your question."

"Well, when you returned from Brussels, it seemed that you two were rather close."

"We're good friends."

"So you're not together? You would have told me, right? We tell each other everything."

She knew Macaire was jealous, and she didn't want to make problems for Lev at the bank. He had already been unfairly demoted. She felt that he was already being victimised and didn't want to make things worse. If Macaire took a dislike to Lev, he could arrange it so that his grandfather, Auguste, who was on his side, would fire Lev. She didn't want to risk losing him again. So she decided to lie.

"No, I'm not with Lev," she said with a look of complete surprise.

"That's what I thought," Macaire replied, reassured. "I think Lev is with Petra."

"Petra? The tall, dark-haired girl in accounting?"

"Yes, I'm sure of it. She's always in our office and she can't keep her eyes off him. All the same, it's better that you and Lev aren't together."

"Why do you say that?"

"It's just that . . . I think I would find it painful."

He tried to place his hand on hers, but she hurried to remove it. She immediately wanted to tell him everything but remained quiet; she didn't want to complicate things. She saw how he looked at her and had no desire to break his heart. She didn't want to hurt him. She didn't want to make him suffer. She felt an immense tenderness for this young man, who was somewhat overwhelmed by his family name but kind and considerate, always talkative, and with whom she was never bored.

Anastasia greatly enjoyed Macaire's company, but if she spent all her afternoons at the Remor after the bank, it was so she could be ready when Lev finished his meetings with Abel. She only agreed to meet Macaire because she didn't want him to suspect what was going on. She always sat facing the window. When Lev was done, he stood on the other side of the street and made a subtle sign. She would pretend that it was time for her to go and would meet her lover on a side street. They exchanged long, deep kisses, kisses that compensated for the many hours spent working so close to each other without being able to touch. They went out to dinner or to the movies, and they ended the day at his apartment, where she often spent the night. Now her mother had given her daughter complete freedom, imagining she was staying at a suite in the Hôtel des Bergues and securing her future.

That evening, as they were having supper in a small restaurant in the Eaux-Vives quarter, Anastasia said to him, "I hear that Petra is making eyes at you."

He burst out laughing.

314

"More than her eyes. I should think about filing a complaint. Who told you?"

"Macaire. I prefer that he thinks you're with Petra rather than learning that we're together."

"I think you're wrong." Lev blushed.

She assumed an air of false severity.

"Don't get too close to Petra."

"If I could tell Petra we're a couple, she'd leave me alone."

"Just tell her you have a fiancée abroad."

He raised his eyes and laughed, then took her hand and kissed it.

He was so terribly happy.

They could see their whole life before them.

Yet, it was all about to collapse.

36

The Banquet Manager

It was Sunday morning, July 1, 2018, and Scarlett and I were trying our luck at the café next to the post office. The owner, after serving our two espressos, told us that Monsieur Bisnard had not yet arrived but should be there shortly. And a half hour later, a man entered the premises.

"Denis, there's a visitor for you," the owner announced to him, pointing at us with her chin.

He approached our table, and we rose to say hello.

"You're the writer?" he asked after I introduced myself.

"And I'm Scarlett Leonas, the writer's assistant. In reality, I'm the one doing all the work."

"It's often that way," Bisnard replied, shaking her hand. "Who told you I would be here?"

"The assistant manager of the Hôtel de Verbier," I explained. "I apologise for intercepting you like this, but we had to talk to you."

"About what?"

"The murder in room 622."

Bisnard looked very surprised. The three of us sat down; he ordered a coffee. We told him everything we knew, which probably convinced him of our seriousness. He asked us to excuse him for a moment and went outside for a short while, long enough to go to his apartment nearby and return with a shoebox.

"I loved working at the hotel. I've kept a few souvenirs."

He opened the box and showed us the relics from his years at the hotel: photographs, menus, and newspaper articles about the sophisticated galas

316

that were held there. Scarlett examined all the items attentively; suddenly, she recognised two men in one of the photos.

"Is that Edmond Rose?" she asked, making the connection with the portrait hanging in the hotel manager's office.

"Yes," Bisnard agreed, "and next to him is . . ."

"Abel Ebezner," Scarlett interrupted before he had time to finish his sentence.

"I'm impressed," Bisnard admitted. "Monsieur Rose and Abel Ebezner knew each other well. Monsieur Ebezner was a regular client of the hotel. Apparently, it was Monsieur Rose who convinced Ebezner to celebrate the bank's annual meeting at the hotel."

"You mean the Gala Weekends," Scarlett said.

Bisnard smiled.

"You're quite well informed."

Bisnard told us that the bank's Gala Weekends were not only very lucrative for the hotel but also provided it with a certain prestige. That success was primarily the result of Edmond Rose's connections; he was the one who had made Abel Ebezner a loyal client.

"Why did this tradition of the Gala Weekend end?"

"The bank said it was a budgetary matter, but in reality, I believe that nothing was the same after what happened."

"After the murder, you mean?"

"Yes. Why are you so interested in this, anyway?"

"Pure chance – a detail that intrigued us. We discovered that room 621A was formerly room 622 and that the number had been changed after a murder took place there. That made us want to look a little deeper."

"It was ridiculous to change the room number," Bisnard said.

"Whose idea was it?" Scarlett asked.

"Monsieur Rose's. However, you have to put his decision in context. In a quiet ski resort, where not much ever happened, the murder caused a shock wave. And especially at the Verbier! The guests felt safe from everything there, in another world – a cocoon, as we say today. From one day to the next, everything changed. A murder! Can you believe it? The following weeks were a disaster – customers cancelled one after the other. The hotel was empty and the ski slope as well. It took us an entire season to get back on our feet. Monsieur Rose didn't want to hear another word about room 622, so he simply decided to get rid of it. He would say, 'Room 622, a room to be forgotten!' To avoid the problem of changing all the room numbers on the floor by putting 623 in place of 622, he decided to rename it 621A. We changed the room number on the door and the reference in the computer, and that was that. Everything was forgotten."

"Who found the body the morning of December sixteenth?" Scarlett asked.

"An intern. Poor guy. He was supposed to bring breakfast up to the room. I recall that I had seen the order come in just before leaving the night before. The order was for a large caviar, two soft-boiled eggs, and a glass of Beluga vodka."

"Caviar and vodka?" Scarlett said with surprise.

"Yes. When he reached room 622, the intern found the door ajar. Since no-one came to answer his knock, he simply pushed it open. That's when he saw blood on the floor and the body."

"You were at the hotel when the body was discovered?"

"No, I was at home. It was a crazy night at the hotel, and I got home late; it must have been one in the morning. My wife was the one who woke me. She said that the police were at the hotel."

Continuing her exploration of the shoebox, Scarlett suddenly smiled at a sheet of paper.

"Is this the programme for the last Gala Weekend?"

"I see nothing escapes you," Bisnard remarked. Scarlett held out the sheet so that I could get a closer look.

EBEZNER BANK – GALA WEEKEND
DECEMBER 14–16

PROGRAMME FOR SATURDAY EVENING, DECEMBER 15

6:00 P.M. • WELCOME DRINKS

Beluga cocktail

7:00 P.M. • OFFICIAL ANNOUNCEMENTS

7:30 P.M. • DINNER

Amuse-bouches
Duck foie gras and home-made jam
Crab ravioli
Striped sea bass in a salt crust and seasonal vegetables
Gâteau Saint-Honoré with crème chiboust
Tea, coffee, and petits fours

10:00 P.M. • COMMENCEMENT OF THE BALL

"Why did you keep it?" Scarlett asked.

"After the murder, during large receptions, Monsieur Rose would wave it at the staff and tell them, 'Never forget that the best-organised events can go terribly wrong. What happened that night is probably the worst thing that can happen to a hotel manager.'"

"But this is the programme for December fifteenth," Scarlett noted. "I thought the murder took place on the morning of December sixteenth. What happened on the night of the fifteenth?"

Bisnard stared at us for a moment before replying.

"The bank reception turned into a disaster."

37

A Concerted Effort

Saturday, December 15, the day before the murder

Standing at the entrance to the Alpes Room, a stunned Macaire repeated, "Levovitch president? But how is this possible?"

"My father voted for Levovitch."

"Your father? But we agreed—"

Jean-Bénédict interrupted his cousin.

"I'm well aware of what we had agreed! But you forgot to share one little detail with us, you filthy little traitor!"

"Jean-Bénédict, what's come over you?"

"What's come over me is that I know everything. You wanted to sell the names of our foreign clients to the tax authorities to bring the bank down."

* * *

One hour earlier, in the Alpes Room

"I have important information to share with you," Tarnogol told the group. "I received this anonymous email an hour ago."

He opened his laptop, and a video played. From its appearance, the video had been taken with a hidden camera. Macaire was on screen, in an empty restaurant (in Milan, judging by subsequent footage). Opposite him was a man in a suit who, to judge by the conversation and the man's accent, was a representative of the Italian tax authorities.

"Do you still want to sell the names of your Italian clients who are hiding money in Switzerland?" the man asked.

"Absolutely," Macaire confirmed without blinking.

"Why would you do that?"

"I've already told you. I was shoved aside when it came to choosing a president. For three hundred years the management of the bank has been handed down from father to son. But my father has always considered me inadequate."

"You understand the consequences of what you are doing? The bank could be investigated by foreign states for tax evasion. Given the fines and the legal costs involved, the bank could be ruined and banned from operating in some foreign markets."

Macaire didn't flinch. He stared at his interlocutor and said, "Our affiliate in Lugano has a number of Milanese clients who cross the border every day to deposit cash. Does that interest you?"

"We're prepared to pay a great deal for your list."

"How much?"

The man wrote a number on a piece of paper and handed it to Macaire. The amount was not visible, but Macaire appeared satisfied with the suggested amount.

Macaire then said, "There's more. I want guarantees of my safety. I want to be able to move here, to Milan, and to have the assurances that I won't be extradited if the Swiss government comes after me."

The recording stopped.

Tarnogol closed the lid of his laptop.

Jean-Bénédict and Horace Hansen looked completely terrified.

"That's the man you're about to name president," Tarnogol said to them.

* * *

"I would never betray the bank!" Macaire insisted to Jean-Bénédict after he reported what had just happened.

"Then explain that video."

"It was a trap. I'll explain everything, I promise. But you have to help me. Time is short."

"Help you what?" Jean-Bénédict asked, no longer knowing what he should believe.

"Become president."

"But, didn't you hear what I said? Levovitch has been named. It's over."

"No, it's not over. It's not over!"

"The vote has taken place. In forty-five minutes, the board will leave the room and go to the ballroom to tell everyone that Levovitch is the new president."

"The vote may have taken place, but no-one knows the results."

"No-one except my father and Tarnogol."

"Your father can be reasoned with. As for Tarnogol, he's not leaving that room alive."

Jean-Bénédict stared at his cousin.

"What? What are you saying? Macaire, you're starting to scare me."

"Levovitch's name won't be announced at nine o'clock in the ballroom; mine will."

With those words, Macaire rushed to the bar and opened the cabinet doors.

"You're going to bring this bottle of vodka to Tarnogol," he ordered his cousin. "Serve him a large glass, and you may as well serve your father a glass as well. But make sure, make absolutely sure you don't drink any."

Macaire stopped talking and observed the shelves before him, horrified. After a moment's silence, he cried out, "It's not possible!"

"What?"

"It's gone."

"What's gone?"

"The bottle is gone. It was here – right here. I'm sure of it, since I'm the one who put it there."

Macaire was stunned. His poisoned vodka had disappeared from the bar.

He had a sudden realisation. Returning from the restroom where he had emptied the good bottle of vodka, he had seen a server carrying a case of bottles.

"What's come over you, Macaire?" Jean-Bénédict asked, confused.

"Come with me," Macaire said, heading towards the service door the employee had disappeared through.

Jean-Bénédict no longer understood what was happening but he followed his cousin obediently. The service door opened on to a storage area where food from the kitchen was kept. Several people were busy inside, rushing back and forth to supply petits fours for the ballroom, where cocktail hour was just beginning. Monsieur Bisnard, the banquet manager, who was monitoring their efforts, caught sight of Macaire and Jean-Bénédict and came over to greet them.

"Can I help you gentlemen?"

"Beluga vodka," Macaire said. "A bottle of Beluga, in the bar, next to the Alpes Room."

"You want Beluga vodka in the Alpes Room?" Bisnard asked, trying to understand.

"No. There was a bottle of Beluga in the cabinet of the bar next to the room, and it's no longer there."

"If it's Beluga you want, that's not a problem," Bisnard reassured him.

He pointed to cases of Beluga stacked against the wall.

"You don't understand. I need the one that was in the cabinet. There was a bottle in the bar, and someone took it."

"One of my staff, most likely. I told them to bring all the Beluga vodka in the hotel back here to make sure we had enough for the cocktail hour. The welcome drink that will be served to the guests is made with Beluga; it was one of Tarnogol's requests."

Macaire recalled what Tarnogol had said when Macaire had brought the envelope from Basel and had been received like a king: "Beluga, the vodka of victory!" Tarnogol had never had any intention of choosing anyone but Levovitch for president. Macaire pulled his cousin aside to speak to him privately.

"We have to check the cases. Help me find the bottle. There's a small red cross on the rear label. You can't miss it."

"What's so special about that bottle?" Jean-Bénédict insisted.

"It doesn't matter."

"If you don't tell me, I won't help."

Macaire had to admit everything to his cousin.

"It's poisoned," he whispered.

"What! You want to poison Tarnogol?"

"I'll explain. It's more complicated than that."

"So, you really were planning to kill him?"

"We don't have time for lessons in morality, Jean-Béné. Help me find the bottle now before something terrible happens. Open them all. We have to find that bottle."

The two men rushed to the cases of vodka and, as Bisnard looked on aghast, they removed all the bottles, one by one, and examined them. Nothing.

"Were there any others?" Macaire asked the manager.

"There are some bottles at the bar in the ballroom."

The two cousins rushed to the ballroom and shoved past the line of bank employees waiting at the bar. Among them was Cristina in a pretty blue dress, who waved her empty glass as she greeted Macaire.

"You have to try this cocktail, Monsieur Ebezner."

Macaire didn't reply but ran over to the bartender.

"You have any Beluga vodka?"

"Of course, everyone's been asking for the Beluga cocktail. Can I make you one?"

"I want to see the bottles."

The bartender, somewhat offended by Macaire's brusqueness, obeyed and handed him the bottle of Beluga placed before him. Macaire grabbed it. The bottle was marked with a red cross. It was his bottle. Terrified, he saw that it was nearly empty. Half the assembled guests had drunk the poisoned vodka.

38

The Announcement

Saturday, December 15, the evening before the murder

It was 6:40 p.m., and no-one had got sick. In the ballroom of the Verbier, the cocktail hour proceeded without the slightest disturbance. Macaire and Jean-Bénédict, in the background, had examined the state of the guests before bowing to the evidence: no-one had been poisoned.

"False alarm," Macaire reported, greatly relieved. "Everything's going to be alright."

Jean-Bénédict was at the end of his tether.

"Everything is alright? How can you be so sure? Maybe the poison takes time to work." He pointed a threatening finger in the direction of his cousin. "I'm warning you, if anybody dies . . ."

"The poison is supposed to work in less than fifteen minutes. They would already be dead. I'm guessing that the bartender served such small amounts that the drinks were harmless."

"Even a small dose could be deadly. You're out of your mind."

"You don't understand. Tarnogol is a threat to the bank. You don't know the half of this story."

"The only threat that I can see is you, Macaire. I'm not going to let you involve me in your criminal affairs. There's nothing more to be done, do you hear me? Levovitch has been appointed. He's the president. What are you going to do? Take a gun and kill him in front of everyone?"

With those words, Jean-Bénédict left the room.

"Where are you going?" Macaire asked.

"I'm returning to the Alpes Room to join the board. Tarnogol and my father must be wondering what I've been doing. And given the way this has been going, I'm not looking forward to anyone remembering having seen us together. You'll sink alone, Macaire. All these years, you've been your own worst enemy. It's your own fault you're not president."

As Jean-Bénédict walked out, Macaire had to admit that maybe his cousin was right. He only had himself to blame. In twenty minutes, Levovitch would be appointed. Macaire would be the laughing stock of the bank, of all Geneva. Worse, he would be considered a traitor, ready to sell his clients to the tax authorities. P-30 wouldn't come to the rescue. On the contrary, P-30 was going to crush him. His life was over.

He returned to his suite, a defeated man. The evening room service had already taken place: the bathroom had been cleaned, and Anastasia's note on the mirror erased. Macaire wondered where she had gone. He had the impression that he was losing control. He knew what he had to do. He had been planning it since yesterday evening.

From the wardrobe, he took out the suit he had had made for his appointment as president. He put it on. He put on his gold cufflinks. On his wrist, he wore one of his best watches, which he had brought just for the occasion. He carefully knotted his tie and buttoned an elegant waistcoat. Inside his jacket, he had had the following embroidered: "M. E., President". He looked at it sadly. He stared at himself in the mirror. He had never looked so good. This is the way he should have become president. This is how he would die. And this is how they would find him. Tomorrow, a cleaning woman would find his body lying on the carpet, covered with his coagulated blood.

He headed for the small safe in the room and took out the pistol. He loaded it and stuck the barrel in his mouth. The gesture calmed him. In a few moments it would all be over, at last. He closed his eyes, pushed the barrel further into his mouth, and placed his finger on the trigger. His last thought was for Anastasia.

Suddenly, there was a banging on the door. And Anastasia's voice could be heard through the wall.

"Macaire? Macaire, are you there?"

He opened his eyes and came to his senses, took the weapon out of his mouth, and put it on the dresser before rushing to open the door.

"Anastasia! I'm so glad to see you. Thank you for being here. Thank you for coming."

He wrapped his arms around her for a long time, then stepped back to admire her face, which was perfection itself. She looked upset; he was, too.

"Macaire, we have to talk about what I read in your journal."

He put a finger to his lips and drew her into his room so they would be out of earshot of anyone who might be listening.

"How is this possible?" she sobbed when Macaire had closed the door behind them. "How could Tarnogol have done that?"

"Tarnogol is the devil."

"Is it true what you wrote? You made a pact? You exchanged my hand for your bank shares?"

"Forgive me, Anastasia. Please forgive me. But at the time, I was desperate. I wanted to marry you so badly – you had told me that you were in love with Lev . . ."

"But how is this possible?" she moaned, not fully understanding what he was saying. She tried to recall how it had all started.

"The engagement ring," Macaire told her. "The sapphire that I offered you fifteen years ago. Tarnogol gave it to me. He told me that, because of that ring, you would agree to marry me."

Anastasia stood there, distraught. None of it made any sense. She wondered whether Macaire had lost his mind.

"You always told me that you transferred your shares so that we would be happy, you and I," she said to him.

"That's true."

"I thought you wanted to get away from the bank, live a different life, not the life of a banker, because you knew how I felt about it."

"No, I gave my shares to Tarnogol so that we could be together."

Anastasia didn't know what to believe. She felt more confused than ever.

"The announcement is in five minutes," she said. "You should go. It's your moment of glory."

"I'm not going to be appointed."

"What?"

"Levovitch is going to be named president."

"Macaire, what are you talking about? That's impossible."

"I've lost."

Looking miserable, his head lowered, he decided to confront his fate. Seeing Anastasia had given him the courage to handle his defeat with dignity.

* * *

It was almost seven p.m. The ballroom at the Hôtel de Verbier was bubbling with excitement. Shortly, the board would announce the name of the new president. All the bank employees had gathered before the large stage at the back of the room; the board members were about to make their entrance.

Macaire, brilliant in his three-piece suit, entered the room. A server greeted him with a glass of champagne. Macaire drained it in one gulp to calm his nerves. He mixed with the joyous throng of employees, drinking a second glass of champagne to help him remain calm.

Suddenly, the room fell silent. Sinior Tarnogol, Horace Hansen, and Jean-Bénédict Hansen appeared onstage. Horace approached the microphone and spoke. "Ladies and gentlemen, the Ebezner Bank board of directors has made its decision. The new president has been appointed, and we are proud to announce that . . ."

He was unable to complete his sentence for, at that moment,

someone in the audience collapsed, dragging with him a tablecloth laden with glassware. Guests nearby rushed to his side, and someone asked that a doctor be called. An uneasy silence settled over the room.

"Is everything alright?" Horace Hansen asked, unsure what to do.

Then a second guest doubled over and fell to the floor. Then another, and another, until the guests were falling like flies, clutching their stomachs and gasping for breath. Before long, the assembled crowd was vomiting on the floor.

39

Unhappy Days

Fifteen years earlier

It was early November, and snow had begun to fall in Verbier. The cold had settled in for the winter.

Lev arrived at the hotel and, with a smile, affectionately observed the façade of the imposing building. He had been in Geneva for three months now. He returned often to spend the weekend in Verbier and visit his father and Monsieur Rose.

Lev entered the hotel's main lobby. Seeing him, Monsieur Rose called out, "The prodigal son!"

Whenever he returned to the hotel, Lev was received like a hero by its owner.

"Hello, Monsieur Rose," Lev said in reply, a little embarrassed by the older man's enthusiasm.

"Follow me, I have good news for you."

Monsieur Rose led him into his office, where he served coffee.

"You'll never guess who came last week. Go ahead, you'll never guess. Abel Ebezner! He wanted to make plans for a Gala Weekend. Well, we discussed it, and he was full of praise for you, effusive praise."

Monsieur Rose had been astonished, although not entirely surprised, by his protégé's rapid ascent. He couldn't help but take a paternal pride in Lev; Monsieur Rose considered himself partly responsible for the boy's success.

"I've been sidelined," Lev announced. "I think there's been some unrest at the bank, and I've been relegated to doing what interns normally do."

"I know. Abel Ebezner told me what happened. He mentioned his father, who is, apparently, very old-fashioned. But Abel also told me that his father is very sick. His kidneys are failing, he—"

"Auguste Ebezner is indestructible," Lev interrupted, "they've been predicting his demise for years."

"Are you going to let me finish? Auguste Ebezner is dying. It's a matter of weeks. Abel told me – confidentially, of course. But I know you won't repeat it. Abel will be announced as the new president during the next Gala Weekend."

"That means Macaire will become vice president."

"Exactly," Monsieur Rose gushed. "And once his son is on the board, Abel Ebezner will no longer feel that his loyalties are torn between the two of you. He told me everything. As of January, he'll officially make you a banker, with your own clients. You understand what that means? You're going to make more money than you've ever dreamed of. You'll be among the leading bankers in Geneva – at your age!"

Lev couldn't help but smile. The promotion would open the doors to Geneva's high society. He would no longer have to hide his relationship with Anastasia; she would no longer have to lie to her mother about his identity. From now on, he was somebody. He had succeeded. His name was going to mean something. And the money! He could ask Anastasia to marry him. The ceremony would be held in a year or two, just enough time to put some money aside. Maybe think about a mortgage, too. Maybe, in a few years, depending on how well he did, assuming he lived up to Abel Ebezner's expectations, he could buy the house on chemin Byron, with the terrace overlooking the lake. In the meantime, he'd rent a magnificent apartment in a fashionable neighbourhood in Geneva, ideally one close to the bank. He liked rue Saint-Léger, very close to the old part of town and opposite the Parc des Bastions.

Monsieur Rose interrupted his daydreaming.

"I've put you in a very good room for this weekend."

"You didn't have to, Monsieur Rose; I can sleep on the sofa at my father's place. Already, the last time . . . It's really too much."

"Come, it's not at all too much. It gives me a great deal of pleasure. We have to celebrate your success."

Lev's father was much less enthusiastic than Monsieur Rose about his son's career. That same day, as they were having lunch together in a restaurant in Verbier, Sol told him, almost reproachfully, "The bank has changed you. You're different."

"Different? How?"

"Different." Sol offered no explanation.

Lev, wishing to change the subject, told his father proudly, "Monsieur Rose offered me a room at the hotel for the weekend."

"Exactly what I've been telling you. You stay at the hotel like a client now. You've gone over to the other side. Perhaps you'd like me to carry your luggage to the room?"

"Oh, stop, Papa, you're being ridiculous."

"Well, tell me about Geneva and your extravagant life down there."

"It's not extravagant, Papa. I work hard to prove myself, but everyone is trying to hold me back."

"I thought you'd already been given responsibilities."

"They took them away. They told me that until I bring in a big client, I have to remain an intern."

"You always want to go faster than the music," Sol said, reproachfully.

"Papa, whose side are you on?"

"Come on, don't get angry. And that pretty blonde you ran off to Geneva with, how is she?"

"Anastasia."

"Anastasia, right. What a charming young woman."

Lev talked about Anastasia at length. He told his father how much he loved her and how happy she made him. He told him about their secret meetings after he had finished for the day at the bank, where no-one knew about their relationship.

Lev's father suddenly frowned.

"You say she's your great love, but that's not something you can hide from others."

"Yes, exactly – it's to protect us."

"Protect you! Did she tell you that? No; if you want my opinion, she's ashamed."

"Ashamed? Ashamed of what?"

"Of you. Of who you really are. Look at us, Lev, we belong to the race of little men."

Hearing his father's remark, Lev struck back.

"No. Anastasia says it's better this way. People wouldn't leave us alone. They detest it when couples are happy together. Why, to get her mother off her back, Anastasia told her that I'm a Russian prince: Count Romanov! And it worked – her mother has left us alone."

Sol, far from finding the anecdote humorous, was annoyed.

"Count Romanov? Why? Because Lev Levovitch isn't good enough?"

"You don't understand. It was a joke. Besides, you should be pleased. I'm doing a great job interpreting the character of Romanov."

"You see," Sol replied, "you'd make an amazing comedian."

"Papa, I don't want to be a comedian. I want to be a banker – have a position, money."

"Oh, really? Because you think that money will make you better and more interesting? Don't forget who you are and where you come from – Lev Levovitch, son of an actor. A banker! When I think that you go around passing yourself off as a count!"

"Count Romanov!" Olga was exclaiming at that same moment, sitting at her table at Chez Roberto, during her weekly lunch with her daughters.

Irina, without understanding exactly what her mother was saying, looked delighted. Seated next to her, Anastasia lowered her head. Olga kept talking.

"I preferred to wait a while before telling you, Irina. I wanted to make sure it was serious. And now you know. Your sister is seeing Count Romanov, and they're madly in love."

"Is he rich?" Irina asked.

"Rich? You mean filthy rich – yes. And richer than that even. He gives charity to the rich. Anastasia, dear, tell your sister where he lives."

"He has a suite in the Hôtel des Bergues," Anastasia said quietly, burying herself deeper in her lie.

"A suite at the Hôtel des Bergues!" Olga shouted. "Can you imagine!"

Irina was furious that her sister had found a husband richer than her own wealth manager. Anastasia was going to overshadow her again.

"You know," Anastasia went on, "money isn't that important. What's important is that he's wonderful, kind, generous, smart, and as handsome as the day is long."

"Tell us the rest," her mother interrupted. "You haven't told us anything."

"It's a large suite," Anastasia mumbled.

"We want to know the details, my daughter. You spend every night there."

"Anastasia sleeps over?" exclaimed Irina, who had never been allowed to sleep anywhere but at home before her marriage.

"Every night," her mother announced proudly. "For a good cause. And so, what about the suite?"

"It's really very nice, very luxurious, with an amazing view of Lake Geneva."

"Is there crystal and jade everywhere?" Olga asked.

"Yes, everywhere."

Olga shivered with delight.

"And he has a job, this Count Romanov?" Irina asked.

"Well," Olga replied, "and this is the best part, he's Abel Ebezner's right-hand man."

"He works at the Ebezner Bank?"

Anastasia wanted to disappear under the table.

"He's one of the bank's great patrons!" Olga exclaimed joyfully. "Abel Ebezner doesn't go to the bathroom without asking Lev's advice. So young and so successful. Sitting on his pile of gold, whipping those lazy employees. Ask your husband, he must know Count Romanov. You could even have dinner together."

Anastasia started to panic.

"It would be best not to talk about it. Because . . . Lev and I haven't told anyone that we're seeing each other. I'm just a secretary. It would look bad at the bank. It could cause problems for him; that sort of thing is frowned upon. Please, Irina, don't mention it to your husband; I don't want to make trouble for Lev."

"My dear," Olga said in a reassuring voice, "you have nothing to worry about. Great men consort with whomever they please. And it's about time to put a stop to this whim of wanting to work. You're going to quit that ridiculous job as soon as you're engaged. Take care of your husband – that's a full-time job."

After lunch, upon leaving the restaurant, Anastasia walked alongside her sister.

"Irina, I lied. You have to help me. Lev isn't a Romanov count. He had a job at the Hôtel de Verbier and now he works at the bank. He's not Abel Ebezner's right-hand man. He's very gifted, but for now he's only an intern."

"So you made it all up? The suite at the Bergues and all the rest?"

"Everything. It was the only way to get Mama off my back. Please, please don't tell anyone. Mama would kill me if she learned the truth; she'd stop me from seeing him."

Irina's face grew bright. She was greatly relieved to learn that her sister was living with a lowly intern, and a former hotel employee at that. Irina's villa with its pool suddenly reappeared in all its grandeur.

"Don't worry; your secret is safe with me."

"Thank you. I'll return the favour."

Irina, enjoying her superior position, couldn't help herself from giving a little lesson in morality to her younger sister.

"You shouldn't waste your time on a worthless little fling."

"I love him. I love him more than anything. I want to spend the rest of my life with him."

"You're being silly, Anastasia. There's more to life than love; think of your future."

"You don't understand, I don't give a damn about money! All I want is to love and be loved."

It was Sunday, the following morning, in Verbier. Lev was having coffee at the counter of the Hôtel de Verbier bar. A man sat down next to him. At first Lev paid no attention to the newcomer. Then, the man spoke to him in Russian.

"Driven away like a peasant, he returns as a prince."

It was Tarnogol. Lev turned to him, surprised, and nodded in greeting. Tarnogol continued.

"Rumour has it that you're destined for a great career at the bank."

"That's only a rumour, Monsieur Tarnogol."

"You're too modest, young Levovitch."

Lev said nothing and turned back to his coffee. He had no desire to speak to Tarnogol and, since he was no longer a hotel employee, he was no longer required to do so. But Tarnogol wasn't done with him.

"You owe me a favour."

"Oh?"

"I saved your life. I allowed you to leave here. Without me, you would still be a hotel employee."

"You had me fired like I was some kind of criminal."

"Come on, you know very well that's not true. If you hadn't wanted to leave here, you wouldn't have lost your temper with me in August. I'm your benefactor."

"I must be dreaming. And what do you expect of me, exactly?"

"I would like you to introduce me to Abel Ebezner."

Lev's curiosity was piqued.

"What do you want with Monsieur Ebezner?" he asked defiantly.

"I want to speak to him. I have money I want to keep safe – a lot of money. I want to deposit it with the bank."

"You don't need me to open an account at the bank."

"Don't be so sure. Auguste Ebezner has principles. He looks at the colour of money. But mine has no colour, if you know what I mean. I know that, if I come with you, Abel Ebezner will be less cautious. I know you have his confidence. It will be tit for tat. Thanks to you, I get to open an account at the bank and, in exchange, you'll get your first big client. Your career will be on its way. There's a lot of money involved."

Returning to the bank on Monday, Lev suggested to Abel that he organise a meeting with Tarnogol. Abel was delighted by the news. He had heard of Tarnogol and his wealth from Monsieur Rose at the Hôtel de Verbier. On Tuesday, in the pink room on the fifth floor of the bank, Abel Ebezner and Lev Levovitch met Sinior Tarnogol, who had travelled to Geneva for the occasion.

"I believe in your bank," Tarnogol explained. "I believe in the stability of this country. I'm happy to entrust you with a portion of my assets."

"And we're very happy to welcome you as a client," Abel assured him.

"This young man next to you," Tarnogol said, pointing to Lev, "is a rare pearl. I would like him to be my liaison at the bank."

"Lev is one of the great hopes of this establishment," Abel acquiesced. "But he hasn't yet been appointed as a banker, strictly speaking. That is to say, he doesn't have his own clients."

"I know," Tarnogol replied. "All the better. He can devote himself entirely to me. By the way, how much does someone have to invest to become a large client at your bank?"

"There are no large and small clients," Abel replied.

"This is what I would like to deposit with your bank. Tell me if that makes me a big client."

Tarnogol grabbed a pad of paper and a pen from the table and wrote down a number, a "1" followed by an interminable succession of zeros. Abel Ebezner was speechless.

"Tell me where I should sign," Tarnogol asked, "and I'll have the funds transferred immediately."

Abel, speaking like a diplomat, said to Tarnogol, "We'd be more than happy to welcome you as a client, Monsieur Tarnogol. However, before accepting your money, given the size of the investment, we'll need some information about its provenance. It's merely a formality, of course. I regret having to burden you with the paperwork, but the banking authorities are constantly on our back to make sure that we verify the origins of the money our clients entrust us with."

Tarnogol looked amused. "Well, to be clear, you want to make sure I'm not using your bank to launder money. Rest assured. Let me have the papers and I'll send them to my lawyers; I'll have them back to you by the end of the week."

The meeting concluded, the news quickly spread through the bank: Lev Levovitch was about to bring in a very large client, one who would make him one of the most important managers in the bank. The information was discussed the following day among the members of the board. No-one – not the Hansens, not Auguste Ebezner – had imagined that Lev would find such a client so quickly.

"You told me you met this Tarnogol in Verbier?" Horace asked Abel, as if to minimise Lev's role in the lucrative deal.

"No, I didn't meet him. I ran into him at the Hôtel de Verbier, where he stays often, but it's through Lev that he approached the bank. Besides, he specifically asked that Lev be his manager."

"That's too much money for an initial client," Auguste opined. "Your Lev is going to find himself in deep water, and if he can't keep up, we're the ones who are going to have to pay for his mistakes."

"A client is a client," Abel protested. "You wanted him to land one for the bank; well, that's exactly what he's done."

"He's a very good-looking man, Lev," Horace remarked with a knowing smile. "Maybe he gave Tarnogol a bit of manly affection."

"You're pathetic, Horace," Abel replied.

"Listen," Auguste interjected. "Let's wait until Tarnogol has signed before getting all worked up over this. Then we'll see what Lev Levovitch is made of."

Two days later, Tarnogol had returned to the pink room. Sitting opposite Lev and Abel Ebezner, he placed on the ebony table a thick envelope containing the different forms.

"As requested, here are the replies to your questionnaires about my money, as well as the documents required for opening an account. Everything has been signed."

"We're infinitely grateful for your thoroughness," Abel Ebezner rejoiced, taking the envelope.

But Tarnogol stopped Abel, placing a hand on the envelope to hold it back.

"One moment, please. You had your requirements, I have mine. Two, to be precise."

Abel frowned. "I'm listening."

"First, I want to make sure that Lev will be my banker."

"I still have to have it confirmed by the board of directors," Abel explained. "But it shouldn't present a problem. You have my word. What's your second request?"

"I want to buy into your bank," Tarnogol announced with a sly smile.

Abel Ebezner's face immediately froze. Lev was speechless.

"The bank is not for sale," Abel said firmly.

"I'm not a man who takes no for an answer," Tarnogol replied.

"And I'm not a man who can be forced into doing something against his will," Abel yelled.

"Let me remind you that the amount I'm prepared to deposit will position you far ahead of your competitors. You can imagine the headlines in all the financial papers at the end of the year, announcing the explosion in the assets under your management."

"I'm aware."

"So, it would seem fair to let me have a piece of the pie."

The tension slowly rose in the elegant salon in which, ordinarily, conversations were only ever cordial. Lev, feeling the situation was getting away from him, was at a loss. He should have been more cautious about Tarnogol; he had fallen into a trap once again. And now, he couldn't turn back. Fortunately, Abel Ebezner avoided any further escalation by suggesting that they take the weekend to think about Tarnogol's request. They agreed to meet the following Monday.

Tarnogol was all smiles when they next met.

"You're right," he confided to Abel Ebezner, "I had time to think over the weekend. It was a ridiculous for me to offer to buy shares in your bank."

Lev breathed a sigh of relief. Abel smiled back at Tarnogol, saying, "I'm very happy to hear that."

"After further consideration," Tarnogol went on, sounding almost light-hearted, "I want to buy all of the bank."

Abel immediately lost patience. "How dare you come into my bank and speak to me in this tone! I think we can end our discussion here."

"You're wrong to underestimate me," Tarnogol replied threateningly. "You don't know what I'm capable of."

"And you're very wrong about me," Abel replied.

Tarnogol burst out laughing. "You know the difference between you and me, Abel? It's that my means are unlimited. I'll end up buying your bank. I'll rename it the Tarnogol Bank and you'll serve me my coffee."

At those words, a furious Abel Ebezner opened the door, inviting Tarnogol to leave the premises.

Turning on his heels, Tarnogol fixed Abel with a last withering stare.

"You'll be hearing from me. You'll regret this insult."

Lev hid his face between his hands; he would be the laughing stock of the bank.

* * *

Two weeks after the incident with Tarnogol, the morning of the last day of November, Auguste Ebezner failed to wake up. The announcement of his death, so close to the Gala Weekend, sent ripples through the bank. Abel Ebezner became president, effective immediately, and his son, Macaire, as tradition dictated, would be named vice president during the Saturday evening ball, assuming his duties as of January 1.

"The youngest vice president in the history of the bank," Macaire announced proudly to Anastasia, at their customary table at the Remor.

"I'm happy for you. How do you feel?"

"It's a great moment in my life. And at the same time, I'm sad to live it alone. I mean, I saw myself being married at this point in my life – with someone by my side."

"You're rather young to be married," she remarked.

"You're never too young for marriage when you find the right person."

She understood immediately what Macaire was implying. She told him she had to meet someone and left the restaurant in a hurry.

That evening, Anastasia and Lev had their first fight as a couple. They were in Lev's studio.

"You have to tell him about us!" Lev said, exasperated. "He's going to ask you to marry him."

"He's going to be so unhappy. It will destroy him. I can't do that to him and ruin his appointment as vice president."

"So, marry him, then, that way you won't hurt him."

"Lev, please, don't be ridiculous. I know these past two weeks haven't been easy for you, after what happened with Tarnogol, but that's no reason to take it out on me, just because you're in a bad mood."

"I'm not in a bad mood. I think you should tell Macaire the truth."

"And break his heart? Why hurt him for no reason? I can keep away from him for the next two weeks. I'll let the Gala Weekend go by and then I'll tell him everything. We can wait two little weeks, can't we?"

"You know, I think you like him. Otherwise, why would you spend so much time with him?"

"Oh, please don't tell me you're jealous. I like him, but only the way you like a friend. He's sweet, kind, he has a heart of gold, he's always supported me. He's the only person who's never hurt me."

"What? What about me?"

"But you, you – Lev, I'm yours. What more do you want?"

"I think you should return home this evening."

"What? Lev, you can't be serious."

"I'm very serious. I'm fed up with being the chump."

"Fine, then you can sleep alone if that's what you want. Let me know when you come to your senses."

She was gone.

For the next three days, there was a glacial silence between Lev and Anastasia, who hardly saw each other. To avoid passing her in the hallway of the bank, Lev would arrive at dawn and leave in the early evening. Anastasia never left her floor, abandoning her customary visits to the office occupied by Macaire, Jean-Bénédict, and Lev. When her day was over, she arranged to leave the bank with colleagues and immediately returned to her mother's apartment. Macaire waited desperately at the Remor, not understanding the reason for her absence.

Anastasia had never felt so sad. She waited, in vain, for a sign from Lev, hoping he would take the first step and contact her. She refused to give in and call or go to his apartment. She felt that he had been rude and that it was his responsibility to apologise.

When Friday rolled around, she was certain he would suggest they do something together for the weekend, but there was no word from him. She spent her two days off bored and alone in her little room.

"What's going on, dear?" her mother asked.

"Lev and I had a fight."

"A fight about what?"

"I don't want to tell people at the bank that we're seeing each other. It could lead to difficulties."

"What sort of difficulties?"

"Macaire Ebezner is going to be made vice president of the bank."

"Macaire, vice president?"

"Yes. And he's very much in love with me. If he knows I'm with Lev, Macaire will get him fired. I'm worried about Lev."

Olga burst out laughing.

"You're worried about him? But he can live off his wealth; you can take off and see the world. Work is just a hobby for him."

Anastasia shrugged. She felt that this was the first serious conversation she had had with her mother. Anastasia wanted to open up to her, tell her the truth about Lev, tell her that he was no more a Romanov than she was a Habsburg. But she decided to remain silent.

"Well, we had a fight, I left, and since then he's been sulking. It's up to him to take the first step, isn't it?"

"It's up to her to take the first step, isn't it?" Lev asked his father, whom he had gone to see in Verbier. "I can't believe she didn't suggest doing something together this weekend."

"All the better, this way we can spend a couple of days by ourselves. Otherwise, you would have stayed in Geneva without ever thinking about your old father."

"I'm serious," Lev replied, failing to understand that his father wasn't joking. "Anastasia should apologise, don't you think? She's so unwilling to say anything about us, I get the impression that she thinks I'm a nobody. You know what, I should take the bull by the horns and tell everyone."

"For what purpose?" Sol asked. "If she doesn't want to tell anyone, that means there's something else going on. Maybe you're not the only one she's interested in. Maybe she really likes this other guy, the Ebezner boy. You're just a Levovitch – he's an Ebezner!"

The couple finally made up the following Wednesday, shortly before the Gala Weekend. That evening, Abel Ebezner, as was customary, organised a reception at his home to celebrate his appointment as president. All of Geneva's high society crowded into the immense residence, where a luxurious cocktail hour and buffet had been organised. Among the guests were Lev, who had been invited by Abel, and Anastasia, invited by Macaire.

Lev and Anastasia ran into each other among the crowd of guests in the living room. As soon as they saw each other, their hearts pounded relentlessly. It was all they could do to suppress their desire and stop themselves from rushing into each other's arms. They said they were going outside to have a cigarette and, once they were out of sight of the others, they held each other and kissed deeply and longingly.

"I came because I knew you would be here," Anastasia said, briefly tearing herself from her lover's lips.

"Me, too," Lev admitted.

Then, with the same voice and at the same time, they said, "Forgive me."

They both burst out laughing.

"I can't live without you," she said.

"Nor can I. I have to talk to you, though. It's important. I've thought a lot these past few days."

Lev stopped because she was shivering: it was freezing.

"Please, what is it?" she begged.

"You're going to catch your death of cold. Meet me in Abel's office in five minutes. The room at the end of the corridor. No-one's there, and it will be warm."

She smiled and kissed him once more.

Lev entered the house first, pretending to mix with the other guests, then he went to the office and waited.

Anastasia did the same. However, thinking she could get away quietly, she hadn't noticed Macaire, who was following her. As she opened the door to the office, he said to her, "Are you lost?"

She jumped.

"Macaire? You scared me. I was looking for the bathroom."

"It's the other door. That's my father's office. But come, let's go in, I want to show you something."

"You don't want to show me in the living room?"

"No, because it's in the office. Come on, go in."

She felt her stomach knot up. Lev was going to be found out. Macaire pushed open the door; no-one was there. Lev must have been delayed by one of the guests.

Macaire and Anastasia entered the room, which was warm and panelled in dark wood. One of the walls was lined with books; opposite was a bay window that looked out over the garden and, before it, a large armchair. The room was dominated by an imposing ebony desk beneath a large painting of the Ebezner Bank on rue de la Corraterie.

Macaire steered Anastasia towards the painting.

"Look. What do you see?"

"I see . . . the bank."

"My bank," he corrected. "In January, I'll be vice president. I'm the sole heir. Think of the future ahead of us."

"Us?" she gasped.

"I want to take care of you, protect you, cherish you."

"Macaire, no, wait . . ."

Without listening, he knelt before her.

"Anastasia von Lacht, I love you. You're the woman of my dreams. I want to marry you."

She felt terribly uncomfortable.

"Listen, Macaire, you know how much you mean to me. But I . . ."

He didn't let her finish.

"I know what you're going to say – that we're too young, that it's crazy. But what's so crazy about it? You know what? I understand that you might be surprised. Think about it. Tomorrow evening, meet me at the Lion d'Or in Cologny at eight o'clock. If you show up, it means yes."

It was time to tell him everything.

"Macaire, I have to be honest with you."

The door to the room opened suddenly, interrupting them. It was Macaire's mother.

"Oh, there you are. Macaire, I've been looking for you everywhere. Come, please, your father is going to make a speech."

They left the room. Macaire turned off the light and closed the door. In the darkness, Lev came out from behind the thick curtains, where he had been hiding. He remained pensive. Did she know that he had heard everything?

Joining the rest of the guests, he ran into Anastasia near the dessert buffet.

"Where were you?" she asked.

"I'm so sorry; I was held up by Abel," Lev lied. "Some people he wanted to introduce me to."

For a moment, he considered telling her that he had heard everything, including Macaire's marriage proposal, but he waited to see whether she would mention it.

For a moment, she considered telling him that Macaire had asked her to marry him and that she hadn't had time to say no, but after their recent drama, she preferred to remain silent. She would settle things herself the following morning.

Realising that Anastasia wasn't going to tell him, Lev decided to set up a date at the same time as Macaire.

"About what I wanted to talk to you about in Abel's office . . ."

"Yes, what was it?"

"Not here. Tomorrow night. Meet me at eight o'clock in the restaurant on the top floor of the Hôtel des Bergues."

"The Hôtel des Bergues?" she said, surprised.

"You'll see. Are you coming over tonight?"

"No, not tonight. I have to see someone tomorrow morning, very early."

"Who's that?"

"It doesn't matter. But it's very important."

* * *

The next morning at seven, Anastasia met Macaire at the Remor.

"Why did you want to see me so early?" he asked, settling into his seat.

He appeared to be in a very good mood. She swallowed some coffee to give herself courage.

"Macaire, you're a very nice guy, I like you a lot, but I'm not coming to the Lion d'Or tonight. I don't want to marry you."

He looked crestfallen.

"You think it's too soon, is that it?"

"No, I'm not in love with you. I'm in love with Lev; we're together. I want to make my life with him."

Macaire turned pale from the shock of the news.

"Lev?" he mumbled. "But you told me there was nothing going on between you."

"I lied – because I didn't want to hurt you – but also so that you would leave him alone. I know there have been problems at the bank because he's cast a shadow over you and Jean-Bénédict."

Macaire refused to believe what she was saying.

"And the drinks after work, here, at the Remor? Why all this circus if you didn't like me?"

"You're the one who came here every day, Macaire. I didn't ask you for anything. Listen to me. I like you a lot, I like spending time with you, but I don't think I tried to mislead you."

"Then what were you doing at the Remor if you didn't want to spend time with me?"

"I was waiting for Lev."

Macaire looked completely undone. She felt he was on the point of collapse.

"I'm really very sorry, Macaire."

"I would never have believed someone could hurt me like this."

"I'm sorry. You know how much you mean to me. I hope we can remain friends. You're someone important to me."

In response, he simply said, "How can your mother accept that you're seeing this good-for-nothing?"

"My mother doesn't know. She thinks Lev is a wealthy aristocrat."

"He won't be able to offer you the life you're looking for," Macaire declared.

"He's the life I want."

"Then, you're wrong! Think about it!"

"I have thought about it."

"I'm going to pretend that this conversation never happened. I'll wait for you tonight at the Lion d'Or at eight o'clock."

"I won't be there. I'll be with Lev tonight."

Macaire's face twisted with pain. He couldn't speak. He fled the restaurant, upsetting the table. Through the window, she watched as he walked quickly back to the bank. But Macaire didn't return to work that morning. He was too agitated to sit at his desk. After wandering around for a while in the old part of town, he decided to go to Bongénie to talk to Anastasia's mother. She was on the second floor, among a collection of fur jackets. Not recognising him at first, Olga thought he was a client. When she realised it was Macaire Ebezner, she looked terrified and tried to hide her name tag.

"Don't worry; I know everything. Anastasia told me. I just wanted to talk to you about a serious matter, Madame von Lacht. It's about your daughter. She's been lying to you about Lev."

At five thirty that afternoon, Anastasia returned to her mother's apartment to prepare for the dinner with Lev that evening. She wondered what he wanted to tell her.

She opened the door to the apartment in a good mood. She knew exactly which dress she was going to wear. There were only two and a half hours to go. She went directly to the bathroom to get ready. When she looked in the mirror, she saw her mother behind her, standing in the doorway.

"There you are, mamochka," Anastasia smiled.

"I'm very disappointed, Anastasia."

"Disappointed in what?"

"I know everything. Your Levovitch boy is nothing but a sewer rat. I forbid you to see him again."

"You can't forbid me from doing anything, I'm an adult. I do as I please."

"You lied to me," Olga screamed. "You lied to me! How could you lie to your mother?"

Overcome with rage, Olga slapped her daughter hard. Anastasia fell to the floor from the shock.

"You're going nowhere," Olga said, before slamming the bathroom door and locking it.

*

That evening at eight o'clock, at the restaurant in the Hôtel des Bergues, Lev sat at a table, waiting nervously. He couldn't stop himself playing with his mother's engagement ring, which he was planning to offer Anastasia. He had decided to ask her to marry him.

At eight fifteen, Anastasia was still not there. He wasn't worried; she wasn't noted for her punctuality. At nine o'clock he realised she wasn't coming.

He looked out over the lake. On the other shore, opposite him, was the hill of Cologny. One of the lights that could be seen shining there was the Lion d'Or. She must be there with Macaire. She had made her choice. He saw the two of them at the table, happy, laughing, eating delicious food and drinking great wines. He put the ring in his pocket and left. It was over.

40

Face to Face

On Sunday, July 1, 2018, after having spoken at length with Bisnard, I went into my office to write. Our discussion had shed new light on the affair.

But my plan failed to account for Scarlett, who didn't leave me alone for more than a few hours. Shortly before noon, she slipped into my room dressed for a walk. She grabbed the pages on the table to see where I was.

"You can't read them yet," I told her.

"Stop trying to drive me crazy, Writer. I'm curious to find out how you're going to tell this story."

"Fine, but don't mix up my pages, I haven't numbered them yet."

"Don't worry, I'm very careful with your work."

There was a knock on the door.

"What's up?" I wondered, concerned.

She went to open the door. A hotel employee entered the room, deposited a wicker basket of food, and then left.

"Are you planning not to leave the room for the next few days?" I asked.

"On the contrary, I'm dragging you out of this hotel suite. It's so beautiful outside, we have to take advantage of it. Get ready, we're leaving."

"Oh really? And where are we going?"

"For a picnic on the mountain. Get ready; I'm going to put the food in my bag."

Scarlett led me to the gondolas. We rose to the first station, from which we walked for a while along the ridge. The panorama was superb. Then, we followed a path that led through the forest and its welcome coolness. We walked along a stream and arrived at a field, from which we had an unobstructed view of the entire Alps. Scarlett, judging that the location was perfect for our picnic, spread a large blanket beneath the shadow of a tree. We sat down side by side, admiring the snow-capped mountains that rose before us. The place was imbued with a sense of absolute serenity.

"When are you returning to London?" I asked Scarlett.

"Next Monday, in eight days. And you?"

"I don't really know. No-one is waiting for me in Geneva. Some people call that freedom; I call it solitude."

"No-one is waiting for me in London, either. Only my work. And, of course, my future ex-husband's lawyer to talk about the divorce."

"So why are you going back to London, then?"

"Because I have to. I have to confront reality. And you? What reality did you escape by coming here?"

It was a moment of intimacy. I decided to tell Scarlett about Sloane, that extraordinary woman I was unable to hold on to.

"So she left you, and instead of fighting you ran away," Scarlett commented.

"You're right."

"Well, don't worry about it, Writer. If she was the one, you'll get together once your book is finished."

"I have no idea."

"You'll see," she assured me.

There was a long silence. Our bodies were closer now, and I could feel the electric tension between us. Scarlett gently touched my hand. Then, she brought her face close to mine. I stopped her just before our lips met.

"Scarlett, it's impossible. I'm sorry . . ."

41

Final Hours

Saturday, December 15, the evening before the murder

It was 7:05 in the evening. The announcement had not yet taken place.

The Gala Weekend reception had ended in chaos. A mysterious sickness had decimated the crowd. The ballroom had turned into a hallucinatory spectacle; guests were writhing on the floor and moaning. It was terrible. Macaire, in the midst of the cries and the crowd, not knowing what to do, decided to take refuge in his room. To avoid having to wait for the elevator, he took the stairs, but he had barely begun his ascent when a voice called him back.

"Is this mess all your fault?"

It was Tarnogol.

Macaire descended the few steps separating him from Tarnogol.

"It's because of me – or maybe because of you, Sinior. You wanted so badly to prevent me from becoming president. Why, really? All these people nearly died because of you."

"We've come full circle," Tarnogol said softly.

"Excuse me?"

"We've come full circle, Macaire. Look where we are: the Hôtel de Verbier during the bank's Gala Weekend. Right where we met for the first time exactly fifteen years ago. And it's all going to end tonight, right here. I have no illusions. P-30 will have my head. This is probably the last time we'll see each other, Macaire."

Tarnogol appeared resigned to his fate. He extended his hand to Macaire to say goodbye. Macaire didn't move, and Tarnogol withdrew his hand. He added:

"Now that I'm about to bow out, I can say that I've wasted my life – always too eager to make money, too eager to run the world, too eager to acquire more power. By always wanting to determine the fate of others, we forget that we can only influence our own. Goodbye, Macaire. Tomorrow, when the hotel returns to life, a single name will be heard between these walls: that of Lev Levovitch. The new president of the Ebezner Bank."

With those words, Tarnogol turned around and descended the stairs. In the background could be heard the chaos in the ballroom and the sirens of the arriving ambulances.

Macaire watched the disappointed old man disappear and wondered whether he himself was going to end up like Tarnogol. That evening, fate had given Macaire a final and miraculous chance to recover the presidency – to repair the breach he had made in his destiny fifteen years earlier when he sold his shares. He was still young then, with his whole life ahead of him. Tarnogol's words resonated in Macaire's head: you cannot influence the fate of others, only your own.

"Sinior, wait!"

Tarnogol stopped and turned around.

"I agree," Macaire told him.

"Agree to what?"

Macaire hurried down the stairs until he reached Tarnogol.

"I accept your exchange, Sinior. Give me the presidency and take back what's yours."

"Are you sure?"

"Yes."

"You're ready to lose Anastasia?"

"A part of me wonders whether I haven't lost her already."

Tarnogol stared at him.

"On Tuesday, she received a very large bouquet of white roses. 'From the neighbour,' she told me. But I talked to the neighbour myself, and she cleared it up for me."

Tarnogol nodded – as if sympathetic.

"Tomorrow, Macaire, you will wake up as president of this bank."

The two men shook hands for a long time. Then, Macaire walked back up the stairs to the sixth floor. Tarnogol's voice called to him once more.

"Macaire, you'll make a good president."

Macaire smiled then. He had the feeling that he had finally won.

In the ballroom and nearby, the commotion and noise continued. Picking their way through the general disorder, the paramedics were busy moving the patients to the hotel entrance for triage.

Anastasia, in the midst of this human scrum, looked desperately for Macaire and Lev. She couldn't find them in the entrance hall or the ballroom. Finally, walking down the corridor that led to the toilets, she found Lev, on the carpet, bent in two. "Lev!" she cried, rushing to his side. "My God, Lev! What happened?"

He was overcome by convulsions, unable to speak. He gasped loudly. She understood then that she was losing him.

* * *

Fifteen years earlier, the Gala Weekend

Friday morning at dawn, Lev left Geneva for Verbier. He had hardly slept that night. The evening before, when he realised that Anastasia wouldn't show up for their meeting at the Hôtel des Bergues, he had returned home, heartbroken, and called his father. Lev had told his father everything: the pain of being rejected, of seeing another chosen in his place. And Sol Levovitch cursed the young woman who had caused his son so much suffering.

"Come to Verbier tomorrow," his father suggested. Lev declined.

"I have no desire to participate in their damn Gala Weekend – and have to mingle with all the bank employees, Anastasia, Macaire, and the rest of them. No thanks."

"Come down; I'll cheer you up. We can go to Zermatt and spend the weekend. It's been a long time since we've travelled together, just the two of us."

Lev didn't really know what he wanted. But he agreed. He told his father he would take the nine thirty train and would be in Verbier around noon.

"We'll have a nice lunch. You'll see, it'll cheer you up," Sol told his son.

Lev felt exhausted. Stretched out on his bed, he had been unable to fall asleep. He closed his eyes for a few minutes, began to doze, and then awoke with a start. Immediately, he started thinking of Anastasia again and twisted up with pain. He simply couldn't understand. He had to talk to her. Before going to Zermatt with his father, he would find her at the Hôtel de Verbier and ask her for an explanation. He watched as the hours slid by. Finally, at around four thirty, he packed his bag. At five, he was on his way to the station at Cornavin. At five thirty, he boarded the first train for Martigny. From there, he would catch a train heading to Le Châble, then take the bus to Verbier.

At five thirty, stretched on the cold tiles of the bathroom in which she had finally fallen asleep, Anastasia awoke. She saw that the door was open. She slipped quietly into her bedroom and grabbed a few items, which she threw into a bag, and rushed to the front door. As she was leaving the apartment, she heard her mother's voice behind her, hidden in the darkness.

"Anastasia, if you go out that door, don't come back."

"Mama, I . . ."

Olga turned on the light; her face was like marble.

"It's time you behaved appropriately for your rank, you filthy little liar."

Anastasia stared at her mother. Olga, realising that her daughter was getting ready to defy her and leave, shouted, "Go! Go join your vagabond and live your miserable life. But I don't want to see you again."

Anastasia rushed out. She ran down the stairs and up the street, into the freezing dawn, her small bag in her hand. She ran as fast as she could in the hope of finding Lev. She reached the shore of Lake Geneva, then crossed the Mont Blanc Bridge. At that time, the streets were empty. She passed the English garden and finally reached Eaux-Vives. A few minutes later, she entered Lev's building. She took the stairs two by two until she got to his floor, then banged on his door. There was no answer. He was probably sleeping soundly. In her haste, Anastasia had left the set of keys he had given her at her mother's apartment. She was stuck outside. She waited for nearly an hour, sitting on the doormat. She knocked again, then finally understood that no-one was home. He had probably gone to Verbier. She rushed to Cornavin station.

At seven in the morning, crestfallen, she took a seat in the second-class car heading to Martigny. As soon as she found Lev, she would explain everything.

At seven fifteen, Lev got off the train in Martigny. During the journey, he had become hopeful. If Anastasia didn't go to the Hôtel des Bergues, she must have had a good reason. She had been kept back or prevented from going. Now he regretted his rash reaction. He had left Geneva so quickly when he should have waited for her by her building. Was she planning to come to Verbier? What if she was waiting for him in Geneva? He thought about taking a train in the opposite direction before deciding that it was better to go to the hotel. She would show up there.

Since there was a short wait before the first train to Le Châble, he decided to have a coffee in the warmth of the Hôtel de la Gare in Martigny. Seated inside, amid the hustle and bustle of the breakfast service, he observed through the window the deserted street and the small square. He had just paid for his coffee and was getting ready to leave when, to his great surprise, he saw his father in the street, a suitcase in his hand. What was his father doing here, and with a suitcase? Was he planning to leave Verbier?

Sol entered the hotel, where he mingled with the other customers. Lev, without revealing himself, watched him attentively. His father crossed the entrance hall. Lev followed. Suddenly, he had the feeling that something wasn't right. But he hadn't the slightest idea what was about to unfold.

42

The Great Reversal

Saturday, December 15, the night before the murder

It was eleven thirty at the Hôtel de Verbier. The place was calm now, but it was the desolate silence that follows a tragedy. In the ballroom, the hotel employees were attempting to wipe away the traces of the evening's chaos.

All of those who had fallen ill, taken to the different hospitals in the region, were safe. The majority remained under observation for the night, a simple precaution given that none of the cases was serious at present. Fortunately, there were no fatalities. The doctors had mentioned food poisoning. Something in the petits fours, probably? The salmon? The foie gras? The police had alerted the health authorities, and samples were being taken from the hotel kitchens. Monsieur Rose, at his wits' end, had all the refrigerators emptied and threw out any food remaining. "I don't want to take any risks," he repeated to his army of cooks, who promised to thoroughly interrogate all of their suppliers. But they couldn't understand what had happened; all the products they used were of the highest quality and freshness.

In his suite on the sixth floor, Lev closed his suitcase, as Anastasia looked on nervously.

"You sure you're okay?" she asked.

Lev had just returned from Sion Hospital. Once the doctors had treated him, he had soon felt normal again. They advised him to remain under observation, but he had insisted on hurrying back to the hotel as soon as possible.

"Everything's fine, Anastasia. Don't worry."

"You're sure you can travel? We can wait until tomorrow."

"We're not waiting any longer. We've been putting this off for too long."

She agreed; he was right. Her bag was by the door; it had been ready for days and had witnessed several failed departures. Now, they were going to leave: disappear together; forget Geneva, and the bank, and everything that had happened over the past fifteen years.

"I don't know what's going on here," Lev said, "but I doubt that this sickness was just a simple case of food poisoning."

"Why?"

"Because I was sick but hadn't eaten anything. I only had a glass of champagne and a few sips of the vodka cocktail, which was disgusting. I didn't even finish it. I can't imagine the hotel serving adulterated alcohol. And what's even stranger, Macaire, Tarnogol, Jean-Bénédict, and Horace Hansen didn't get sick."

"Are you sure?" she asked.

"Certain. I saw them. Everyone was bent in two with cramps except them."

"What does that mean?" she asked aloud, thinking of Macaire's notebook in which he described his dark plans to regain control of the bank.

"I have no idea," he replied. "But I think something very strange is going on, Anastasia. I don't know what, but the sooner we leave this place, the better I'll feel."

They would leave in an hour. Alfred had been alerted. He would pick them up at one of the hotel's service entrances so no-one would see them. He'd drive them to the airport near Sion, where a private plane would be waiting. Everything had been planned.

"A private plane to where?" Anastasia asked.

"You'll see." Lev smiled.

Anastasia smiled back. Her hand in her pocket, she played with the engagement ring Macaire had offered her. She suddenly realised that she couldn't simply leave like a coward without saying goodbye. She wanted to end their relationship the way it had begun, here, in this hotel, fifteen years earlier.

"I have to take care of one more thing," she said. "Finish packing. I'll be right back."

Back in his room, Macaire was jubilant. Seated in his chair, he observed with emotion the bearer shares that an anonymous hand had slipped under the door. Tarnogol had kept his word and returned to him what he was owed. After fifteen years, he would finally resume the position that was rightfully his.

There was a knock on the door. Macaire put the shares in the safe before opening it. It was Anastasia. She looked exhausted; he soon understood why.

"Come in," he told her, as if she were a stranger. She entered the room, sat in an armchair, and placed on a low table an object she had taken from her pocket, as if she no longer wanted it. Macaire immediately recognised the sapphire ring he had offered her when he asked her to marry him. It had been years since he had last seen it.

"It's over," she told him.

"I know."

She was shaken by his response, which she hadn't expected.

"I know you're seeing someone, Anastasia. Last weekend you weren't with your friend Veronica in Vevey. I know because, before leaving for Madrid, I wanted to send you a box of your favourite chocolates. I thought it would make you happy. I found Veronica's phone number in the old address book that you keep, and I called her to get her address. But Veronica had no idea what I was talking about. She told me she hadn't seen you in a long time. And the flowers weren't from the neighbour. There's someone else in your life."

Macaire had spoken calmly, looking at Anastasia with such intensity that she had to turn away.

"Why didn't you say something, then?" she asked.

"Maybe because as long as I didn't speak to you about it, I could hope that it wasn't true. When I returned from Madrid on Sunday evening, I asked Arma to stay with you at the house until Monday because you didn't like being alone. But, in reality, I asked so she could keep an eye on you – so that I could come here without wondering whether you were sleeping with someone else."

They looked at each other in silence. It was almost midnight. Macaire understood that he had lost Anastasia. Tarnogol had given with one hand and taken with the other.

"I was happy with you," he said.

"So was I."

After hesitating, he asked her, without being sure he wanted to hear her response, "Who is he?"

"It doesn't matter."

"You're right, it doesn't matter. Love is less alchemy than the work of time. In fact, it's mostly work. I hope you work hard so you can love and be loved."

She let a tear roll down her cheek. She loved him, but in the way she might love a brother, not a lover. She smiled and allowed herself to be overcome with memories of their youth – of the good man he had been. They looked at each other for a long time.

Suddenly, energetic knocks on the door made them both jump. "Macaire, open up!" Jean-Bénédict shouted. "I know you're in there."

Macaire turned pale and told Anastasia to hide in the bathroom. Then he opened the door to his cousin, who rushed into the room.

"Do you want to know what just happened? Tarnogol just came to see me. He gave me a letter of resignation. He's leaving the bank, effective immediately. He said that his shares have been returned to you and that he's voting for you to become president. With my vote and his, you'll be the new president. Congratulations, Macaire!"

A victorious smile spread over Macaire's face. Anastasia, from the bathroom, where she heard everything, smiled as well. She was happy for him. They would rebuild, each in their own way. But Jean-Bénédict then announced, "Except . . . I'll be the president!"

Macaire frowned. "What are you talking about?"

"For three hundred years, the Hansens have been treated as next to worthless by the Ebezners. You always considered yourselves to be superior, but that's over. Now, the Ebezner Bank will become the Hansen Bank, starting January first. My name will appear on the building on rue de la Corraterie. Because you're going to give me the shares that Tarnogol gave you. And those shares, added to my own and those of my father, will make us untouchable. The bank will belong to us from now on."

"You've completely lost your mind!" Macaire shouted.

Jean-Bénédict burst out laughing.

"You're the one who's out of his mind, Macaire. You've always been a loser. You wanted to betray the bank, you tried to kill Tarnogol, and you poisoned everyone, you lunatic. I should tell the police, but I won't if you immediately turn your shares over to me."

"You have no proof."

"Are you really willing to take that risk? For now, everyone believes that the smoked salmon wasn't fresh. That's where it will end. But all I have to do is tell the police everything I know. The investigation won't take long; the hotel cameras must have caught you putting the bottle of vodka in the bar. The banquet manager saw you search for it later like a maniac. If I talk, everyone will corroborate my claims. I can see the headline now: 'Macaire Ebezner, Poisoner!' Obviously, I'd also distribute the video of you trying to sell the client list to the Italian tax authorities. Quite the scandal, I'd say!"

Macaire closed his eyes and collapsed into an armchair.

"It's over for you, Macaire," Jean-Bénédict said.

Macaire had no choice. After some hesitation, he went to the safe and took out Tarnogol's envelope. Jean-Bénédict took it and opened it, delighted to find that the documents were inside.

"You can't be president," Macaire said. "My father expressly barred any board member from succeeding him."

"But thanks to you, the Hansen family now holds the majority of the shares. It's up to us to appoint or fire the president. Now we control the bank, and we decide its fate. Naturally, you will publicly approve these changes. And, of course, you will resign from the bank. In fact, I think it would be in your interest to leave Geneva and settle somewhere else. With everything your father has left you, money won't be a problem. You should take advantage of the situation and make a new life for yourself. I don't want to see you again, cousin."

Macaire was shaking. Jean-Bénédict patted his cousin's shoulder condescendingly.

"You made the right decision. Tomorrow morning, I'll organise a press conference to announce the changes. I'll read out Tarnogol's letter of resignation and explain that you're leaving the bank for personal reasons, leaving me in charge. People will think you have cancer and feel sorry for you; that's not so bad. Well, goodnight, dear cousin. Sleep tight."

"Check and mate," Macaire said to himself, stifling a sob. "I've lost everything."

Anastasia rushed back to Lev's room.

"Anastasia, what's going on?" Lev asked upon seeing the look on her face.

"Lev, it's terrible."

"What the hell is going on?"

"It's Macaire; he's done something very foolish."

She burst into tears from the strain. Lev held her in his arms to comfort her.

"Macaire wanted to kill Tarnogol by poisoning the vodka, but the bottle was mistakenly used to prepare cocktails for the guests."

"So everyone was poisoned?"

"Yes."

"But why was no-one killed?"

"Macaire thinks that the amounts served were too small to be fatal. We're caught in some kind of terrible drama. Jean-Bénédict discovered Macaire's plot and he's blackmailing him so he can take control of the bank. He's forcing Macaire to resign so he can become president."

Anastasia remained silent for a moment, as if she was thinking.

"Only one person can stop this," she said.

"Who?"

"Tarnogol. I'm going to talk to him."

"Now?"

"He resigned," she explained. "He knows he's being threatened and he's probably packing his bags right now. I have to talk to him before he leaves the hotel. Macaire told me that Tarnogol was in the next room."

"Tarnogol is dangerous," Lev warned.

"I know."

"Let me go with you."

"No, Lev. Don't get involved in this, please. It's between Tarnogol and me. He . . . he stole a part of my life. It's because of him that I married Macaire. It's because of him that you and I . . ."

She interrupted her sentence. She didn't want to talk any longer. She went out to the hallway and knocked on the door of the adjacent room. No answer. She bent down. After a few moments, she saw a shaft of light, as if someone had just got up and turned on the lamp.

She leaned against the wall and said, quietly to avoid alerting the rest of the floor, "Tarnogol, I know you're in there. Open the door."

After a short while, Tarnogol opened the door,

"What's all this about?"

"We have to talk, you and I," she said, entering the suite.

She stared at Tarnogol like an angry lioness. She had a brief vision. She recognised those eyes. She recalled what she had said that morning in Geneva to Lieutenant Sagamore: "*The eyes don't lie.*" She suddenly understood and rushed at Tarnogol.

43

Personal and Confidential

Fifteen years earlier, the Gala Weekend

Anastasia arrived at the Hôtel de Verbier in the late morning. Rather than joining the joyful gathering of her colleagues, she ran up and down the hotel looking for Lev. She looked in the bar, the meeting rooms, the pool; she went from floor to floor, all the way to the top, where she found the employees' rooms, where he had brought her a year earlier. The room where they had made love for the first time – where they had promised never to leave each other. She knocked on the doors, but none were opened to her. In her desperation, she called out, "Lev! Lev!" – but there was only silence. She returned to the great hall and questioned all the hotel employees and whomever she ran into from the bank; no-one had seen Lev.

Finally, she stood by the entrance to the hotel, examining the cars that came and went. Suddenly, she saw Sol Levovitch arrive in a taxi. She ran outside and rushed down the stairs leading to the hotel.

"Monsieur Levovitch!"

He turned around. She had last seen him at the end of the summer and now found him pale and thin.

"Anastasia?"

He glared at her angrily. She was the one who had turned Lev's head. Before, Lev had never dreamed of leaving. He was happy with his life, always smiling, always content. She was the one who separated him from Verbier; she was the one who had turned him into a banker, turned him into a different person.

By his look, Anastasia could tell that Sol knew something.

"Monsieur Levovitch, I have to talk to Lev."

"You caused him a great deal of suffering last night."

"That was a terrible misunderstanding. I was supposed to meet him, but I was held against my will. It's a long story, but I absolutely must speak to him. Where is he?"

"I'm afraid it's too late."

"Monsieur Levovitch, it's very important. I have to speak to Lev. Tell me where he is; he's all I have left in my life. Please!"

"Unfortunately, he's gone. I don't know where he is. He wouldn't tell me anything."

Her eyes filled with tears.

"If you see him, I beg you to tell him that I must speak to him. My mother prevented me from leaving last night. Tell him it was my mother. He knows her; he'll understand, right away."

* * *

By ten p.m. that evening, Anastasia still had no news of Lev.

She had spent the day in her magnificent room in the hotel, paid for by the bank. She had never had a room like that all to herself. She'd spent the night a few times in luxurious mountain resorts with young men from important families whom her mother hoped she would marry. And there was her time with Klaus, of course. But for the first time, this room was hers alone. She didn't take advantage of it; she was at her wits' end for lack of news from Lev. The past few weeks she had imagined herself in such a room with him, between these sheets, in the immense marble bath. Where was he?

Suddenly, there was a gentle knocking on the door.

"Anastasia? It's Macaire."

She went to open the door.

"Is everything okay? I didn't see you during the day."

"Okay."

He noticed her eyes; they were red.

"You've been crying?"

She started sobbing. Macaire entered the room and held her, trying to comfort her.

"I feel so bad, Macaire," she said.

"You feel bad? Where? Do you want me to call a doctor?"

"Nothing a doctor can cure. I'm heartbroken."

"I know how that feels. I feel it as well. I really thought you were coming to meet me at the Lion d'Or last night."

They no longer spoke. Words were no longer needed – or adequate. They sat on the edge of the bed and stayed that way for a long time; she cried all the tears her body had to give, and he suffered in silence, knowing she was so close and yet so far. Finally, as he was leaving, he said to her, "Anastasia, I can't imagine living without you."

"Macaire, I . . ."

"Tell me you don't love me, that I don't mean anything to you."

"You mean something, but not the way you want, not in my heart."

He grimaced. Then he begged, refusing to accept the situation for what it was.

"Please, think about it. We could be so happy together. I'll make you happy. I'll protect you. You'll have everything you need. Tell me you'll think about it, that there's some hope for me."

She didn't have the strength to reply.

"Tomorrow night at the ball, I'll be living one of the most important moments of my life. I need you to be there, at my side – at least as a friend."

"I'll be there," she promised.

When Macaire finally left the room, she sat at the small table. In the drawer she found paper and envelopes engraved with the hotel's crest. She wrote two letters. One was for Lev, the other for Macaire, the two people who had meant the most to her in her life. Two short letters, so that she could say what she had to say. Two letters, as if she could write her destiny.

*

It was near midnight when she left the room, the two envelopes in her hand, and went down to the hotel's reception area. The place was deserted. There was no-one there but a disturbing silhouette, who stared out through the large revolving door. It was Sol Levovitch, who hadn't moved since she last saw him, desperately waiting for his son. They had argued in Martigny, and Lev had stormed off, furious. Sol had to talk to his son. He had to tell Lev everything. Suddenly, a voice called out.

"Monsieur Levovitch?"

He turned around; it was Anastasia. She smiled sadly.

"Monsieur Levovitch," she said, handing him the letter addressed to Lev. "Can you give this to Lev as soon as you see him? It's very important. It concerns our future, his and mine."

"You can count on me," Sol promised.

"Tell him that I'm going to apply for a job as a chambermaid in this hotel – that I'll be here waiting for him for as long as it takes."

Sol Levovitch, without knowing quite why, agreed. He saw there was a second envelope in her hand and that it was addressed to Macaire.

"Do you want me to give that letter to someone?" he asked innocently.

"It's . . . it's for a hotel guest, Macaire Ebezner. I don't know his room number."

"I can have it brought up to him. Well, only if you want."

"It's late," she remarked.

"It will be done first thing tomorrow morning."

"It has to be given directly to him. It's extremely important."

"It will be done."

She hesitated. It would be cowardly not to give it directly to Macaire, but she knew that he would read it in front of her and begin his entreaties all over again. She no longer had the energy for his histrionics. She gave Sol the letter and walked away.

Sol Levovitch went to his office. He opened the envelopes and read the letters.

He read Anastasia's letter to Lev. He was stunned, overcome with pain. Then he read the letter for Macaire and decided there might be something he could do.

He grabbed a magnifying glass and scissors and a tube of glue. He took the two letters and carefully cut the first line out of each. Once that was done, he rummaged around in the administration office, where he ran both letters through the colour photocopier. The machine spat out two new letters; the results were perfect. Without a magnifying glass, it was hard to tell that the text apparently written with a blue ballpoint was only a copy.

Soon after Sol had returned to his observation post at the entrance of the hotel, Lev arrived.

"Lev," he said, greeting him from the reception hall, "you're back, finally. I was very worried."

Lev glowered at him.

"I've only come back to get Anastasia. I have to talk to her."

"Wait – *we* need to talk."

"What do you want? Do you want to tell me what kind of game you're playing?"

"I'm very sick, Lev."

"Sick? How?"

"I have cancer. I don't have very long to live."

"Why should I believe you?"

"Because it's the truth."

Sol was aware that his son was furious with him. He imagined Lev going away, far away, and the thought terrified him. He was all Sol had. He didn't want to die alone. He didn't want to spend his last months without someone at his side. That was his greatest fear. A few months, that was all he was asking. His son would then have his whole life to find another Anastasia. There were so many other women, and he had only one son. With that thought, Sol put his hand in his pocket and decided to put his plan into action. He was a coward, and he knew it.

"I didn't want to worry you given all that's happened," Sol said, "but

I saw Anastasia this evening with someone else. She was laughing, she looked happy. She looked like she was in love."

"I don't believe a word you're saying."

"Someone called Macaire," Sol added. "He's the one you told me about, no? The one she met last night at the Lion d'Or, right? Just now I intercepted two letters that Anastasia left at reception, one for you and the other for Macaire."

Sol took out the two envelopes, which he held in his hand.

"Give them to me," Lev demanded.

"After I saw Anastasia with that young man, I suspect it'll be bad news."

"Give them to me!" Lev said and snatched the letters from his father's hand.

He opened them at once, read them, and blanched. Furiously, he crumpled the letters and threw them against the wall. His father picked them up and pretended to read them for the first time.

Dear Macaire,

I love only you. Let's get away from here. Far from Geneva. I don't care about your great future at the bank, I don't care about money. All I want is to be with you. I'll always love you.

Anastasia

My dear Lev,

I should have had the courage to tell you to your face, but I'll write it instead: I don't want to be with you. That's why I didn't come to meet you last night. You should have understood. Contrary to what you think, we have no future together. Please don't be angry with me. You know that I don't want to hurt you. I hope you'll forgive me.

All my love,
Anastasia

"She wants the money," Sol said with an air of discontent. "You're just a poor man and a poor man you'll stay. I'm very sorry, but you're just a Levovitch, my son."

Lev, under the strain of his suffering, felt he was about to fall. He straightened up and staggered away, as if he had been shot, in the direction of the hotel's wide entrance.

"Where are you going?" his father asked.

"For a walk."

"Wait!"

"I need to be alone."

Lev walked through the doors and down the steps, his father at his heels.

"Wait, Lev!" his father pleaded, fearing his son would do something foolish.

But Lev ran off into the night. His footsteps beat against the fresh snow; the cold air whipped his face. He screamed as loudly as his lungs allowed – screamed as if he had lost everything. He began to run, without a goal, mindlessly, and ended up on Verbier's main street. The village was quiet. He lit a cigarette, walked a while in the darkness, and found a bar that was still open. Through the glass, he saw her, alone at the bar. His heart beating, he walked through the door to join her. She didn't notice him at first. He sat down next to her; she suddenly turned her head and smiled. He smiled back.

"Hello, Petra."

"Hello, Lev."

He ordered vodka for the both of them and drank it, staring into the young woman's eyes, which burned with desire. Anastasia wanted Macaire; let her have him. Lev could have any woman he wanted. He would replace her with a snap of his fingers. He would show her who Lev Levovitch was and that he wasn't ashamed of his name. He leaned towards Petra and kissed her. She returned his kiss with passion, breaking in only to whisper, "I've waited so long for this!" They kissed again.

The night was theirs.

44

Night

In the middle of the night, the hotel slept.

The light in the sixth-floor hallway suddenly went dark. The shadow that had flipped the switch moved carefully in the darkness, its steps muffled by the thick carpet. It paused briefly before the door of each room to examine the number, before finally stopping. This was the one. Room 622. The shadow slipped its hand into its coat pocket and took out a gun. With a gloved hand, the shadow knocked softly on the door of the suite – just loudly enough to awaken the occupant.

There was a noise. Light escaped from beneath the door. The occupant got out of bed. Then steps could be heard inside the room.

The shadow put a finger on the trigger of the weapon. When the door opened, it would have to fire – and aim well.

Death was getting ready to strike.

45

Goodbyes

Fifteen years earlier, the Gala Weekend ball

In the hotel ballroom, a few minutes before seven p.m., Anastasia, resplendent in a midnight-blue dress, mingled with the other bank employees. She was looking for Lev, but she didn't know whether he had arrived at the hotel yet. He had been assigned a room, but according to the receptionist, he hadn't checked in yet. She wondered whether he had gone back to Geneva. Suddenly, someone grabbed her hand. She turned around, filled with hope. It was Macaire.

"I'm so happy you came," he said, interpreting her presence as a sign of hope. He smiled broadly.

"Macaire, I . . . Did you get my letter?"

"Your letter? What letter?"

She looked deep into his eyes, trying to determine whether he was playing at being a fool.

"You sent me a postcard?" he joked. "There's no need for letters when we can talk face to face. I want to tell you that you're the most beautiful woman here tonight, Anastasia."

"Thank you."

"Will you let me have the first dance?"

She simply nodded.

"Come, they're going to start."

He led her in the direction of the dais, and they made their way through the small crowd already assembled, who were trying to position themselves in front of the other guests. Soon, everyone fell quiet, and the bank's board of directors, with Abel Ebezner at its head, strode on to the stage through a concealed door.

Lev left Petra's room, where he had spent the day.

"Hurry up," she urged him gently as he waited by the elevator. "We're going to miss everything."

She smiled. He didn't react. He was exhausted and didn't seem to be his usual self. She attributed it to the alcohol from the previous night – which hadn't prevented them from making love.

"Are you alright?" she asked in the elevator. "You don't look happy."

"I'm okay," he assured her.

She smiled and kissed him. The doors opened on the first floor. They walked hand in hand towards the ballroom.

Abel had just finished his solemn speech, his very first as president of the bank. He invited the new vice president to join him. When Abel pronounced his name, Macaire was filled with a sense of immense pride. It was one of the greatest moments of his life. He walked up to the stage to be officially appointed by his father, who, following tradition, handed Macaire his bearer shares. Before the assembly of bank employees, his father presented their new vice president, and Macaire was applauded for a very long time.

Macaire was the man of the evening. Stepping down from the dais, galvanised by the moment, he gathered up his courage and, approaching Anastasia, standing in the front row, he grabbed both her hands, pulled her to him and kissed her.

She immediately freed herself from his embrace, terribly embarrassed. Looking around her, she saw Lev. He glared at her and bent towards Petra, who was standing next to him, and kissed her. Anastasia's face fell, and Lev kissed Petra again, delighted by the effect it had.

He was glad to be able to avenge himself – glad that he was able to hurt Anastasia the way she had hurt him.

Macaire, oblivious to all this, was caught off guard by his own boldness; he wasn't sure whether or not Anastasia had welcomed his kiss (she didn't return it, but she didn't try to escape either). He was, however, relieved to see Lev with Petra. Macaire then said to Anastasia, "You see, I told you they were together."

Anastasia, weakened, gathered her strength to stop herself crying in front of them all. She pushed through the guests and rushed from the ballroom. Overcome by uncontrollable sobbing, she went up to her room to take refuge. She had lost him.

They had lost each other.

Back in the ballroom, Macaire was upset by Anastasia's reaction. In his hand, he held shares in one of the largest private banks in Switzerland, but this left him indifferent. All he wanted was to be loved by Anastasia. He wanted to find her.

He had a hard time leaving the ballroom. Everyone wanted to say hello, wish him well, toast him with a glass of champagne. He would have gladly sent them all away, but he was unable to set aside his good manners, and it was fifteen minutes before he was able to extricate himself and leave the room.

He rushed to the staircase to reach Anastasia's room. It was then that he ran into Tarnogol, who was coming down the stairs towards the ballroom. Macaire, who didn't recognise him immediately, simply said, "Good evening, sir."

Tarnogol stopped and stared.

"Something wrong, my young friend?"

"A matter of the heart," Macaire replied, happy that someone had noticed he wasn't feeling too good.

"It happens," Tarnogol said.

Macaire looked at him.

"Have we met?"

"No, I don't think so."

"Yes," Macaire suddenly realised. "You came to the bank a few weeks ago."

"Do you know the bank?" Tarnogol asked.

"Do I know it?" Macaire replied, amused by the question. "I'm Macaire Ebezner." He extended his hand to Tarnogol. "I'm the new vice president."

They exchanged a warm handshake.

"I'm Sinior Tarnogol. Pleased to make your acquaintance. I don't like seeing a handsome young fellow like yourself looking so sad. Is there something I can do for you?"

Macaire sighed. "Oh, only if you could make it so that the woman I love returned my affections. Her name is Anastasia. I'd give anything to be with her."

46

The Morning of the Murder

Six thirty in the morning. The Hôtel de Verbier was dark. Outside, it was pitch-black and snowing heavily.

On the sixth floor, the doors of the service elevator opened. A hotel employee appeared with a breakfast tray and made his way towards Room 622.

When he reached the room, he noticed that the door was ajar. Light spilled through the opening. He knocked but there was no response. Finally, he decided to go in, assuming that the door had been left open for that purpose. He walked in and let out a scream. Running from the room, he went to alert his colleagues and call for help.

As the news spread through the hotel, the lights went on, floor by floor.

On the carpet of room 622 lay a corpse.

PART THREE

Four Months After the Murder

April

PART THREE

Four Months After the Murder

47

The New President

It was twelve thirty on the first Tuesday in April. Macaire's session with Dr Kazan had just begun. The window overlooked Place Claparède, planted with tall trees whose foliage was slowly emerging. Geneva was becoming green again. Spring was about to begin.

"It's been four months since my cousin Jean-Béné was killed, and the police still don't have any leads," Macaire complained in the psychiatrist's office, slumped in the large chair.

"How do you feel about it?" the doctor asked.

"My cousin's murder or the fact that the investigation is going nowhere?"

"Both."

"You know, I didn't mention it to the police, but our relationship had deteriorated."

"Oh? Yet, you got along well with him."

"Right before his death, we'd exchanged words."

"What do you mean?"

Macaire remained silent. He looked out the window and appeared to be daydreaming.

"Are you certain you're okay, Macaire?"

"Yes, yes. I'm fine. Sorry, I'm a bit preoccupied at the moment – the bank and all that. Now that I'm president, I'm deluged with responsibilities. Meetings, cocktail parties, all kinds of dinners."

"How do you feel about returning to seeing me only once a week? Is that enough?"

"Absolutely. It was good to see you twice a week after Papa died. But now, I feel I'm able to deal with things."

"Deal with what?" Kazan asked him.

"My solitude. Without Anastasia, I feel very alone."

"Do you miss her?"

"Every day. You know I keep thinking about that Saturday of the Gala Weekend, when she came to see me in Verbier and I lost her. It was my fault."

"You still believe it was your fault?"

"I told you, Dr Kazan, I made a pact with the devil: Anastasia in exchange for the presidency. I lost my wife and secured my position."

Kazan sighed noisily to signal his disapproval.

"Macaire, you know I cannot accept this story of a pact with the devil. You yourself are far too rational to believe in it."

"You see, that's the reason why, for all these years, I never told you why I sold my bank shares to Tarnogol. I was certain you wouldn't take me seriously. Besides, as a psychoanalyst you're not supposed to judge your patients."

"Very well," Kazan replied, as a form of concession. "Tarnogol, the devil, made a pact with you fifteen years ago: your bank shares for Anastasia's love."

"Exactly. I accepted. That was the night of the grand ball. My father had just given me my shares, and I ran into Tarnogol, who offered to exchange them for the thing I wanted most in the world: Anastasia's love. And, that night, Anastasia literally fell into my arms."

"And fifteen years later," Kazan continued, trying to untangle the story, "Tarnogol – the devil – offered you a new pact. Is that it?"

"Yes. Two days before the election, last December, Tarnogol told me that I would become president if I gave up Anastasia. At first, I refused. Then, on the Saturday night, I accepted, at the Hôtel de Verbier. And today I'm president, but alone – exactly as Tarnogol had predicted."

"Macaire, I'm trying to help you be rational, for your own good. Do you really believe the devil, in the form of Tarnogol, might have done this?"

"I know you don't believe me. But explain this to me, then: that Saturday, as the presidency was slowly slipping away from me, Anastasia came to the Verbier to support me, to be by my side on one of the most important days in my life. She wrote a tender message on the bathroom mirror in lipstick. Don't tell me that that's not the behaviour of a woman in love!"

"Well, yes," Kazan conceded.

"At that moment, Levovitch was about to be appointed president. When the official announcement was delayed by the poisoning, aware that I had only one chance at the presidency, I accepted Tarnogol's pact. A few hours later, Anastasia left me, and I became president. So, explain all that to me, Dr Kazan, if it's not the work of the devil!"

Kazan didn't know what to say, and Macaire continued.

"What happened that night surpasses everything you could imagine, Doctor. I can't tell you anything more. You wouldn't believe me."

"You mean the night of the murder?" Kazan asked, suddenly circumspect. "What happened that night? You always said that you were sound asleep, that you had taken sleeping pills."

"I know things, Doctor – things that even the police probably don't know."

After a moment's silence, Kazan asked, "Macaire, why did you agree to the pact if you didn't want to lose your wife?"

"Because I let my ambition get the better of me. And, at that moment, I had the impression that I had already lost Anastasia."

"Why?"

"Because I could sense that the flame had gone out in our marriage – that we didn't share anything any longer. I was wrapped up in my work at the bank; she was busy with I have no idea what. The last few years, we only went out for social events. Always surrounded by others, always among large groups of people – never alone. In fact, we avoided being alone together. Each of us, in our own little corner, began tending our own secret garden, but we were incapable of cultivating one together."

"That's a nice image."

"During the last year, I felt alone when I was with my wife. And when we weren't together, we didn't miss each other."

"The absence of that sense of loss, if I may say so, is a terrible sign for a relationship."

Macaire nodded and went on.

"What a strange invention – the couple – which always ends up making us feel alone when we're together. So, that Saturday evening, I asked myself why I was fighting for a woman I had already lost – a woman who had betrayed me."

Kazan opened his eyes very wide.

"Your wife had had an affair?"

"Yes."

"How do you know?"

Macaire evaded the question. "A day doesn't go by that I don't relive that Saturday night when I gave her up to become president. I ask myself what would have happened if I had fought for her. I wouldn't have been named president, and then what? I would certainly have left Geneva with her. I would have won her back; we would have rebuilt our relationship. But I let her leave."

"Macaire, excuse the pun, but I want to play the devil's advocate for a moment. Why do you suppose that your wife wouldn't have left anyway, given that you believe she had a lover?"

"You may be right. But at least I would have tried to fight. I would have shown that I was prepared to sacrifice everything for her. Giving up was my downfall. You know, Doctor, I believed my ambition was to become president of that damn bank, but now that I am president, I realise that my ambition is to be loved. And that's a much more difficult goal to achieve."

When the session was over, Macaire returned to the bank on foot.

He was feeling melancholy, and walking did him good. He followed rue Jean-Sénebier then crossed the Parc des Bastions, following its main footpath.

It was a day of brilliant sunshine, and the air was soft and delicious. In the trees, the birds were loudly celebrating the coming of spring. A carpet of crocuses coloured the lawn, where beds of tulips flowered. The crowd filled the benches and the terrace of the restaurant, and by the high gates separating the park from Place de Neuve, the chess tables were full. Macaire observed this small world and thought of Anastasia. There had been no news in four months.

To his friends, his family, or anyone who questioned him, he explained that she had left him and gone away. In general, his interlocutors assumed an air of discomfort. Over the weeks that followed her disappearance, Macaire had had to undergo similar exchanges with friends, neighbours, shopkeepers, even the postman.

"Say hello to your wife, Monsieur Ebezner."

"She left me."

He concluded that he didn't have many friends since no-one seemed concerned by his condition; no-one had invited him to dinner to give him something else to think about. Most people didn't ask questions. Aside from a few displays of more or less well-meaning curiosity, people were mostly indifferent.

Macaire crossed place de Neuve, then followed rue de la Corraterie, which began between the Rath Museum and the ramparts of the old city. He finally arrived at the bank.

Upon entering the venerable building, he was greeted deferentially, as he was every day.

"Hello, Mr President!" sang the chorus of tellers.

Macaire replied with a cordial nod.

"Hello, Mr President!" intoned the obsequious bootlickers who crossed his path in the bank's large entrance hall.

"Hello, Mr President!" cackled those who entered the elevator with him, moved by such proximity.

At every floor someone entered or left the elevator saying "Hello, Mr President." Macaire, alone now, finally reached the top floor and headed towards his father's old office, which was now his. In the ante-chamber, installed behind her desk, Cristina, who had moved with him and now kept watch over the room, greeted him with a broad, friendly smile.

"Hello, Mr President."

"Cristina, when are you going to stop calling me 'President'?"

"Never. You're the president now."

He smiled before entering his office, closing the door to indicate that he didn't want to be disturbed.

He sat in his armchair. He felt lost. Before him, on his desk, was a photo of Anastasia that he hadn't had the courage to remove. The police hadn't really shown much concern about her departure. Shortly after Jean-Bénédict's murder, Lieutenant Sagamore of the Geneva Judicial Police had shown up to question Macaire at home. The police were con-cerned about a possible link between the murder of Jean-Bénédict, the poisoning at the hotel, and the break-in that had taken place at Macaire's home.

"What link is there?" Macaire had asked, perplexed.

"The robbery, the poisoning, and the murder all took place within forty-eight hours and are connected with the Ebezner Bank," Sagamore replied. "How's your wife?"

"I've no idea. I haven't had any news."

The lieutenant frowned. Macaire was careful not to mention his pact with Tarnogol. His wife had disappeared on the night of the mur-der, and he had become president of the bank. Obviously, he would have liked the police to locate her, if only to assure him that she was alright. He had hired a private agency, but in spite of their exorbitant fees, the investigators had found no trace of Anastasia. Surely, the police would be more effective. It was then that Macaire admitted to Sagamore that Anastasia had left him.

"I'm sorry to hear that," the lieutenant replied.

If Macaire had preferred not to involve the police in this matter, it was because the investigators were unaware that Anastasia was at Verbier the night of the murder. He couldn't help thinking about the message she had left him that night and wondering: what had Anastasia done?

48

The Police Investigation

Monday, July 2, 2018.

I had spent the morning in my suite so I could review the elements of the investigation – or maybe to avoid Scarlett after our aborted kiss the night before. I was fascinated, amazed, and charmed by her. But whenever I closed my eyes, I thought of Sloane. Tired from pacing aimlessly like a lion in its cage, I stopped for my first cigarette break of the day. I poured myself a cup of coffee and went out onto the balcony to smoke and get some air. I found myself face to face with Scarlett, who was also on the balcony, sitting in an armchair in the sun. She was reading *Gone with the Wind*.

"Well, well, the writer emerges from his den."

She got up and leaned against the railing that separated our two balconies. I offered her a cigarette, which she accepted.

"You can even come over to this side of the railing," I said. "I have a pot of hot coffee; can I offer you a cup?"

"No, thank you. I'm staying on my side; it's safer."

She pretended to grasp the railing tightly and laughed uncomfortably.

"I'm very sorry about yesterday . . . that I tried to get you . . . Well . . ."

I interrupted her.

"Don't be sorry about anything, Scarlett. It's all my fault."

She smiled sadly and hurried to change the subject.

"I made a few calls this morning. Bisnard mentioned an investigator by the name of Favraz, with the Judicial Police in the Valais, who had questioned him at the time of the murder."

"I remember, yes."

"I found Favraz. He's still working with the police in the Valais. He's now head of the crime squad. I even managed to talk to him."

"And?"

"We can see him this afternoon at four in Sion – if you're interested, of course."

"Of course, I'm interested!"

At four p.m., Scarlett and I presented ourselves at the headquarters of the Judicial Police in Sion.

"You're the writer?" Favraz asked as he ushered us into his office.

"That's him," Scarlett replied for me, as she was now accustomed to doing.

"And you're writing a book about the events at the Hôtel de Verbier?"

"Somewhat reluctantly, but yes. We're trying to understand what happened back then."

"Forgive my language," Favraz replied, "but it was a shitshow. I clearly remember getting to the hotel with the other officers. The municipal police and the state police were already there. The hotel was sealed, but the area was already crawling with onlookers. You can imagine how news like that travels in a small place like Verbier. Half the village was gathered in front of the building, along the police barricades. They kept asking about the murder. In the lobby, the hotel employees were in a panic. The manager was beside himself. The journalists were going to milk the story for all it was worth, and his season was fucked."

"What did you do once you arrived?" Scarlett asked, hanging on his every word.

"I went to the sixth floor. I made sure that room 622 was off limits while we waited for the forensic team, to avoid contaminating the crime scene. Then we went around all the rooms on the floor, hoping to find witnesses."

"So you were the one who led the investigation?" I asked.

"No. It was finally turned over to the Judicial Police in Geneva."

"Geneva? Why?"

"Because it was obvious that the murder was connected with the Ebezner Bank. The crime took place in Verbier, but the roots of the investigation were in Geneva. And when the police in Geneva asked to take over, no-one was against it."

"Why were you so convinced that the investigation should focus on Geneva?" I asked.

Favraz hesitated. His reply was opaque.

"Because of what we found in room 622."

"And what did you find?"

"I've already told you too much," Favraz said.

"Or not enough," Scarlett replied.

"At the time, only a small number of police offers knew what was going on. It's the police in Geneva who have the information you want. It's still their investigation, because the case hasn't been closed yet. I don't want to confuse the issue."

"Do you have a contact in the Geneva police department?" Scarlett asked.

"At the time, the inspector in charge was Lieutenant Philippe Saga-more. He was about forty years old, so I'm sure he's still working. Contact him; you can give him my name."

I wrote the name down as Scarlett continued.

"Getting back to the morning of December sixteenth, you were at the hotel and you questioned potential witnesses? Is there anything you can share with us?"

"Most of the time, there's something distinctive about the scene of a murder. It may sound strange, but no matter how many cops are around, it's usually calm, silent – the calm after the storm, so to speak, or after death. But that morning, on the sixth floor of the hotel, I discovered an exception to the rule. I'd never seen such commotion before."

49

The Morning of the Murder

Sunday, December 16, seven thirty a.m. Macaire's deep slumber was interrupted by someone knocking on the door. He awoke with difficulty. The knocking became insistent. Finally, he got up and wrapped himself in his bathrobe. In the entrance hall of his suite, as he was about to open the door, he stepped on a piece of paper. Someone had slipped a note under the door. At first, Macaire thought it was a message from the hotel, but then he recognised the handwriting: it was from Anastasia. His heart pounding, he read the letter, several lines written in haste.

> *Macaire,*
>
> *I'm leaving for good. I'm not coming back. Don't try to find me.*
>
> *Forgive me. I'll always live with the weight of what I have done.*
>
> *Anastasia*

Suddenly, there was more knocking. Macaire slipped the note into his pocket and went to open the door. A uniformed policeman stood there. The hallway was filled with noise and confusion.

"What's going on?" Macaire asked.

The policeman stared at him suspiciously.

"You didn't hear the racket that's been going on for the past hour?"

"I took some sleeping pills last night," Macaire explained, looking visibly comatose.

"Someone was killed during the night."

"What? Who?"

Macaire understood nothing of what was happening. Everything around him was spinning, and he had a headache; it was like a bad dream.

"Who died?" Macaire asked.

"A guest on this floor. You didn't hear anything during the night?"

"No, nothing. But I told you, I took a couple of sleeping pills."

Macaire wanted to walk down the hallway to see what was going on, but the policeman prevented him.

"For now we're asking everyone to remain in their rooms. Keep your door open, please. A police inspector will speak to you within the hour."

From the doorway, Macaire saw Lev, also by the entrance to his room, observing the commotion.

"Lev, what's going on?"

"It's Jean-Bénédict. He was found dead this morning."

"What? Jean-Bénédict is dead? What are you talking about?"

"A hotel employee found him dead – shot."

Macaire, overcome by the shock, returned to his room and sat on the couch. This was the best news possible. He couldn't get over it. If Jean-Bénédict was dead, then he would be president, right? Was Tarnogol's prophecy coming true? He had lost Anastasia but he was going to become president. At last!

A policeman in a suit, rather young-looking and athletically built, appeared at the door of Macaire's suite.

"Inspector Favraz, Judicial Police," the policeman said, flashing his badge. "Can I ask you a few questions?"

Macaire invited the young man into the room. When requested, Macaire showed his identification to the policeman and told him what position he held at the bank. Carefully writing everything down in a notebook, the inspector explained that Jean-Bénédict had been shot during the night. Macaire was terrified.

"You didn't hear anything?" the inspector asked, surprised.

"I was sleeping."

"Two shots were fired a few metres from your head, and you slept right through it?"

"Sleeping pills. What time did it happen?"

"We don't know yet. I was told many of the guests got sick last night. Did that include you?"

"No. I didn't drink the cocktail."

Macaire bit his tongue. The policeman stared at him suspiciously.

"Why did you mention the cocktail? I was told it was food poisoning."

Suddenly, the conversation was interrupted by loud noises from the hallway. Inspector Favraz left immediately to see what was going on. Macaire, from the doorway of his suite, saw the policeman rush to Horace Hansen's room, before rushing back out. "He's had a heart attack! Call the medics." After several minutes of confusion, two paramedics appeared and were guided to Horace Hansen's suite, where they remained for a long time. Finally, he appeared, lying on a stretcher, inert, pale as death, an oxygen mask on his face. Inspector Favraz was helping the paramedics, holding an intravenous drip in his extended arm. They entered the elevator, and the doors closed behind them.

In the elevator, Favraz, watching Horace Hansen's face, had the impression that he was trying to say something. Favraz brought his ear close to the man's mouth and heard the old man murmur, "Levovitch president, Levovitch president." Favraz, not understanding what Hansen meant, wrote down the enigmatic words so as not to forget them.

Day was dawning slowly over Verbier. The blue lights of the emergency vehicles lit up the front of the hotel. Around the main entrance was a throng of gendarmes, police inspectors, dog handlers, and a forensics team. Behind them, contained by plastic tape, were dozens of curious onlookers and journalists, impatient to discover what had happened.

393

"One of the big executives of the Ebezner Bank was murdered," could be heard. A murder in Verbier – that had never happened before.

Observing the confusion from the large bay windows, Monsieur Rose and a few employees were lamenting the fact that there would be far fewer reservations now. It was the start of the ski season, and no-one would want to come to a hotel where a murder had just been committed. The hotel risked going bankrupt.

* * *

Four months later, at the start of April, in his presidential office at the Ebezner Bank, Macaire was thinking about that dark December Sunday, which had seen the disappearance of two generations of Hansens. A few hours after the murder of his son, Horace Hansen died from cardiac arrest at the hospital in Martigny. The brutal death of Jean-Bénédict had been a fatal blow. As for Sinior Tarnogol, the third member of the board, he had simply disappeared. He had left Jean-Bénédict a letter, later found in the safe in his room, which stated that he was resigning, effective immediately, and that his shares should be given to Macaire Ebezner.

And, in the weeks following the murder of Jean-Bénédict Hansen, Macaire also acquired the shares belonging to his father. The board having been dissolved, the lawyer responsible for executing Abel Ebezner's will had to acknowledge that the old man's wishes could no longer be respected and, therefore, his shares would be given to his sole heir.

Macaire had become the de facto president of the Ebezner Bank because he held the majority of its capital, which made him one of the richest and most powerful men in Geneva. He was admired and envied. But his reputation had suffered. He owed his newfound glory to the murder of his cousin. In addition, the police investigation seemed to be going nowhere, and although nothing directly incriminated Macaire, everyone he passed in the street had to wonder what had happened the night of December 16 in room 622 at the Hôtel de Verbier. Did Macaire Ebezner kill his cousin to get control of the family bank?

Macaire, aware of the rumours, forced himself to ignore them. Those in his immediate entourage continued to bow and scrape as usual, while those he passed in the city, whatever they might be thinking, rushed to greet him respectfully, practically kissing his feet. There was a very specific reason: because Jean-Bénédict had been an only son and had no children, he and Horace had died without heirs. The Hansen clan had been eradicated. The bank's by-laws stipulated that in such cases, their shares would be repurchased by the bank and then transferred to two new members of the board appointed by the president.

For the first time in three hundred years, there would be no Hansen on the Ebezner Bank board of directors. For all the young wolves of the financial industry, this was a unique opportunity. Macaire was now the most celebrated man in Geneva, and they were all fawning over him.

Macaire, Abel's unloved son, had become the most powerful Ebezner of all. The richest. The greatest. How did he feel? Bored. Disgusted. He had never really cared about the bank. Now that he had reached the summit, he recalled why, fifteen years earlier, he had sold his shares. He had been happy only with Anastasia. Without her, his life was empty. He wanted to find her. He wanted to win her over.

Where was she?

At that same moment, fifteen hundred kilometres from Geneva, on the island of Corfu, Greece, Anastasia emerged from the emerald sea and grabbed the towel she had left on the beach. She was happier than ever before, and it showed. She was sublime, magnificent, radiant, bathed in sunlight and Lev's love. She dried herself and walked towards the impressive house that rose up behind her, protected by rocks and overlooking the Ionian Sea.

When they had arrived in December, they had been in the grip of passion – the passion of rediscovery, of being together all the time, of not having to hide. They could walk hand in hand to the old town of Corfu or along the beach. And the house! Anastasia had never seen anything like it.

Lev had wanted everything to be perfect, and it was.

Lev had wanted them to be beautiful; they had emptied all the high-end boutiques in Athens. "We'll dress for dinner every evening!" he told her. She thought the idea was marvellous. Their bedroom, as large as a living room, gave way to two dressing rooms and two very large bathrooms. Each enclosed in their own bath, they parted so that they might rediscover each other, more beautiful than before, more sweet-smelling, more discriminating – even more sublime.

It was a lengthy ritual, and they took their time. Their senses awakened, they felt the excitement of their rediscovery rise as the hour advanced.

Lev applied a facial tonic, then took a long shower, after which he examined every centimetre of his sculpted physique. He arranged, shaped, cut, and hunted down the slightest imperfection, closely examining any rebellious hair.

Anastasia loved her bathroom kingdom. She plunged into the immense bathtub, filled with pleasantly hot and perfumed water. She had arranged candles all around her and read for a long time in this peaceful environment. This was followed by the ritual of curling her hair. Next, she tended to her nails, hands, and feet. Of course, she had to find a dress, and never the same one twice, as Lev had insisted: "When you run out, there'll be more!" A steady stream of gifts was delivered to the house.

Lev was generally up at dawn. He would go for a run across the island's hills and then work in his small office on the ground floor.

Once she was up and dressed, Anastasia joined him, and they would have breakfast together in the kitchen early in the year or on the terrace when the weather turned mild. They ate cheesecake, Greek pastry, and croissants still warm from a boulangerie that delivered to the house every morning.

After walking on the empty beach, Anastasia climbed the stone steps that led up to the house. When she arrived on the terrace, Alfred brought her coffee, some water, and some cut fruit.

"Thank you, Alfred," she said, smiling, as she took the cup from him. "You must have read my mind. When is Lev coming back?"

"By late afternoon," Alfred replied, looking at his watch.

Since their arrival in Corfu, Lev would travel regularly to Geneva at the request of Macaire, who thought Lev was living in Athens. Lev had explained to Anastasia that he couldn't run away like a thief in the night. It would raise suspicions, he had said. Anastasia didn't understand what suspicions he was referring to. It didn't matter. Lev's brief absences were deliciously unbearable; she desired him more when he returned, loved him more, felt more passionate towards him. Who would have thought it possible?

Besides, it would only be for a few months. At least, that's what Lev had said. At first, he was planning to resign quickly, then he changed his mind, arguing that he couldn't abandon his clients from one day to the next. "It wouldn't be professional," he explained. "What good is it to be professional when you're going to quit?" she had asked. "It's a matter of principle," he said.

Alfred's voice awakened Anastasia from her thoughts.

"What would you like to eat this evening, Madame? We've just received some fresh fish and some magnificent lobsters."

"How about spaghetti with lobster?" she suggested.

"That sounds like an excellent idea."

She looked at the sea, which offered itself to her. She couldn't believe that they were living here now, she and Lev, in this dream of a house, with its private cove and staff to take care of their every need. She hoped she would never have to leave.

In Geneva, on the top floor of the bank, Cristina pushed open the door to Macaire's office.

"Lev is here," she announced.

"Have him come in," Macaire replied, rising from his chair to greet Levovitch.

Lev appeared in the room. They fell into each other's arms.

"Hello, old friend! I'm pleased to see you."

"The pleasure is mine, Mr President," Lev responded with a smile.

Macaire burst out laughing.

"None of that between us, please. I know how much I owe you. I haven't forgotten that you were prepared to give up your shot at the presidency and leave the way clear for me."

Macaire pointed to a pair of armchairs, and they sat down.

"Can I offer you a small glass? A whiskey?"

"Yes to a whiskey," Lev replied.

Macaire reached out and grabbed an imposing crystal decanter. He poured some of the contents into two glasses and the two men toasted each other conspiratorially.

"You wanted to see me?" Lev asked.

"Yes. How are things going in Athens?"

To justify his departure, Lev had explained to Macaire that he couldn't remain in Geneva now that Macaire was president. He needed a change of air. He needed to renew himself, and he needed some new projects. They had agreed, largely to ensure a smooth transition with his clients, that Lev wouldn't announce his departure immediately – that he could work remotely and return to the bank at regular intervals. His lengthy absences would be explained by a new focus on foreign business.

After Lev made a brief summary of the situation, Macaire said to him, "Listen, I've thought a lot about what you told me – your resignation, the feeling that you were done in Geneva. But to be honest, I still need you at the bank. It's a question of stability. You have some of the bank's biggest clients in your portfolio. I'm afraid they'll go elsewhere if you leave. The bank has already been badly shaken by Jean-Bénédict's murder, and your departure would be bad for business."

"You want me to stay?" Lev said, surprised. "To be frank, I don't really want to."

"You've been approached by another bank, is that it? How much are they offering you? I'll double it! I need you here!"

"No, I hadn't planned to join another bank. I just want a change of scenery. And besides, you're president now; you've got your office on the sixth floor. If I return, it won't be the same if I'm alone on the fifth."

"Lev, why don't you take over the bank's office in Athens? You could develop it even further. You have a large Greek clientele, it would make perfect sense. You could continue to manage all your clients from down there. It would be easy to return to Geneva or anywhere in Europe if necessary."

"The bank's location in Athens isn't very good," Lev objected. "I don't want to spend my days there."

"You could work from home if you want. You won't have to go to the bank more than once a week to make sure that everything is going well."

Lev hesitated. Macaire insisted.

"Don't leave me hanging," he implored. "You're one of the pillars of this bank. I can't begin my presidency by losing my best manager. How would it look? Please, Lev."

"Okay. But I'm not signing on for more than a year."

"A year will be fine," Macaire assured Lev, looking at him with gratitude. "And if you're satisfied with the arrangement, you can continue as long as you want."

Lev accepted. The two men sealed their agreement with a handshake and clinked their glasses once more.

When Lev left, Macaire allowed a self-satisfied smile to spread across his face, betraying his feelings of superiority. As he had suspected, Lev's weakness was his kindness. The first part of the trap had closed on him.

Macaire opened the first drawer of his desk and took out the letter he had received a few days earlier – an anonymous letter that had made him spit out his coffee when he read it for the first time. On the paper was a single line:

Anastasia has run away with Lev Levovitch.

50

Geneva (Part 1)

With Favraz's help, we had managed to obtain a meeting in Geneva with Lieutenant Philippe Sagamore. So, on Tuesday morning, July 3, 2018, Scarlett and I travelled to Geneva for the day.

"I can see why the police in the Valais turned the case over to Geneva," Scarlett said. "Because they're going to waste an hour and a half travelling every time they have to question someone!"

"You're definitely the most cynical investigator I know."

The road from Verbier to Geneva passed along Lake Geneva. In between her observations of the scenery, Scarlett read some of the articles she had collected about the murder.

"I've been going over this file for days," she complained. "I get the impression that we're missing something. All the journalists claim that Jean-Bénédict Hansen was widely liked. People only had good things to say about him."

"And yet, there's at least one person who wanted him dead."

"To find out who, we have to find out why."

"Hopefully Sagamore can help. A good job you managed to convince him to meet with us. You're very persuasive, Scarlett."

"Oh, not really. It was your name that opened the door. At first, on the phone, he was rather guarded. He wanted to know how I had heard about him. When I gave him your name, he immediately became very cordial. It seems that he liked the television series adapted from one of your books. I have to watch it one of these days."

I was amused by the reference.

"Bernard and the movies, that was something," I explained. "He was the one who got the series going."

"Bernard liked movies?" Scarlett asked.

"He loved them. He was a brilliant film critic. He had seen everything. He knew all the films, all the actors. And after the success of my second novel, several producers wanted to buy the rights for a movie adaptation. Bernard was the one who took care of it; I had a few good laughs about that."

"Tell me!" Scarlett insisted.

* * *

Paris, a few years earlier
Bernard was a man difficult to impress. When the producers and movie studios appeared at the door to his office in Paris to purchase the rights to adapt my second novel, he remained calm. I, on the other hand, was awed by the people who showed up and the amounts of money they offered. Bernard was much more reserved. Largely because of his immense cinematic knowledge, he found faults everywhere.

After the meeting, he never failed to trash the various names that had been mentioned – the producer, the director, the actors – reminding me that even the best of them had made very bad movies. "Better no film than a bad film," Bernard said to me.

At first, I couldn't understand why he was so suspicious. Then, I finally understood the reason for his caution: I had entrusted him with managing the film rights, and he didn't want to disappoint me.

He refused to sell the rights to a producer who intentionally failed to leave a tip for the coat checker in a Parisian hotel after having spent hundreds of euros on lunch to impress us, because he didn't want to work with a tightwad.

He dismissed an American director, very popular at the time, who insisted on buying the rights, because he didn't want to come to Paris to have lunch with us.

"I'm sure he's very busy," I remarked to Bernard. "You can understand why he's unable to travel from Los Angeles to Paris just for a lunch."

"If he really wanted the rights, he'd come. If he doesn't, it means that he doesn't really want to make this film, and he'll abandon the project at some point. And you, you'll end up with nothing. Don't let yourself be impressed, Joël."

Bernard turned down a Hollywood studio that made us a fantastic offer.

"All the same, Bernard," I said, "we're talking about several million dollars!"

"There's more to life than money, Joël; you need ambition as well. All of the movies produced by this studio lately have been terrible."

The highlight of these adventures involved a phone conversation organised between Bernard and one of the most influential directors in Hollywood. For the occasion, an emissary from the Paris office of the director – who spoke no French – had been sent over to translate the conversation. When the call was over, visibly quite impressed, the translator said to Bernard, "Monsieur de Fallois, do you realise that you've just spent forty-five minutes on the phone with Monsieur So-and-So? Monsieur So-and-So never has time for anyone, but you, he gave you forty-five minutes. Can you imagine!"

Bernard replied with a disappointed pout, "No, I didn't know that. I'd like you to explain it to me. Because if you had said that I had just spent forty-five minutes on the phone with the great Alfred Hitchcock, then, yes, I would have been very impressed. If you had said that I had just spent forty-five minutes on the phone with the great Buster Keaton, then, yes, I would have been very impressed. If you had said that I had just spent forty-five minutes on the phone with the great Charlie

Chaplin, then, yes, I would have been very impressed indeed. But this Monsieur So-and-So – I don't really see why I should bat an eyelid."

* * *

In the car, Scarlett laughed. "Did he really say that?"

"Yes."

"And how did it end?"

"We finally opted for a television series. Because that was the format most suitable for the novel. Bernard had been reluctant at first. For him, television was inferior to film. He would say, 'Film is the seventh art!' And then he learned about the advantages of modern television series over film; the same budgets, directors and actors, but with the benefit of an extended running time. When he saw the early footage for our series, Bernard said to me, 'Television is the new cinema.'"

As we had agreed with Sagamore, Scarlett and I arrived at the headquarters of the Judicial Police in Geneva in the mid-morning. The lieutenant was waiting for us in the lobby. He recognised me at once and greeted us warmly, before leading us to the third floor and inviting us into his office.

"So, Favraz sent you?"

"We've been trying to understand what happened in room 622 at the Hôtel de Verbier," Scarlett explained.

"I'd like to know what happened there myself," Sagamore replied. "What do you know, exactly?"

I decided to reveal our hand.

"We know that the police found something in room 622 after the murder. But what was it?"

Sagamore smiled.

"You're very well informed. Can I offer you some coffee?"

51

The Mole

Late in the afternoon of the first Tuesday in April, four months after the murder, at the headquarters of the Judicial Police, boulevard Carl-Vogt, Lieutenant Sagamore was being lectured by Hélène Righetti, commander of the Geneva police.

"Look, Lieutenant, it's been four months since the murder, and you still have nothing?"

"The case is more complicated than it seems," Sagamore tried to explain.

"Lieutenant, let me remind you that you're the one who wanted to put the Geneva police in charge of the case."

"After the discovery we made in the dead man's room," Sagamore pleaded, "it was obvious that the investigation had to be conducted from Geneva."

"And I supported you in convincing the police in the Valais to turn the case over to you," Commander Righetti interrupted, wishing to cut short any objections.

"I'm grateful to you for that," Sagamore assured her.

"Good, then you can show me how grateful you are by solving this case, Lieutenant. Because, right now, I look like an idiot, and so do you."

"Commander, I'm convinced that we need to focus on Geneva and that the case is connected with the Ebezner Bank. The break-in at Macaire Ebezner's home, shortly before the murder, was no coincidence. Then there was the food poisoning at the hotel, which prevented them from announcing the election of the new bank president. And then, later that night, one of the members of the board of directors is murdered. Everything is connected; we just have to find out how."

"You have a suspect, I presume?"

"No-one we can really pin this on, Commander."

Righetti let out a deep sigh.

"Did you search the bank?"

"No, just Jean-Bénédict Hansen's office."

"If it's all connected to the bank, as you claim, why didn't you search the whole building?"

"There was no need to search it, Commander. I have something better. I have a mole inside the bank."

"Excuse me?" Righetti said, startled. "You put a mole inside the bank without asking me first?"

"Purely by chance," Sagamore explained. "The mole has been there for months. The finance squad has been conducting a secret operation with the support of the Federal Police. There is evidence of embezzlement at the most senior level of the bank."

Righetti rolled her eyes.

"Do what you want, Sagamore, but close this case, and do it quickly."

With those words, the commander left Lieutenant Sagamore's office. Seated at his desk, he looked for a long time at the large wall display on which he had recorded all the elements of the investigation. He then checked his watch. The mole was due to arrive for a debrief any moment. He picked up the phone and called the finance division, one floor below. She was there. He asked her to come up to talk about the case.

As for the mole, her involvement had begun a little more than a year ago, right after Abel Ebezner's death, when the anti-money-laundering division of the Federal Police had issued an alert concerning large amounts of money of uncertain provenance being moved among banks in Geneva.

The investigation, conducted jointly with the Geneva Judicial Police's fraud squad, had targeted the Ebezner Bank and quickly homed in on Sinior Tarnogol. But the more the police had tried to pin Tarnogol down, the more they found themselves up against a brick wall: all their information was from the past fifteen years and the only property they could link him to was a town house at 10 rue Saint-Léger. Before that, nothing – as if the man simply hadn't existed. His identity papers were limited to a passport from a former Soviet republic whose archives had been partly destroyed, which had made it impossible to trace his history. On the strength of this passport, Tarnogol had obtained a residence permit by bribing a less-than-scrupulous employee in the Census Department of the Canton of Geneva. The employee had recently renewed this permit for a new ten-year period; the investigators had easily been able to find and expose him.

But the employee had been unable to provide the slightest bit of information on Tarnogol, about whom the investigators still knew next to nothing. In the months that followed, their attempts to tail him had proven fruitless. Tarnogol seemed capable of evaporating into the background. His network was very limited, which was unusual for a man as rich as he was. He had no friends, no family, no relations. The only connections that they had been able to establish pointed to Macaire Ebezner, who had transferred his family bank shares to him, and Lev Levovitch, who, it seemed, had introduced Tarnogol to Abel Ebezner fifteen years earlier.

The previous summer, after six months of frustration, it had been decided that a member of the fraud squad would be placed inside the Ebezner Bank to investigate clandestinely. One of the squad's recent recruits had the perfect profile: she had studied finance and had worked at a bank before joining the police. She had the necessary experience to fool everyone.

For the operation to succeed, they would need to work with someone with access to the highest levels of the bank.

* * *

June of the previous year

The large greenhouse of the Geneva Botanical Gardens was deserted except for a man waiting on the small bridge overlooking the pond. He was nervous. He wondered what the fraud squad wanted from him. Yes, he had intentionally overlooked a few things on his tax forms. But who didn't? And why have him come here? Leaning against the railing, he watched two turtles swimming peacefully between the white water lilies.

After making sure that the man was definitely the one they were expecting, the two inspectors – the mole and the head of the fraud squad – emerged from behind the large flowering bush where they had been hiding and walked across the bridge.

The man the police had approached was Jean-Bénédict Hansen; he had appeared to be the most discreet and reliable director at the bank. In the secrecy of the large greenhouse, with the only witnesses being the multicoloured goldfish and the freshwater turtles, the head of the fraud squad had explained the reasons for the meeting at some length.

"Infiltrate the bank?" Jean-Bénédict remarked as he stared at the mole.

Of course, the mole had revealed nothing of the true nature of her mission inside the bank and used a pretext that had been prepared in advance.

"We're investigating the possible laundering of drug money by bank clients who haven't yet been identified. We require absolute secrecy, even from the board of directors."

"Rest assured," Jean-Bénédict replied, suddenly pleased to find himself at the heart of an intrigue such as this.

"Do you think you can arrange for me to be hired by Sinior Tarnogol?" the mole asked.

"That's complicated. He doesn't want a secretary. He's a very secretive man. And he has no clients. It would be best to work for one of the managers. That would be more discreet. In fact, my cousin Macaire is overloaded with work right now. Ever since his father died, he's let himself fall behind. I could always tell him that I hired a secretary to assist him."

"Are you speaking of Macaire Ebezner?" the head of the fraud squad asked.

"Yes, do you know him?"

"Only by name."

That very day, when he returned to the bank, Jean-Bénédict went to see Macaire in his office and enacted the bit of theatre he had rehearsed with the investigators.

"Dear cousin, I have found you a rare pearl! A secretary who can help you get things under control. Solid experience and everything. With her help, you won't have any further problems with your clients."

"Oh, Jean-Bénédict, you're my saviour!" Macaire thanked him. "To be honest, I'm drowning in work."

The mole arrived at the bank a few days later. She was initially placed in the office shared by all the secretaries on the wealth management floor, but after a few days, she asked Jean-Bénédict to move her. She needed a more secure location, at the centre of the action, where she wouldn't be constantly spied on by her colleagues. She suggested the antechamber leading to the offices of Macaire Ebezner and Lev Levovitch (the only known links to Sinior Tarnogol). Jean-Bénédict, taking his new role very much to heart, went off to persuade his cousin.

"Say, Macaire, why don't you suggest that your new secretary move into the office in front of your own? She could help you get on top of things without anyone realising that's what she's doing. You know how news travels around here . . . it wouldn't be very good for your election as president."

Macaire was convinced by the argument. And the mole was transferred to the antechamber. During the following months, she tried, through Macaire and Levovitch, to track Tarnogol's activities – in vain.

* * *

In this late afternoon in April, at the headquarters of the Judicial Police, someone knocked on the door to Lieutenant Sagamore's office.

It was the mole.

It was Cristina.

52

Cristina

Cristina entered Sagamore's office. She was dressed in a suit that she had worn that day to the bank. But she had removed her jacket and undone her tight bun, letting her hair fall to her shoulders. Her service weapon, in a leather holster, was hooked on her belt, along with her badge.

"I'm exhausted," she said to Sagamore. "I've been posing as a secretary at the bank since June. I get the feeling I've got two jobs now."

"Well, if it's only a feeling . . ." he answered, and he started to laugh loudly.

"I'm glad you find it funny, Philippe. You know, I'd like to have a life, meet a guy, that sort of thing."

"You'll meet one, don't worry, and you'll get a promotion into the bargain – as soon as we've solved this murder."

"Is that why you wanted to see me?"

"Yes, I'd like to go over the case with you."

"Oh, please, Philippe, I was getting ready to go home, take a bath, and have a quiet dinner."

"You'll have a quiet dinner with me. I'm ordering pizza."

Cristina resigned herself. It had been ten months since she had begun her infiltration of the bank, and she wanted to conclude the investigation as badly as Sagamore wanted to solve the murder.

She examined the large wall displaying different elements of the case. She took a photo held in place by magnets and examined it carefully.

"Let's go. Let's rearrange the pieces of the puzzle."

*

A few hours later, after night had fallen over Geneva, the offices of the crime squad were empty and dark except for Lieutenant Sagamore's. At a corner of a table, Cristina and the lieutenant finished their meal of pizza and tiramisu. Facing them stood the immense whiteboard on which they had reconstituted the investigation item by item.

As Cristina eagerly attacked the container of tiramisu with a spoon, she examined the first quarter of the board, which described the facts as they were known. It was labelled "Timeline of the Murder". Beneath the title, they had attached, with small magnets, photos of Jean-Bénédict's body along with a diagram of the sixth floor of the Hôtel de Verbier, on which they had written the names of the guests.

621: Horace Hansen
622: Jean-Bénédict Hansen
623: Sinior Tarnogol
624: Lev Levovitch
625: Macaire Ebezner

Just below that list, they had placed the following note:

Jean-Bénédict Hansen was killed at around 4 in the morning in room 622 of the Hôtel de Verbier. Two 9-mm bullets practically at point-blank range. His body was found at 6:30 in the morning by a hotel employee who had brought his breakfast.

Sagamore, swallowing the last slice of pizza, stood up.

"Based on the position of the body, we have to assume that the murderer knocked on the door, Jean-Bénédict Hansen got up, put on his bathrobe to open it, and then – bam! bam! He had no chance of escaping. This wasn't a threat, or a robbery, or an argument that went wrong; it was an assassination. There's no doubt about that. The guy who did it wanted to eliminate Hansen."

"It could have been a woman," Cristina suggested. "You can't exclude that possibility."

"True," Sagamore agreed. "But statistics show that in the vast majority of cases, the killer is a man."

"And they also show that, when a woman does kill, it's often with a gun."

"Point taken. In any event, it's impossible to know whether the murderer left right away or entered Jean-Bénédict Hansen's suite. There are no signs of ransacking, no footprints, no evidence of forced entry. And let's not forget that it's a hotel room; there are traces of DNA absolutely everywhere."

"What does the ballistics report say?" Cristina asked.

"We pulled the bullets from the body intact, but they didn't tell us much. If we find the weapon, at least we might be able to identify it by comparing it with the barrel markings on the bullets."

Cristina looked at the bottom of the board, which was mostly empty, displaying only a page that was blank except for a single word: "Witnesses???"

"Still, it's hard to believe that there were no witnesses," she said.

Sagamore agreed but then added, "Some of the guests were hospitalised after the food poisoning."

"Including me!" Cristina reminded him; she had spent the night at the hospital in Martigny. "Do you think the poisoning was intended to get the guests out of the hotel so the murderer wouldn't have to worry about being seen?"

"It's hard to say. All we know is that none of the guests on that floor that evening heard anything. Before his heart attack, Horace Hansen had time to explain to the police that he was deaf as a post; he wore a hearing aid during the day but removed it before going to bed. Macaire Ebezner said that he had taken powerful sleeping pills, which was confirmed by his doctor. Lev Levovitch and one of the human resources managers at the bank insisted that they had heard absolutely nothing.

Another guest reported that he was awakened briefly by a noise, but since he didn't hear anything else, he went back to sleep without asking any questions."

The lieutenant then pointed to a diagram of the ground floor of the hotel.

"After ten p.m., access to the hotel is restricted to the main entrance. There are two cameras on it along with a security guard. The guard stated that he didn't see anyone that night. The security footage confirms it."

"What about the other exits?" Cristina asked, pointing to what appeared in the diagram to be different doors leading to the outside.

"All the exits are locked at night, except for the emergency exits, which open only from the inside. No-one could have entered the hotel that way."

"Unless they had an accomplice," Cristina noted. "Someone could have opened the door from the inside and let them in. Then at least two people would be involved. But I don't buy that idea. The murder feels like it was spontaneous. Killing Jean-Bénédict Hansen in a hotel with a gun implies some kind of sudden impulse. He had to die that very night. That sounds like someone acting alone, someone isolated, desperate."

Sagamore smiled.

"So, you're getting back to my conjecture, the only element in this whole business that I'm sure of."

"And what's that?"

"That the murderer was inside the hotel. He – or she – was a guest, someone from the bank or invited by the bank; whoever it was, it was someone who was already on the premises."

"And who then fled using one of the emergency exits?" Cristina suggested.

"It's possible. Unfortunately, it was snowing heavily that night and we weren't able to pick up any tracks around the hotel. But I don't think the murderer did flee the hotel. He killed Hansen and returned to his own room before pretending to be surprised the next morning. The murderer was there, in the hotel, right in front of us. I'm sure of it."

Cristina remained quiet, thoughtful. Then she asked him, "Who was the last person to see Jean-Bénédict Hansen?"

"Sinior Tarnogol. I know because hotel security came up to his room on Saturday night, a few hours before the murder."

Sagamore took from the board an excerpt from the statement made to the police on the morning of the murder by the hotel's head of security, and gave it to Cristina to read.

Saturday evening, December 15, at 11:50 p.m., I was called because of a commotion in room 623. I immediately went to the room in question, where I was met by a man who assured me that everything was okay. I thought that maybe it was the wrong room. There was no noise in the corridor. Everything appeared to be quiet. I didn't insist and left. I told the manager just in case I needed to go back. It had been a strange evening, and it was better to be cautious. But there was no follow-up call. The night was calm. Then, the next day, a body was found in room 622.

"The head of security is certain," Sagamore continued, "that the man who opened the door to room 623 was Jean-Bénédict Hansen. The head of security recognised Hansen later from a photo. But 623 was Tarnogol's room."

"And Jean-Bénédict Hansen was staying in 622. What does that mean?" she asked.

"You'll see," Sagamore said, pointing a finger at the next section of the board, labelled "Suspects".

Beneath the title hung two photos. One was of Lev Levovitch, the other of Macaire Ebezner. Each of the pictures was accompanied by a short explanatory note.

Lev Levovitch

Had been known as Abel Ebezner's right hand; the old man considered him his spiritual son.

The board was about to elect him the new president. Jean-Bénédict Hansen seemed opposed to that choice, preferring his cousin, Macaire Ebezner. Lev Levovitch decided to leave Geneva shortly after the murder. He gave up the suite he had been living in at the Hôtel des Bergues for the past fifteen years. To go where? Why the sudden departure?

"We know that Levovitch has significant property holdings," Sagamore noted. "A house in an upscale New York suburb, an apartment in Athens, and a house in Corfu."

"Based on my information," Cristina added, "he's in Athens. He claims that he needed a change. He was in Geneva today; I saw him at the bank. He came to see Macaire, who convinced him not to resign. Macaire put Lev in charge of the Athens office, and he'll continue to manage his clients from there. In my opinion, managing the Athens office is a pretext found by Macaire to keep up appearances for the bank's customers. Macaire might be president, but the real star has always been Levovitch. If he resigns, it's going to hurt the bank."

Sagamore wrote with a marker on the board, next to Levovitch's photo: "Athens?" Then he pointed to the note for Macaire.

Macaire Ebezner

Home burglary: he's lying about the contents of his safe. He claims it held important bank documents, which he placed there to protect them in the event of a fire, but this is not very credible. There could be a connection with the death of his cousin.

He was seen in the hotel's kitchen rummaging around in the cases of vodka with Jean-Bénédict Hansen. No connection with the poisoning of the guests has yet been made.

414

He has a licence for a 9 mm pistol, the same type that was used
for the murder. He agreed to a ballistics check of his weapon; the
rifling on the barrel doesn't match that of the weapon used to kill
Jean-Bénédict Hansen.

No proof that would enable us to charge him.

Sagamore had only displayed the names of Lev Levovitch and Macaire Ebezner. Cristina was surprised that the lieutenant hadn't included Tarnogol.

"You said that Tarnogol was the last person to have seen Hansen alive," she remarked. "And hotel security came up to investigate the 'commotion' in his suite, where Hansen was found. And right after the murder, Tarnogol dropped out of sight, his only explanation being the letter of resignation he left behind. Why isn't Tarnogol on the list of suspects? I can't imagine you simply forgot."

Sagamore smiled slyly.

"I'm getting to it," he promised before continuing with the commentary on his whiteboard.

From the names of the two suspects highlighted by the lieutenant an arrow had been drawn leading to the last part of the board: "Motive: The Presidency?"

"Why kill Jean-Bénédict Hansen?" Sagamore asked. "According to his wife, he had no enemies and had never received any threats. The only motive I can think of is in connection with the presidency of the bank."

"It was Levovitch's name that should have been announced by the board that Saturday evening in the hotel ballroom," Cristina reminded him. "We have the report from that police inspector from the Valais, who stated that he clearly heard Horace Hansen say, 'Levovitch president.'"

"Right, but he'd had a heart attack," Sagamore objected. "I'm not certain that an investigating magistrate is going to take that evidence into consideration."

Cristina wasn't entirely convinced and went on with her argument.

"We could easily imagine that Levovitch killed Jean-Bénédict because Jean-Bénédict wanted to prevent him from becoming president, hoping to see the position go to his cousin Macaire. We know that Jean-Bénédict Hansen was a minority voice on the board, because Sinior Tarnogol and Horace Hansen supported Levovitch. Isn't it possible that, after Levovitch was elected but before the announcement was made, Jean-Bénédict Hansen informed Macaire of the result? And that Macaire, who knew he was threatened by Levovitch, had planned for this eventuality? Perhaps he then poisoned the vodka served in the cocktail so that the announcement would be delayed, to buy himself time."

"Unfortunately, you have no proof to support your theory," Sagamore retorted.

"Macaire Ebezner and Jean-Bénédict Hansen were seen in the kitchen rummaging around in the vodka crates," Cristina reminded the lieutenant. "Perhaps Levovitch discovered after the poisoning that Jean-Bénédict Hansen was plotting against him, and killed Hansen in revenge."

"And then leaves for Athens?" Sagamore remarked. "Your hypothesis doesn't make sense."

"Do you have a better one?" she asked.

"Yes. I think that Macaire Ebezner killed Jean-Bénédict Hansen to ensure that he would become president."

"But Jean-Bénédict Hansen did everything he could to help his cousin become president," Cristina remarked.

"Two days before the murder, Anastasia Ebezner, Macaire's wife, was hit by a car in front of the Hôtel des Bergues. I questioned the doctor who attended her at the hospital. It was Jean-Bénédict Hansen who was driving; he stated that he had forgotten to turn on his headlights and hadn't seen her. The next morning, a day before the election, Anastasia Ebezner surprised a burglar in the house. None of this can simply be coincidence."

"You think the burglar could have been Jean-Bénédict Hansen?" Cristina asked.

"It's a possibility. Maybe he wanted to put pressure on Macaire, first by going after his wife, then by breaking into his safe, perhaps looking for compromising information."

"Any news on Anastasia?" Cristina asked.

"No. I tried to locate her but without success. I questioned everyone who knew her, but she didn't really have any friends. And, honestly, I don't see a connection with our investigation. On the day of the break-in, she left a note for her husband telling him she was leaving him. She wanted to take advantage of her husband's absence to take off. It's just another break-up story that doesn't really concern us here."

"To get back to the investigation," Cristina said. "I really don't see what motive Macaire Ebezner would have had for killing Jean-Bénédict Hansen."

"Because Macaire discovered the truth about his cousin."

"The truth?" she said, with surprise. "What truth?"

Sagamore's face assumed a more serious expression.

"Cristina, there's an aspect of this investigation that I've kept hidden from everyone, except for the members of my team and the head of police in the Valais. It's the main reason why the Valais police turned the case over to us. It's probably the key to this entire investigation."

"Well, spit it out, then!" Cristina urged him.

"I think everything goes back to the initial investigation, the one that began before Hansen's murder, the one you joined ten months ago when you infiltrated the bank. I think it's all connected."

Cristina didn't look convinced.

"I don't see what you're driving at, Philippe. Besides, you never explained why Tarnogol isn't on your board if he really is at the heart of the investigation."

"Do you like surprises?" Sagamore asked.

"Not much."

"Then you're not going to like this."

Sagamore then placed a piece of paper on the last open part of his diagram. On it was written "Who is Sinior Tarnogol?"

Cristina read the words aloud. In reply, Sagamore simply went to a small metal cabinet in which he kept several folders. He removed a large opaque plastic bag.

"The morning of the murder, as soon as I was informed, I went to the Hôtel de Verbier."

"I know that," Cristina remarked. "We saw each other there that day. You arrived from Geneva, and I arrived from the hospital."

Sagamore shook the bag he held in his hand.

"I found this in Jean-Bénédict Hansen's suite, at the bottom of a wardrobe."

Sagamore thrust his hand into the bag. Everything inside had been analysed by the forensic team several months earlier, which meant it could be handled without compromising the evidence. The first object that Sagamore removed was a long coat, which he put on. The coat was stuffed in different locations in such a way as to lend the wearer a strange type of corpulence. At first, Cristina didn't understand what the disguise was supposed to mean. Then the lieutenant removed what looked like a silicone mask and put it on his face. Cristina suddenly stepped back, terrified. How was it possible? The man who stood before her was no longer her colleague, Philippe Sagamore, but Sinior Tarnogol.

Tarnogol had never existed. He was a creation of Jean-Bénédict Hansen.

* * *

That evening, in Lieutenant Sagamore's office, Cristina spent long minutes studying the silicone face she held in her hands. She couldn't get over it – it was a fake of absolutely extraordinary quality; the care and talent with which it was made were light years from anything she

418

had ever seen before. It was unlike any of the masks sold in specialist shops. This one was made with great attention to detail and one-of-a-kind technology. The roughness of the skin was impressively authentic. The individual hair follicles had been inserted perfectly. The colour of the skin gave an impression of life. It was truly terrifying. The silicone used was extremely fine, perfectly moluding itself to the form of the wearer's face, even the lips and eyes. It reacted to movement as if it were natural skin – the nose, the wrinkles and folds of the face moved with absolute realism. The mask was clearly the work of a highly skilled professional. It was unlike anything she had seen before.

She was speechless. Once the shock had passed, she listened to Sagamore detail the various elements he had collected to prove the shared identity of Jean-Bénédict Hansen and Sinior Tarnogol. For each of them, he posted a sheet of paper on the board.

Item 1
Hotel security is called for a "commotion" in room 623, Sinior Tarnogol's room. Inside, Jean-Bénédict Hansen opens the door and assures them that everything is okay.

Item 2
A bag containing clothing as well as a silicone mask of Tarnogol's face is found in Jean-Bénédict Hansen's suite.

Item 3
Inside the mask, hairs belonging to Jean-Bénédict Hansen were found.

Item 4
Tarnogol lived in a town house at 10 rue Saint-Léger, purchased through a shell company based in the British Virgin Islands and directly tied to JBH SA, the personal holding company of Jean-Bénédict Hansen.

Item 5

A search of the town house at 10 rue Saint-Léger led to the discovery of personal effects belonging to Jean-Bénédict Hansen.

Item 6

The schedules of Hansen and Tarnogol reveal that they frequently travelled at the same time.

Item 7

It was Jean-Bénédict Hansen who was, on behalf of the board, in charge of organising the Gala Weekend. And, as if by accident, he and Tarnogol were given neighbouring rooms. By using the balcony, Jean-Bénédict would have been able to move from one room to the other without anyone noticing anything. Jean-Bénédict entered room 622, and a few moments later Sinior Tarnogol left room 623.

Item 8

The breakfast that Jean-Bénédict Hansen ordered the morning of his murder included eggs, caviar, black tea, and a small glass of Beluga vodka. According to employees at the Hôtel de Verbier, this was Sinior Tarnogol's preferred breakfast.

Item 9

Tarnogol mysteriously disappeared after the murder of Jean-Bénédict Hansen.

Item 10

A letter of resignation, signed by Tarnogol, was found in Jean-Bénédict Hansen's safe along with the shares sold by Macaire Ebezner to Sinior Tarnogol fifteen years earlier. Most likely, Hansen wanted to find a way to get rid of his bothersome persona and get hold of the shares.

Cristina was stunned by what she had learned.

"Jean-Bénédict Hansen was leading us on from the start," she said, reviewing the various items displayed on the board.

"That would explain why you discovered nothing about Tarnogol in six months at the bank," Sagamore remarked.

Cristina was furious with herself; she had been taken in like an inexperienced cadet. From the start, Jean-Bénédict Hansen had been manipulating her. For fifteen years, he had been deceiving them all.

53

Geneva (Part 2)

"Until the April after the murder, no-one knew about this," Sagamore explained to us, "aside from a handful of colleagues within the crime squads of the Valais and Geneva police departments, and they were sworn to secrecy. Cristina was the first person I spoke to about all this. And she was a big help in sorting things out."

Sagamore had prepared a pile of documents for us. He spread them out on the table so we could examine them.

"Is this the file for the murder investigation?" I asked. Sagamore nodded yes.

"You can look at it, but you can't take it with you; and remember, I didn't show you anything."

Among the documents were photos of the Ebezner home and a room with a broken window.

"Is this the break-in that took place two days before the murder?" Scarlett asked.

"Yes, how did you know?"

"We spoke to the Ebezners' neighbour," Scarlett said. "But let's get back to your investigation. You were saying that by April, four months after the murder, you had no conclusive proof."

"Well, not much."

"Any leads? Or a suspect?"

"Just a personal conviction that the murderer had uncovered Jean-Bénédict Hansen's double identity."

"And when you say 'murderer', were you thinking of someone in particular?"

"Macaire Ebezner. During the Gala Weekend, he found out that Jean-Bénédict Hansen was really Tarnogol and had been manipulating him for fifteen years. He understood that it was his cousin who was preventing him from becoming president. He decided to eliminate him, killing two birds with one stone – by killing Jean-Bénédict Hansen, he also killed Sinior Tarnogol. It meant the board of directors was in no position to hurt Macaire; the remaining member of the board, Horace Hansen, was not a man of great character. Ebezner knew that the presidency was his if he got rid of his cousin. So, on the night of the fifteenth of December, he put his plan in motion. He just had to leave his room and knock on the door three rooms away. When the occupant opened the door, he fired two shots and returned to his room. Even if he was heard, even if someone on the floor woke up and went into the hallway to see what was going on, he would have had time to return to his room and swallow a sleeping pill, as he did every other night. A solid alibi that was later confirmed by his doctor. The weapon used for the crime? Most likely it was an unregistered gun bought second-hand from an individual. Macaire told the police that he owned a registered gun, even willingly agreeing to a ballistics check, pretending to be naïve to fool everyone around him. But he is an accomplished marksman. I know because I found out that he practised frequently at a shooting range outside Geneva."

Someone knocked on the door. It was an inspector, who had come to ask his superior about an urgent matter.

"Please excuse me a moment," Sagamore said, leaving the room.

He disappeared into the hallway with his colleague. Scarlett grabbed her mobile and began to take pictures of the documents on the table.

"Are you crazy?" I said, stopping her. "You can't do that."

"This is a gold mine, Writer. Sagamore told us we couldn't take the file with us. Hurry up and help! Take photos of whatever you can. Each one of us takes a pile."

I obeyed. It was now or never if we were going to get crucial information about the investigation.

54

The Music Box

Anastasia had slept badly. For the first time since her arrival in Corfu, she awoke long before Lev. It was still dark outside. For a moment, she looked at her lover as he slept peacefully, then she got up. She drew a bath and stayed in it for a long time. She was worried. She had the impression that clouds were beginning to gather over their little Greek paradise.

The night before, she had been happy to see Lev when he got back from Geneva. They had eaten dinner in the large dining room, lit with candles. Everything was perfect. Still, she had the feeling that something wasn't right.

"Did everything go okay in Geneva?" she asked.

"Yes," he assured her.

To judge by the way he looked away when he replied, she knew he was lying. She decided to dig deeper.

"You said you had a meeting at the bank."

"Yes."

"With clients?"

"With Macaire. He wanted to see me."

"Macaire? Why?"

"He asked me to postpone my resignation. He says that my departure risks destabilising the bank. He offered me the Athens office, said I could manage my portfolio from there."

"I hope you refused."

"I had to accept."

It was their first argument in Corfu. She told him that he had promised to quit the bank, and he replied that nothing would change, that he could work from Athens.

"We were supposed to come to Corfu to be together," Anastasia reminded him.

"We will be together! This doesn't change anything. It's only once a week. I can do the round trip to Athens in a day."

"I get the impression that you don't want to leave the bank."

"It's just that I don't want to raise any suspicions."

"Suspicions? What suspicions?"

He was evasive.

"I want us to be left alone. No more problems."

"If you wanted us to be left alone, you would have resigned. The bank can get by without you."

"It's more complicated than that."

"Lev, sometimes I get the feeling that you're hiding something from me."

He laughed, as if she wasn't making sense.

"I'm not hiding anything, really. What would I hide? I have to work, Anastasia."

"You have enough money not to have to work."

"That's what I haven't told you. I'm not as rich as you think."

To divert her attention, he poured more wine. She knew he was lying. And it wasn't like him to talk about money.

"Do I have to remind you that you were living in a suite at the most luxurious hotel in Geneva?"

"The suite at the Bergues is nothing compared to this house, with the staff, the dresses . . ."

"Lev," she interrupted, "I don't care about any of that. I don't care about money, I've always told you that. We could live in a barn, without a penny, and I'd be perfectly happy. And if we need money, I'll work. I could get a job at a boutique in town. I'd be very happy."

Lev burst out laughing. He seemed to take great delight in her last remark. He rose from the table, took Anastasia by the hand, and led her out on to the terrace. In the mild spring evening, they could hear the sea and the gulls. In the distance the lights from the town glittered. It was a dream. He wrapped his arms around her, and she felt good again – until she awoke at dawn.

In her bath, Anastasia was lost in thought. Why couldn't Lev sever his ties with Geneva? She was convinced he was lying to her. She was convinced he was hiding something.

Lieutenant Sagamore had slept badly. He woke up at dawn as usual. At first, he thought it was far too early to get out of bed; he still had two good hours of sleep ahead of him. But after fifteen minutes of day-dreaming, his eyes staring at the ceiling, he quietly got up.

In the darkened kitchen of the family apartment, Sagamore made himself some coffee. Cup in hand, he walked over to the window, watching the empty street. The investigation was getting to him. He thought about his conversation with Cristina the night before in his office. In spite of all the proof he had shown her, she had told him, "I don't think Jean-Bénédict Hansen could have been Tarnogol."

Sagamore was surprised by her reaction.

"Look, Cristina, between the silicone mask and the hair found inside – there's a DNA match with Jean-Bénédict Hansen – and Tarnogol's town house, which belongs to Hansen; the objects found there that belong to Hansen; and even the breakfast of caviar, eggs, and vodka ordered by Hansen in his room, what more do you need?"

"I agree, it's all pretty convincing," she admitted. "But how could Jean-Bénédict Hansen have been seen with Tarnogol if Jean-Bénédict *was* Tarnogol?"

"Did you see them together often?" Sagamore asked her.

Cristina thought for a moment.

"No, not really," she replied, suddenly uncertain. "I never saw them together . . . except that Saturday evening at the Gala Weekend in the ballroom. They were side by side on the stage, while Horace Hansen was getting ready to make the announcement."

"He had an accomplice," Sagamore said. "Someone who looked like Tarnogol wore the mask and stood by Jean-Bénédict's side so he wouldn't be suspected."

Cristina recalled that, at the moment of the announcement, Tarnogol and Jean-Bénédict had remained silent while Horace took the microphone. If Tarnogol didn't have to speak, any accomplice would have sufficed. Nonetheless, she was still doubtful.

"I'm sure you'll find dozens of employees at the bank who'll claim to have seen Jean-Bénédict Hansen and Tarnogol together. And how could Jean-Bénédict have fooled everyone during board meetings?"

"It was his accomplice who was present at those meetings. All they would have to do is assume the right accent – somebody from Eastern Europe – and not talk too much."

Cristina was not totally convinced by this either.

"I didn't know Abel Ebezner," she said, "but from what I've been told, I get the impression that he wasn't the type of man to let himself be conned easily. Tarnogol is a perfect deception. It required intelligence, talent, and unusual presence of mind. I don't think Jean-Bénédict Hansen was capable of that."

"Unless Jean-Bénédict Hansen's genius was such that he pretended to be less brilliant than he actually was and fooled everyone around him. That would be proof enough of his talent. He was completely above suspicion."

Cristina considered Sagamore's comment carefully.

"Were you able to trace the mask?" she asked. "Find out who made it?"

"I tried, but no luck. The specialists in the region I questioned said they had never seen anything like it. It's cutting-edge technology. It's Hollywood quality."

Cristina's doubts had destabilised Sagamore. That morning, in his kitchen, after thinking about their conversation again, he made a decision that would change the direction of the investigation.

He got ready for work, set the breakfast table for his wife and their two children, who were still asleep, and went to the police headquarters on boulevard Carl-Vogt.

Sagamore believed that only a small circle of police officers were aware of the existence of the bag found in Jean-Bénédict Hansen's room. He was wrong about that.

Macaire Ebezner had slept badly. It was eight thirty in the morning in Cologny when he walked into the kitchen in his bathrobe, his hair uncombed. Arma was making toast and poaching eggs for the third time – her employer was an hour and a half late for his usual routine. Since becoming president, he would have breakfast at seven sharp every morning. He always appeared in a splendid three-piece suit from his wardrobe, which had been completely refreshed to suit his new position. He would have his coffee and eggs with a slice of wholewheat toast (to maintain his figure) while reading the newspaper. At 7:20, at the latest, he left the house to go to the bank.

"Is everything okay, Moussieu?" Arma asked, surprised to see Macaire in the kitchen so late.

"Up at dawn, went back to sleep, didn't hear my alarm," Macaire summarised grumpily as he sat down at the table. Arma immediately prepared a cup of strong coffee for him.

"I didn't want to knock," she said as she placed a steaming cup before him. "I should have. It's my fault you're late."

"It's not important."

He wiped his hand over his face. He was pale.

"Are you sick, Moussieu?"

"No, I'm worried."

"Worried?"

"In a way."

"Is it the bank?"

Macaire didn't reply and drank his coffee. He was tired; he needed a good night's sleep. In spite of his sleeping pills, for the past two months he kept waking up every morning at dawn. He'd open his eyes, overcome by an anxiety that he couldn't shake and which prevented him from going back to sleep.

Arma kept talking, but he wasn't listening. He wolfed down his breakfast and went off to his bedroom. He needed to think calmly, but there was no calm. At the bank, he was constantly interrupted, and at the house, Arma was always after him out of concern for his well-being. He sat at his desk. In front of him were a few bank documents he was supposed to sort, of little interest; photos of Anastasia; and a miniature music box. He picked it up with a mechanical gesture before putting it down as if the object had burned his fingers. He thought of what had happened two months earlier, an evening in mid-February. That was when he started having insomnia. He had gone to the opera in Geneva after receiving, by mail, a ticket for Tchaikovsky's *Swan Lake*. Discovering the invitation, he immediately understood: it was Wagner; he wanted to get in touch with Macaire again.

* * *

Mid-February, two months after Jean-Bénédict's murder

The intermission was almost over. The bell could be heard. The audience at the Grand Théâtre in Geneva quickly returned to their seats. Act III of *Swan Lake* was about to begin.

In the empty foyer, two men were seated on a marble bench, side by side.

"I thought I was no longer in active service," Macaire said, "that I was too exposed because of my job as president."

"That's true," Wagner said. "I simply wanted to congratulate you on the success of your last mission for P-30. We're rid of Tarnogol, and you're president of the bank."

"Thanks," was all Macaire said in reply, not understanding the allusion to Tarnogol.

After a short silence, Wagner said, "Macaire, I want to ask you a question, if you don't mind."

"Please, go ahead."

"Why kill Jean-Bénédict Hansen with a gun? Why take such a risk?"

Macaire sat there for a moment, unable to speak.

"What? I didn't kill Jean-Béné!"

Wagner smiled.

"Okay, well, I only asked out of curiosity. I thought you might have followed the Horace Hansen example. That was much cleaner."

"Horace Hansen died of a heart attack," Macaire reminded him.

"A heart attack!" Wagner repeated. He seemed to find the response amusing.

"I don't understand what you're getting at," Macaire responded angrily.

"Please don't pretend to be so innocent. I know that you're very talented in concealing your actions. You killed Horace Hansen. You used the vial of poison, the first one I gave you. A heart attack after twelve hours, completely untraceable, the perfect crime. You got away with the perfect crime when it came to the father. However, the son? That was a bloody mess."

"But I had no part in any of it, Wagner. If I had killed someone, it would have been Tarnogol."

Wagner laughed quietly.

"I'm aware of that as well, Macaire. Don't take me for a fool."

"Aware of what?"

"That your cousin, Jean-Bénédict, was Sinior Tarnogol."

"What? What are you talking about?"

"Come on, Macaire, not with me. I know that Tarnogol never existed; he was a creation of Jean-Bénédict Hansen. He had been impersonating Tarnogol since the beginning."

"But what the . . . what are you talking about?" Macaire muttered in confusion.

Faced with his incredulity, Wagner realised then that Macaire knew nothing of what had happened.

"The police didn't say anything to you?" Wagner asked, surprised. "In Jean-Bénédict's suite there was a silicone mask – of Tarnogol. Tarnogol never existed! It was all one big hoax."

Macaire stared at Wagner. For a second, he wondered whether Wagner had been sent by the police to feed him some cock and bull story and try to tease out anything he might know about Jean-Bénédict's murder.

"I don't believe a word of what you're saying, Wagner. I spent fifteen years with Tarnogol; believe me, he was real. And if what you say is true, why wouldn't the police have mentioned it?"

Wagner didn't dispute this. He stood up and extended his hand to Macaire.

"I didn't come to argue with you. I wanted to apologise for the way I acted back in December. You've got a lot more backbone than I thought. If you need P-30 one of these days, for whatever reason, we'll be there for you."

With those words, Wagner took from his pocket a small packet, which he offered to Macaire. Macaire simply stared at it. Wagner said to him, "It's a gift. Open it."

Inside the package was a small wooden music box that was activated by turning a tiny handle. On the front, the following was engraved: *Swan Lake, Act II, Scene 10.*

"If you need me, simply turn the handle and let it play. I'll come running." And with that, he walked away.

* * *

431

In his small office, two months later, Macaire went over his last conversation with Wagner. Since that day, being president had left a bitter taste in his mouth. The intoxicating sensation of power had been ruined. Had P-30 orchestrated the deaths of Jean-Bénédict and Horace Hansen? Was Macaire involved, even indirectly, in some terrible plot? Was he sitting on a throne of blood? He didn't know what to believe. It worried him, the whole thing. He could no longer sleep soundly – as if he had something to reproach himself for.

He returned to his room to get ready for work, then left the house to go to the bank. He was now very late. He made up an excuse. When his car left the grounds of his property, it was nine thirty.

It was nine thirty in the morning. Sagamore felt it was a reasonable hour for an impromptu visit and pressed the intercom of the house on rue des Granges, in the heart of Geneva's old town. After he identified himself, the massive wood gate opened, and he entered the interior courtyard, holding in his hand the bag he had brought from police headquarters. At the far side of the courtyard was the main door to the building. An employee greeted the lieutenant. He presented his badge and repeated what he had said on the intercom.

"Lieutenant Sagamore, crime squad. I've come to see Charlotte Hansen."

The employee nodded respectfully and led the inspector inside. They crossed a long hallway; the floor was white marble, the walls covered in expensive fabric. Sagamore had been to the Hansen home several times before, yet he remained impressed by the luxurious decorations. The room into which he was ushered resembled a museum. The employee offered him tea or coffee, which he politely declined, then left him alone and went to alert the lady of the house.

Sagamore had come to see Charlotte Hansen and tell her what he had discovered about her husband. It was a decision he had made that very morning at dawn. He felt it was the best way to provide fresh

impetus for the investigation. For if Jean-Bénédict had indeed impersonated Tarnogol for fifteen years, Sagamore had a hard time believing
that Jean-Bénédict's wife would know nothing about it. She might even
have been his accomplice. He knew that her reaction when presented
with this revelation would reveal the truth. It was time to play his trump
card.

The door to the living room opened and Charlotte Hansen appeared.
He hadn't seen her in a while, and she appeared to have lost weight.

"Hello, Lieutenant," she said, shaking his hand vigorously. "Do you
have any news about my husband's murder?"

They sat in two armchairs facing each other, and after a rapid summary of the investigation, Sagamore decided to take the plunge.

"Madame Hansen, I'm wondering how well you knew your
husband . . ."

"What?" she said, clearly worried.

In response, Sagamore simply removed the silicone mask from his
bag and put it on. Charlotte's reaction, one of terror, was similar to Cristina's the previous day.

"Tarnogol," she murmured, fearfully. "What . . . what does this
mean?"

Sagamore removed the mask.

"We found this in your husband's hotel room at the Verbier. We
have good reason to believe that your husband and Tarnogol were one
and the same – that he invented Tarnogol and was impersonating him
all these years. He deceived everyone – including you, apparently."

Charlotte remained silent for several moments. She then reacted to
the shock by questioning the policeman's claims, assuring him that he
was mistaken. Sagamore told her about the town house on rue Saint-
Léger, which had been bought by a shell company owned by Jean-Bénédict
Hansen. Charlotte, still in a state of shock, continued to deny Sagamore's allegations. To support his claims, he showed her the bank
documents he had brought with him. He then presented several objects

in transparent plastic bags: business cards, some in the name of Jean-Bénédict Hansen, others in the name of Sinior Tarnogol; a shirt embroidered with the initials *JBH*; a lighter; cigars; a bottle of cologne.

"Do you recognise these?"

"Yes. That's the cologne my husband used, the cigars he smoked, one of his shirts, his lighter – I recognise it, it's a Dupont, and he was very fond of it. There's nothing surprising about finding all this in his hotel room."

"We found them in the town house at 10 rue Saint-Léger," Sagamore clarified. "Madame Hansen, that town house is only a few minutes from here, and the bank is close as well. You have to admit, it's quite convenient. Your husband could move from one place to the other, under an assumed appearance, without anyone suspecting anything."

When his visit was over, Sagamore returned to his unmarked car, parked on the place du Mézel. Cristina was sitting in the passenger seat, waiting for him. She had called in sick to the bank that morning so she could work on the investigation.

"Well?" she asked Sagamore as he got into the driver's seat.

"Well, we'll have to wait and see how she reacts," he replied, as he observed the entrance gate of the Hansens' town house, not far away.

55

Secrets

That same day, in the late afternoon, in the Ebezner home in Cologny, Arma was pacing outside the door to Macaire's office, under the pretext of dusting, trying as best she could to listen to the conversation taking place within. But unfortunately she heard nothing. All she knew was that it was connected with the murder of Monsieur's cousin.

Madame Hansen had come to the house earlier, very nervous, trembling, in fact. She didn't appear to be her usual self. Monsieur had immediately led her into his office and they had locked themselves in. It must be serious, then. He never received anyone in there.

Inside the room, Macaire and Charlotte were whispering, aware of the gravity of the situation.

"How could Jean-Béné have been Tarnogol?" Macaire repeated, unable to believe the possibility. "It's impossible! I saw them together."

"Often?"

The question shook Macaire's certainty. Considering the matter, he realised that, over the years, he had rarely seen the two of them together.

"Tarnogol wasn't at the bank much," he noted. "He always seemed to be coming and going, which makes sense now. But there were the board meetings. Jean-Béné and Tarnogol were both there; how could they have been the same person? Did Jean-Béné have an accomplice, someone who assumed Tarnogol's appearance?"

"So, you think it's really Jean-Béné who created all this?"

"I have no idea," Macaire confided. "Given what the police showed you, I would like to have some information to prove the contrary.

Unfortunately, there are no members of the board still alive who could help us sort this out."

There was a moment of uneasy silence. Then Macaire asked Charlotte, "Did you bring Jean-Béné's appointment book?"

With a nervous gesture she pulled a leather notebook from her handbag. Macaire opened it to the week before the Gala Weekend.

"During the night of Monday, December tenth, to Tuesday, the eleventh, I saw Tarnogol," he explained. "I was with him at three in the morning, after I returned from Basel, where I had gone to do him a favour."

Macaire put his finger on the corresponding box in the appointment book.

"It says he was in Zurich. I remember that Monday. The day when all this madness started. I recall that he left the bank for some so-called meeting in Zurich. And shortly afterwards, Tarnogol shows up in my office, on the pretext of having come to see Levovitch, and asks me to go to Basel to pick up an envelope for him."

"So Jean-Bénédict would have needed to have rapidly changed his appearance?"

"You told me that the town house on 10 rue Saint-Léger belonged to . . ."

"The police discovered that. He never spoke to me about it."

"He had plenty of time to leave the bank as Jean-Bénédict, change his appearance at the town house on rue Saint-Léger, and return as Tarnogol. It's a walk of less than ten minutes between the two locations. So that night, returning from Basel, thinking I was with Tarnogol, I was with Jean-Béné."

"And I thought he was in Zurich," Charlotte said.

Macaire was in a state of shock. Jean-Bénédict's planner was still open. Macaire slid his finger over to Tuesday, December 11, where Jean-Bénédict had written: "Dinner with Macaire."

"That Tuesday evening, Jean-Béné and I had worked out a plan together in my dining room, a plan to neutralise Tarnogol on the night of Thursday, December thirteenth."

"Neutralise Tarnogol?" she choked. "What are you saying?"

"After the Association of Bankers dinner, I was supposed to walk with Tarnogol along the Rhône, empty and dark at that time of year. Jean-Béné, driving his car, was supposed to pretend not to see us, and I was to prevent a collision with Tarnogol by pulling him towards me. He would have owed me his life and would have backed me for president."

Charlotte stared at Macaire uneasily.

"And what happened that night?"

"For some strange reason, Tarnogol didn't stay for the dinner. What a coincidence, right? As if he were aware of our plan."

"That was the night Anastasia was hit by Jean-Bénédict. I was at an organ concert with my sister, and Jean-Béné was supposedly as sick as a dog."

"He wasn't sick," Macaire revealed. "What time did you leave for your concert?"

"Early, because we had dinner before the performance."

"As soon as you left, Jean-Béné went to the Hôtel des Bergues disguised as Tarnogol. I ran into him there; he walked in front of me. Then Levovitch told me that Tarnogol was ill and had asked him to take his place at the dinner. When I think about it now, I realise that it was all intentional. After leaving the hotel as Tarnogol, Jean-Béné hid in his car on the quai des Bergues, where he resumed his normal appearance, and waited, as we had agreed in our plan."

"But why?"

"So I could see him at the end of the dinner and wouldn't suspect his secret. He would have played dumb and asked me where Tarnogol was. But I think he had something else in mind: getting rid of Levovitch."

"Levovitch?"

"I think that Jean-Béné, alias Tarnogol, asked Levovitch to replace him at the dinner for a very specific reason. He suspected that

Levovitch, after the evening, would take a walk on the quay to stretch his legs – which is what happened. When Jean-Béné saw us, him and me, in front of the hotel, he didn't hesitate for a second: he wanted to run Levovitch over – to eliminate him. It was the perfect crime; there were no witnesses. And if Jean-Béné was questioned, he had a solid alibi that you would have confirmed: he had spent the evening sick in his bed. As for me, he would have assured me that he had thought I was with Tarnogol and that he had only carried out the plan that I had orchestrated. I couldn't have said anything because I was in it up to my neck. But his plan hit a snag. Anastasia walked in front of his car just as he pulled on to the quay, and he hit her instead."

"But why would he want to kill Levovitch?"

"To become president himself. Jean-Béné already had ample power at the bank because he was a member of the board alongside his father. He must have had a plan to undermine my father's last wishes and take control of the bank officially. But he couldn't carry out his plan with Levovitch around. Levovitch was always too powerful."

After hearing his explanations, Charlotte Hansen turned pale and remained silent for a long time.

"I don't believe it," she said softly.

Macaire drove in the final nail.

"That evening, after the accident, you joined us at the hospital, then we all came here, do you remember?"

"Yes, absolutely."

"How did you get to the hospital?"

"I took my sister's car. She was parked next to Victoria Hall. I wanted to get to the hospital quickly, so she gave me her keys, and we agreed that I would return the car the following day."

"So, when you left here, that night, Jean-Béné was in his car, and you were in your sister's car?"

"Yes, that's right . . . Why do you ask?"

"Because, right after you left, Tarnogol appeared at my door wanting to talk to me. So much for being sick, he was suddenly as fresh as a daisy. Then, throughout the weekend at the Hôtel de Verbier, I never saw Jean-Béné and Tarnogol together, until the moment of the last board meeting on Saturday afternoon. Right from the start, it was Jean-Béné who was running the show."

When Charlotte Hansen left Macaire, she was more shocked than when she had arrived. Leaving the property, at the wheel of her car, which stalled several times because of her nervousness, she didn't notice the unmarked vehicle parked discreetly on the chemin de Ruth, which had followed her throughout the day.

Back home, Macaire was exhausted. He thought about his last conversation with Wagner, in February; the man hadn't lied about Jean-Bénédict.

Macaire grabbed the music box and stared at it. "If you need me, simply turn the handle and let it play," Wagner had said. Macaire took the little handle between his fingers and turned it. After a few turns, metallic notes played the well-known melody from Act II, Scene 10, *of Swan Lake*, and a piece of paper slowly emerged from the music box's toothed roller. On the paper was a telephone number. Macaire decided it was time to ask for help.

At that same moment, in Corfu, beneath the late afternoon sun, Anastasia and Lev were swimming in the turquoise water of the Ionian Sea. Anastasia stopped a moment to look at the cove and the village in the distance, clinging to the cliff side. She seemed pensive. Lev went to her and took her in his muscular arms.

"Everything okay? You've been quiet all day."

"I'm fine."

"Is it because of our discussion yesterday? If you really don't want me to take over the Athens office, I won't."

"Please don't worry. I'm fine, I promise."

439

She kissed him to keep him from talking.

But she was bothered. She felt he was hiding something from her. She couldn't stop thinking about the pistol, the gold pistol, that she had put in her bag in Geneva and hadn't found there when she arrived in Corfu. The only person who had access to the bag had been Lev, in his suite at the Verbier.

She had never dared talk to him about it. Mostly because she didn't really want to know. Every time she thought of that gold pistol, she recalled what had happened four months earlier at the Hôtel de Verbier when Jean-Bénédict had threatened to take the presidency of the bank away from Macaire and she had discovered the truth about Sinior Tarnogol.

56

Under Surveillance

It was early May. In the heat of mid-afternoon, Anastasia strolled around the historic centre of Corfu. Lev was gone for the day. Since accepting the position at the Athens office of the Ebezner Bank a month earlier, he had left Corfu every Tuesday morning early and returned for dinner. That Tuesday, however, at Macaire's request, Lev had gone to Geneva to update him on the situation.

Fifteen hundred kilometres away, back in Geneva, bathed by a warm spring sun, on the terrace of the Red Ox Steak House, boulevard des Tranchées, Macaire and Lev were finishing lunch. They were the last customers. They had arrived late because Macaire didn't want to miss his biweekly appointment with Dr Kazan, and he had chosen this restaurant because it was next to his psychoanalyst's office.

"I'm very glad that you're happy in Athens," Macaire said to Lev. "It's a nice city, I assume?"

"Very. I'm comfortable there."

"Where do you live, exactly?"

"In the Kolonaki neighbourhood, near Mount Lycabettus, not far from the centre of town."

Macaire glanced at him with false complicity. Lev looked at his watch.

"I have to leave soon to catch my flight, unless there's something else you want to discuss with me."

"No, I think we've covered everything. Thanks for coming all the way over."

The two men shook hands, and Lev left.

* * *

Macaire left the restaurant, but rather than head for the bank, he walked up rue de l'Athénée to the Parc Bertrand, then sat on a bench along one of the paths, as Wagner had told him to do. A few minutes later, Wagner appeared and sat next to Macaire. They pretended not to know each other, and Wagner buried himself in the paper he had brought with him.

"I slipped the box into his bag," Macaire said.

"He didn't notice anything?"

"He was in the toilet."

Wagner smiled with satisfaction. "In a few hours, we'll know exactly whether Levovitch really is in Athens and whether Anastasia is with him."

"Thanks for your help, Wagner."

"P-30 owes you this, Macaire."

* * *

That evening, in Corfu, as the sun was setting, Lev and Anastasia were drinking a glass of wine on their terrace, admiring the sunset. An employee lit the candles around them; dinner was about to be served. The two lovers were too absorbed in each other to notice, about ten metres away, the man watching them from the large rocks overlooking the house; he was photographing them with a telephoto lens.

Back in Cologny, at that moment, in the Ebezner home, Arma was finishing preparing dinner.

"Are you hungry, Moussieu?" she asked Macaire as he opened a bottle of wine.

He filled two glasses and handed one to Arma.

"I'm hungry," he replied, "but I don't feel like eating alone. Would you care to join me?"

Arma, surprised by the proposal, stood there in silence. Then she collected herself, muttered a quick "Thank you, thank you," and headed to the pantry to add an additional table setting.

"Come on, Arma, you've worked enough for today. I'm taking you out. How about the Lion d'Or?"

"That's too fancy for me." She frowned. "I'm in my apron."

"No, no, you're fine. You'll see."

"I can't go to dinner like this," she insisted. "Some other time."

"Why don't you take something from Anastasia's wardrobe? Her clothes are all still there. You're about the same size, aren't you? Take whatever you like. And take your time, I'm not in any hurry."

Arma obeyed and walked upstairs. She entered the large marital bathroom, where everything was still in place. She did her face, then her hair. She chose a dress from the wardrobe, something simple and elegant. She found a pair of matching shoes: heels, but not too high. When she worked up the courage to look at herself in the mirror, she was afraid she might look ridiculous. But that wasn't the case. In fact, she looked rather pretty.

"Wow! Arma," Macaire exclaimed, who had come upstairs to see what was going on. She turned as red as a tomato.

"Do you think this will be alright?"

"You look . . . amazing."

Her heart was beating wildly. Moved by his reaction, she followed her boss solemnly. He drove her in his sports car to the restaurant, and when they arrived, he opened the door for her gallantly. They were seated at a table on the terrace, facing one of the most beautiful views in Geneva.

"Is this where you came with Médéme?" Arma said, observing the panorama.

"Yes."

Arma at once regretted having mentioned her and quickly changed the subject.

"I've never seen anything so beautiful," she added. She smiled at Macaire, who smiled back.

* * *

Ten years earlier

Arma passed through the open gate and discovered the immense residence that rose up before her at the end of the path. She had never been to Cologny before, much less to the chemin de Ruth. She had been very impressed by the size and style of the homes she had seen as she approached. She rang the bell; a very beautiful young woman greeted her with a smile. It was Anastasia.

"Hello, Médéme," Arma presented herself timidly. "I've come about the ad."

"Come in. We've been waiting for you."

Arma was led into the living room. She felt uncomfortable sitting on the beautiful couch. A man entered the room. Arma thought he was magnificent.

"This is my husband, Macaire," Anastasia said.

"Hello, Moussieu," Arma greeted him, greatly impressed. "I'm Arma."

"Thank you for coming, Arma," Macaire smiled. "The agency told us you're a rare pearl. We've just moved here, and we need someone full-time to manage the house. You're young, but you have good references. Would you be okay with a short trial period?"

"It would be an honour, Moussieu."

* * *

Ten years later, Arma couldn't get over the fact that she was sitting opposite Monsieur in this restaurant, which she had often heard discussed. She marvelled at the dishes she was served that evening, the wine, the dessert platter. She wanted the evening to last forever; but when it was time to leave, Macaire said to her, "Thank you, Arma."

"For tonight?" she said, surprised.

"For everything."

He drove her to her home, in the Eaux-Vives quarter, and escorted her to the entrance of her building, at the angle of rue de Montchoisy and rue des Vollandes. She was shaking as she entered her apartment. He was smiling as he walked in the door at his home.

Returning to Cologny, Macaire spent some time in his bedroom office. He lit a cigar, pensive. Suddenly, the house phone rang, late as it was. He picked up, and at the other end of the line, he heard a melody, one he would recognise anywhere: *Swan Lake*. It was Wagner.

Without losing a second, Macaire got into his car and drove to a public phone box in the centre of Cologny. He dialled the number hidden in the music box. After it rang once, Wagner picked up.

"I'm in Corfu. I've found them."

"Corfu? Anastasia and Lev are in Corfu together?"

"Yes. I have photos. I'll send them to you."

Macaire hung up, his heart beating fast. So the anonymous letter was true. Anastasia had left him for Lev. Macaire felt the rage rise up inside him. The hour of vengeance had arrived. And he knew exactly what he was going to do.

57

Geneva (Part 3)

By the time Sagamore returned to his office, Scarlett and I had managed to photograph everything. We were sitting quietly, like two children who had just done something they shouldn't have.

"Forgive the interruption," Sagamore said. "A small emergency I had to take care of."

"We understand," Scarlett reassured him.

"Where were we?"

"You were telling us about your investigation, which wasn't going anywhere, your doubts, the pressure from above."

He drew our attention to a large photograph of a whiteboard on which the entire investigation had been laid out.

"I've kept this diagram for almost two years," Sagamore told us. "Before taking it down, I took this photograph to remind me of everything I had found."

Scarlett and I had carefully examined every item on that diagram, which would turn out to be very useful later on.

"What's this ring?" Scarlett asked, pointing to a photograph on the board of a ring set with what looked to be a sapphire.

"Back then it was one of the keys to advancing my investigation. For four months, the investigation stalled; it went nowhere. Then, in mid-April, we came across this ring. Cristina found it."

58

Goodbye Levovitch

Arriving at the bank that morning, Macaire hadn't felt so calm in a long time. Ever since Jean-Bénédict's death, and in spite of becoming president, Macaire had the feeling that he was no longer in control. He had been battered by the succession of events: Anastasia's disappearance, the anonymous letter that told him she had run away with Levovitch, then the information that Tarnogol was a creation of Jean-Bénédict's. He had been so upset that he had stopped sleeping or eating. He had asked himself a thousand questions and replayed the film of the past fifteen years over and over again in his mind, trying to bring back the most distant memories, trying to understand how it had all been possible.

He had imagined the most unlikely theories. He had even begun to wonder whether Anastasia and Jean-Bénédict had been lovers all that time and whether, fifteen years earlier, they had both planned some terrible deception: whether Jean-Bénédict had, in the guise of Tarnogol, tricked him into exchanging his shares for Anastasia's love and making a fool of himself. Anastasia, as part of the plan, had pretended to fall madly in love with him, and Jean-Bénédict had gained the shares. Had she acted out of love? For the money? The dividends Tarnogol received every year were enormous. The bank earned hundreds of millions of francs in annual revenue, a large part of which was redistributed to the shareholders. Had Jean-Bénédict promised a share of the money to Anastasia?

During those weeks, Macaire felt mentally tortured. He felt like a puppet. But as of two nights ago, ever since his call to Wagner, Macaire had the feeling that the wheel was finally turning: he was getting ready to resume control of the situation. He had located Anastasia and, most important, he had confirmed that she had run away with Levovitch. The anonymous letter was accurate. He wondered who could have known – and who had sent it. But it really didn't matter. What mattered now was vengeance. Macaire was finally able to focus his rage.

Levovitch had underestimated him, taken him for a fool and ridiculed him for months: Lev hadn't left Geneva because he needed time for himself; he hadn't settled in Athens. He was living in a house by the sea in Corfu, where he was playing house with Macaire's own wife! Levovitch had planned it all from the beginning. He had turned down a chance to become president to make it easier to run off with Anastasia. Had he been in cahoots with Jean-Bénédict? Were they in it together, all three of them? Had Lev and Anastasia killed Jean-Bénédict?

Macaire struggled to keep his mind from running over these thoughts. He had to concentrate on the matter at hand: destroying Levovitch and sullying his name and his reputation.

That morning Macaire had coldly put his plan into action. He called it Operation Goodbye Levovitch. It was a simple idea. Based on what Charlotte had told him, the police were certain that Jean-Bénédict, alias Tarnogol, had had the help of an accomplice inside the bank. Jean-Bénédict couldn't have done it all by himself, if only because he needed a double during board meetings. Macaire was going to make Levovitch that accomplice. The police would pick him up at his dream house in Corfu. He would leave in handcuffs. His downfall! From now on, if Levovitch was on the front page of the papers, he would no longer be in the company of the French president but stepping out of a police van at the Geneva court building. Maybe they would even pin Jean-Bénédict's murder on him, who knows? Levovitch would be condemned to life in prison, and Anastasia, now alone, would come crawling back, begging Macaire's forgiveness.

At the bank, he patiently waited for Cristina to leave the office for her customary morning break. As soon as the coast was clear, Macaire walked down to the next floor without being seen.

He slipped into Levovitch's office, which, notwithstanding his departure to Greece, had remained unchanged. He opened one of the drawers of Levovitch's desk and placed two items that would incriminate him inside. One was the embroidered handkerchief with Sinior Tarnogol's name on it, which Macaire had stolen the night he returned from Basel. The other was the engagement ring Anastasia had returned to him before leaving, now concealed inside the handkerchief. The ring was the one that, fifteen years earlier, had sealed the pact with Tarnogol. It was Tarnogol who had given the ring to Macaire the night they met at the Hôtel de Verbier, assuring him that the woman to whom he offered it would love him in return. And Macaire, so in love, was desperate enough to believe him. Macaire hid the handkerchief in a pile of folders and left quickly.

When Cristina came back from her break, Macaire was on the phone. The door to his office was wide open, and she could hear the conversation.

"I'm sure, Lev," Macaire said into the receiver, which continued to buzz in his ear, "that I gave you the Stevens folder. Are you sure you didn't take it with you to Athens? I see. Well, I'm very upset. Okay, keep me posted."

Macaire hung up and sighed noisily, as if he was terribly annoyed.

"Everything okay?" Cristina couldn't keep herself from asking.

"Levovitch has misplaced a client folder. That's the problem when you're on the road all the time. I gave him some important documents . . . and now I can't find them. He told me they're not in his office in Athens."

"What about his office here?" Cristina suggested. "Do you want me to go downstairs and have a look?"

"I hadn't thought of that," Macaire admitted. "I'll come with you; it'll be easier that way."

A few moments later, Macaire and Cristina returned to the fifth floor and their old offices. They entered the one that had been used by Levovitch. Macaire immediately went to the cabinet. Cristina headed for the desk. Suddenly, she stopped, motionless. Macaire, who was watching her, asked, "Everything alright, Cristina?"

"I don't know."

Macaire, satisfied with his ruse, approached her.

"You found the Stevens folder?"

"No, I found this handkerchief with a ring wrapped up in it."

Macaire read the embroidery: "Sinior Tarnogol". "What's this supposed to mean? And this ring? Why did Levovitch keep Tarnogol's handkerchief and ring in his office?"

"It looks like a woman's ring," Cristina remarked, observing the diameter of the ring. "And the stone is rather feminine. Looks like a sapphire. I don't remember seeing Tarnogol wearing a sapphire."

Macaire, sensing that his deception wasn't working, went deeper into his lie.

"You know, now that I see the ring, I'm sure I saw Tarnogol wearing it as a necklace, on a gold chain. I remember it clearly: I was at his home and I was really surprised to see it. That's how I remember it."

Cristina stared at her boss.

"You went to Tarnogol's home?"

Macaire bit his tongue. He had said more than he should have.

* * *

At the end of the day, at the headquarters of the Judicial Police, boulevard Carl-Vogt, Lieutenant Sagamore invited Macaire into an interrogation room.

"Thank you, Monsieur Ebezner, for taking the time to stop by," Sagamore said. "Please excuse the surroundings, but we don't have an available meeting room."

"Don't worry about it, Lieutenant. It's always interesting to see the other side of things. Like being in a police series."

Sagamore smiled. "You said you found a ring belonging to Sinior Tarnogol in Lev Levovitch's office at the bank. Is that correct?"

"Well, my secretary found it. We were looking for a folder, and she came across it. And she's the one who suggested I get in touch with you."

"Yes, I spoke to her not too long ago. She told me that you recognised the ring. Is that correct?"

Macaire sensed that he would have to play the game carefully if he was to get out of this hornets' nest.

"Well, first of all, Charlotte Hansen, Jean-Bénédict Hansen's widow, informed me several weeks ago that her husband had been impersonating Sinior Tarnogol and that Tarnogol had always been nothing more than a big hoax."

"Yes, that's our opinion as well," Sagamore confirmed.

"I have to admit that the news really shook me up. Especially because I was very close to my cousin. Since then, I haven't stopped trying to piece together this puzzle, looking back on all the time I spent with Tarnogol. That's why, when I saw the ring, it came to me in a flash."

"You recognised it because Tarnogol had worn it, is that it?"

"Yes, exactly."

"And where did you see him with this ring?" Sagamore asked. "At the bank?"

Macaire hesitated. He had no wish to explain to the police what he had planned at Tarnogol's town house. But he couldn't very well change the story he had given to Cristina either. If Sagamore questioned her, the two versions had to be the same.

"I saw him wearing it around his neck on a chain one day when I went over to his home. I was surprised to see it, a woman's ring, that's why I remember. At the time, I thought it was just a memento of some old love affair or something like that."

"Why did you go to see Tarnogol?" Sagamore asked.

Macaire assumed a detached air.

"He invited me. I don't think it was any special occasion. It was

451

shortly before the election of the new president; I guess he wanted to meet with the potential candidates."

"Monsieur Ebezner," Sagamore interjected, "excuse me for bothering you with this, but could you describe to me in detail the interior of Sinior Tarnogol's town house?"

Macaire was surprised at the question. He wondered whether this was a test to catch him in a lie. Sagamore had certainly searched Tarnogol's premises and knew the arrangement of the interior. Macaire decided to provide an exact and detailed picture of the house.

"It was at night; we had dinner together, rather late. A cold buffet. Very elegant. Salmon, caviar, wonderful food. Everything was very refined."

"The interior," Sagamore interrupted. "Can you describe the interior? The furniture, the different rooms?"

"I recall that when I entered, there was the elevator and a very broad staircase in white marble. I only saw the living room in which Tarnogol received me. That was on the first floor. There were at least three rooms in a row, separated by movable walls. The one we were in was covered in rich tapestries. I recall the couches; they were very comfortable, in blue velvet. There was a round table near the window, on which the food was presented. It looked like a Louis XVI. Or Louis something, but an antique for sure."

"Anything in particular strike you as unusual? Some object, maybe – a painting, a sculpture?"

Macaire took a moment to think about the question.

"There was a very large painting on one of the walls, very long, which represented a view of Saint Petersburg. I remember it well because Tarnogol talked about it at length, before giving me the story of his family origins."

When Macaire had concluded his statement and left the interrogation room, Sagamore went into an adjoining room where, through a video link, Cristina had been able to witness the interview.

"So, what do you think?" Sagamore asked her.

"I have no idea. He seems to be telling the truth. Or he's a terrific actor. But I can't help but wonder whether he was Jean-Bénédict Hansen's accomplice – and whether he was the one who pretended to be Tarnogol when he and Jean-Bénédict Hansen had to appear together. Now that Macaire knows that his cousin has been revealed, he's getting rid of evidence by putting it in Levovitch's office. We're lucky he asked me to rummage around in the office drawers and that I was the one who found the handkerchief and the ring. I have a hard time believing it was just a coincidence."

Sagamore agreed.

"You think his description of the town house was accurate?"

"Hard to say," Cristina conceded.

During the search after the murder, the police had discovered an empty building. The furniture had disappeared, as if someone had wanted to erase any trace of its presence. All the investigators found was a box that had been left in a cabinet, containing items belonging to Jean-Bénédict Hansen. A neighbour told them that the movers had taken everything the Thursday before the murder. But it had been impossible to contact the moving company.

Sagamore made a face.

"I can't help feeling there's something important we're missing," he said.

"If only the ring could talk!" Cristina sighed, shaking the evidence bag containing the ring found in Levovitch's desk drawer.

Sagamore thought that was a very good idea.

"I know someone who can help us," he suddenly shouted. "Come on, get your things."

Ten minutes later, Sagamore's unmarked car pulled up outside of a small second-hand jeweller's in the Pâquis neighbourhood. Although it was late, the shop was still open. The owner, a man named Frank, was a bit of a character, who, in the past, had been somehow involved with stolen diamonds. Since then he had worked for the police, occasionally serving as an informer whenever his former acquaintances asked him to fence stolen jewellery.

Sagamore and Cristina entered the empty shop, and Frank greeted them jovially.

"Lieutenant, delighted to see you. Have you come to pick out a watch?"

"I've come for information," Sagamore replied, placing the ring on the counter.

"What do you want to know?"

"Can you trace the ring for me?"

Frank looked doubtful.

"Well, that would appear to be difficult, Lieutenant. But I can have a look."

Frank took the ring and studied it with a loupe.

"It's not a very valuable ring. It's not a real sapphire."

"Anything else?" Sagamore asked.

Frank took some time to carefully inspect the stone. He sat at his desk, changed the loupe, and examined the stone under different light sources.

"It looks like there's an inscription in the setting, but it's hidden by the stone."

"Can you read any of it?"

"No, I'd have to remove the stone."

"Do it," Sagamore instructed.

Frank did as he was asked. He removed the stone from the setting and was able to read the inscription on the inside of the ring: *Kaham Bijoutier, Geneva – 4560953.*

* * *

Kaham was an elderly jeweller who, for decades, had had a shop on rue Étienne-Dumont, in the heart of Geneva's old town. The hours of business were irregular and uncertain, and Sagamore had to wait a long time before the jeweller decided to finally open the boutique. The interior was dark and dusty. Entering the shop, Sagamore imagined that old Kaham probably hadn't sold anything in a very long time.

"I'm Lieutenant Philippe Sagamore," he said as he flashed his badge.

"Police?" the old man said, surprised at Sagamore's presence.

"Yes. Crime squad. I'm investigating a murder."

The old man shrugged, giving no indication of whether the shrug meant he was uninterested or simply hadn't understood. Sagamore showed Kaham the ring, whose stone was now no longer attached to its setting.

"You want me to repair it?" Kaham asked.

"No, this ring came from your shop. I need to know who bought it."

Quite surprisingly, the question was easy to answer. Kaham, who considered his creations unique, had carefully numbered each of them. The reference, along with the name of the buyer, was registered in a series of large accounting books that had piled up over the years. After looking through his interminable inventories, year by year, Kaham suddenly placed his finger on a line and shouted victoriously. He had found the buyer. Sagamore hurried over to read the record: "4560953 – gold ring with blue zircon. Buyer: Sol Levovitch."

Back in Corfu, it was morning still. Anastasia was having a late breakfast on the terrace. Opposite her, Lev read the paper. He looked happy and carefree. She didn't dare speak to him about what continued to gnaw at her. She couldn't help thinking about what had happened, a few hours before the murder, when she had discovered that Tarnogol was an imposter.

59

Sinior Tarnogol

Five months earlier, Saturday, December 15, shortly before
midnight, four hours before the murder

Anastasia had just witnessed Jean-Bénédict blackmailing Macaire: he
would give Jean-Bénédict the presidency and, in exchange, Jean-
Bénédict would remain silent about the fact that his cousin had poisoned
the vodka used for the cocktails. She returned to Lev's room and told
him everything.

"Only one person can stop this," she said.

"Who?"

"Tarnogol. I'm going to speak to him."

"Now?"

"He resigned from the bank, he knows he's being threatened, and
he's probably packing his bags right now. I have to speak to him before
he leaves the hotel. Macaire told me Tarnogol was in the room next to
yours."

"Tarnogol is dangerous," Lev warned her.

"I know that."

Her response surprised Lev.

"Let me go with you."

"No, Lev. Don't get involved with this, please. It's between Tarnogol
and me. He . . . he stole a part of my life. It's because of him that I married Macaire. It's because of him that you and I . . ."

She broke off from what she was saying. She didn't want to talk. She
went out into the hallway and knocked on the door next to theirs.

Lev remained in the suite, overwhelmed by panic. For the first time in the fifteen years that he had been orchestrating this deception, it was beginning to get away from him. He had no choice but to open that door. He rushed to the balcony and climbed over the railing and onto the balcony next door, which led to Tarnogol's room, where the tall French window remained open.

Anastasia, in the sixth-floor hallway, banged on the door. No answer. She bent down and, after a few moments, saw a shaft of light, as if someone had just woken up and turned the lights on.

Lev had quickly removed his clothes to wrap himself in a bathrobe when he heard Anastasia's voice through the door: "Tarnogol, I know you're in there. Open the door."

Lev grabbed the silicone mask and put it on. He held the bathrobe closed to hide the difference between the silicone and the skin on his neck. His disguise was far from perfect, and he was neglecting the most fundamental rules his father had taught him. But he had no choice. He went to the door. He knew deep down that this would be the moment of truth.

The door opened and Anastasia found herself facing Tarnogol, dressed in a bathrobe, obviously having just got out of bed.

"What's going on?" Tarnogol asked.

"We have to talk, you and I."

Tarnogol stepped aside, inviting her inside. She stared at him like an angry lioness and, suddenly, had a sudden flash of insight: she recognised his eyes. She recalled what she had said that very morning, in Geneva, to Lieutenant Sagamore: "The eyes don't lie." Suddenly she understood and rushed at the man standing before her.

In room 622, the room next to Tarnogol's, Jean-Bénédict Hansen was exultant. The bank was his. He was in the process of placing the shares taken from Macaire in the safe when he heard a noise from the other side of the wall. There seemed to be some commotion in Tarnogol's room. He heard a woman's cry and a thud against the wall. He ran to the phone to alert hotel security, then into the hallway to see what was going on. The door to Tarnogol's suite was open. Inside, a struggle was taking place. Slowly he approached the door and found something he had not expected. Anastasia was shaking Lev by the collar of his bathrobe. There, on the carpet, lay a silicone mask that looked like Tarnogol's face.

"What the . . .?" Jean-Bénédict said.

Anastasia, realising that someone was present, let go of Lev. He looked at Jean-Bénédict helplessly as he picked up the mask.

"You?" Jean-Bénédict said, stupefied. "All these years, it was you? Tarnogol was a fake?"

He held the mask up to Lev's face. Lev stood there, petrified. His secret had been discovered.

"It's incredible," Jean-Bénédict said admiringly, "absolutely incredible."

He walked towards them, a threatening glimmer in his eyes. At that moment, a member of the security team appeared at the door to the room.

"Everything alright in here?" he asked. "A guest complained that he heard shouting."

"Oh, everything's fine here," Jean-Bénédict said with a broad smile. "We were rehearsing a play. Did we make too much noise? If so, I'm very sorry."

Jean-Bénédict walked over to the guard and, smiling broadly and patting him on the shoulder, assured the man that everything was fine. Jean-Bénédict then shut the door in the guard's face. Turning back to Lev and Anastasia, Jean-Bénédict stared at them coldly. They both looked terrified.

"How extraordinary this evening has been!" Jean-Bénédict said with considerable enthusiasm.

With those words, he put on the silicone mask and admired his reflection in the mirror on the wall.

"Amazing! Simply amazing. You've fooled us for fifteen years, Lev. I want to know everything. I want to know how you did it."

Jean-Bénédict removed the mask and walked towards the living room area.

"Come over here. Sit down," he ordered.

They obeyed and sat side by side on the couch. Anastasia was terrified and, in a kind of reflex, grabbed Lev's hand. Jean-Bénédict didn't fail to notice the gesture.

"Well, well, my little lovebirds! It gets better and better. Better and better."

He opened the minibar and grabbed a bottle of champagne.

"Mind if I serve myself?" he asked Lev. "Or should I ask Tarnogol?"

Jean-Bénédict shook the silicone mask and started to laugh, then opened the champagne and drank from the bottle. He licked his lips ostentatiously and shouted, "Champagne! Champagne for Sinior Tarnogol, the greatest imposter the world has ever seen. And now, Lev, talk. I want to know everything."

* * *

Fifteen years earlier, Friday morning of the Gala Weekend

That morning, Lev had left Geneva at dawn to return to Verbier. The night before, Anastasia had stood him up, skipping their rendezvous at the Hôtel des Bergues.

Arriving in Martigny, since he had a short wait before the arrival of the train to Le Châble, where he would catch the bus to Verbier, Lev decided to have a coffee in the warmth of the Hôtel de la Gare. Sitting inside, among the bustle of the breakfast service, he observed the empty street through the window. Suddenly, to his great surprise, he saw his father appear, walking in the half-light with a suitcase in his hand. He entered the hotel and mingled with the other customers. Lev, without going to greet his father, kept his eyes on him. Sol Levovitch crossed the room, heading for the toilets, and disappeared. Lev decided to follow him. He had a feeling that something wasn't right. He entered the toilets, but there was no-one there. He saw then that one of the stall doors was closed. His father was inside – with his suitcase, in the process of rummaging around for something. What could he be doing in there?

Lev waited.

Suddenly, the door opened. Lev stood there, hypnotised. He couldn't believe it. The man standing before him was Sinior Tarnogol.

"Papa," Lev said, still shocked.

Tarnogol brought his hands to his neck and carefully removed the silicone face he wore. The operation took time. Slowly, from behind the mask, Sol's face appeared.

"You're Tarnogol?" Lev muttered. "It was you all this time?"

Sol nodded.

"Tarnogol and a few others. That's why Monsieur Rose hired me. I could use the multiple identities I had developed to pose as a customer and track down any problems with the service."

Lev realised, to his horror, that some of the hotel guests he had served over the years had never really existed. Rather, they had all been one and the same person: his father.

Sol Levovitch was a great actor. He had deceived absolutely everyone. All those years he had given life to characters who were truer than nature. Thanks to Monsieur Rose, Sol had finally been able to give free rein to his genius. He had silicone masks custom-made by the best artisan in the region, a man based in Vienna who provided masks for the biggest film studios.

Lev took the mask and examined it. It was staggeringly realistic: the nose, the placement of the hair, the way the silicone blended in with the skin around the eyes and mouth. The illusion was perfect.

When the shock had passed, Lev reconsidered Tarnogol's behaviour towards him over the years and asked his father for an explanation.

"If you're Tarnogol, why did you betray me to Monsieur Bisnard at the bank's Grand Ball last year?"

"All the other hotel employees had seen you. They were furious. I wanted to put an end to your foolishness while there was still time – before you were labelled a disgrace to the hotel or the situation got out of hand. It would have cost you your job. And, to be honest, I saw the way you looked at all those bankers, all those powerful men. And I felt small. I was jealous of them. When I realised that you had lied about your identity to pretend that you were part of that world, I couldn't take it any longer."

"And then?" Lev asked, still trying to understand.

"Last spring, after Anastasia left for Brussels, you were miserable. I couldn't speak to you. I was frustrated. I asked you several times to have dinner with me, but you wouldn't. Remember?"

"Yes."

"I then said to myself that maybe Tarnogol might succeed where I had failed. I chose Tarnogol rather than another of my characters because he seemed to be the best match for the banking world, in my opinion at least. Tarnogol asked you to dinner, and you accepted."

"I couldn't refuse his invitation," Lev replied in his defence.

"It doesn't matter. What's important is that I spent a wonderful evening in your company. I discovered that by becoming Tarnogol I could be the father figure full of good advice that I can't be when I'm myself, sitting opposite you. Remember how last summer you told me that you had received an offer from the bank? It drove me crazy. I didn't want you to leave; I made a ridiculous scene to dissuade you from leaving, and you stayed. I then regretted it because it was clear to me that your place was no longer at the hotel but in Geneva."

"So you returned to the hotel as Tarnogol and arranged to get me fired."

"Yes, Monsieur Rose was in on it. I told him I would drive you crazy and demand that you be let go."

461

"So it was all just one big act?"

"That's one way of putting it. By chance Anastasia happened to arrive and took you with her. I was sad about it, but Tarnogol was happy for you."

"But why this masquerade at the bank? Why this business of opening an account and then buying the bank?"

"Monsieur Rose told me that you had been sidelined by Auguste Ebezner and needed your first big client to become a banker on your own. I told myself that Tarnogol was the right man for the job. Each of my characters has a genuine fake passport, made in Berlin by an exceptional counterfeiter. I need them to register at the hotel. I thought all I needed to open an account at the bank was to set up a meeting. I had my passport in my pocket, so it seemed like child's play. I figured I could delay the transfer of the cash, which didn't exist in the first place. I mentioned that there were problems with various banks. By the time the transfer failed, you would have become an official banker with other clients and you would have been untouchable."

"But the meeting at the bank didn't go as planned, did it?"

"Exactly. I named an astronomical sum of money, and Abel Ebezner asked me to sign all those documents. I didn't expect that. At the same time, I had to play the game until the end. I went to the next meeting with all the documents – blank – in the envelope. I knew they wouldn't open the account. I only wanted to gain time, for you, to help you. So I had the idea of adding a requirement that Abel Ebezner couldn't agree to: that he sell Tarnogol part of his bank."

"But you made me look like an idiot!" Lev said angrily.

"I'm sorry about that. I just wanted to help. I'm going to fix everything, you'll see. I'm getting ready to return to the hotel as Tarnogol. Monsieur Rose has kept a room for me next to Abel Ebezner's, and I'm going to tell him . . ."

"You're not going to do anything!" Lev exploded. "You're going to forget Tarnogol."

"I'm going to convince Abel Ebezner to make you a banker. Let me do it, please."

"But, regardless, I'll be a banker as of January, once Macaire officially becomes vice president. I don't need your help, don't you understand? I don't need your help!"

"Well, that's the problem."

"What?"

"That you no longer need my help. You've always needed me; I'm your father. But now you're on your own. You no longer need me, and that's hard to accept."

"I don't believe it; it's all a big farce."

"It wasn't a farce!"

"Call it a clown show if you prefer," Lev replied, deeply hurt by the lies. "All those clients who spent their time praising me, who made me feel proud of my work – it was all a giant scam. You and Monsieur Rose must have had a good laugh; you didn't give a damn about me, either one of you."

"No, Lev. Those characters helped monitor the quality of the service at the hotel."

"It was simply a way to keep me there."

"No, no, not at all."

Lev was beside himself with anger. He felt betrayed and humiliated.

"You and your ridiculous obsession with being an actor. It wasn't a banker who killed Mama, it was an actor. It was you and your ridiculous performances – that's why she left. She's dead because of you."

"Lev, no, please. Forgive me, I thought I was doing the right thing."

"You've ruined everything," Lev screamed. "You're nothing but a clown."

"I'm not a clown!"

"If you're not a clown, then what are you, in your costume?"

"I'm your father."

"I'm not sure you're the father that I wanted."

Hearing those words, Sol, profoundly hurt, slapped him. Shocked by the gesture more than by the force of the blow, Lev raised a hand to his cheek.

"Forgive me . . ." Sol begged, immediately regretting his behaviour.

Lev moved towards the exit.

"Wait," his father cried. "I did it for a good reason, all of it. There's something I've never told you . . ."

But Lev was done listening. He ran out. He wanted to disappear. Most of all, he needed sympathy. He needed Anastasia and had to find her. He jumped on the first train to Geneva. And as he travelled from Martigny to Geneva, the train going in the opposite direction, leaving the city from the end of Lake Geneva, was taking Anastasia to Martigny, on her way to Verbier to find Lev.

Lev spent the day wandering around Geneva. There was no-one home at Olga von Lacht's apartment. No-one at his apartment either. He waited at the Remor for a very long time. He went to all of the places in Geneva that she loved – in vain. Desperate, he returned to Olga's apartment, but it was still empty. He waited for a long time by the staircase for someone to come. At around seven p.m., Madame von Lacht showed up, back from work. As soon as he saw her, Lev prepared himself to play the part of a Romanov. But before he could open his mouth, Olga began to yell.

"How dare you show up here, you piece of garbage? You filthy little shit."

And with those words, she began to beat Lev with her handbag.

"Madame von Lacht, stop. What's got into you?"

"Get out, you shit. You're nothing but vermin – an imposter. I know everything."

"Please, Madame von Lacht, I have to talk to Anastasia. I've spent the day trying to find her."

Olga withheld her final blow. Anastasia wasn't with Lev? Where had she gone, then? Olga decided to take advantage of the occasion to drive a wedge between Lev and her daughter.

"Anastasia doesn't want to see you any more. She's in love with someone else. Someone rich. Someone powerful! Not some miserable baggage handler. Get out of here, do you hear me? Go!"

Lev left without saying anything more.

That evening, after wandering around for hours, Lev, overwhelmed by the events of the past twenty-four hours, finally returned to the Hôtel de Verbier.

It was past midnight when a taxi dropped him in front of the hotel. In the reception area, he ran into his father, who appeared to be waiting for him. And the old man, desperate to keep his son near, gave him the letters he had falsified to make him believe that Anastasia loved Macaire.

He knew it was a cowardly act. Not even Tarnogol would have stooped so low. But he was no longer Tarnogol. He was simply Sol.

And Lev, deeply wounded by what he believed to be a break-up letter, had gone off to drown his sorrows in Petra's arms.

* * *

Fifteen years later, in room 623 of the Hôtel de Verbier, Jean-Bénédict interrupted Lev's story.

"What's this business about the letters?"

Anastasia repeated the explanation she had given to Lev when they were finally together again, a year earlier, after Abel Ebezner's funeral.

"I wrote letters. One to Lev, to tell him I loved him, and the other to Macaire, to make him understand that I didn't have any feelings for him. But Lev's father, to whom I had given the letters, changed them."

"He cut out the names and switched them," Lev added. "I ended up with the break-up letter and thought that Anastasia wanted to spend her life with Macaire. The following evening, during the Gala Ball, I saw Anastasia and Macaire kissing, which confirmed what I had read, as far as I was concerned."

"It was Macaire who kissed me!" Anastasia protested, still feeling the need to defend herself fifteen years after the fact. "I didn't see it coming."

"I have no memory that you objected," Lev said in return.

"Come, come, my little lovebirds," Jean-Bénédict interjected, "stop squabbling. I want to know what happened afterwards, and why your father, Lev, switched the names on the letters so you would doubt that Anastasia loved you."

"Because he was very ill and didn't want to die alone."

* * *

Fifteen years earlier, in the hotel ballroom

After seeing Anastasia and Macaire kissing, Lev took revenge by doing the same with Petra. Anastasia, distressed by the discovery of his new conquest, hastily left the room.

Within the happy crowd, Lev, to whom Petra was clinging tightly, felt that he was about to collapse. Seeing Anastasia again, especially witnessing the kiss between her and Macaire, had shaken him badly. It was one thing to learn from the letter he had read that she did not love him; it was quite another to see her with another man.

Lev also left the ball. He didn't feel right among all those bankers. Maybe his father was right: the bank had changed him. He wanted to become a hotel employee again – to live here once more, in this bubble; to never again leave the hotel. He finally had to admit that the only person who had always looked out for him was his father.

Leaving the ball, he ran into Monsieur Rose, who was clearly aware of what had happened between Sol and his son.

"Lev, I have to talk to you. It's about your father."

"I know; he wanted to do the right thing and help me by impersonating Tarnogol."

466

"That's not what I wanted to talk to you about. Lev, your father has cancer."

Lev turned pale. This time, his father hadn't lied to him.

"So he's not making it up?" Lev said.

"He's dying," Rose confided.

"Why didn't he say anything before?"

"He didn't want to upset you. He thought he would get better. Unfortunately, there's nothing more to do. He's going to die, and you're all he's got. He only has a few months."

Lev wanted to find his father, to embrace him. He didn't want to waste a second of the time remaining to them.

Sol was supposed to be at the hotel that evening. But Lev couldn't find him in his office, and none of the employees Lev questioned had seen him. Lev thought his father had to be in his apartment. Lev went there and knocked on the door, but no-one answered. The door wasn't locked, however, and Lev let himself in. The place was deserted. He called out: no answer. It was clear his father wasn't home. Lev went into the bedroom to double-check. It was empty as well. But instead of leaving the room, Lev stayed. He felt he needed to know more about his father. He opened the large wardrobe facing the bed. To his surprise, he found, on a shelf, a series of silicone face masks placed on mannequin heads: the faces of hotel guests he had served. Below, a pile of objects used as accessories for the characters: watches, jewellery, glasses, cigarettes. And, among them, was the leatherbound notebook his father kept so carefully, in which he wrote down all his ideas. Lev opened it and discovered in its pages sketches and annotations about the customers he had served. His father had drawn the faces, had moulds made from the drawings, and finally had masks made from the moulds. Lev discovered that the characters really existed: Sol had made extensive notes about their personal histories, their language tics, their preferences, and their requirements as guests of the hotel to maintain consistency whenever they appeared.

Lev looked at all the masks and observed the one representing

Tarnogol. He was fascinated. He grabbed it and put it on in front of the vanity mirror, which dominated the room – the mirror where, for years, his father had transformed himself so he could blend in, incognito, at the hotel. Lev realised that his father had taught him everything: he knew the gestures and poses, he knew how to change his voice by projecting it further. He realised that, for the past year, he himself had enacted a similar fraud by pretending to be Lev Romanov. Really, all he had done was put into practice what his father had taught him. He was an actor, from a long line of actors: the Levovitches.

Half of the wardrobe was used for the clothing worn by his father's characters. Lev found Tarnogol's clothes without difficulty and put them on. They were lined with fabric and polyester foam to add weight and curve the silhouette. The effect was astonishing.

He put the mask on his face. The plastic adhered to the contours of his jaw, moulded to his eyes and lips. He arranged the grey hair and thick eyebrows. The result was incredible; he was Sinior Tarnogol. He spent a few minutes trying to talk and move in his new physical carapace. He realised he could perfectly imitate the character Sol had created for Tarnogol, just as Sol had taught him. Lev realised that his father had prepared him to take over the role. He understood then that his father was not simply a gifted actor; he was a dramaturge, the soul of the theatre personified – a great artist.

As Tarnogol, Lev looked at himself in the mirror for a long time. He felt proud – proud to be a Levovitch. He wanted his father to see him like this. He wanted to show Sol that the son was like the father, that Lev was no different.

If his father wasn't there, he had to be at the hotel. Lev went back. Leaving the apartment, he was careful to take with him his most precious possession, which hadn't left his pocket since the previous evening: his mother's engagement ring, which he had planned to offer Anastasia at the Hôtel des Bergues.

*

Returning to the Hôtel de Verbier, Lev at once understood how real his new identity was: the employees saw him as the regular and somewhat notorious guest he appeared to be and greeted him with deference. Lev enjoyed showing them a contempt worthy of Tarnogol. It was an opportunity to practise his voice and his accent, screaming "Get out of the way, will you!" at any employee who crossed his path. Beneath the silicone mask, Lev marvelled as he imagined the expression on his father's face if he were to see him now. But Sol was nowhere to be found. Having wandered around the large lobby, Lev walked outside to smoke a cigarette.

At that moment, Macaire was leaving the first-floor ballroom, his bank shares in his hand, to return to the hotel's lobby. Without Anastasia, his evening was ruined. He felt sad and alone, ready to give all the gold in the world to be with her. He needed to get some air, so he walked outside.

Lev, seeing Macaire exit the hotel, looked at him with fury, before realising that Macaire didn't recognise him.

"Good evening, sir," Macaire said politely, as he came up to Lev.

Lev saw that he looked sad. He questioned him, reproducing Tarnogol's voice and accent.

"Something wrong, my young friend?"

Macaire turned, happy that someone had noticed he wasn't feeling too good.

"A matter of the heart," he replied.

"It happens."

Macaire looked at him.

"Have we met?" he asked Tarnogol.

"I don't think so."

"Yes, you came to the bank a few weeks ago."

"Do you know the bank?" Tarnogol asked.

"Do I know it?" he replied, amused by the question. "I'm Macaire Ebezner." He extended his hand to Tarnogol. "I'm the new vice president."

They exchanged a warm handshake.

"I'm Sinior Tarnogol. Pleased to make your acquaintance. I don't like seeing a handsome young fellow like yourself looking so sad. Is there something I can do for you?"

Macaire sighed.

"Oh, only if you could make it so the woman I love returned my affections. Her name is Anastasia. I'd give anything to be with her."

Hearing those words, Lev understood that Macaire didn't know he had been chosen by Anastasia. He had never received the letter she had written him. Anastasia wanted to spend her life with him, but he knew nothing about it. And since she had fled the ballroom after their kiss, he probably felt rejected. Lev realised he had an opportunity to play Macaire, not realising for a second where it would all lead. In the guise of Tarnogol, Lev said to Macaire, as if in confidence, "I can help you with Anastasia."

"How?" Macaire implored, visibly prepared to do anything.

"It will be expensive. I'm not sure you have what's required."

Macaire shook the envelope he held in his hand.

"Do you see this? These are shares in the Ebezner Bank. Do you know what they're worth, even the annual dividends? Trust me, I have enough to pay for your services. How much do you want?"

"Are you ready to make a pact with the devil?" Tarnogol asked.

The word terrified Macaire, but he didn't back down.

"I'm ready for anything!"

Tarnogol, responding accordingly, said to him, "Your shares for Anastasia."

There was a moment of silence. Macaire appeared to hesitate before collecting himself.

"I accept. If you can deliver Anastasia, I'll give you my shares. I don't care about money, Monsieur Tarnogol. All I want is her love."

* * *

Fifteen years later, Lev was almost relieved to be able to reveal the secret he had carried with him all that time. He explained it to Jean-Bénédict Hansen.

"I had nothing to lose. At first, I saw it as no more than a bad joke, before realising that maybe it was my master stroke. Getting myself named vice president – can you imagine the insult to Macaire who, I was convinced, had stolen Anastasia from me? And then, if it worked, I would be immensely wealthy for a man of my age. That night, I thought I was taking Macaire for a ride. In reality, I took myself for a ride."

* * *

Fifteen years earlier

Macaire entered his room at the Hôtel de Verbier, followed by Tarnogol.

"Sit down," Macaire said, showing Tarnogol to an armchair as he seated himself behind a small desk. Macaire opened a drawer, took out a sheet of paper and a pen, and began to write a contract: a few lines in which he transferred his shares to Sinior Tarnogol.

"Is this contract valid?" Tarnogol asked. "I don't want any tricks."

"Don't worry," Macaire reassured him. "I studied law at university; I know what I'm doing. The contract is perfectly valid."

He put the document in the safe along with the shares.

"If, as you have promised, I obtain Anastasia's love, I'll give you the signed contract together with my shares."

"How can I be sure that you'll keep your word?"

"I'm a man of my word," Macaire replied. "You can count on me."

The opportunity was too great, and Lev decided to go for it. If it worked, it would be the deal of the century. He put his hand in his pocket and, touching his mother's ring with his fingers, said, "Meet me in fifteen minutes in front of the elevators on the third floor."

*

Fifteen minutes later, Macaire stood nervously in the third-floor hallway, where Anastasia's room was located. Suddenly, a concealed door opened, and Tarnogol appeared.

"You're the devil," Macaire said, shaking his head.

"Follow me." Tarnogol led Macaire into a service corridor known only to the hotel employees.

Unseen by anyone, Tarnogol removed the ring from his pocket and placed it in Macaire's hand. Lev had a moment of hesitation at giving up his mother's ring. But he figured that if his subterfuge failed, he would get it back. And if it worked, he would have enough to buy the biggest diamonds for the rest of his life.

"Offer the ring to Anastasia," he told Macaire. "Ask her to marry you. She'll accept."

Macaire rushed to Anastasia's room. When he got to the door, he stood there, motionless, not daring to knock.

On the other side of the door, Anastasia, prostrate on her bed, cried in desperation. Deceived by Lev, who had clearly chosen Petra, and rejected by her mother, who wanted nothing to do with her, Anastasia felt abandoned by everyone. Once the Gala Weekend was over, she wouldn't even have a home. She didn't know what was to become of her. She was even considering throwing herself out the window to put an end to it all.

Suddenly, there was a knock at the door. She rose to open it. Before her, kneeling, was Macaire, who presented her with a sapphire ring.

"Anastasia von Lacht, will you marry me?" he asked.

She barely hesitated. It wasn't her heart that responded but her fear of being alone in the world and, especially, her need for kindness, the visceral need to be loved. She had suffered years of being dragged around by her mother in search of a husband, and then the successive failures of her relationships with Klaus and then Lev; she wanted to be cherished and live in peace.

"Yes," she said, and raised Macaire so she could embrace him. "Yes!"

A few steps away, hidden by the angle of a wall, Tarnogol observed them. Beneath his mask, Lev was crying.

* * *

Fifteen years after these events, in room 623 of the Hôtel de Verbier, Anastasia suddenly realised what had happened.

"So, the ring that Macaire offered me was the ring you planned to give me?"

"Yes, my mother's ring."

She covered her mouth with her hands in a gesture of despair.

"I gave it back to Macaire a little while ago."

"That's okay," he assured her.

Anastasia was unable to hold back her tears. Jean-Bénédict Hansen stood there, shocked by the story he had just heard.

"Macaire kept his promise," Lev went on. "That same night, he gave me the contract and the shares. A month later, Tarnogol took his first steps as a member of the board of directors, and I, Lev Levovitch, was made a banker by Abel Ebezner, who never suspected a thing. Tarnogol was supposedly travelling all the time, and I was often meeting with clients, either at the bank, elsewhere in Geneva, or abroad. It wasn't hard to juggle their two schedules. We rarely had to cross paths. The money from the dividends allowed me to do the groundwork for the character: I had enough to pay off an employee at the Immigration Office to obtain, based on a fake Soviet passport that my father had had made, a real residence permit for Tarnogol, who settled in Geneva. He moved into a town house at 10 rue Saint-Léger, which he rented at first, then bought. It was nothing more than a stage set; only the entrance, the staircases, and the living rooms on the first floor, visible from the street, were furnished. The rest has always been empty and unoccupied."

Jean-Bénédict rose and took a few steps around the room.

"It's wild, Lev! You're a genius. An absolute genius. Do you realise you fooled all of us? A week ago, you terrified poor Macaire by promising to make Lev Levovitch president. That was brilliant. Once you were elected president, Tarnogol could have resigned from the board, and no-one would ever have been the wiser. And you, you would be president of the bank, the first ever who wasn't an Ebezner."

"Not quite. I wanted to drive Macaire into a corner to convince him to make the opposite exchange: the presidency in exchange for Anastasia. I had found Anastasia at last, after fifteen years that were like crossing a desert. I wanted Macaire to leave us alone. If she left him, he would have caused problems, from blackmail to suicide; he was capable of ruining everything."

Jean-Bénédict stared at Lev.

"Macaire almost killed you."

"I know."

Jean-Bénédict burst out laughing.

"This story is insane. Well, the most important thing is that I now have Tarnogol's shares, which Macaire so kindly transferred to me. As for you, Lev, or should I say, Tarnogol, you've just handed me your letter of resignation. I'm delighted to learn that you're planning to disappear. As for Macaire, he too is going to leave the bank, appoint me president in his place, and transfer Abel's shares to me. When my father dies, I'll have all the bank's shares. I'll be the most powerful banker in Switzerland. So, how is it going to turn out for Lev? You're going to play Tarnogol one more time tomorrow. We're going to call a press conference with Tarnogol, Macaire, my father, and me. We're going to announce that Macaire has been elected president, but he's going to resign immediately and give me his shares, and immediately after him, you're going to announce that you're resigning as well. If the press asks any questions, if they ask why, make something up. Then I'll let you leave. I never want to see you again. I'll leave you in peace, and you can spend your life somewhere with Anastasia. That's what you want, isn't it?"

"Agreed. That's all I'm asking."

Jean-Bénédict left room 623 to return to his own.

"And now?" Anastasia asked Lev when they were alone in the room.

"Now, we leave and never return. Don't worry, I've taken care of everything."

At three in the morning, that same night, shortly before the arrival of the morning shift at the hotel, two shadows left room 624.

Without a sound, they slipped down the stairs, their steps muffled by the thick carpeting. They went down to the ground floor and followed a service corridor, at the end of which was an emergency exit. Lev pushed the door. Outside, it was snowing heavily, and a blast of frigid air entered the building. Before them was a narrow, snow-covered road. Alfred was there, waiting in the cold. Behind him was a large black sedan with the motor running. Lev held the door to let Anastasia out, but she said to him, "Wait, I have to go back."

"What?"

"I have to do something. It's important."

"Anastasia, no . . . we have to leave before someone finds us."

"Lev, please. It's important."

He sighed.

"Hurry up, then."

She went back inside. Lev let the door close and stood in the cold with Alfred. Outside, there was no risk of being seen.

They waited a long time. Their hair was covered with snow; they shivered, pulled their collars up. Then the door opened again, and Anastasia appeared. Lev held the door so that it couldn't shut.

"Finally. Where were you?"

She stared at him for a moment before answering.

"I had to do it."

"Let's go," Alfred said, opening the car's rear door. "We can't wait around."

Anastasia climbed into the vehicle before turning around to find that Lev hadn't budged and was still holding the door open.

"Alfred, you know what you have to do."

The chauffeur nodded affirmatively.

"Aren't you coming with me?" Anastasia asked, uneasily.

"I have to stay here."

"No, Lev, please don't, there's going to be trouble."

"I can't let the bank fall into the hands of Jean-Bénédict Hansen. I at least owe that to Abel Ebezner."

In spite of her protests, he went back into the hotel, closing the door behind him. The car took off with Anastasia and, in the darkness of night, left the hotel and then the town of Verbier, proceeding down into the valley to the airport at Sion, where it drove directly on to the runway. A private jet was waiting, ready for take-off.

A few minutes later, the plane took off with Anastasia on board, heading for Corfu.

60

Saint Petersburg

Sagamore had travelled from Geneva to Verbier. His first stop was the local police station.

"You're chasing a ghost," he was told by the head of the police, a pudgy man whose crown of grey hair showed that he was a few months from retirement.

"Why is that?" Sagamore asked.

"Sol Levovitch has been dead for years."

"I know. I want to know who he was. Over the phone, you told me you knew him."

"This a small village, Lieutenant, everyone knows everyone here. Sol Levovitch was friendly, good-natured; everyone liked him. He's been dead a while, though. Why are you interested in him?"

"Because I'm wondering whether there's a connection between him and the murder of Jean-Bénédict Hansen."

The chief of police lifted his head, intrigued.

"The murder in room 622?"

"Yes. During our investigation, we found a ring that belonged to Sol Levovitch."

"But he's been dead for at least ten years."

"Fourteen," Sagamore specified.

"You know, he has a son, a big shot at the Ebezner Bank; he was at the hotel the night of the murder."

"I know. That's why I came."

Sagamore was convinced that the ring found in Levovitch's drawer had a connection with the case. Cristina, however, didn't agree, and the night before they had argued the ins and outs of the matter at some length.

"We found a ring belonging to his father in a drawer in Lev Levovitch's desk. Nothing that would incriminate him," Cristina remarked.

"A ring that was wrapped in a handkerchief belonging to Tarnogol and that Macaire Ebezner told us he saw Tarnogol wearing around his neck."

"What if Macaire is lying?" she asked.

Sagamore had felt that that possibility was one more reason to keep digging. Either Macaire was telling the truth and Levovitch was involved in the case, or Macaire was lying, which incriminated him. Concluding that the local chief of police wasn't going to be of much help, Sagamore said he was going to the hotel to question the manager.

"I'll come with you," the chief of police said, delighted to be part of an investigation that was more interesting than handing out parking fines.

In his office, Monsieur Rose had coffee brought for the two officers.

"Sol Levovitch? I knew him well. A well-regarded employee. I met him in Basel. He was working at the bar of Les Trois Rois. I offered to hire him and his son, and they both came here. Lev, his son, worked at the hotel before joining the bank. A very talented young man."

"What did Sol Levovitch do at the hotel?" Sagamore asked.

"He worked on quality control," Rose explained. "He was my eyes and ears, so to speak. He was good at it, very good. He didn't miss a thing."

"According to my research, he had been an actor. Is that correct?"

"Yes. For years he tried to get ahead, but without success. So he gave up his acting career for something a bit more stable."

"I found a former colleague of Sol Levovitch from the time he worked at Les Trois Rois. Sol told him that he had been hired at the Hôtel de Verbier to work as a kind of mystery client, using his talents as an actor and various disguises to uncover any oversights or problems with the staff."

Rose stifled a laugh.

478

"That's absurd, Lieutenant. I run a hotel, not a circus."

Sagamore didn't insist and went on with his questions.

"What sort of man was Sol Levovitch?"

Monsieur Rose frowned, as if he didn't understand the meaning of the question.

"He was pleasant, a hard worker, and honest. I don't really see what you're driving at with such questions, Lieutenant."

Sagamore then showed the ring to Monsieur Rose.

"Recognise this ring?"

"No. Should I?"

"It belonged to Sol Levovitch."

"Where did you find it?"

"It doesn't matter."

Sagamore's reply was sharper than he had intended, and Monsieur Rose realised that something wasn't right. But he didn't fish for details. He simply said, "Is there anything else I can help you with, Lieutenant?"

"Not right now," Sagamore said and thanked Monsieur Rose. "Here's my card. If you remember anything else, please call me."

"About what?" Rose asked, somewhat confused.

"About Sol Levovitch."

Sagamore and the chief of police left the hotel. From the window in his office, Monsieur Rose watched them get into the car. So the ring had finally shown up. The ring, which had meant so much to Lev and Sol that it had led to their estrangement and poisoned what little time was left to them.

* * *

Fifteen years earlier

It was the end of January. Monsieur Rose and Sol Levovitch were together in the small private room of L'Alpina Restaurant. Suddenly, the door opened, and Tarnogol entered the room. He closed the door behind him to make sure that no-one could see them and, unbuttoning his shirt to grab the ends of the mask, rolled it up and off his head, revealing Lev's face.

Monsieur Rose and Sol burst out laughing. Lev joined them at the table, and Monsieur Rose served champagne.

"What are we celebrating?" Rose asked. "You told me you had important news."

"Yes; on Wednesday, Sinior Tarnogol sat for the first time at a meeting of the bank's board of directors."

They clapped. Sol was overcome with a sense of pride.

"The student has surpassed the teacher," he said.

"No-one realised?" Monsieur Rose asked.

"No-one. You should see Abel Ebezner; he's furious. He said he'd contacted his lawyers and they're going to contest the transfer of his son's shares."

"Be careful, this could lead to problems down the road," Sol said.

"Don't worry," Lev reassured him. "I wanted to see how far I could go. I managed to get a seat on the board; the joke has lasted for a while. I've thought about it. I'm going to let Macaire have the shares. They can be sold back to him for quite a bit of money. Then Tarnogol will disappear forever."

The two men approved, relieved that Lev was putting an end to the hoax before he was found out.

Sol looked at him admiringly. "In any case, it's incredible that you managed to convince them. Macaire transferred his shares to you! Do you realise what you've done? If that's not proof of a great actor . . . How the hell did you do it, Lev? Tell me."

"I exchanged them for the ring."

"What ring?" Sol asked, suddenly concerned.

"Mother's ring."

Sol turned pale.

"The . . . your mother's ring? You gave your mother's ring to Macaire Ebezner?"

"You always told me it wasn't a real sapphire, that it wasn't worth anything."

"But it has sentimental value! You think like a damn banker. So that's the kind of man you've become: a materialist, obsessed by money."

"But Papa, isn't that what you wanted?"

There was silence in the room. Sol trembled with rage. Overcome by his anger, he banged his fist on the table. A glass tipped over.

"What I wanted! For the love of God. For you to get rid of the only thing that remained of your mother?"

"No, not that, that I'm an actor! I took over your role; in fact, I even went further with it. I'm in the process of pulling off the performance of a lifetime – a performance as large as life."

"You did it for the money," Sol said. "You wanted to take control of the bank."

"Of course not. I did it to prove to you that we were part of the same tradition, that I was an actor too."

"Enough!" Sol yelled. "I don't want to hear any more. The son I raised would never have done this. Go on, get out. Return to your bank. Go count your money. Go back to your empty banker's life."

*   *   *

While Lieutenant Sagamore was in Verbier, Cristina had taken time off from the bank to make enquiries at the Hôtel des Bergues. Since the discovery of the ring, Sagamore seemed to be leaning towards the Levovitch theory. She walked up to the front desk of the luxury hotel and put on her best smile, hoping that she could discreetly conceal that she was a detective.

"Hello, I'm Monsieur Levovitch's secretary. He's staying in one of your suites."

The employee made a sign with his head to indicate that he knew who she was talking about.

"How can I help you, Madame?"

"It's about the suite Monsieur Levovitch was renting, which he recently gave up. It seems that he left a few things behind."

"What's he missing?"

"Some files. Paperwork. Probably stuck in the back of a drawer. Would you mind if I had a look around? Monsieur Levovitch would be very grateful."

"Impossible, Madame. The suite is currently being rented. But I'll ask the other employees if the cleaning staff found anything and put it aside. I'd be very surprised if hadn't already been sent to Monsieur Levovitch, though."

The employee picked up the phone to talk to the general manager. Cristina stood there anxiously. After a brief exchange, he hung up.

"Nothing was found in Monsieur Levovitch's suite after his departure. I was told that all his belongings were taken away by the movers."

"Thank you so much. I'll call them right away. Would you happen to have the name of the company? I have the information back at the office, but I'd like to avoid having to go back there; it'll save me time."

"Please ask the concierge; he's the one who handled the move."

Cristina waited at the hotel bar while the concierge located his exchanges with the moving company on his computer. He joined her at the bar and placed a sheet of paper on the counter.

"This is all the information we have."

"Thank you," she said, grabbing her phone to call the company.

She talked to an administrative assistant, who quickly gave her the information that was available. Then Cristina called Sagamore.

"Philippe, where are you?"

"I'm returning from Verbier. I'm about to get on the autoroute to Martigny."

"Then hold on tight to the wheel because I'm about to give you some good news."

Two hours later, Sagamore's unmarked car parked in front of a large warehouse in the industrial area of Carouge. It was here that the movers, at their client's request, had stored all the personal effects taken from his suite at the Hôtel des Bergues.

Sagamore and Cristina showed their badges to the warehouse manager and were taken to the room rented by Levovitch to store his belongings. A bulb on the ceiling cast a dim light across the objects stacked up in piles.

"This is all furniture," Cristina noted. "The moving company told me they brought only boxes from the hotel."

Sagamore swept his torch over the objects in the room. There were tables, lamps, rugs, and blue velvet couches.

"The furniture matches Macaire's description of Tarnogol's living room," Sagamore noted.

In a corner, he saw some old framed posters for Sol Levovitch's shows. Next to them, on a Louis XVI table, the lieutenant found a bound book with yellowed paper. He flipped through it and came across sketches of different characters, together with detailed notes. He turned the pages until he came across a picture of Sinior Tarnogol.

"I think I've found something."

"So have I," she replied. "Bring your torch over here, please."

Sagamore stepped across the room and held the beam of his torch in the direction of a picture resting on two chairs. They both immediately knew what they were looking at.

"The view of Saint Petersburg that Macaire told us about," Cristina remarked.

They realised then that they had been looking in the wrong places – and that it was Lev Levovitch who had been pretending to be Sinior Tarnogol all those years.

61

Geneva (Part 4)

In his office, Sagamore took a break and drank a glass of water.

"So, it was Lev Levovitch who was masquerading as Tarnogol all those years?" Scarlett said.

"Yes. Cristina's intuition was right. He did an amazing job concealing his activities. I was eager to find out how and why. But for weeks we couldn't find Levovitch. After the discovery at the warehouse, I tried to locate him but without success. I got the impression that he had slipped between our fingers like an eel. He had completely disappeared from circulation. He didn't show up again in the Athens office, where the local police were working on the case. His apartment in the Greek capital had been sold a long time ago. We couldn't trace his movements. He didn't show up on any of the airline manifests, so he must have been travelling under a false identity. In Geneva, the bank was under surveillance, and Cristina was keeping an eye on things – but nothing. And as far as I could tell, the last person to have seen him was Macaire Ebezner."

62

Problems

In Geneva, at the Ebezner Bank, Sagamore questioned Macaire in his office.

"As I've already told you," Macaire repeated, "Lev resigned a month ago."

"How did he let you know?" the lieutenant asked.

"He told me he didn't want to continue, that's all," Macaire replied, not understanding the question. "He said he had tried to leave several times before and stayed mostly to please me, but in the end he had had enough."

"What I meant to say was did Levovitch tell you he was resigning in person?"

"Yes."

"Levovitch was in Geneva?" Sagamore asked, surprised.

"Yes, obviously. Why do you ask?"

"When was that?"

"I told you, about a month ago. I no longer recall the exact date."

"He came here, to the bank?"

"No, we met in town."

"Where?"

"At the restaurant in the Parc des Eaux-Vives. After lunch. We had coffee on the terrace."

Macaire felt his heartbeat accelerate, but he forced himself to remain calm. Obviously, he couldn't tell the police what had really happened that day or what Levovitch had said to ensure his silence.

* * *

One month earlier

Macaire had just completed his session with Dr Kazan. As he left the building, a man in a suit was waiting for him.

"Hello, Monsieur Ebezner."

Macaire stared at the man. It took him several moments to place him.

"You're Levovitch's chauffeur."

"Yes. Monsieur Levovitch would like to speak to you."

Alfred pointed to the grey sedan behind him and opened the passenger door. There was no-one in the back seat.

"Where's Levovitch?" Macaire asked.

"He's waiting for you."

Macaire frowned.

"What's with all this cloak-and-dagger stuff? Why doesn't he show his face? He can call my secretary and make an appointment! I'm the president of the Ebezner Bank, you know!"

Alfred, without raising an eyebrow, offered Macaire a small card. It was printed with the name Sinior Tarnogol. Below were the words: "The hour of truth."

"What's this supposed to mean?"

"Come, Monsieur Ebezner," Alfred encouraged him gently.

Macaire reluctantly complied.

The car crossed central Geneva and drove along quai Gustave-Ador to the Parc des Eaux-Vives. They went through the gateway and continued on until they reached the restaurant. Lunchtime service was over, and the car park was deserted. There was no-one around except, a few steps away, seated on a bench, a familiar silhouette. It was Sinior Tarnogol.

Macaire stepped out of the car and approached him, stupefied. Tarnogol removed his silicone mask, and Lev's face appeared.

"So, it was you!" Macaire cried. "Tarnogol was you!"

Lev nodded.

"The police think it was Jean-Bénédict. I . . . I don't know how you did it but . . ."

"That's good," Lev interrupted. "That way everyone's happy. You, you're the president, that's what you wanted. Me, I was able to put an end to this deceit."

"Did you kill Jean-Béné?"

"I was going to ask you the same thing."

There was a silence, during which the two men looked at each other. Then Lev said, "I'm resigning from the bank, Macaire. I wanted to say goodbye."

"Goodbye?" Macaire reddened. "You're joking, I hope. You're not getting out of this so easily, Lev. I know you're with Anastasia."

Lev looked shaken.

"How did you find out?"

"It doesn't matter. I have a few aces up my sleeve as well."

"Listen, Macaire, I just wanted to tell you that I'm leaving the bank effective immediately. Everything on my end has been taken care of. I've already sent all my files to our people at the Athens office. I'm leaving for good. Don't try to find me."

Macaire laughed.

"Do you think I'm going to let you disappear like that?"

"We made a deal, Macaire. Anastasia for the presidency. You got the presidency."

"I made a deal with Tarnogol," Macaire said.

"I am Tarnogol."

"No, no – you're only Lev Levovitch!"

Lev shrugged as if none of this mattered. He was about to walk over to the car when Macaire said to him, "I know you're in Corfu. In a villa by the sea."

"Come and visit us since you know the address," Lev replied, unflustered.

"The police are going to show up," Macaire threatened. "To arrest you."

"You won't do anything," Lev said. "For Anastasia's sake."

"For Anastasia?"

"On the night of the murder, I helped her escape. While we were outside, about to leave, she decided to return to the hotel. She said she had to go back upstairs, as if she meant the sixth floor. I waited outside; it was a while before she reappeared."

"What are you saying?"

"I don't know," Lev replied. "But let's keep the police out of it."

Macaire, struck by this disclosure, then said, "On the morning of Jean-Béné's murder, I found a note in Anastasia's handwriting slipped under the door of my room, that said, as I recall, something like this:

"Macaire,

I'm leaving for good. I'm not coming back. Don't try to find me.

Forgive me. I'll always live with the weight of what I have done.

Anastasia"

* * *

To Lieutenant Sagamore, Macaire simply said that he had met Lev at the restaurant in the Parc des Eaux-Vives and that Lev had resigned, effective immediately.

"Is Lev in any trouble?" Macaire asked the officer.

"There's a warrant out for his arrest," Sagamore replied. "If you speak to him, if you see him, you have to let me know right away."

At that moment, in the heart of the lively and joyous old town of Corfu, Anastasia was seated on the terrace of a small café she was fond of. Once a week, in the late morning, she would come here. She sat at a table, ordered a tomato salad, cucumbers and feta, then a cup of Greek coffee. She watched the people crossing the small flower-covered square. She would spend the afternoon observing the silhouettes that passed by: the locals, always in a hurry; the tourists, trundling to and fro; and the couples. They were the ones she watched most closely, the couples who walked, who kissed, who argued – vibrant and alive.

For a while now, she had had the unpleasant feeling that she and Lev were imprisoned in a bath of formaldehyde. She wasn't sure how long it had been going on. Perhaps it was time for them to leave Corfu. She loved the house, she loved the island; she felt good there and wanted to come back for their holidays. She was happy, but it had been almost six months, and she couldn't imagine staying there for the rest of their lives. What would they do there? For the first time in her life, she experienced a tinge of boredom.

For six months, they had been happy from morning till night – six months of a perfect life, outside time, six months without a single false note from Lev or the army of employees who watched over the two of them. Six months of absolute perfection. But, she had realised, one tires of perfection.

Six months of breakfasts with caviar. Sometimes she thought, with a tinge of nostalgia, about Macaire with his head in his paper, some of which he would read out to her from time to time, muttering, "Can you imagine, chouchou!" as he munched on his toast, his fingers covered in jam. Six months locked in an intricate ballet with their silent servants. Sometimes she thought of Arma and her jovial impertinence. She wondered how they were doing. She wondered what was going on in Cologny.

She liked to cook, but on Corfu there was a cook and a pastry chef, and neither of them let her lift a finger. In Cologny, she had always been involved in the upkeep of the house, often helping Arma with her work. In Corfu, Lev was against her pitching in. "Don't waste your time," he would say to her, "we have people for that."

She began to dream of a project with Lev: opening a bar, for instance. She would be in the kitchen; he could wait on tables. Chez Lev & Anastasia – they would make a fantastic team. She had mentioned it to him, but Lev didn't take the idea seriously, too obsessed with creating what he thought was a paradise. But eventually paradise gets monotonous. Eve ended up eating that apple because she was looking for a good reason to leave.

So, once a week, when Lev had left for work in Athens, she took her bicycle and went into town. Alfred insisted on driving her, but she wouldn't hear of it. She felt free only on her bicycle. She would wander around the small streets of the old town, then sit at her table and observe the couples, wondering which of the women she would like to be.

That day, on the terrace of the restaurant, Anastasia took a piece of paper and a pen from her bag and finished the letter she had begun that morning. The desire had overcome her quite suddenly, and she had decided not to repress it. Her letter finished, she reread it several times. Then she folded it and placed it in an envelope before going to the post office. An employee behind the counter asked her, "Where is it going?"

"Geneva, Switzerland."

63

Letters

A week passed. One afternoon, Macaire returned home early but in a bad mood; he was scheduled to attend a fashionable cocktail party that evening and had no desire to go. As he entered, he ran into Arma, who was waxing the banister.

"Hello, Moussieu," she greeted him, looking at him tenderly.

Macaire examined her for a moment.

"Tell me, Arma, are you free this evening?"

"Yes, Moussieu! Do you want me to stay late?"

"No, I would like you to accompany me to a cocktail party."

"A cocktail party?" she repeated, looking uncomfortable. "Where?"

"At the Museum of Art and History. It's for major donors, and the bank is one of them. It'll be in the interior courtyard. It should be nice."

"Oh lá lá," Arma said, worriedly. "That's fancy."

"Yes, a little."

"But I have nothing to wear. You need fancy clothes."

"Take something from Anastasia's wardrobe."

"You want me to steal from Médéme again?"

"Yes, *go steal from Médéme*. Médéme is no longer here. And she's never coming back."

After hesitating, Arma asked, "Moussieu, can I get ready in the large bathroom? There are some beauty products there and I . . ."

"Use the bedroom and bath as much as you like, Arma. I don't need them."

Arma didn't have to be told twice. She hurried upstairs and made a pilgrimage to Anastasia's very large wardrobe. She looked over the dresses, touched the costly fabrics, admired the snakeskin shoes. She chose an outfit that looked chic on her but not excessively so. She made sure the waist was right. It was perfect.

"Now to get cleaned up," she declared, determined to scrub herself like a casserole dish for the occasion.

She locked herself in the bathroom. She shoved her face into the soft bathrobes she had so often cleaned and ironed, marvelling every time at how comfortable they were. She sniffed the bath salts and the body lotions. She drew a bath and lounged in it for a long time, hidden behind a mountain of foam, applying all the creams and soaps she happened upon.

When it was time to leave and she had decided to reveal herself to Macaire, he was unable to hide his emotion.

"Arma, you're . . ."

"Ridiculous," she concluded.

"Sublime," he corrected.

She smiled. And this made her even more lovely.

When they arrived at the museum, they joined the crowd of guests who were noisily talking in the interior courtyard. Candles had been arranged around the fountain.

"Oh, it's magnificent," Arma sighed. "I don't think I've ever seen anything so beautiful."

As they mingled with the guests, Macaire gave his arm to Arma, and everyone was buzzing about the woman accompanying President Ebezner.

That evening, for the first time in years, not only did Macaire not feel alone, but he enjoyed himself, even though he usually found such gatherings dull and uneventful. Arma attacked the champagne at once, which had a liberating effect on her. She then turned to the buffet, fascinated by the tastes, shapes, and presentation. She didn't hesitate to interrupt Macaire in his conversation to shove her most recent discovery into his mouth. "Taste this, Moussieu!"

She made him laugh. She lit up the night. When the party was over, since he didn't want the evening to come to an end, he led her through the cobblestone streets of Geneva's old town. They found a bar, sat at the counter, and ordered something to drink. Macaire couldn't recall ever having done anything like this with Anastasia.

Around midnight, Arma said to Macaire, "Moussieu . . ."

"Stop calling me that. I'm no longer Moussieu."

She stared at him curiously.

"Who are you then?"

"I'm Macaire."

"Ahhh! And what should I call you?"

"Macaire."

She began her sentence again.

"Macaire . . ."

"Yes?"

"I think I drank too much."

Arma fell asleep in the car on the way to her apartment on rue de Montchoisy. Macaire led her to the elevator then, finding the key to her apartment in her handbag, carried her to her bed, where he deposited her. The following morning, when she opened her eyes, she saw him sitting on a chair, sleeping in an uncomfortable position.

"Macaire?" she called softly.

He opened one eye. She looked at him tenderly and extended her hand to touch his arm.

"You spent the night watching over me?"

"Yes."

"Was it romantic?"

"No, it was not romantic at all. I was afraid you would choke on your own vomit."

They burst out laughing. Macaire realised that it had been a long time since he had laughed like that. Suddenly, without thinking, he bent over and kissed her.

*

That same day, in Corfu, at the post office, the employee behind the window informed Anastasia that she had received a letter. He had replied, general delivery, as she had suggested. She took the letter and returned to her customary café. She sat at the table, ordered, and tore open the envelope.

Anastasia,

Your letter made me so happy. It's been months that I've wondered where you had gone – if you were okay. And for months I've been asking myself thousands of questions.

Why didn't you give me any news? Why come to Verbier during the Gala Weekend and enter my room at the hotel to leave me a love letter, then treat me with such contempt?

I hope one day to see you again – to talk about all this.

I waited for you. I'm not waiting any longer.

But there is a question that's been haunting me, and I have to ask it now, Anastasia: was it you who killed Jean-Béné?

I hope you will write back.

I don't even know if you're still in Corfu. Maybe you've gone somewhere else now that Lev has resigned from the bank.

Tenderly,
Macaire

She raised her eyes. Lev had resigned from the bank? But what was he doing then, when he went to Athens every week?

At that moment in Geneva, Lev was playing with fire. He knew it. If the police stopped him, it was all over. He was pensive. He wondered how he had let it go on this long. He found himself thinking of that December fourteen years ago.

* * *

494

December, fourteen years ago

The Gala Weekend was approaching.

It was almost a year since Lev had lost Anastasia and gained Macaire's shares.

It was almost a year since Lev had begun his double life as himself and as Sinior Tarnogol, a member of the board.

It was almost a year since his father had stopped talking to him. Sol was getting visibly weaker; he could no longer work and was receiving palliative care at a clinic in Martigny.

Lev lived a life of extreme solitude. He was the first to arrive at the bank and the last to leave. His role took up all his time and all his energy. But his objective was in sight: within a month, his bonus would allow him to buy the house on chemin Byron, the one with the extraordinary view that Anastasia had dreamed about. He had promised to offer it to her, and now, he was about to succeed.

The house would fix everything. He would bring his father there, make sure he was comfortable. He would say, "Look, Papa, it was my talent as an actor that enabled me to buy this." And then, with the house, he could win back Anastasia. The house was their future.

She was supposed to marry Macaire in February. He was convinced she would understand her error and break off the engagement. He couldn't imagine it any other way. He couldn't imagine that they could fail to end up together, the two of them. They had promised themselves to each other – for life.

*   *   *

Thinking about those moments fourteen years later, Lev still experienced pain in the depths of his heart. He and Anastasia had finally been reunited, but how long would it be before their past suffering was erased completely? And that didn't take into account what was about to unfold, involving the investigation into the murder of Jean-Bénédict.

The head of the local police showed up at the Hôtel de Verbier a few minutes after receiving the call. It was a gardener, busy pruning the roses, who had noticed the object. In the meantime, curious hotel employees had gathered around the flower bed to observe the scene.

"Don't touch anything!" the police chief ordered, as his round silhouette trotted over to the site.

The gardener pointed at his discovery, and the chief of police knelt to get a closer look.

"Damn, it's not possible!" he muttered.

He grabbed his radio and asked the station to send over the Judicial Police at once.

64

Geneva (Part 5)

"It was the Judicial Police in the Valais who notified us," Sagamore explained, recalling the events. "I immediately went to Verbier. I wanted to see it with my own eyes."

"What had the gardener discovered?" Scarlett asked impatiently.

"A small gold pistol, whose grip had been engraved with a name: *Anastasia*."

"Anastasia, as in Anastasia Ebezner?"

"Exactly. It was unlikely to be a coincidence. We immediately had the weapon analysed in the police lab in Geneva. The extent of corrosion indicated that it had been outside in the snow and the elements for several months, and unfortunately, they couldn't do a complete ballistics check. It was, however, a 9 mm."

"Like the weapon used for the crime," I said.

"Like the weapon used for the crime," Sagamore confirmed.

"And what did you do?" Scarlett asked.

"I had to find Anastasia. For the past few months, no-one had seen her."

"You had never considered her a suspect before this?" Scarlett asked.

Before answering, Sagamore rifled through his documents and pulled out a report on the robbery, which he held out to us.

"Anastasia's disappearance didn't concern me," Sagamore explained, "because on the day of the robbery at the Ebezner home, I had found a note she had left for her husband. She wrote to tell him she was leaving him. This was confirmed by the maid, a woman named Arma, who told me that her employer was having a very serious extramarital affair with a man and was planning to leave with him. To my mind, it all fitted together."

"Did you know who her lover was?" I asked.

"At the time, no. To be honest, I didn't dig too deep because I didn't see the connection with my investigation. But I then discovered that it was Lev Levovitch. Quite the coincidence, wasn't it? The two people I was looking for were together. But at the time, since I wasn't aware of this, I had to question my lead suspect."

"Macaire Ebezner," Scarlett said.

"Bullseye."

65

The Woman with the Golden Gun

In the interrogation room at police headquarters in Geneva, Macaire stared uneasily at Lieutenant Sagamore, who had placed a gold pistol, wrapped in a plastic bag, before him. He recognised it at once.

"Judging by your expression, I imagine that you're familiar with the weapon," Sagamore said.

Macaire nodded. "The gun belongs to my wife, Anastasia. Where did you find it?"

"In the garden of the Hôtel de Verbier. Near an emergency exit. Judging by its condition, it's been outside for several months."

"Is it the weapon used for the crime?"

"That's what we're trying to find out. Monsieur Ebezner, why did your wife own a weapon?"

"I gave it to her. There were a series of break-ins in Cologny. She was afraid, she wanted to be able to defend herself, especially when I was travelling for business and she was alone in the house."

"The weapon isn't registered," Sagamore noted.

"Like most of the weapons sold from one individual to another," Macaire replied. "The law doesn't require me to do so. I bought it at a weapons fair in Zurich."

"When was that?"

"A few years ago."

For a moment, Sagamore studied the man in front of him. The silence made Macaire uncomfortable.

"Monsieur Ebezner, do you have any idea how your wife's gun happened to turn up in Verbier?"

"None. I'm as surprised as you are."

"Come on, you have to admit that it makes sense. Your wife owned an unregistered weapon. You brought it with you to Verbier before the election. It could always turn out to be useful."

"Lieutenant! I can't allow you to make such insinuations."

"Then give me a better explanation."

"I don't have one. I don't understand how the gun ended up in Verbier."

"Did your wife go to Verbier during the bank weekend?"

"My wife? No, why?"

Sagamore didn't reply directly to the question.

"Monsieur Ebezner, where is your wife?"

Macaire turned white.

"I don't know," he lied. "She left me, as you know. I haven't had any news of her since December."

Sagamore knew he wouldn't get anything from Macaire. Besides, the lieutenant hadn't brought the banker in to get a confession but to study his behaviour. If Macaire Ebezner was mixed up in the murder, Sagamore would soon find out.

After Macaire left police headquarters, Sagamore immediately called Cristina.

"Macaire just left. I sent a team to tail him; another is watching his house. Keep an eye on him at the bank."

"Understood. Any news from the lab about the gun?"

"Well, it's a 9 mm alright, like the gun used for the murder, but with all the rust and corrosion, they can't tell for sure whether it was the weapon used for the crime."

"Shit. What do you think?" Cristina remarked.

"I think that the murderer is Macaire Ebezner or his wife."

"What motive would Anastasia have had?"

"I'm not so sure, but it is her gun, and she disappeared after the murder. That's enough to raise a lot of questions. In any case, I've contacted her mother and sister. Maybe they can help."

Sagamore hung up and examined the whiteboard opposite his desk, to which he had added Anastasia's photo. The gun had been found near one of the hotel's emergency exits. Based on the hotel's floor plan, this was the exit nearest the stairs, leading directly to a narrow road. Sagamore was certain the murderer had left through that door. Had they dropped the weapon accidentally as they ran out? Had they thrown it into the snow to get rid of it, sure that no-one would find it before the snow melted and they were already far away?

He looked at Anastasia's photo again. Did she kill Jean-Bénédict Hansen?

Olga von Lacht assured Sagamore that she didn't have the slightest idea where her daughter was.

"In any case, I'm not happy that she left her husband. It's a terrible thing."

"Did Anastasia tell you she was planning to leave him?"

"No," Olga lied.

"So, how do you know that she left her husband?" Sagamore asked.

"Macaire told me, obviously."

Olga didn't understand the intent of the question. As far as Sagamore was concerned, there was a grim logic to it: he wondered whether Macaire had managed to get rid of his wife. Was she a problematic witness to what had happened? But Sagamore put that idea aside after speaking with Irina. She told him that Anastasia had always been her mother's favourite.

"She spent her time pampering and protecting her," Irina explained. "It was always about her."

"Do you know where your sister is now?"

"No idea. Probably in the sun somewhere, living the good life with her banker."

"Her banker? What banker?"

"Lev Levovitch. They were having an affair. During lunch one day, Anastasia showed us a gold bracelet he had given her. She said she wanted to leave with him. I'm sure they're together. Anyway, that's what I told Macaire Ebezner."

"Oh?"

"I wrote him an anonymous letter in early spring. I ran into him once, very sad, still in love. I said to myself that he had a right to know."

* * *

That afternoon in Corfu, Anastasia was swimming in the Ionian Sea. Lev watched her adoringly from the terrace, where he was reading the paper and drinking coffee. She looked at him and burst out laughing.

"Are we going to stare at each other forever?" she shouted. "Put your bathing suit on and join me."

"I'm coming. As soon as I finish the paper, I'll be there."

Back in Cologny, Macaire arrived home in a fury.

"Back already?" Arma said, surprised to see him hurtling into the hall.

Macaire didn't even bother to reply. He went directly to his room and closed the door. The situation was serious. Evidence had been building against Anastasia: her presence at the hotel the weekend of the murder, her gun found in the garden. Macaire couldn't stop thinking about what Lev had told him when they met for the last time in the Parc des Eaux-Vives: Anastasia and he had left through an emergency exit, but she had suddenly gone back inside. She had gone back upstairs to kill Jean-Bénédict; then she had left the note under Macaire's door, gone back out through the emergency exit, got rid of the gun, and fled.

He opened his safe and took out the note that had been slipped under his door on the morning of the murder, as well as the letters sent from Corfu. He threw them all into the metal wastepaper basket and burned them. He had to destroy everything. Watching the letters burn, Macaire was overcome with sadness. He had loved her so much. She was the love of his life. He couldn't bear the idea of seeing her in trouble. He had to warn her. He needed help.

He grabbed the music box sitting on a shelf and turned it to release the telephone number. He memorised it, then left the room quickly.

"What's going on, Macaire?" Arma asked, as he rushed by.

He didn't bother to reply. He jumped into his car and drove off at high speed. He drove down chemin de Ruth in the direction of Cologny. The police who had been watching the house followed.

Sagamore was in his office at police headquarters when he got the call.

"Lieutenant, Ebezner ran into his house, stayed there ten minutes, and has just left. He looks like he's in a hurry."

"He's making a run for it," Sagamore said. "Follow him, and make sure he doesn't see you. We have to know where he goes. I'll join you."

Sagamore left his office and rushed down the stairs to the underground car park. He jumped into his unmarked car, put the emergency light on the roof, and drove through town as fast as he could, his siren blaring.

Macaire didn't go far, however. He parked near the centre of Cologny and crossed the lawn of the small park until he reached a phone booth.

Sagamore was driving down rue de la Confédération when he was informed of the situation.

"A phone box? Get them to trace the call. I want to know who he's calling."

"Wagner," Macaire said from the booth. "I need your help; it's about Anastasia."

"What's going on?"

503

"The police found a gun that belonged to her near the Hôtel de Verbier."

"What?" Wagner said, surprised. "How is that possible?"

"It's a long story. Everything points to her, Wagner. She was at the hotel on the weekend of the murder, it's her gun that was found, she left me a note that looks like a confession. But I know she had nothing to do with the murder."

"How can you be so sure?"

"She told me. Well, she wrote to me from Corfu. We wrote to each other; I sent my letters to general delivery."

"Anastasia wrote to you?"

"Yes, she wanted to tell me she was thinking about me, that she hoped I would forgive her for what she had done."

"What she had done? Do you mean killing Jean-Bénédict Hansen?"

"No. I asked her whether it was her. She assured me it wasn't."

"Let me see what I can do," Wagner replied. "I'll be in touch."

They hung up.

"He hung up," one of the detectives observing the scene announced to Sagamore. "They're trying to trace the call but it's going to take a while."

The lieutenant was now driving at high speed along quai Gustave-Ador.

"Stop him," he ordered.

In Cologny, the police rushed Macaire as he was leaving the phone booth.

Wagner sat there, thoughtfully, the receiver still in his hand. He hadn't seen the figure behind him, who had been present for the conversation. It was Alfred.

"What are you doing, Monsieur Levovitch? You promised me it was over."

504

Lev lowered his head. He cleared his throat to get his voice back, "There's nothing else I can do, Alfred."

"But, Monsieur, you're going to lose everything! You're playing with fire and you're going to burn your fingers."

"You don't understand, Alfred. I can't stop."

* * *

Fourteen years earlier

In mid-February, the day the papers for the house on chemin Byron were signed, Macaire and Anastasia went together to the city hall of Collonge-Bellerive.

Lev, returning from the lawyer, had seen them from his car as they left the building. They looked happy. It was all over, then, for good. He would never be the man by her side. He would never be her husband.

Lev, broken-hearted, made his way to the large house that was now his. The rooms were all empty – except for the bedroom, in the middle of which could be found a small table with a telephone. He picked up the receiver and decided to call the only person he had left in life: his father.

At the hospice in Martigny, the nurse who answered sounded grim.

"Monsieur Levovitch, we've been trying to reach you since morning. Your father isn't doing so well. You should come now."

Lev jumped into his car and drove quickly to Martigny without worrying about the speed limit. When he entered his father's room, Monsieur Rose was already there. Judging by the tears that flowed down his cheeks, Lev understood that his father was dying. Lev moved towards the bed and kissed the face of the man he would never see again.

"I'm sorry about mother's ring. I'm so sorry for what I did."

"Don't regret anything, Lev," Sol said with difficulty. "I'm very proud of you. You've done something few actors are capable of doing: you've brought a character to life."

505

"We're Levovitches," Lev whispered. "A great line of actors."

"A great line of actors," his father said with a smile.

Sol held the large leather-bound book in which he had described all his characters. Using the little strength he had left, he offered it to his son.

"Don't let my characters die with me, my son."

"I promise."

"Make them live forever. That way, I'll live forever in you."

His father smiled and went to sleep, now at peace.

That night, returning to Geneva, Lev spread a can of gasoline over the ground floor of his new house and lit a match. Then, without waiting for the firemen, he left and went to the Hôtel des Bergues.

"I'd like to rent your largest suite," he said to the receptionist.

"For tonight?"

"Forever."

66

Rupture

Anastasia, wrapped in a bath towel, left the beach and walked to the house. She wondered why Lev hadn't joined her in the water. She had seen him leave the terrace and assumed he was going to get changed, but he hadn't returned.

She entered the house and was surprised to find it empty. Neither Lev, nor Alfred, nor any of the staff were there – as if everyone had disappeared. It was all very strange. She called out, but there was no reply.

She walked upstairs to the bedroom and found Lev sitting on the bed. She noticed at once that something wasn't right.

"Lev, what's going on? Why didn't you come to the beach?"

Without saying a word, he looked at her ominously.

"Lev, what is it? Why are you looking at me like that?"

"So you wrote to him?"

"You went through my things?"

"You're still in love with him, aren't you?"

"What? Of course not, no!"

"Then why did you write to him?"

"Because I wanted to tell him what happened."

"What happened? I must be dreaming. What made you think you had to tell him anything?"

"He's been a friend for fifteen years," she replied.

"He's your husband!"

"He's always treated me with respect and kindness. I'm angry with myself for leaving him the way I did."

"Oh, so now you have regrets!"

"Lev, don't take that tone with me. It's not a question of regret but remorse for hurting someone who has always been good to me."

"You know, Anastasia, it's strange, because for six months you haven't mentioned divorcing him."

"Maybe because for six months you haven't thought to ask me to marry you. I've been waiting for fifteen years. What are we doing in Corfu, really? Sealed in this house, pretending to be in love from morning till night. We're not building a life together, Lev!"

"We share our love."

"That's not a plan. What are we building together?"

"What did you build with Macaire?" Lev asked, awkwardly.

"But I'm no longer with Macaire! Your biggest weakness, Lev, is that you don't have enough self-confidence. The only person who doesn't admire you is you."

There was a lengthy silence.

"Anastasia, did you kill Jean-Bénédict?"

"Did I what . . . ? Obviously, no. Where on earth did you get that idea?"

"The police found a gun engraved with your name on it in the hotel garden."

"My gold pistol?"

"What was your gun doing in Verbier?"

"It was in my bag when I left Geneva. I didn't want to leave it there. It was only when I arrived in Corfu that I realised it was gone."

"So your gun mysteriously disappeared?" he asked, sarcastically.

"It disappeared in your room at the hotel," she replied. "My bag never left the room. Maybe Sinior Tarnogol took it? Oh, but I'm forgetting, you're Tarnogol."

"Are you insinuating that I killed Jean-Bénédict?"

"That's what you're accusing me of, isn't it? You're full of accusations today. When were you planning to tell me that you resigned from the bank?"

"Who told you? Macaire?"

"Since when have we been keeping secrets, Lev? You resign from the bank and you don't tell me? Where do you go every week when you leave for Athens and your so-called office?"

"I go to work for myself, for us."

"Meaning?"

"Managing my money, taking care of my investments. Our investments, I should say. I'm doing it all for us, so that we can live on our island without worrying about anything."

They stared at each other. Anastasia looked sad.

"I'm suffocating on this island. I feel as if we're about to lose each other, Lev."

She left the room.

* * *

At police headquarters, Sagamore was questioning Macaire; the lieutenant went hard on him. The number dialled from the phone booth was an unregistered prepaid mobile – it was impossible to trace it to the person on the other end of the line and therefore impossible to locate them.

"Who did you call?" Sagamore repeated. "Anastasia? Are you protecting her?"

"No, I already told you. I don't know where she is."

"Then who? Who was it? I'm warning you, Macaire: I'm going to charge you with Hansen's murder."

"But I didn't kill him. Why would I?"

"To ensure you became president. The board decided on Levovitch. But Hansen's death tilted things in your favour."

"I didn't kill my cousin," Macaire assured Sagamore.

"So tell me who you called."

Macaire had no other choice than to tell him the truth.

"I called a man named Wagner, an agent with the Swiss intelligence services. I was upset by the discovery of the gun at the hotel; I wanted to help Anastasia and thought Wagner could help."

"Why do you want to help Anastasia?"

"Because she was in Verbier on the weekend of the murder," Macaire explained, overwhelmed.

"Your wife was at the hotel at the time of the murder?"

"Yes."

Sagamore sat down in front of Macaire.

"So, who is this Wagner character?"

Macaire was at the end of his tether. His nerves were shot. He couldn't sleep and when he did, knocked out with sleeping pills, he had nightmares. It was time to get things off his chest.

"Because of me, people are dead!" he shouted.

"So you killed Jean-Bénédict Hansen?" Sagamore asked.

"No! Of course not. I did play a role, however, in the double murder of a retired couple in Madrid."

Sagamore was at a loss; he didn't know what to believe. He opened the door of the interrogation room and looked at Macaire.

"You can go."

"Really?" Macaire said, surprised, rising from the chair.

"I spoke to the retired couple you savagely murdered. They're doing very well. They say hello, by the way."

Macaire looked as surprised as Sagamore had – which confirmed the detective's intuition: Macaire was telling the truth. But what did it all mean? None of the lieutenant's contacts at the Confederation's Federal Police and Information Services had ever heard of P-30 or their dealings with foreign tax authorities. The only thing Sagamore knew for sure was that Macaire, consciously or not, was at the heart of the affair. Sagamore had decided to keep the banker under surveillance, convinced that he would lead them somewhere. The lieutenant didn't have to wait long – only until the following Tuesday.

At noon that day, Macaire left the bank on foot. A detective with the surveillance team followed at a distance. The two men walked along rue de la Corraterie to place de Neuve, then crossed the Parc des Bastions, finally reaching place Claparède, where Macaire entered a building. He climbed to the third floor and disappeared behind a door.

A few moments later, Sagamore, alerted by his colleague, arrived at the same door. He read the sign next to the door: a psychoanalyst.

Sagamore didn't immediately make the connection. Then, suddenly, it came to him. He stood there, stunned. Now everything made sense.

67

Le Dôme

That Tuesday afternoon, July 3, 2018, Scarlett and I returned to Verbier. Our meeting with Sagamore had been very rewarding. At the Hôtel de Verbier's reception desk, Scarlett had the staff print all the photographs we had taken in the police station; we then went and sat at the bar to go through them together. Suddenly, I said to Scarlett, "It's at this very black marble counter that I saw you for the first time, ten days ago."

She smiled.

"And look where we are now – neck deep in a criminal investigation. Say, do you talk about me in your book?"

"I don't know whether I'll publish this book, Scarlett."

"But, Writer, you have to. I'm sure we're about to solve the case."

"And discover what the police couldn't see?"

"We're good investigators," she noted. "And everyone is going to want to read your book. Can you imagine? A novelist solves a criminal investigation at a hotel in the Swiss Alps."

"I no longer have a publisher, as you may recall."

"You'll find another one," she assured me.

"Impossible. After Bernard, all the others would seem insignificant."

"So what are you going to do? Stop writing?"

"I have no idea."

We sat in silence for a moment. I then got up to go to my room.

"Are we dining together, Writer?" Scarlett asked. "I'll buy you a drink here before dinner. Let's say eight o'clock? And we'll eat afterwards. I'm dreaming about the pasta I had the other day."

"No, thank you, I need to work on the book."

She looked at me with a mixture of sadness and disappointment.

"Why do you always do that, Writer? I suggest keeping you company, and you systematically refuse."

"You know why, Scarlett."

"I know. But I'd like things to be different."

"If things were different, I wouldn't be a writer."

"Well, sometimes I would prefer it if you weren't a writer."

"If I weren't a writer, we wouldn't be together at this very moment."

I went up to my room and stepped out on to the balcony for a cigarette. I thought of Bernard. The penultimate time I saw Bernard was a Monday in mid-December in Paris. We had lunch at Le Dôme and, as always, ordered John Dory and a glass of wine. We talked about our projects. I recall saying to Bernard, "I have several ideas for books. In any case, the next one will be about you."

He burst out laughing before replying. "I'll have to live a very long time."

We then got into his old Mercedes, and he drove me to the Gare de Lyon.

The day after that day filled with promises, he fell terribly ill at café Le Mesnil, downstairs from his office – the café in which, every morning, he dunked his bread into his coffee. An ambulance was dispatched to take him to hospital.

68

Check and Mate

In Corfu, one sun-drenched morning in mid-June, Anastasia and Lev were having breakfast on the terrace. Suddenly, a group of Greek police in uniform arrived from the beach. At their head was a man in civilian clothing. Anastasia and Lev looked at each other uneasily. The police remained below, and the man in civilian clothes walked alone up the steps that led to the house. Anastasia recognised him.

"Lieutenant Sagamore . . ."

"Hello, Madame Ebezner. Hello, Monsieur Levovitch."

Judging by the way Sagamore looked at them, Lev understood that the lieutenant had come for him.

"How did you find me?"

"I followed you from Geneva on Tuesday. From place Claparède to the private plane terminal at the airport."

"You were in Geneva on Tuesday?" Anastasia said. "Lev, you told me you were in London. What were you doing in Geneva?"

Lev didn't answer her. Sagamore continued: "Ever since the start of the year, Monsieur Levovitch, you've been going to Geneva every Tuesday, on a private plane. I was able to trace your movements."

"I have my sessions with Dr Kazan," Lev said.

"You're seeing Dr Kazan?" Anastasia asked, surprised. "Why didn't you tell me?"

"Monsieur Levovitch, you haven't been seeing Dr Kazan," Sagamore interjected. "You *are* Dr Kazan."

Levovitch appeared greatly surprised by Sagamore's accusation. Nonetheless, he said he was deeply concerned by the whole matter and wanted to assist the police. He had coffee brought out for Sagamore and for the police on the beach.

"It appears that you recommended Dr Kazan to Macaire Ebezner," Sagamore said.

"Absolutely," Lev confirmed, "he's an excellent therapist."

"And how did you meet him?"

"At a party at the Hôtel de Verbier. That was years ago. I found him fascinating. He agreed to take me on as a patient although he was already fully booked."

"Give me the names of some of his other patients," Sagamore demanded.

"How should I know? Kazan kept that information confidential."

"Stop this nonsense, Monsieur Levovitch. Dr Kazan has never existed!"

"I don't understand what you're insinuating. He has his office at 2 place Claparède."

Sagamore placed a file on the table and opened it. Inside were three sheets of paper, which the detective showed to Lev and Anastasia. They were photocopies.

"These are pages from a notebook belonging to your father, Sol Levovitch. We found it in a warehouse you're renting."

Each page included a drawing and a description.

The first represented Sinior Tarnogol.

The second represented Dr Kazan.

The third represented Wagner.

Looking at the drawings, Anastasia shuddered, and Sagamore noticed. Lev stood motionless.

"Those are my father's drawings. He could draw well and he liked observing people."

"Explain to me," Sagamore said, "who was Sinior Tarnogol?"

"A member of the bank's board of directors," Lev replied casually. "And a long-term client of the Hôtel de Verbier, all of which I'm sure you already—"

"Stop talking to me like I'm an idiot!" Sagamore interrupted, irritated now. "Tarnogol was a character invented by your father, Sol Levovitch, an actor. And the same is true for Dr Kazan and Wagner!"

"I don't know this Wagner," Lev said. "He's supposed to be a member of the intelligence services, which doesn't surprise me. At one time, with all the rich foreign businessmen staying at the hotel, it had become a nest of spies. These people were all guests of the hotel. But why don't you ask them directly?"

"Because they've mysteriously disappeared from sight," Sagamore hissed. "At the same time as you did."

"Lieutenant Sagamore," Lev said, in a very relaxed tone of voice, "I'm afraid you're looking in the wrong place."

Anastasia had a vacant expression on her face and had grown pale. She understood everything now. She didn't say a word, fearing she would incriminate her lover. But her face spoke for her. Sagamore said to her, "Madame Ebezner, we found a weapon belonging to you at the scene of the crime."

Anastasia remained silent. She was terrified.

Sagamore continued.

"I know you were at the Hôtel de Verbier on the evening of the murder. Can you explain why?"

She had begun to crack. She was edgy, nervous, and she began to cry. Sagamore got up from his chair. He made a sign to the Greek police, who joined them on the terrace. Sagamore then said, "Anastasia Ebezner and Lev Levovitch, I'm arresting you for the murder of Jean-Bénédict Hansen."

The police surrounded Lev and Anastasia and handcuffed them before leading them away. Lev was afraid but didn't show it. Anastasia was in tears.

It was all over.

The gates of their Greek paradise closed behind them.

PART FOUR

Three Years After the Murder

September

69

The Fall

It was autumn in Geneva.

In a supermarket in the city centre, Anastasia was in the fruit aisle. Her sister, Irina, joined her. They were both working in the same store. Irina had found the job for her sister.

"Give me a hand," Irina said, "we need someone at the register."

Anastasia followed her sister obediently. Irina had been very good to her. After all that had happened, she had given her a place to stay until she found a small apartment in Servette. Gradually, she began to make a new life for herself.

The end of Corfu, three years earlier, had been the end of everything. Since then, she had left Lev. And she had divorced Macaire. The procedure was very simple. She had given up everything – hadn't even demanded any settlement. All she wanted was for the marriage to be dissolved and to be able to draw a line under the last fifteen years of her life.

She felt very alone. Irina often said to her, "You'll find someone soon enough, don't worry about it." But Anastasia had no wish to find *someone*. She wanted to find him – him. She wanted to find Lev, the dreamy young baggage handler at the Hôtel de Verbier. She didn't want Lev Levovitch the banker, or Dr Kazan, or Wagner, or Sinior Tarnogol.

* * *

Three years earlier, mid-June
Immediately after their arrest in Corfu, Lev and Anastasia were extradited to Geneva. But the case didn't go very far. Lev, with the talent of

519

the greatest of lawyers, dismantled the accusations against them piece by piece.

There was no concrete proof to link them to the murder of Jean-Bénédict Hansen. They were at the Hôtel de Verbier that night, yes, but so were many other people. And Anastasia's pistol? She said she had lost it, and in any event, corrosion had damaged it so badly that it was impossible to formally prove that it was the weapon used for the crime.

"Like you, I would like to understand what happened in room 622 of the Hôtel de Verbier," Lev assured Lieutenant Sagamore.

"Don't play games with me, Levovitch! Jean-Bénédict Hansen found out that you were Tarnogol, isn't that right?"

"That I'm Tarnogol?" Lev said, offended. "You've been repeating this nonsense to me ever since you landed in Corfu. What does it mean to be Tarnogol? You're you, and I'm me."

"Stop your clowning, Levovitch. We know everything."

"You have no proof for your theory."

"We found this ring, which belongs to you."

"You found a ring that belongs to me, which I got from my mother, and which was in the drawer of my desk at the bank. I don't see anything special about that."

"A witness claims that this ring was in Tarnogol's possession."

"Your witness is mistaken. A single witness isn't much to go on. It's even possible that the witness was paid off."

"Furniture belonging to Sinior Tarnogol was found in a warehouse you rented. The movers who brought it there formally identified the objects."

"I lent my warehouse storage space to Tarnogol."

"You *are* Tarnogol!" Sagamore repeated in frustration. "He was a character invented by your father. Just like Wagner and Dr Kazan. We have their descriptions in your father's book."

"I've already explained this to you several times. They were guests of the hotel. Check the hotel's reservation register; you'll see that I'm telling the truth. My father made sketches of guests. In any case, I'm shocked to learn that Kazan had no medical degree. I hope you find that charlatan."

"You're only making things worse for yourself, Levovitch."

"Quite the opposite. I take exception to this arbitrary arrest, and it's going to have disastrous consequences for you, Lieutenant."

Anastasia had replied to Sagamore's questions with the same coolness.

"What was I doing at the hotel the night of the murder? We had planned to run away together, Lev and I. I felt like a coward for leaving my husband with nothing more than a cheap note on the bed in our room. So I came to the Verbier to tell him in person."

Sagamore found that Anastasia's claims matched what Macaire Ebezner had already told him.

"You admit that it's rather strange running off in the middle of the night," Sagamore remarked.

"After I spoke to Macaire, I had no wish to remain at the hotel. For what? So he could beg me and make a scene to keep me from leaving him? So he could blackmail me with suicide? I wanted to get out of there as quickly as possible."

"Why didn't Lev Levovitch leave with you that night?"

"He wanted to finish the Gala Weekend. The big announcement had been delayed by the food poisoning. And then he wanted to leave the bank the right way – not run off like a thief in the night."

The questioning kept going around in circles. Finally, Sagamore had no choice but to let them go. Together they walked out of the police headquarters on boulevard Carl-Vogt in Geneva. They walked along the pavement for a while, and when they were out of earshot of anyone, Anastasia looked at Lev. She was angry.

"Who are you? Lev Levovitch? Dr Kazan? Sinior Tarnogol? Wagner?

I no longer know to whom I'm talking. I know that you lied to the police, Lev. But your charm won't work on me. I want to know why you did it."

Lev looked grim.

"I hadn't planned to keep Tarnogol's character alive for very long. But the day my father died, I decided to extend the charade. As long as Tarnogol was alive, my father would be, too, in a way. Gradually, I began to enjoy it. Being Tarnogol, fooling everyone at the bank, was an intoxicating experience. During board meetings, I felt a rush of adrenaline. And Abel Ebezner was furious with Macaire over the whole thing, and I have to admit that, deep down, I enjoyed that."

"But it wasn't enough for you – you added Dr Kazan!"

"Macaire was looking for a shrink. I immediately saw it as an opportunity to bring to life another of my father's characters: Dr Kazan, physician and psychoanalyst from Berlin. I had a big advantage because the bank shares held by Tarnogol gave me all the money I needed to cover my expenses. So, using a false identity, I rented an apartment on place Claparède, which I transformed into a doctor's office. I even ordered a brass plate for the door and had a new phone line installed. Who was going to check?"

Anastasia was stunned.

"And Wagner – this business about the intelligence services. That was you as well?"

Lev nodded. There was no point in denying it any longer.

"It was all a fabrication: Wagner, P-30, his so-called missions. There never was a double murder in Madrid. That poor computer technician is doing fine. In exchange for some cash, he and his wife agreed to fake their own murder and let me take some pictures, fake blood and everything."

"But what did you get out of all this?" she asked.

"The satisfaction of controlling Macaire's life. I felt he had taken from me the thing I valued most in life: you. Thanks to Dr Kazan, I understood how Macaire thought. Every time Wagner sent him on a mission outside Geneva, it took him away from you. But when we found each other again, you and I, at Abel's funeral, I decided to put an end to the masquerade. Wagner explained to Macaire that when he became president, he would have to give up his missions."

"But if you cared so much about me, why did you ignore me all those years?"

"Because I thought that you were the one ignoring me – that you didn't want to see me again. Fifteen years of silence: that's where it got us."

"Lev, did you kill Jean-Bénédict because he discovered your secret?"

"No."

"I don't know whether I can believe you. There have been so many lies."

"Ask me whatever you like."

"What happened the week before the murder? Did you really plan to leave with me?"

"That's all I dreamed about, Anastasia. But I knew that Macaire would make our life impossible – that is, unless I could get him to swap the presidency for you."

"You mean in the same way that he transferred his shares to you?"

"Yes. I knew how badly he wanted to become president. He was prepared to do anything to get the position. It was the best way to get him to leave us alone. I was on good terms with the editor-in-chief of the *Tribune de Genève*. I promised to arrange an interview with the French president in exchange for a made-up story in the weekend edition."

"The article claiming that Macaire would become president?"

"Yes, I wanted Macaire to be floating on air. It would make his fall easier later on. The next day, a Monday, very early in the morning, I went to the bank as Tarnogol and arranged things so that our secretary, Cristina, would intercept a contrived phone call that would lead her to assume that Macaire was not going to be elected president. I had five days until the new president was appointed."

"But we were together that morning," Anastasia remarked.

"You were still asleep. I returned to the Hôtel des Bergues as soon as my act was over. Then all I had to do was bide my time and keep stringing Macaire along. The whole thing went like clockwork. As Tarnogol, I was able to push him to breaking point. As Wagner, I was able to discover the plan Macaire and Jean-Bénédict concocted to narrowly miss running over Tarnogol after the dinner for the Association of Bankers of Geneva. That was the reason Tarnogol didn't show up for the event."

"But I saw you together, you and Tarnogol, in the hallway of the Hôtel des Bergues!"

"Alfred wore Tarnogol's costume that night," Lev explained.

"So, on Friday morning, when we were at Cornavin station together, and you told me that Tarnogol was going to prevent Macaire from being elected, you had no intention of leaving with me?"

"It was Macaire who prevented his own election – because he resisted me. On Friday morning, as Wagner, I found out that Macaire was convinced that he could persuade Tarnogol to back him for president. He appeared to be dead set against accepting Tarnogol's offer of the presidency in exchange for you. I had to find a way to get him to change his mind. So I had to delay our departure. I used the time to look for compromising material I could use against him by organising a break-in."

"What! You were the robber?"

"Alfred, to be precise – on my orders."

"Alfred!" she gasped, realising that on the day of the robbery she had recognised Alfred's eyes without being able to identify him. "How could you . . ."

"Alfred had spied on Macaire and had seen the combination to the safe. I wanted to get Macaire's notebook to put pressure on him. I didn't know what was in the notebook but I assumed it must be important for him to spend so much time on it and store it in his safe. Alfred would take advantage of our rendezvous at the station to grab the notebook – except that the notebook was no longer in the safe. So he called me to ask what to do. Since I suspected you would return home, I told him to wait there and surprise you, scare you a little. I wanted Macaire to think that the secret service was going to go after him if he wasn't elected to the president."

"How could you do that, Lev?"

"I did it for us."

"You did it for you," she replied.

They stared at each other in silence. Lev saw a taxi and signalled for it to stop.

"Come. Let's go somewhere we can talk in peace."

But she backed away.

"I'm not going with you, Lev."

"Anastasia . . ."

"Go. I beg you!"

He did as she said. He poured himself into the waiting taxi and disappeared. She waited until he was out of sight and burst into tears. She was alone again. She walked around and soon found herself at the place du Cirque. She then saw the Café Remor, where she had spent so much time after she and Lev had first met. Not knowing where she should go or what she would do, she entered the café. She stopped short at the entrance; inside, sitting at one of the tables, a man was staring at her. It was Macaire.

She sat down across from him. They sat there in silence for a very long while. Then she said, "I'm sorry for everything."

"I'm sorry, too."

"How are you?"

"Much better. I've got my life back in shape. I'm very much in love."

"I'm happy for you."

They talked a while and decided they both wanted a quick divorce. It was time to turn the page. Before separating, Macaire asked her, assuming a tone of confidentiality, "Anastasia, is there something I should know? Did you kill Jean-Béné?"

"No," she assured him. "Why would I do such a thing?"

"What about the note you slipped under my door?"

"As I was leaving the hotel, leaving everything behind, I thought you should know. I wanted to tell you that you meant something to me in spite of everything."

"*In spite of everything*?" Macaire broke in, deeply annoyed. "That's elegant."

"I didn't have the life I wanted, Macaire. I should never have married you. I wasted your time, and I regret it. Time is precious; life is so very short. What's important is that your love is real – that you love with all your heart."

"So you never loved me, is that it?"

"I never loved you the way you wanted to be loved. That's why I wanted to ask your forgiveness."

She kissed Macaire on the cheek and left.

Three months had passed.

It was a beautiful evening in early September on the place de Neuve, where the Grand Théâtre was located. There was a large crowd for the premiere of *Nabucco*. It was a new adaptation of Verdi's opera that was said to be absolutely exceptional; all of Geneva's high society was there that evening.

Among the crowd were Macaire and Arma, who had arrived hand in hand to take their place in one of the best loges in the theatre. During the intermission, Macaire wanted to get some air, while Arma preferred to remain in the loge. He went outside on to the plaza in front of the theatre and ran into Lev. The two men burst out laughing.

"Cigarette?" Lev offered.

"Why not?" Macaire accepted.

They moved away from the other theatregoers and sat on the stone steps, admiring the Parc des Bastions. Macaire then turned to Lev.

"Thanks, Wagner."

Lev smiled.

"Thanks for what?" he asked.

"You made me happy. On each of my missions I felt so alive. I had the impression that there was something more to life. Those moments, even if they weren't real – I truly lived them."

Lev hesitated, then asked, "You're not angry with me?"

"Quite the contrary! You know, after Anastasia left, it was hard. Then I realised that this was my chance to rebuild my life: to learn from my mistakes and live a life that was more in line with my character. I got engaged to Arma. I'm happy."

"That's great news," Lev exclaimed. "I'm very happy for you."

"Thanks, that means a lot to me. With Arma, it's a love like nothing I've ever experienced before. I hope you'll come to the wedding."

"Of course."

"Thank you, brother. We're really like two brothers, don't you think?"

"It's true. I've been closer to you these past fifteen years than almost anyone else. Will you invite Tarnogol to the wedding as well?"

Macaire burst out laughing.

"How did you manage to pull that off? It's amazing."

"My father taught me everything. But it was mostly a question of circumstance. You didn't recognise me when we crossed paths in front of the hotel, and I wanted to see how far the charade could go. It went much further than I had anticipated."

"And Dr Kazan? Was he one of your father's characters, too?"

"Yes. One day you opened up to me – I don't know if you remember. You were overwhelmed by what Tarnogol had done, felt ignored by your father, and suffered terribly for it. I saw an opportunity to bring Dr Kazan to life."

"There was a spontaneous connection," Macaire said.

"And it lasted more than ten years."

Macaire smiled.

"And Wagner? Where did you get the idea?"

"One day you told Kazan how much you dreamed about a life that was less monotonous. You wanted action – you didn't want to spend your life in an office. And so, at the meeting of the board, where my character Tarnogol presided, Abel Ebezner explained how the federal police were asking the bank to help them with an investigation by Scotland Yard into money laundering."

"The Diamond Wedding Operation."

"Yes. The board decided to follow up on Scotland Yard's request, which was top secret. I had the idea of bringing Wagner, from my father's book, to life. He was an agent of the intelligence services who often stayed at the Hôtel de Verbier to spy on wealthy foreign guests. Wagner asked you to send him information that the board had, in reality, already sent to the real federal police."

"That's why the newspaper article made Wagner's claims seem so credible."

"Exactly. That was an unexpected gift. After that, I decided to create a universe around Wagner. And, because P-30 was supposed to be a clandestine investigative department, I didn't need to demonstrate ties with any official agency."

"But still, you knew that I had bought a gun," Macaire noted.

"You told Dr Kazan, which meant you told me and Wagner."

"And the letter from the president of the Confederation?"

"A forgery – which I fabricated."

"And my reports to the Federal Council?"

"What Wagner referred to as 'reports' were nothing more than long letters sent by mail, to which the administration replied by standard letter, as it does with everyone who writes to the government. With respect to your missions, I simply had to send you traipsing all over Europe at the bank's expense. Your reports about tax administration buildings generally ended up in a bin at the Grand Théâtre. As you know, the murder in Madrid never took place. As for the lawyers who served as intermediaries with the agents for foreign tax offices, they were my lawyers in those countries and they were in on the ruse."

"And the tax authorities?"

"Actors."

"And Perez, the agent for the intelligence services in Madrid?"

"Also an actor."

"Well, well," Macaire said. "Sometimes we can be really dumb."

"No," Lev said. "When we really want to believe in something, we see what we want to see."

Macaire agreed.

"You know, Lev, I don't regret anything about what happened the past fifteen years. Thanks to you, I really lived!"

"I'm glad I was able to tell you how it happened," Lev confided.

"You managed to live four lives."

Lev smiled. There was a moment of silence, then Macaire asked, "Lev, what happened in room 622 that night in December?"

"I don't know. I don't know who killed Jean-Bénédict."

From the foyer, the bell summoned the audience back to the theatre.

"Before we go back inside," Macaire said to him, "I have one final question. It was Wagner who put me on your trail to Corfu. But if Wagner was you, why would you do that?"

Lev sighed and smiled sadly. He knew from the start that by running off with Anastasia, he risked changing their relationship. He knew that the thrill of getting back together they had experienced in Geneva, the passion for the forbidden, for novelty, the need to see each other constantly, to adore each other when they were together and despair when they were apart, all of that would be jeopardised by their constant proximity once they were together for good in Corfu. He had to admit it: doing nothing all day long was boring. Sometimes, they began to grow tired of each other. To prolong their mutual passion, they had to work at it: the beautiful clothes, the refinement, the candles, the preparations, the primping and pampering, always being one's best. It was the only remedy for the dissolving power of routine that all lovers experience when, after having been two distinct lovers, they become no more than a couple. It was the beginning of the great winding down, the neglect of the self and the other, the end of the magnificent lie that had allowed them, until then, to be perfect, beautiful, impeccable, always happy, always alert, and which was suddenly slipping away: comfortable clothes, stretch pants, the pot belly, the three-day beard, the bad breath. "Darling, can you bring me some toilet paper, please?" The supper tray before them as they watched the evening movie. Falling asleep like two sacks on the couch, the television on, their mouths open, snoring loudly. Never! Lev had promised himself – not with Anastasia. He'd rather die.

To guard against that outcome, he needed an enemy. He needed the jealous husband to land in Corfu and create a scene, allowing Lev to go somewhere else and find himself once more – start from the beginning again. A couple that is always new is a couple that never grows bored.

To Macaire, he simply said, "I think Corfu was always destined to fail." They rose.

"You're not bitter?" Lev asked Macaire.

"Are you joking?" Macaire smiled.

The two men shook hands fraternally. There was something triumphal in Macaire's gaze. Suddenly, he unbuttoned his shirt and revealed to Lev a microphone fixed to his chest with adhesive tape. Plain-clothes police rushed from the shadows and grabbed Lev. Sagamore was among them.

"That's what I would call a confession, Monsieur Levovitch," Sagamore told Lev before pushing him into an unmarked car.

* * *

Three years later, Anastasia often thought of those events. She had learned about the arrest in the papers, like everyone else. She had followed the trial closely and had even attended in person when she was able to, and she had kept all the articles that were published about it. She had hoped that Lev would be okay. He always had been in the past, after all. Although she didn't believe in God, to her surprise she had begun to pray.

Three years later, though she hadn't seen him since, she couldn't help thinking about him all the time. On Sundays, she walked from the neighbourhood of La Servette, down rue de Chantepoulet, to Lake Geneva and the Hôtel des Bergues. She found a bench and sat there looking at the majestic building. She examined the fifth floor of the façade, especially the windows of the suite where he had lived. She wondered who was staying there now. Then she continued her walk around quai du Mont-Blanc to the Hôtel Beau-Rivage. She settled into an armchair in the lobby and ordered a black tea. She continued thinking about him. She saw him again, right here, eighteen years earlier, pretending to her mother that he was Count Romanov. Then she unfolded the article in the *Tribune de Genève*, from the time of the trial, that she kept in her handbag. There was a large photograph of Lev, still handsome, arriving at court, and right below that this article:

FALL OF STAR BANKER LEV LEVOVITCH

Lev Levovitch was found guilty by the Court of First Instance of Geneva of fraud, practising medicine without a licence, and breach of trust. The banker had assumed a false identity within the Ebezner Bank's board of directors and had misled Macaire Ebezner, the current president of the bank, for years. Levovitch was condemned to four years in prison without parole and the forfeiture of all his assets. He can no longer work in banking.

70

Poisoned

Wednesday, July 4, 2018.

In my suite at the Hôtel de Verbier, Scarlett was buried in newspaper clippings. She had examined all the reports of Levovitch's trial, which the papers had made the most of. I sensed her impatience: she felt we were near the end of our investigation.

"I've gone over it all again, Writer, and I always come to the same conclusion: Levovitch is the murderer."

"Yet the court didn't find him guilty."

"Yes, because of a lack of evidence," she added.

"Don't play with words. If there is no evidence, he's not guilty. You know how it goes: innocent until proven guilty."

"What bothers me is why they found Tarnogol's belongings in Jean-Bénédict Hansen's room. What did Hansen know? What was his connection with Levovitch? I'm convinced that that's the key to the case."

"In what sense?"

"For example, we don't know who is responsible for the poisoning at the Gala Weekend – or why it happened. We know that Macaire and Jean-Bénédict were seen going through the crates of vodka in the kitchen, but Macaire Ebezner swore to the police that he was looking for a specific bottle, and Jean-Bénédict Hansen wasn't around to give his version of events."

Scarlett was set on questioning Macaire Ebezner, but since our brief meeting at the bank, our requests for an interview had gone unanswered.

"What is certain," she continued, "is that neither Macaire Ebezner nor Jean-Bénédict Hansen was poisoned; their names don't appear on the list of those hospitalised that evening."

She waved the list in question, which we had found in the police report.

"And Levovitch?" I asked.

"He *was* poisoned," she said, pointing to his name underlined on one of the pages.

She went back to the list of names. Suddenly, her face froze.

"Oh, my God!" she shouted.

"What is it? What did you find?"

"Oh, my God!" she repeated. "Look."

She circled a name with red pen and gave me the paper.

"Arma, Ebezner's maid," Scarlett said. "She was poisoned. Arma was at the Hôtel de Verbier on the weekend of the murder!"

71

Arma

Scarlett's discovery meant another round trip to Geneva on July 5 to speak to Arma again. We found her in the early afternoon near Lake Geneva. It was very hot. We walked a bit to the bridge and sat on a bench in the shadow of trees on Rousseau Island. Geneva was never so beautiful as it was in summer, a luxuriant green, bathed in a sun that cast emerald reflections on the lake and made it seem like the Caribbean.

"Arma, we know what happened," Scarlett said.

"What do you know?"

"You were at the Hôtel de Verbier on the weekend of the murder. You were poisoned on the Saturday night and wound up in the hospital. It appears that this detail escaped the police at the time, because it doesn't show up in the file."

Arma lowered her head.

"Why did you go to the hotel that weekend?" I asked.

"I wanted to help Macaire with the election. It was supposed to be one of the great moments of his life, and I wanted to be there. For a whole year I had been looking forward to his appointment."

"Did he know you were there?"

"No, obviously not. It's unlikely he would have allowed me to attend. All I wanted was to stand quietly in a corner of the room to be present at his triumph. I had taken time off from work so I could be there; I had asked for the weekend several weeks earlier. I arrived in Verbier on the Friday; I had reserved a small room in a cottage. On the Saturday evening, I got dressed and joined the cocktail party in the hotel ballroom. No-one asked me any questions."

"And what happened then?"

"Well, I was a little nervous, so I asked for a cocktail. A while later, at the time of the announcement, I suddenly felt very sick. Everyone was very sick. I ended up in the hospital. I wasn't released until Monday morning, and that's when I learned about the murder."

"So no-one knew you were at the hotel that evening?" Scarlett asked.

"No-one. Except Macaire, much later. That's why he left me. As I told you the other day, it's because of what happened at the hotel that I lost him."

"He left you because he found out that you had gone to the hotel?"

"No, he left me because he thought I had killed Jean-Bénédict Hansen."

Arma burst into tears. Scarlett and I looked at each other, intrigued.

"Why would he think that?"

Arma didn't reply. She grabbed her bag and fled in tears.

We absolutely had to find out what had happened. The only person who could answer our questions was Macaire Ebezner. We knew that he wouldn't see us at the bank. Based on what Arma had told us, he was now living in an apartment on quai du Général-Guisan. So we waited in front of the entrance to the building until late afternoon, when he would return from work. When he finally arrived, he grew angry when he saw us.

"You again! I thought I had made myself clear."

"Monsieur Ebezner, we absolutely must speak with you."

"I have nothing to say."

"It's about Arma. We know where she was on the weekend of the murder."

Ebezner couldn't refuse our request. He led us into his immense apartment and showed us to the living room; the bay window offered a magnificent view of the Jet d'Eau.

"So you've continued to stick your noses where they don't belong," Macaire said to us.

"We've been investigating," Scarlett corrected. "And we've discovered that your former maid and companion, Arma, was at the Hôtel de Verbier on the weekend of the murder."

"How did you find out?"

"She's on the list of people hospitalised after the poisoning. The police seem to have missed that detail. I'm curious to know how you found out she was at the hotel."

* * *

December, a year after the murder

It was a Thursday, late afternoon. In the house in Cologny, Arma, diamonds in her ears and dressed in a leopard-skin-patterned dress, upbraided the maid.

"Come on, you can do a better job with the floor, can't you?"

"Pardon, Médéme," the employee whimpered.

"Pardon, pardon! It's easy to ask me to pardon you all the time, but you have to apply yourself a little."

The front door to the house opened, and Macaire appeared, obviously in a very good mood. Arma wrapped herself around his neck and covered him in kisses. Whenever they greeted each other, Macaire realised that he had never known anything like it with Anastasia. He felt so much happier now. He was a new man.

"How was your day, darling?" she asked.

"Very good. I cancelled my meetings for tomorrow. We're going on a long weekend. There was snow in the Alps, and I want to take advantage of it. And some buyers are coming to look at the house on Saturday; I have no desire to have them underfoot. I'll let the broker deal with them by himself."

Still clinging to his neck, she asked, "Where will we go on the weekend?"

"I want to go to Verbier."

"Oh, yes, Verbier! Where? The hotel?"

"To tell the truth, I'm hesitating. It's only been a year since Jean-Béné's murder."

"You have to forget about all that. Chase those horrible memories away. You're not going to deprive yourself of the hotel all your life, are you?"

"I don't know . . ."

"Come, dear. All that magnificent luxury. We'll lock ourselves in the room, make a big fire, and sit on the couch staring into the flames."

"Okay, if you want," he agreed.

After removing his coat, he went into the living room and served himself a whiskey. He drank it by the window, looking at the snow that was slowly falling on the frozen lawn. He let his thoughts wander. He thought of Anastasia. It still happened from time to time. He wondered where she was, what she was doing – whether she was happy. He was no longer in love with her, but he loved her in spite of everything. Once you've loved, you love forever.

In all likelihood because they had discussed the Hôtel de Verbier, he remembered the note written in lipstick on the bathroom mirror:

I'm here, my love.
A.

Suddenly, he wondered about that simple *A*. His wife had always ended her letters from Corfu with *Anastasia* – the note slipped under the door of his hotel room as well. He suddenly recalled a line from one of the letters: "I'd come to the Verbier to break up with you, not to write you love letters." He then thought of what Arma had said to him in the hallway: "We'll lock ourselves in the room, make a big fire, and sit on the couch staring into the flames." They had never been at the hotel together. How could she know that the suites had a fireplace and a comfortable couch just opposite? His glass fell from his hands.

Hearing the sound of breaking glass, Arma ran into the living room. She found Macaire looking pale.

"My dear, what happened?"

"It was you! You were at the hotel on the weekend of the murder! You pretended to be my wife; you entered my room and left a note in lipstick to make me think it was Anastasia."

"No. I heard how much you liked that shade of lipstick. So I had a cousin in Paris buy me some. I brought it to the house so you would notice me, but you never did. I had just finished writing that note on the mirror when I heard the door to the room open. I hid in the wardrobe, leaving the lipstick on the sink."

"What the hell were you doing at the Verbier?"

"I wanted to help with your election. I was so proud of you. It was your big day. That's why I asked for the weekend off. I wanted to be there for your coronation. I reserved a small cottage in the village months in advance. Meanwhile I discovered that Anastasia was going to leave you and that you wouldn't find her at home when you got back. I wanted to tell you I loved you – that you could be with someone who really loved you! I went to the reception desk at the hotel and told them I was your wife. The employee didn't even ask me any questions and gave me a key to your room. But you weren't there, so I left that note on the bathroom mirror and hid to see your reaction. But when you finally returned to your room, I hesitated. I was afraid you would find me ridiculous. And then, suddenly, a man called you from the balcony, and, obviously, I had to stay hidden. I thought it would be better to love you from a distance; I was afraid you would reject me. I was only your maid, after all."

Macaire was dumbfounded. He needed another glass of Scotch, and this time, he swallowed it in one gulp. He then asked, his voice trembling slightly, "Arma, did you steal Anastasia's gold pistol?"

She looked at him in silence. Then she began to cry,

"I found it in the luggage Anastasia had hidden in her wardrobe before her departure with Levovitch. I don't know why I went through her things – probably because I wanted to find out where they were going. I was hoping to find an airplane ticket or a hotel booking. But I found the gun. At first, I was afraid that Anastasia wanted to kill herself. She was so fragile at the time, I thought she was going to do something terrible, like Romeo and Juliet. I was planning to get rid of the gun, throw it in the lake or something like that. But I was afraid someone might see me and that they would think I was a criminal. Then I thought about a ravine in the mountains, where no-one would find the gun. So I took it with me to Verbier."

"Arma," Macaire asked somewhat in shock, "did you kill Jean-Bénédict?"

"No! I promise you I didn't kill him."

"So – so what the hell did you do?" he asked, suspecting that Arma wasn't telling him everything.

"On Saturday afternoon, when I was hiding in your room, I heard you talking with Wagner. I knew that Tarnogol was giving you trouble – that he was threatening your position. Returning from the balcony, you said you were going to kill him. But I didn't want you to go to prison. You would never have survived there. You would have lost everything; you would have ended up killing yourself. I couldn't let you do that. I had to do something. It would be better for me to be condemned instead of you. I told myself that it was a sign from God: I had found the gun and had come here with it because I was supposed to use it. The time had come to prove to you how much I loved you. I wanted to illuminate your life with an act of courage. And then, everyone would have known. I would have told the judge and the jury; they would have written about it in the papers. What greater proof of love could there be? I would no longer be a simple cleaning woman; I would be the angry lover – the Bonnie Parker of love. That day was going to be a turning point in my life. So, at six o'clock, I mingled with the bank employees in the ballroom. I had the gun in my handbag and had decided that as soon as Tarnogol appeared, I would shoot him – for you, my love! But obviously I was very nervous, so I had a vodka cocktail to give myself courage. I had several, in fact; you have to when you're going to kill a man. But then I began to feel sick. Shortly after the board arrived, I began to throw up. When the ambulance arrived, I left the room; I had to get rid of the gun before I fainted and they found it on me. I wandered around the corridors until I came to a window. I opened it and threw the gun into some bushes covered with snow. At the time, I wasn't thinking that the snow would melt. I wasn't thinking about anything. Once I'd got rid of the gun, I fainted. When I opened my eyes, I was in the hospital in Martigny."

Not knowing what to believe any longer, Macaire chased Arma out of the house and locked himself in his bedroom office. There, his phone in his hand, he stared at the business card Lieutenant Sagamore had given him.

* * *

"But, in the end, you didn't call the police," Scarlett said in Macaire's living room. "Why?"

Before replying, Macaire rose from his armchair to rummage around in the drawer of a cabinet locked with a key. He took out a folder, which he handed to us.

"I preferred to find out for myself. Here's Arma's hospital record for the night of the murder, as well as a report from the doctor who examined her. I've kept them all this time, thinking that I might need them one day."

Scarlett looked over the documents.

"It says that Arma was hospitalised on Saturday, December fifteenth, at eight fifteen at night, and left the hospital on Monday morning. The poisoning was quite severe, and she was on an IV drip the whole time she was in the hospital."

"When the murder took place," Macaire continued, "Arma was in the hospital in Martigny, which is a half-hour drive from Verbier, with an IV in her arm. It seems to me to be a reasonably solid alibi."

Scarlett agreed and said, "You did this research after you found out she'd been in Verbier. That doesn't explain why you didn't call the police at the time."

"Because if Arma had killed Jean-Bénédict, if she'd done it to protect me, then it meant that her love for me was unlike anything I had ever experienced before."

"But after discovering that it wasn't her, you didn't want to get back together with her?"

Macaire gazed into the distance, as if he was ashamed of his reply.

"I realised that I was with her for the wrong reasons. She was merely a pale imitation of Anastasia – her ghost. The only woman I've ever loved is Anastasia. But Tarnogol was right. His prophecy turned out to be true: I had become president of the bank, but I ended up alone."

"Tarnogol never existed," I interjected.

"And yet," Macaire replied, "he was there."

72

Endgame

Scarlett and I left Macaire Ebezner and Geneva without having got much further in our investigation. We still hadn't identified the murderer. Back in Verbier, we locked ourselves into my suite to examine, once again, all the pieces of the puzzle. We spent hours going over all the elements of the case, ordering cheeseburgers and fries up to the room for supper, which we ate while pulling out and rereading documents from the file that we had already gone over several times.

We had missed something – but what?

At two in the morning, we stared at the wall on which we fixed three sheets of paper with the names of the three potential suspects:

Anastasia   *Lev*   *Macaire*

Scarlett sighed as she looked at a picture of the board from the original investigation by Lieutenant Sagamore, which indicated those same three names as suspects.

"We've come to the same conclusion as the police," Scarlett said. "We're stuck at exactly the same point in the investigation."

We were exhausted – and, I have to admit, a bit discouraged. But we had to keep going.

"Coffee?" I suggested.

"I'd love some."

I turned on the espresso machine. Scarlett methodically arranged all the items from Sagamore's board, going over the items we had illegally photographed. For more than an hour, she examined each of the documents Sagamore had collected. We again brought up the presence of hotel security in room 623 and came across an excerpt from the statement made to the police on the morning of the murder, by a man named Milan Luka, the hotel's head of security.

On Saturday evening, December 15, at 11:50 p.m., I was called because of a commotion in room 623. I immediately went to the room in question, where I was met by a man who assured me that everything was okay. I thought that maybe it was the wrong room. There was no noise in the corridor. Everything appeared to be quiet. I didn't insist and left. I told the manager just in case I needed to go back. It had been a strange evening, and it was better to be cautious. But there was no follow-up call. The night was calm. Then, the next day, a body was found in room 622.

After giving me the statement to read, Scarlett added, "The report specifies that the man who greeted the head of security in room 623 was Jean-Bénédict Hansen, whom Luka recognised from a photo."

She stopped, suddenly lost in thought.

"What is it?" I asked.

"The head of security said there was a 'commotion'."

"Yes, so?"

"That implies some kind of fight, no?"

"Yes, more or less. Or a noisy argument."

"So that implies that Jean-Bénédict Hansen wasn't alone in room 623. At the time, it didn't mean much to Sagamore, because he thought that Jean-Bénédict Hansen was Tarnogol. So, there was nothing surprising about the presence of Jean-Bénédict Hansen in room 623 – Tarnogol's room. But Tarnogol was, in reality, Lev Levovitch. Sagamore overlooked that detail."

"Jean-Bénédict had an argument with Tarnogol – which means, with Levovitch!" I said, understanding where Scarlett was going with this.

She agreed.

"On Saturday, December fifteenth, Jean-Bénédict Hansen had an argument with Levovitch. A few hours later, Jean-Bénédict was found dead."

* * *

Milan Luka hadn't worked at the hotel for years, but after a few searches on the web, we were able to find him. He was running his own surveillance company, Luka Security, located in Sion.

So the following morning, Friday, July 6, 2018, after a few hours' sleep, we went to visit Luka at his office in central Sion. He was a man of about fifty, well built and, from the look of him, not easily approachable, but, as it turned out, pleasant enough. He received us graciously when we showed up at his office out of the blue. We had the feeling that he was moved to be talking about his years at the hotel.

"I was very happy there. I arrived in Switzerland when I was very young and was lucky enough to meet Monsieur Rose. He knew how to inspire confidence so you would always give him the best of yourself. I was hired as part of the security team and was later put in charge. I owe him a great deal."

"Why did you leave the hotel?"

"I left after Monsieur Rose died. It wasn't the same without him. And to be honest, for a long time I had wanted to leave and start my own company. But I remained loyal to Monsieur Rose. Even though, after the murder, things at the hotel changed a lot."

"What do you mean?" Scarlett asked.

"The hotel was a special place – a haven for the guests. Perfect peace and serenity. After the murder, nothing was the same. Monsieur Rose was very affected by it all, especially by what happened after: Lev

Levovitch's trial and sentence. It devastated Monsieur Rose, who had been so proud of Levovitch. If you heard Monsieur Rose talk at the time, Levovitch was his hero. Monsieur Rose even thought Levovitch would be named president of the Ebezner Bank. But, unfortunately, his hero fell from grace in the worst possible way. That was a terrible shock to Monsieur Rose. It's what killed him."

"How so?"

"He killed himself some time after Levovitch was sentenced – a bullet in the mouth from his army revolver. It was terrible. He was found next to a bunch of newspaper clippings about Levovitch's fall. That was a very tough time for me."

"What can you tell us about the murder in room 622, Monsieur Luka?" I then asked.

The former head of security told us about the chaos on the Saturday evening after the poisoning of the crowd, and the discovery of the body the next morning.

"I was one of the first to be notified. I immediately called the police and restricted access to the floor so as not to destroy any possible evidence."

"You were at the hotel on the morning of the murder?" I asked, surprised.

"Yes, why?"

"Because you were already there on Saturday evening; you went up to room 623 at 11:50 p.m."

"I should have gone home that night, at the end of my shift, but after the poisoning, Monsieur Rose was very nervous, and I stayed. At night we generally work with only a single security guard, which had always been enough. But in light of the circumstances, I thought it better to provide some backup, just in case."

"Where were you that night?" I asked.

"The night guard was at the reception desk, as always, to keep an eye on the main entrance, the only way in. I was asleep in my office; I had to get some rest, I'd had an exhausting day."

"So no-one could have come in from the outside?"

"No, except through the main entrance. That was the rule at night at the hotel, that all the other entrances had to be closed. We had to be careful. The hotel had a large number of very rich guests, with jewellery and cash."

"But someone could have entered through one of the emergency exits, assuming there was someone on the inside to help them," I noted.

"*Assuming there was someone on the inside to help them*," Monsieur Luka repeated before remarking, ironically, "thieves could also have landed a helicopter on the roof of the hotel. We were pretty cautious for a quiet town like Verbier. What exactly are you getting at?"

"Monsieur Luka," Scarlett said, "we believe you may have seen something important a few hours before the murder."

"What does that mean?"

She showed him the excerpt from the police report.

"On Saturday, December fifteenth, you intervened in room 623."

"Yes, I recall. A client had called the reception desk, and they called us. Something had happened – some shouting, I believe."

"Who was the guest who made the call?"

"I never found out. I don't think the name was ever mentioned. And back then the telephone network wasn't computerised; we didn't know which room a call came from. I still don't understand where you're going with this."

"Who did you find in room 623?"

"Monsieur Hansen. I already told the police."

"It didn't surprise you that you didn't find Monsieur Tarnogol there?" I asked. "It was his room, not Hansen's."

"The security team is not supposed to know precisely who is in which room. They give us a room number and we go up to see what's going on, that's all."

Scarlett then played our trump card.

"We think there was someone else in that room. If you read the papers at the time of the trial, you'll know that Sinior Tarnogol never existed – Lev Levovitch was pretending to be him. Which means that Levovitch had two rooms assigned to him. That night, when you went upstairs, Jean-Bénédict Hansen and Lev Levovitch were there in the room. Isn't that right?"

The former head of security sighed. He rose from his desk and went to the window, as if he wanted to avoid meeting our eyes.

"It's true. Lev was in the room. A woman as well."

"Why didn't you tell the police?" Scarlett asked.

"Because Monsieur Rose asked me not to say anything. After the incident, I told him what had happened, and he ordered me not to mention that Lev was in the room. Monsieur Rose always wanted to protect him."

* * *

All the evidence led us back to Lev Levovitch.

Scarlett and I looked at the names of the three suspects on the wall of my suite:

Anastasia   *Lev*   *Macaire*

Even if, according to Milan Luka, Anastasia – as we deduced the woman mentioned by the former head of security must have been – was in room 623 with Lev and Jean-Bénédict Hansen, we concluded that she didn't commit the murder.

"Since we now know that Arma had Anastasia's gun, we can eliminate Anastasia from the list of suspects," Scarlett suggested.

"True," I conceded. "And we also know that Arma got rid of the gun as the poison took effect, around seven p.m. We can be certain, therefore, that it wasn't the weapon used for the crime."

Scarlett removed Anastasia's name from the wall. That left Macaire and Lev.

I continued, "Our suspect had to have access to a weapon. We know that Macaire had access to one."

"Yes, but Levovitch can't be ruled out," Scarlett reminded me. "Given his fifteen years of deception, if he had needed a gun, he could surely have got one without too much trouble."

She was right about that. She went on, "I'm with Sagamore: the murderer was in the hotel and didn't leave the hotel after the crime. When the police thought he was outside, he was within the walls of the hotel."

"He could have fled through the emergency exit, like Anastasia," I said.

"We've looked around and studied the plans for the building. The path taken by Anastasia to leave the hotel was the only way to get out without being seen. The murderer would have had to know the building well."

"We can assume that the murderer had carefully prepared his plan."

Scarlett made a disapproving face.

"Be serious, Writer. If he had been planning to eliminate Jean-Bénédict Hansen for months, he wouldn't have done it with a gun in a hotel. It looks like something spontaneous, improvised. By the way, that's also what Sagamore thinks, and it seems very logical to me."

"So what are you thinking?" I asked.

"If the murderer used the emergency exit to flee, it means he was familiar with the hotel. Only an employee would have known that. So either the murderer never left the hotel after the murder or he was very familiar with the layout. There doesn't seem to be any question about it now. Who could have easily gained access to a weapon? Who knew the hotel inside and out?"

"Levovitch."

"Levovitch," Scarlett confirmed. "And the motive was very simple. Jean-Bénédict Hansen had discovered, the night before the murder, that Levovitch was Tarnogol. Levovitch killed Hansen that night to protect his secret."

"That almost works," I said. "If Levovitch killed Jean-Bénédict Hansen because the latter had discovered the truth about Tarnogol, why was evidence connecting Hansen and Tarnogol found in Hansen's room?"

"Levovitch could have put it there to cover his tracks," Scarlett suggested.

"I'm not convinced. We're overlooking something."

It took us several hours to figure it out. We went back over the evidence from every angle, and there was, indeed, one thing that stuck out. And late that night, while she was deep in a pile of documents spread across the floor, Scarlett called out, her face suddenly bright.

"But of course! Why didn't we think of it before?"

"Think of what?"

"It's been right under our noses all this time."

Without further explanation, she went over to her laptop and typed on the keyboard. When her search was over, she raised her eyes from the screen, both proud of and stunned by her discovery. She then left my suite and ran down the stairs, as if she couldn't bear waiting for the elevator. I followed, not entirely understanding what was going on. We got to the ground floor and crossed the empty lobby. The night guard had momentarily left the reception area, and Scarlett took advantage of his absence to walk behind the desk and slip into the hotel's administration corridor. She quickly found the office of the hotel manager. She pushed open the door, certain no-one would be in the room at that late hour. But we were surprised to find the light on – and a man, sitting in an armchair.

Scarlett stared at him, speechless. She recognised him at once. In spite of the years that had passed, he hadn't changed. He looked just as he did in the newspaper photos.

"Lev Levovitch . . ." she said. "But . . . what are you doing here?"

"Then you know everything," he said.

73

The Murderer in Room 622

That night Lev Levovitch told Scarlett and me what had happened in the months before the murder.

"After Abel Ebezner's death," Lev explained, "I got back together with Anastasia. I was finally happy. I had only one thing in mind, to quit impersonating all those characters and make a life with her. But I felt she was hesitant about leaving Macaire. She didn't want to hurt him; she was worried he might kill himself. I decided to act under the guise of Tarnogol. Fifteen years earlier, I had succeeded in what I thought was the deal of the century: I had obtained Macaire Ebezner's shares by pushing Anastasia into his arms. I was convinced that all I had to do was put pressure on Macaire for him to agree to give up his wife in exchange for the presidency. Five days before the Gala Weekend, when it seemed clear that he was going to become president, Macaire discovered that Tarnogol wanted to vote for Levovitch instead of him. At first, Macaire reacted as I had suspected he would: he collapsed. I wanted to play him, push him as far as he could go until he had no choice but to exchange Anastasia for the presidency. But Macaire had no intention of giving up his wife or the presidency. He clung to them both in spite of my scheme. So I had to activate my plan of last resort: to have the board elect Levovitch but prevent the announcement from being made at the very last moment – to force Macaire's hand."

"You would have been better off running away with Anastasia," Scarlett said, pragmatic as ever.

Lev smiled.

"You're absolutely correct. Perhaps I stayed out of a sense of pride. I wanted to get the better of Macaire."

"And your plan to prevent the announcement at the last minute?" I asked Lev. "Was that the reason for the food poisoning?"

"Absolutely. I was the one who poisoned all those poor people. By then, I had Macaire running in circles. Two days earlier, Wagner had given him the poison, which was only water and which Macaire was supposed to use to get rid of Tarnogol. I had plenty of opportunity to make sure he failed to poison Tarnogol and to force him to accept Tarnogol's proposal. But Macaire didn't go through with that plan. So Wagner, under the pretext that the poison would take too long to act, gave Macaire a bottle of what was supposed to be poisoned vodka, which he would place in the bar next to the first-floor conference rooms, where the board met. All I had to do was wait until Macaire was distracted to grab the bottle and make Macaire believe that he had lost it."

"But was the bottle really poisoned?" Scarlett asked.

"Of course not. I didn't want to take any risks. I had prepared everything in advance, for months. I made sure that the cocktails with Beluga vodka would be served before the grand ball to confuse Macaire if necessary. Then I arranged it so that a bottle of vodka to which I had added a fairly strong purgative wound up in the hands of the bartender. I had marked the bottle with a cross, like Macaire's bottle, so that Macaire would think it was all his fault. The purgative would take effect quickly, and the chaos would force them to shut down the event. But I had miscalculated the dosage. When I realised, at six thirty, that the purgative wasn't having the effect I had anticipated, I called Alfred. He mixed in with the guests and was told to faint noisily just as the announcement was being made. But he didn't have the time to carry out the plan, because before he could do so, one of the guests collapsed, pulling down with him a tablecloth and everything on the table. Then other people fell sick around him, and soon, everyone began to fall like flies.

I myself pretended to be sick to avoid suspicion. The plan went perfectly after that. Macaire finally agreed to give up Anastasia in exchange for the presidency. All we had to do then was leave. Except for one thing: Hansen got involved, and everything went wrong."

"How so?" I asked.

"Macaire, convinced he might have killed all the bank's employees with the poisoned vodka, opened up to his cousin. But his cousin decided to blackmail him: Jean-Bénédict wanted the presidency in exchange for his silence. Anastasia, however, caught wind of their conversation and, hoping to call Tarnogol to the rescue, discovered that it was me playing a character. We argued. Jean-Bénédict Hansen surprised us. And then he, too, discovered my secret."

Lev stopped for a moment. There was silence in the room. He then turned to Scarlett and asked her, "How did you find out?"

"That the murderer was Monsieur Rose? Because he was able to come and go inside the hotel without being noticed. Because he had a weapon." She pointed to the picture showing Rose in the uniform of a lieutenant-colonel. "I just checked online; all high-ranking officers in the Swiss army are assigned SIG Sauer P210 9 mm pistols, like the gun used for the murder. And he had a motive: he wanted to protect you. A few hours before the murder, the hotel's head of security came up to room 623. Apparently, it was a false alarm. But the head of security told the police he had reported the incident to the hotel manager, given everything that had happened that night. I assume that as soon as Monsieur Rose found out that there had been an incident in room 623, he grew concerned. He knew that 623 was Tarnogol's room. And he knew that you were Tarnogol. We know from the reports of your trial that Tarnogol was a character invented by your father at Monsieur Rose's request to play the part of a mystery client. Your father was dead, so Monsieur Rose was the only one who knew that you were Tarnogol. And when Monsieur Rose learned that Jean-Bénédict had discovered your secret, he realised you were in danger."

* * *

Monsieur Rose was pacing in his office at the hotel. He was visibly upset. Lev looked at him, distraught.

"Don't worry, Monsieur Rose, I have things under control."

"Under control? I've asked you to stop playing with fire. I knew you would end up getting caught. Do you realise that you risk going to jail and paying an enormous monetary settlement? Your career is going down the drain. They'll take everything you have."

"Jean-Bénédict agreed to keep quiet if I play the role of Tarnogol one more time tomorrow, during the press conference, to name Jean-Bénédict president. Then I'll disappear for good."

"And you think the police won't find you?"

"No-one will know a thing," Lev assured him.

"Look, Lev, for someone so intelligent, how can you be so naïve? Do you think Macaire Ebezner is going to accept losing his bank to his cousin because of some grotesque blackmail attempt? It's going to end badly."

After a lengthy silence, Lev said, "Monsieur Rose, rest assured, I've taken care of everything."

"That doesn't reassure me at all. What have you planned?"

"You'll see, the whole thing is going to explode in Jean-Bénédict Hansen's face. It will serve him right, too; he's always been two-faced. He's been dreaming of taking over the bank for years, all the more so since Abel Ebezner's death. So I took out, how can I put it . . . some insurance at his expense."

"Insurance?"

"I knew that the truth about Tarnogol would end up being discovered. In fifteen years, banking practices have changed a great deal. Fifteen years ago, very few questions were asked about financial transactions, but that's no longer the case today. I realised that the authorities would end up sticking their noses into the matter. So I decided to protect myself. I collected objects belonging to Jean-Bénédict to place them in Tarnogol's town house. I then arranged it so that their schedules would coincide, like that Monday evening when I sent Macaire to Basel; I knew that Jean-Bénédict was in Zurich. I also sold him the town house on rue Saint-Léger, which I had purchased through a shell company, for next to nothing. He thought he was investing in a real estate fund. I told him the returns were sensational, and he trusted me entirely. He moved funds into the shell company and ended up owning a building in Geneva without realising it. He never asked any questions, especially because he made so much money on the deal. But it was money I had put into it myself, so that he wouldn't ask any questions. All that is to say that I was ready to erase my tracks if it turned out to be necessary. There was only one last thing for me to do."

"What?" Monsieur Rose asked.

"Hide Tarnogol's mask in Jean-Bénédict's room."

A short while later, Lev went up to Jean-Bénédict Hansen's room on the pretext of wanting to prepare for the press conference the following day.

"What do you want to talk about at this time of night?" Hansen groaned. "I was just about to go to bed."

"We have to make sure that everything is in place," Lev said. "The journalists are going to ask questions; we have to agree what to tell them."

Suddenly, there was a knock on the door. "Again?" Hansen complained. "What's all this about, bothering people in the middle of the night?"

He opened the door, furious, but calmed down when he saw it was Monsieur Rose.

"Excuse me, Monsieur Hansen," said Monsieur Rose. "I know it's very late, but the circumstances are unusual. After all, you, on behalf of the board, are in charge of organising the Gala Weekend. I absolutely must speak to you."

"What's going on?"

Lev, while Jean-Bénédict was temporarily distracted by their visitor, discreetly unlocked the tall French windows to his room.

"Inspectors from the health department are still in our kitchen. I'd very much like you to meet them so they can confirm for you that the poisoning had nothing to do with the food that we prepared."

Jean-Bénédict didn't look very enthusiastic, but Monsieur Rose insisted, and he ended up agreeing. Lev left room 622 to return to his own while the two men headed for the elevators.

In the dark of night, Lev, with a bag in his hand containing a silicone mask of Tarnogol along with the jacket he wore, climbed from his balcony to the balcony of room 623 – Tarnogol's room – then to room 622, entering Jean-Bénédict Hansen's suite through the unlocked window. From Jean-Bénédict's comb, Lev took a few hairs; he placed them inside the mask, which he hid in a wardrobe. He then used the room telephone to call reception and order a breakfast for the following morning identical to the one Tarnogol usually had: eggs, caviar, and a small glass of vodka.

* * *

"What was the point of all this?" Scarlett asked.

Lev answered, "During Hansen's press conference the next day, I would have publicly accused him of having pretended to be Tarnogol for fifteen years and betraying the bank. From Geneva to Verbier, all the proof was in place. I would have said that I had been conducting an investigation for several months and had discovered that he was the owner of the town house on rue Saint-Léger and that all they had to do was check his room and examine what he had hidden in his wardrobe and his safe – where Macaire's shares had been deposited. The trap would have closed on Jean-Bénédict."

I then interjected, "But Monsieur Rose knew that, thanks to your plan, if he eliminated Jean-Bénédict Hansen, you would be sheltered forever, because everyone would have assumed that he had been Tar-nogol. So, in the middle of the night, without anyone seeing him, he shot Hansen twice, killing him. Rose protected you like you were his own son. That was a gesture of total love."

Lev agreed, clearly moved. Finally, he confided, "Monsieur Rose finally admitted everything to me one evening, in Geneva, when he came to offer his support during my trial. He was sick over the crime he had committed. He felt that it was all his fault – that by killing Hansen, he had precipitated my fall. He was very hard on himself. He kept repeating that I was going to lose everything because of him. My sentence destroyed him. He ended up by killing himself a few months later. He had made me his legal heir."

"He left you the hotel," Scarlett said. "That means you're the manager – the elusive manager I've never succeeded in meeting since my arrival here."

"Yes. When I learned you were making enquiries about the murder in room 622, I was uneasy at first. Then I told myself that it was an opportunity to get it all off my chest."

"Monsieur Levovitch, where's Monsieur Rose's revolver now?" I asked.

Levovitch smiled.

"It was taken by the police after Monsieur Rose's suicide. No-one ever made the connection with the murder at the hotel. Since I was his heir, a policeman contacted me one day, long after I had been let out of prison, to tell me that I could come to get his gun. I told him I wasn't interested. The policeman then told me, 'If you don't claim it, we're going to destroy it.' So I said to him, 'Destroy it, then.' And that's what they did. The police destroyed the only proof incriminating Monsieur Rose. That was my way of protecting him. How far are we willing to go to defend the ones we love? That's a way to measure the meaning of one's life."

74

Learning to Turn the Page

Monday, July 9, 2018, Hôtel de Verbier.

There was a knock on the door of my suite. It was Scarlett. I detected a note of sadness in her smile. Behind her, a hotel employee was carrying her bags.

"Is it time to leave already?" I asked.

"Yes."

"I'll go with you down to the lobby," I said, trying to postpone our goodbyes a while longer.

In the elevator, she said to me, "You never told me what happened after Bernard fell ill, downstairs from his office."

* * *

Paris, January 1, 2018

Bernard was briefly hospitalised. Then he was allowed to return home. The doctors advised him to rest. But suddenly, his condition worsened, and he had to be readmitted to the American Hospital in Neuilly.

On January 1, I took an early train from Geneva to Paris; I had been told that Bernard was very ill. When I arrived, I rushed to the hospital. I was very worried. Having known him as a man who had always been so energetic, I was afraid to find him in pain, in his robe, looking haggard in his bed. As I pushed open the door to his room, my heart was pounding in my chest. And there he was, looking as he always had, seated in a chair in a shirt and tie, smiling. He looked better than I had ever seen him.

"Joël, you went through a lot of trouble for nothing. As you can see, I'm doing fine."

I wondered why I had been told that he was doing so poorly while now being reassured that this wasn't the case. We talked a while; then, since he was expecting someone, he suggested I go out and enjoy the rest of my day.

"Calm down, Joël," Bernard assured me with a smile I'll never forget. "We'll see each other tomorrow."

That was our last time together.

The following day, he was gone.

A man who had always loved clowns, he had played his last, magnificent joke on me.

* * *

Scarlett wiped a tear from her eye.

The elevator doors opened on the ground floor, and we crossed the lobby.

"We never found out what finally happened between Lev and Anastasia," Scarlett said. "Did they go their separate ways? How sad."

"I think it turned out well."

As we reached the reception desk, Lev Levovitch came to meet us.

"Madame Leonas," he said to Scarlett, "it was a pleasure to have met you."

"The pleasure is all mine," she replied, shaking his hand.

At that moment, the assistant manager, whom we had met a few days earlier, appeared.

"This is Monsieur Alfred Agostinelli, the assistant manager of the Verbier," Lev said.

"Your former chauffeur?" Scarlett asked.

"The very same," Lev smiled. "And if you'll allow me, I'd like to introduce my wife, who also works here with me."

A beautiful blond woman approached us. It was Anastasia. We said

558

hello; then two children, about ten years old, came running across the lobby to join their parents. Edmond and Dora, the son and daughter of Lev and Anastasia.

"How did you get back together?" Scarlett asked. Anastasia took her husband's hand and smiled.

* * *

Several years earlier, a few months after Lev's release

These were the first days of the new year. It was a sunny winter afternoon in Geneva, and Olga von Lacht walked into the lounge of the Beau-Rivage. She sat in an armchair and ordered a black tea. The woman sitting next to her, hearing Olga's voice, raised her eyes from her paper.

"Mama?" said Anastasia, surprised.

"Hello, my daughter."

It had been a long time since they had last spoken – since Anastasia's departure for the last Gala Weekend, when she had left to join Lev.

"How did you know I would be here?" Anastasia asked.

"The apple doesn't fall far from the tree."

After a silence, Olga continued, "I wanted to speak to you, Anastasia – to tell you that I want you to be happy. You don't look like you are."

"Thank you, Mama. I'm trying."

"Try harder."

Anastasia looked away. Her mother couldn't help herself from using this as an opportunity to criticise her daughter.

"You have no children, but I hope you will one day."

"With whom?" Anastasia asked.

She couldn't help herself and began to cry. Olga took her daughter in her arms and said to her, softly, "He's the one you love. You know, I believe we love only once in our life; it's an opportunity we can't afford to waste."

559

Olga held her daughter's face in her hands and dried her tears.

"You know what I've always wanted for you and your sister?"

"That we marry rich men."

"No. That you be at peace."

A few days later, Olga arrived at the Hôtel de Verbier to find Lev.

"It seems that you're the new manager," she said to him.

"How did you find out?"

"Don't underestimate me. I always know what's going on around me."

Levovitch couldn't help but smile. She looked at him in silence for a while.

"You know, Lev, for me you're just a sewer rat. But for my daughter, you're Count Romanov. And isn't that what's important, really?" Olga smiled then, the first time he had ever seen her do so. "You're made to be together, the two of you. Go to Geneva, win back my daughter. You'll both be happy here. Life is short, Lev. You have to make sure it ends well."

* * *

It was time for Scarlett to leave. A taxi was waiting in front of the hotel. We walked down the front steps together.

"I've grown attached to you, Scarlett."

"Me too, Writer. I know that we'll meet again one day."

She kissed me on the cheek.

"Thanks to you, I feel that I've got to know Bernard."

"If the readers feel the same way, then the book was worth all the effort."

She smiled.

"Writer, can I ask you one last question?"

"Of course."

"Are you heartbroken? Is that why you write?"

"Maybe. And you, are you heartbroken?"

"Well, if you are, I am as well, since I'm one of your characters."

"Scarlett, I wanted to say that . . ."

The sound of a door opening interrupted my sentence.

It was Denise; she had returned from her holiday. It had been two weeks already. I hadn't even noticed the time pass. I heard her shout, "The kitchen is a mess!" Then she was in my office.

"Joël, what happened here? Your apartment is upside down. It looks like you haven't been outside in two weeks."

She looked at my computer screen, the papers on my desk, and the notes stuck to the wall.

I said, "I wrote a novel. I was completely wrapped up in the story."

She looked stunned. "You haven't moved from your apartment in two weeks?"

She grabbed a bunch of pages.

I warned her, "I haven't had time to correct them yet."

She read:

The Enigma of Room 622

On Saturday, June 23, 2018, at dawn, I put my suitcase in the boot of my car and set out on the road to Verbier. The sun was just above the horizon, bathing the empty streets of central Geneva in a powerful orange halo. I crossed the Mont Blanc Bridge before driving along the flowered shore to the United Nations and then taking the autoroute in the direction of the Valais.

That morning, everything seemed marvellous: the colour of the sky appeared new, the landscape on either side of the autoroute more bucolic than ever before; the small villages scattered among the grapevines and overlooking Lake Geneva could have been taken from a postcard. I left the autoroute at Martigny and continued

*along the winding local road, which, after Le Châble, climbs all the
way to Verbier.*

"You imagined you were going to the mountains?" Denise asked
me. "You're the devil, Joël."

Through the window, she suddenly noticed the ashtray on the balcony, overflowing with cigarette butts.

"All those cigarettes – it's really disgusting. You could have at least
emptied the ashtray."

"I spent a lot of time on the balcony."

"That's no reason not to empty the ashtray. And the kitchen is a wreck."

She then glanced at the notes I had stuck to the wall.

Sloane
22/6: a day to forget
622: a room to forget

"June twenty-second is the day you broke up with Sloane," Denise said.

"Yes. Much of the book is inspired by Sloane. You'll understand
when you read it."

Denise read another note.

"I guess this Scarlett Leonas, originally from London, is also inspired
by your English friend."

"Bingo. *Leonas* is an anagram of *Sloane*."

"Why did you name her Scarlett?"

"After Scarlett O'Hara in *Gone with the Wind*, Bernard's favourite
book. The novel is filled with references to him. Verbier, for example,
was a place he loved. The chauffeur, Alfred Agostinelli, gets his name
from Proust's secretary. And Scarlett, with an S as in *solitude:* the solitude I always feel and that drives me to write. With Bernard, I felt less
alone. Then Bernard left, and Scarlett showed up."

*

Denise made me take a walk around Parc Bertrand so that I would get out of the house for the first time in two weeks. She said she needed to straighten out the apartment, but she really wanted to read my new novel.

I stepped outside and walked into the park. I knew that by finishing this book, a part of me was saying goodbye to Bernard. I would have liked him to be with me, in this park, so we could walk side by side one last time. Surrounded by the birds singing, I suddenly seemed to hear the sound of his voice answering the question that I had asked myself ever since his departure.

Where do the dead go?

Wherever they can be remembered. Especially in the stars. For they continue to follow us, they dance and shine in the night, just above our heads. I raised my eyes to the blue sky above. I was alone but calm. And at that moment, I ran into Sloane, who was in the middle of her run and now standing in front of me. She stopped, smiled, and removed her headphones.

"I just got back from holiday, two weeks," she said. "I've reflected about us a lot. I think perhaps I wasn't very considerate."

"Me, too."

I felt my heart pounding.

"Maybe we could go out and have a drink tonight. If you're free, that is. I know you were very busy with your book."

"I finished my book. I have all my life ahead of me."

She smiled again.

"Till tonight, then," she said.

She walked away. I sat on a bench, looked at the park around me, and reconnected with the world. Suddenly, I felt very happy.

Life is a novel whose conclusion we already know: in the end, the hero dies. The most important thing is not how our story ends, but how we fill the pages. For life, like a novel, must be an adventure. And adventures are life's holidays.

A NOTE FROM THE TRANSLATOR

Translation is a process that unfolds in stages. Interpretation is a first step toward translation, but it is not translation itself. The interpretive process is a form of exploration and, as such, must often account for elements that are not purely linguistic: pragmatic, cultural, social, phatic, or rhythmic, for example. With this in mind, and once we are clear about the sense of a text – which can be the book as a whole, a chapter, a paragraph, a sentence or sentence fragment, even a word—we can move forward into the second stage of translation, which is the (re)writing of a text. The intensity and extent of these various interpretive maneuvers varies widely, depending as they do on the nature of the text at hand and the status of the original work – when it was written, its purpose, its history, past translations (if any), and so on.

With respect to *The Enigma of Room 622*, what is required of the translator is less a form of analysis, the kind associated with a highly technical or academic work, philosophy or history, for example, than an understanding of the interactions among Dicker's characters and an easy fluency in translation that enables them to sound real, believable, and convincing in their speech. Consequently, word choice, vocabulary, diction, sentence structure, and cultural references must reflect these requirements and, most importantly, appear credible to the English-language reader.

For the translator, the practical challenge, then, is to find a voice for these characters, one that reflects their reality as foreign characters in a foreign environment – modern-day Switzerland in this case. We are not creating or recreating American or English protagonists who happen to be sojourning abroad but foreigners who, mysteriously, happen to speak the same language we do. So, an element of their foreignness must cling to them – their speech, their behavior, their names and titles. It is why Macaire is Monsieur and not Mr and why Anastasia is Madame and not Mrs.

To complicate matters, in the case of *The Enigma*, we have a set of nested stories, and what could be seen as alternating registers or degrees of fiction. There is, of course, the crime and its resolution. Around this hidden core circle a victim (initially undisclosed) and several suspects and their interactions. For long sections of the novel, the voice of the narrator, Joël, drops away and we are immersed in the world of the bank and its employees – Macaire, Jean-Bénédict, Lev, Tarnogol – and their families, friends, and lovers. And weaving in and around this group and the murder itself, we have Joël and Scarlett, who have become amateur sleuths in service of a story – the kind of story that, as Joël tells Scarlett, could arise from the flimsiest of threads, from almost nothing in fact. These two characters stand at one remove from the crime both in time and space, and so their voices must be distinct from those of Macaire and company. Then there are the passages narrated by Joël (or "Joël") that describe his beginnings as a writer and his friendship with Bernard de Fallois. But these events inhabit yet another narrative space; they are both fictional and real, that is non-fictional, because they did take place, outside the novel, in Joël Dicker's life, but they are also fictions, in a sense, because they are narrated by a fictional character in a novel about a crime that is also (presumably) a fiction and, ultimately, a pretext. And, of course, at the end, we realise that it has all been a game of smoke and mirrors – the murder, the mystery, the characters – they have all been written into the story to show how stories can be made. We are then confronted with the problem of authenticity. Joël Dicker, the author, and Bernard de Fallois, his publisher, are real characters in a quasi-autobiographical novel narrated by a writer who greatly resembles Joël Dicker, who may even be Joël Dicker. Or not. And in this way, the novel turns in upon itself, like the ever circling spirals of a gastropod shell.

Embedded within the structure of a crime novel, we find a kind of autofiction, a memoir by the protagonist-author, a retelling of his life, the origin story of a writer; he could be any writer but happens to bear a close resemblance to the author whose name appears on the cover of the book you are reading. However, and perhaps most importantly, this "fictional" memoir by a fictional writer, is a real form of homage to Bernard de Fallois, the guide, mentor, and close friend of Joël Dicker, author.

Robert Bononno